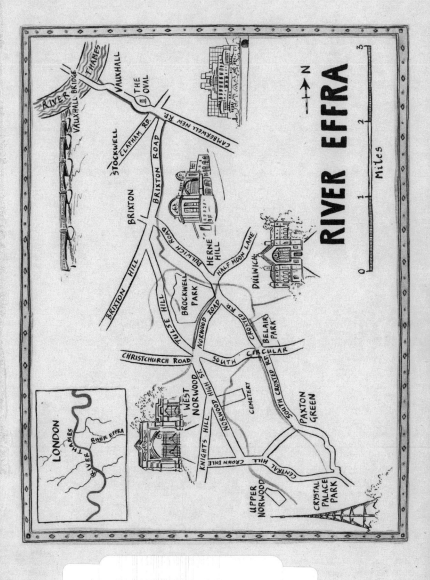

RIVER EFFRA

N

0   1   2   3
Miles

D0186136

PENGUIN BOOKS

Saturday Requiem

Saturday Requiem

NICCI FRENCH

PENGUIN BOOKS

PENGUIN BOOKS

UK | USA | Canada | Ireland | Australia
India | New Zealand | South Africa

Penguin Books is part of the Penguin Random House group of companies
whose addresses can be found at global.penguinrandomhouse.com

First published by Michael Joseph, 2016
Published in Penguin Books, 2017

001

Set in 11.7/13.9 pt Garamond MT Std
Typeset by Jouve (UK), Milton Keynes
Printed in Great Britain by Clays Ltd, St Ives plc

A CIP catalogue record for this book is available from the British Library

B-FORMAT ISBN: 978–1–405–91861–9
A-FORMAT ISBN: 978–1–405–93089–5

www.greenpenguin.co.uk

MIX
Paper from
responsible sources
FSC www.fsc.org
FSC® C018179

Penguin Random House is committed to a
sustainable future for our business, our readers
and our planet. This book is made from Forest
Stewardship Council® certified paper.

To Kersti and Patricia

She isn't afraid. Being stabbed doesn't cause a stabbing pain. It had felt more like a punch, with an ache flowing through her body in waves, and then her legs had given way and she was on the floor, her knife rattling on the hard surface.

She hadn't realized it was happening, even though it was with her own knife. She'd stolen it and kept it beneath her mattress and brought it with her, tucked into her waistband. But it had all gone wrong.

Now she is slumped on the tiled floor, her back against the wall. Her bare feet are wet and warm with her own blood.

She hears a voice and a light is switched on. Two strip lights hang from chains, giving out a dim, sour glare. One of them, the one on the left, flickers and buzzes. She looks down at her blood with a detached interest. It isn't red, more like a sort of maroon, and it looks sticky and thick. Her head sinks back and she looks upwards.

She hears rushing feet, rubber soles squeaking on the tiles. All she sees at first is the green fabric of their scrubs. The faces lean in close, she feels hands on her body, clothes being cut away, muttering voices.

'Where did she go?'

The woman doesn't say anything. She tries to shake her head but it feels like too much effort.

'Where'd you get the knife?'

The question doesn't seem worth answering. More footsteps. She hears a man's voice. One of the doctors. The Asian one. He sounds calm. A light shines on her, into her eyes, so that when it moves away, the darkness looks purple and swirly.

'Messy,' he says. 'But it's all right. Where's the other one?'

'There,' says one of the nurses, pointing at a smeared footprint. Several

1

more lead out into the corridor and down to the right, then fade away. The corridor is dark but the disturbance is attracting attention. From behind bars, there are groans and cries. Someone shouts for help, the same phrase over and over: 'Get me. Get me.' She is an old woman and that is what she always says, in a shout or a whimper, when she is awake and afraid, sometimes for the whole night. An orderly stands looking at the last footprint, then into the darkness down the corridor. He hears running footsteps behind and looks round. Two more orderlies in their white scrubs and T-shirts. One of them rubs his eyes. He has been asleep.

'What do you think?'

'She'll be in rec,' says the man.

'How do you know?'

'The floor's locked down. There's nowhere else.'

'You bring the meds?'

He held up a syringe.

'Have you got enough?'

'For a fucking horse.'

'She'll be really wired.'

'There's three of us.'

'Has she got a knife?'

'She dropped it. It wasn't hers.'

'She might have another.'

They pad down the corridor. Looking into the shadows on either side, listening for a movement. The only light is from the moon, in stripes through the bars and across the corridor.

'Can't we get the lights on?'

'Only from downstairs.'

The wind blows outside and rain splatters on the windows, like it's being thrown, then a pause, then thrown again.

The recreation room isn't really a room, but a space at the end of the corridor where it widens out into an area with chairs and a sofa. They can see the glow of the TV on the walls, as if a fire is burning. The men speak to each other in whispers.

'Shall we wait?'

'There's only one of her.'

'You saw what she did back there.'

'Are you scared?'

'I'm not scared.'

At first they can't see anyone. The TV is silent but still on, a shopping channel, a flash of cheap jewellery. Empty chairs, a low table with an open magazine. They see a shape in the corner, hunched up, arms folded around itself. In the light of the TV they can make out the tattoos along the arms – faces, stars, spirals. One of the arms is stained dark. The head is bent down, hair obscuring the face. She is murmuring something they can't make out and begins to move her head down, then up again, each time banging it back against the wall. One of the orderlies steps forward.

'Calm down. We'll take you to your room.'

She continues her low murmur. It isn't clear if she even knows they are there. The orderly steps closer and she lifts her head and her thick mat of hair parts. Her eyes are as bright and fixed as those of a cornered animal. His skin prickles and for a moment he falters. In that pulse of hesitation she flies forward. It isn't clear whether she is going for him or whether he is in the way. He falls back over the table with her on top of him. He lets out a scream. The other two orderlies try to drag her off. One eases his arm round the woman's neck and pulls harder and harder but the man underneath is still crying out. An orderly raises his fist and punches her hard in the ribs, again and again. They all hear the soft thud of each blow, like a mallet sinking into earth. At last she releases her grip and they pull her away. Her whole body flexes and flaps even as they try to hold her still.

'Pin her down.'

They turn her over onto her front. One grasps each arm and the third sits on her back but she still kicks at the air. He pulls the plastic tip off the hypodermic needle with his teeth.

'Keep her still.'

3

He jabs the needle into the woman's thigh and eases the lorazepam slowly into her. He tosses the needle to one side and lies down across her legs, holding them still. She wriggles under him, squealing and crying. He smells her: tobacco, sweat, the hot reek of fear, almost like sexual excitement. At first there is no change but then, after a minute, the movements and the sounds fade away and the body seems to die under him. He counts slowly to twenty, just to make sure. They stand up and step back, panting, from the prone body on the floor.

'Are you all right?'

One of the orderlies raises a hand to his neck. 'She bit me.'

'She's fucking strong. Three isn't enough.'

'It wasn't her fault. They came for her.'

'They'll come worse for her next time.'

ONE

The wind tunnelled down the road towards Frieda Klein and the rain fell steadily. She walked through the darkness, trying to tire herself out. This time of night, the small hours when the streets were almost deserted and foxes scavenged in the bins, was when she felt London belonged to her. She reached the Strand and was about to cross over to get to the Thames when her mobile vibrated in her coat pocket. Who would ring at this time? She pulled it out and looked at the screen: Yvette Long. Detective Constable Yvette Long.

'Yvette?'

'It's Karlsson.' Yvette's voice was loud and harsh in her ear. 'He's been hurt.'

'Karlsson? What happened to him?'

'I don't know.' Yvette sounded as if she was holding back tears. 'I just heard. It's all a bit confused. Someone's been arrested, Karlsson's in hospital. He's being operated on. It sounds serious. I don't know any more. I had to call someone.'

'Which hospital?'

'St Dunstan's.'

'I'm on my way.'

She pushed the phone back into her pocket. St Dunstan's was in Clerkenwell, a mile away, maybe more. She hailed a taxi, and stared out of the window until she saw the grimy upper floors of the hospital ahead.

The woman at Reception couldn't find anyone called Karlsson on the system. 'Try A & E,' she said, pointing to the right. 'Across the courtyard. There's a corridor directly ahead.'

At A & E Reception, Frieda had to join a queue. A man at the front was asking why his wife hadn't been seen yet. She'd been waiting for two hours. More than two hours. The receptionist explained to him very politely and very slowly how the queues were managed according to urgency. Frieda looked at her phone. It was twenty past four in the morning.

The man seemed reluctant to leave. He restated his complaint more loudly, then got into an argument with a tracksuited teenager behind him whose right hand was wrapped in a grubby dishtowel. An old man in front of Frieda turned round to her and sighed. His face was greenish-grey. 'Bloody waste of time,' he said. Frieda didn't reply. 'My wife made me come. It's just my arm. And my indigestion.'

Frieda looked at him more closely. 'What do you mean? What do you feel like?'

'It's my indigestion.'

'Describe it.'

'Like a clamp round my chest. I just need some Alka-Seltzer.'

'Come with me,' said Frieda, and she dragged the confused man to the front.

The man at Reception stopped his complaint and looked round. 'There's a queue.'

Frieda pushed him aside. 'This man may be having a coronary,' she said.

The receptionist looked puzzled. 'Who are you?'

'Coronary,' said Frieda. 'That's the word you need to hear.'

And then there were a few minutes of shouting and banging doors and the man was lifted onto a trolley and suddenly it was calm again and Frieda and the receptionist were looking at each other.

'Is he your father?'

'I'm here about Malcolm Karlsson,' said Frieda. 'Chief Inspector Malcolm Karlsson.'

'Are you a relative?'

'No.'

'Are you a colleague?'

'No.'

'Then I'm sorry. We can't give out information.'

'Actually, I was a colleague. We did work together.'

The woman looked doubtful. 'Are you a police officer?'

'I was employed by him and he's a friend.'

'I'm sorry.'

'At least let me know his condition.'

'Excuse me, could you please step aside? There are people waiting for treatment.'

'Do you have a supervisor?'

'If you don't move aside, I'll call security.'

'All right, call security, I can –'

'Frieda.'

She looked round. Yvette was out of breath, her cheeks flushed. She fumbled in her bag, produced her badge and showed it to the receptionist. Frieda saw that her hands were trembling. The receptionist took the badge and examined it closely, as if it might be a prank. Finally she gave a sigh. 'Through the door on the far side of the waiting room and ask there. Is this woman with you?'

'Sort of,' said Yvette.

'Please take her with you.'

'Nobody knows anything,' said Yvette. She pushed open a swing door out of the waiting room and the two women almost collided with a uniformed officer.

'Is Karlsson here?' said Frieda.

The young man looked at Frieda in puzzlement and Yvette held out her badge. 'How is he?'

7

'Not well.'

'Is he in danger?'

'Danger?' said the officer. 'He's along there. In the cubicle at the end.'

Frieda and Yvette walked past the other cubicles. From one came the sound of a woman sobbing. They reached the final cubicle, screened with a blue curtain. Yvette looked at Frieda questioningly. Frieda pulled the curtain back. All at once, Frieda saw a young female doctor and, on the bed, Karlsson, half sitting up, in his white shirt, his tie, and the trousers of his suit, with one side cut almost away to reveal a bruised and swollen leg.

'I thought . . .' Frieda began. 'We thought . . .'

'I've broken my fucking leg,' said Karlsson.

'They've got him,' said Yvette. 'He's in custody. He'll pay for this.'

'Pay for what?' Karlsson glared at them both. 'I fell over. He started to run and I started to run and tripped over a broken paving-stone. It's the sort of thing you get up from and brush yourself down and keep on running but it turns out I'm an old useless fucking idiot. I fell and heard it, like a stick snapping.'

'Yvette phoned me,' said Frieda. 'We thought it was something terrible. I mean really terrible.'

'What does this look like?' Karlsson looked at the young doctor. 'Tell them. It's a fractured what?'

'Tibia and fibula,' said the doctor.

'There's going to be an operation,' said Karlsson. 'With nails and screws.'

'We're waiting for the consultant. He should be on his way.'

'Does it hurt?' said Yvette.

'They gave me something. It's strange. I can still feel the pain but I don't care about it.' There was a pause. Karlsson looked down at his bruised shin. Frieda could see now that it wasn't quite straight. 'It's going to be weeks. Months.'

The doctor looked embarrassed. 'I'm going to see what's happened to the consultant,' she said. She pushed her way through the curtain and they were left alone.

'Can we get you something to eat or drink?' asked Yvette.

'Better not,' said Frieda. 'Not if they're going to operate.'

When Karlsson next spoke, he sounded woozier, slurred, as if the drugs were taking hold. 'This is all your fault.'

'Me?' said Frieda. 'I haven't seen you for weeks.'

'You got me reinstated,' he said. 'You and your friend Levin. If you hadn't done that, I'd be safely at home.'

'I don't think it's exactly –' Frieda began, but Yvette interrupted her.

'Who's Levin?'

'Frieda was going to jail,' said Karlsson. 'You know. And I was going to be disciplined or fired or arrested or all three. The reason none of this happened is that a man called Levin appeared.'

'From the Met?' asked Yvette.

'I don't think we're supposed –' began Frieda, but Karlsson interrupted.

'Oh, no. Not him.'

'Home Office?'

'He never said. He was keen on Frieda. Interested. But he never said why.'

'He said I owed him. But I don't know what that means.'

'It's dangerous,' said Karlsson, 'owing someone a favour. I've sat across the table from people who said, "I was just doing it for a friend." I'd point out that they'd killed someone and they'd say, "But I owed him." As if that was a defence.' He sank back on the bed. The effort seemed to have tired him. 'So you haven't heard from him?'

'I didn't say that. In fact, he recently left a couple of messages on my voicemail.' He'd left four, asking her in an amiable voice to call him as soon as she could. 'I haven't got back to him yet.'

Karlsson didn't seem to be paying attention. 'The doctor talked about screws and bolts in my leg.'

'You said that.'

'I'll set the alarm off going through Customs.'

'Probably.'

'So Levin's going to steal you away from me.' Karlsson spoke dreamily.

'Nobody's stealing Frieda away,' said Yvette. 'The police aren't going to employ her again. Not after last time.'

'Thanks, Yvette,' said Frieda. 'Not that I want to be employed.'

'I'll always employ you,' said Karlsson.

'That won't be possible.' Yvette sounded cross now.

'This is just the drugs talking,' said Frieda. 'You need some rest.'

Karlsson shifted on the bed and flinched. 'What I need is some more drugs. What day is it anyway?'

'Saturday,' said Frieda. 'But not yet dawn.'

'I hate Saturday.'

'Nobody hates Saturday.'

'That's the thing. You're supposed to like Saturday. Going out on Saturday and getting drunk and having so-called fun. It's compulsory.'

'Well, you won't be going out tonight,' said Frieda.

'Now that I can't, I almost want to.'

Karlsson was speaking drowsily and before anyone could reply he was asleep.

TWO

It was midday on the following Monday, wild and wet, rain streaming down the windowpanes so that it was impossible to see the swollen grey sky beyond. Frieda had seen two patients and made notes, and now she had time to go to Number Nine for a quick lunch before her afternoon sessions. In the past few months, ever since the last terrible summer, she had taken pleasure from the steady pattern of her life: her little mews house with its open fire, the work here in her consulting room and at the Warehouse, the small circle of friends, the hours spent alone and in silence, making drawings in her garret study or playing through chess games. Gradually the horror had receded and now it stood far off, on the rim of her consciousness.

She picked up her coat and slung her bag over her shoulder. She was going to get wet, but she didn't mind that. As she pushed open the door into her anteroom, the first things that she saw were the shoes: brown brogues, old. Then the legs, stretched out in their brown corduroy trousers, ending in blue socks. She opened the door fully.

Walter Levin sat up straighter in the armchair and pushed his spectacles back up his nose. He beamed at her.

'What are you doing here?'

Levin stood up. He was wearing a tweed jacket with large buttons that reminded Frieda of men's clubs, open fires, wood-panelled rooms, whisky and pipes. When she shook the hand he held out, it was warm and strong.

'I thought we could have a chat.'

'No, I mean, literally what are you doing here? How did you get in from the street?'

'A nice woman was coming out as I was coming in.'

'I don't believe you.'

'Does it matter?'

'Why couldn't you have rung to make an appointment, like a normal person?'

'I tried that and it didn't work.' He raised his eyebrows at her. Frieda didn't reply. 'Can I carry your bag for you?'

'No, thank you.'

He took his coat from the back of the armchair and buttoned himself into it, then wound a checked scarf round his neck. 'I have an umbrella,' he said genially.

'I'm probably going in a different direction from you.'

'I'm here to ask you to dinner.'

'Dinner?'

'Not just any dinner.' He patted his pockets vaguely, one after the other, then bent down to look in the leather briefcase at his feet. 'Here we are,' he said, pulling out a cream envelope and handing it over to Frieda.

She slid out a thick card. In gold-embossed letters she was cordially invited to a gala dinner at a hall near Westminster on the coming Thursday. An auction of promises to raise money for the families of soldiers fallen in the line of duty. Black tie. Carriages at ten.

'What is this?'

'A gathering of the great and the good.'

'Is this the favour?'

'It's an introduction to the favour.' He took off his glasses and rubbed them against the hem of his scarf. His eyes were cool, like pale brown pebbles.

'Can't you just tell me?'

'It isn't necessary. Shall I send a car for you?'

'I can make my own way.'

Frieda waited until he was gone before leaving herself, walking out into the wild February day with a sense of relief. Water was running down the sides of the streets and collecting in puddles on the pavements. The shapes of buildings dissolved. All over the country there were floods; a deluge. She walked fast, feeling drops of rain slide down her neck, and soon was at Number Nine, enveloped in its warmth, the smell of coffee and fresh bread. She pushed the thought of Thursday evening away from her.

After Dory is sewn up, they put her into bed with a drip in a private ward, full lockdown. They don't want her talking to other patients. Or prisoners. Patients. Prisoners. Even the guards get confused with the distinction and drift between one word and the other. It doesn't change the reality, whichever word they use. She is at the far end of wing D, by a window. Two owls hoot at each other the whole night. Dory can't separate the sound from the sounds in her head, from the sounds in her dreams, from the memories of her own screams as Hannah pushed Dory's own knife into her, their faces so close they were like lovers.

But she knows that Mary needs to be told. Mary will know what to do. Hannah will be dealt with.

THREE

The party was at a gentlemen's club in St James's. Women were excluded, except on special occasions. When Frieda entered the hall, she was dazzled by the chandeliers, the glint of jewellery, the gleam of light off the wine glasses. She heard the noise, a bray of voices, little screams of laughter. She smelt perfume, leather, money.

'Splendid,' said a voice.

Levin was beside her, putting a flute of champagne into her hand, tucking her arm through his, leading her into the crowd, murmuring niceties, his eyes behind their glasses darting this way and that. There were men wearing medals and ribbons. Levin pointed out a senior politician and her portly husband, whose speech was already slurred, a sprinkling of CEOs, a general.

'Is everyone head of something?' asked Frieda.

'Apart from you.'

She glanced at him suspiciously. His face was bland. He introduced her to a woman who was something important in finance but, before she could say a word, led her away again. Dinner was announced. They sat at a table with the head of a company that made solar panels, a lawyer who said she specialized in divorce settlements, a man with beautiful silver hair and an aquiline nose, whose name and job Frieda never discovered, an architect with a glass cane, and the architect's wife, who drank too much and kept poking the silver-haired man with her forefinger whenever she wanted to make a point. They ate scallops, then duck lying on a daub of pomegranate, plums and tiny yellow mushrooms. Frieda couldn't stomach it and drank only water. She thought about sitting by her fire with a bowl of soup, looking into its flames, hearing the wind and rain outside. The man at the table next to her pushed his chair back and rammed into her.

'Sorry,' said a familiar voice.

Frieda turned and found herself staring into the florid face of Commissioner Crawford, the man who had wanted to discipline Karlsson, who had dismissed her, who had wanted her sent to jail. He gazed at her, still chewing slowly. He glanced back at the people at his table and found them watching with interest. He fixed a smile to his face. 'I didn't expect to see you here.'

'I didn't expect to see myself here.'

'What brings you?'

'I'm here as a guest.'

'Aren't you going to introduce us?' asked the woman at his side.

Crawford frowned and introduced them.

'And how do you two know each other?' asked the woman, playfully. 'Business or pleasure?'

'Neither,' said Crawford, and turned back to Frieda. 'Are you up to something?'

'Don't worry,' said Frieda. 'I won't do anything to embarrass you.'

'I'll be the judge of that.'

She turned back to her table and saw Levin watching her with a speculative air. There was a break before the auction of promises. Levin came round to her chair and said, 'Let's mingle, shall we?'

He led her to the long table at the end of the room where they were serving coffee, one hand lightly under her elbow. 'I was considering bidding for a weekend cookery course in

Wales. What do you think?' His expression altered. 'Ben. I didn't see you there.'

Frieda's immediate impression of the man he was addressing was that he seemed larger than life. He was broad-shouldered, barrel-chested, chestnut-haired, white-toothed, tanned, exuding an air of bonhomie and genial, slightly flashy charm. He made Levin look small and plain and he towered over the people around him. He laid his hand on Levin's shoulder. 'You do pop up in the most unlikely places.'

With an equable smile, Levin introduced him to Frieda as Ben Sedge. His eyes were very blue. He took her hand in his firm grasp. 'Bidding for anything?' he asked, looking around. 'The prices are a bit steep for me.' He bent slightly towards Frieda. 'More money than sense, wouldn't you say?'

'It's in a good cause, I suppose,' said Frieda. She noticed that Levin had slipped away.

'So they say. You're not a journalist, are you?'

'No.'

'What do you do?'

'I'm a psychotherapist. What are you?'

'I'm a police detective,' he said. 'Best job in the world.'

Before Frieda could say anything else, Levin reappeared. He handed her a cup of coffee and put his hand under her elbow once more. 'If you'll excuse us,' he said to Sedge, and led Frieda back into the centre of the room.

'I think we'll give the auction a miss,' he said. 'If that's all right.'

'Are we leaving?'

'Yes.'

'So why did we come?'

He blinked at her. 'I wanted you to meet Detective Chief Inspector Sedge.'

'Why?'

'I'm interested in him.'

'What's that got to do with me?'

He dipped his hand into his breast pocket, brought out a small card and handed it to her. 'Nine tomorrow morning, please. Then I'll tell you what your favour is going to be.'

FOUR

At half past eight the next morning, Frieda left her house and headed east across Fitzroy Square. The sun was shining out of a blue sky. When she had first moved to the area, one of her neighbours had been an old woman who had lived there since she was a little girl. Frieda used to do her shopping for her sometimes and Doris talked about how the area had changed. 'Along Warren Street it was all second-hand-car dealers,' she used to say. 'Car dealers and criminals.'

By the time Frieda had moved in, the car dealers were long gone. The grand houses around the square had been broken up into dingy little offices, for solicitors and travel agents. Now the solicitors had moved on, travel agents were as obsolete as lamplighters, the square had been pedestrianized and spruced up, and the offices had been turned back into town houses. They were occupied by TV celebrities, who complained about the possibility of paying tax on the millions that their houses were now worth. Frieda wondered whether it was time to move to wherever the car dealers and criminals now lived.

Levin's address was just a short walk away. Frieda could visualize it like a geometric game, touching four leafy squares: Fitzroy, Bedford, Bloomsbury and Queen Square. She walked through them one by one, turning off the last down a shady, almost hidden street of narrow houses. She looked at the dark green front door. Could this really be Levin's office? She pressed a little plastic buzzer. The door was opened by a young woman with short, spiky hair, dressed in a blue and white striped shirt and blue trousers, with heavy black leather boots. She smiled at Frieda. 'You don't recognize me,' she said.

Frieda paused for a moment. 'Yes, I do.'

'Where from?'

'Your other office. In Chapel Market.'

'That's right. I let you in. When Walter interviewed you.'

'It wasn't exactly an interview.'

'I'm Jude. Follow me.'

Inside, it was a normal terraced house, with framed engravings on the wall. Ahead there were stairs, and to the side of them, the corridor led to a kitchen. Jude opened the door to the left and showed Frieda inside. 'Can I get you tea or coffee?' said Jude.

'No, thank you.'

'Then I'll fetch Walter.'

She left the room and Frieda heard her walking up the stairs. She looked around. It was like a million other ground-floor rooms in London, a front room and a back room knocked together. There were two little fireplaces and two mantelpieces. It had all the components of a home – pictures on the wall of landscapes that looked vaguely rural, a sofa and two chairs, a low coffee-table – but it was clear that nobody lived there. The glass in the window that gave onto the street was frosted. There were none of the fragments of an actual life, no ornaments on the shelves, no books, no magazines. Instead, there were files everywhere, box files and cardboard files and plastic files, piled on the floor, arranged on shelves. Two filing cabinets – slightly different colours and slightly different shapes – were jammed together against a wall. At the far end, there was a stripped-pine desk with a computer and a printer and another laptop.

'So you found us?' said a familiar voice. Frieda looked round. It was Levin. With him was another man, with heavy, puffy features, wearing a grey suit and a dark tie. He looked at Frieda with an expression that was bored, as if he were waiting to be impressed and didn't expect to be.

'This is Jock Keegan,' said Levin. 'He used to be a policeman.'

'What are you now?' asked Frieda.

'He's working with us,' said Levin. 'Did Jude offer you tea?'

'I'm fine.'

'Let's make ourselves comfortable.'

Levin and Keegan sat on the sofa. Frieda took a wooden chair from the desk, placed it opposite them and sat.

'It feels like you're interviewing us,' said Levin, with a smile.

'I think I should warn you about something,' said Frieda.

'Really?'

'If what you want from me is some sort of profiling, I need to say that I've got no interest in it. I don't believe in it and I don't do it. If that's what you want, then you should get someone else.'

There was a pause. Levin and Keegan looked at each other.

'I'm not exactly sure what you mean by profiling,' said Levin. 'But at this point I feel we could go in two different directions. You could keep making guesses about what you think I want you to do and what you would say if I did. Or, on the other hand, I could simply say what I want you to do. I think the second option would probably be quicker.'

'All right.'

'Did you enjoy last night?'

'It wasn't really my kind of thing.'

'I didn't think so. But you met, or encountered, DCI Sedge.'

'Yes.'

21

'Was his name familiar to you?'

'No.'

'Do you know about the Geoffrey Lester case?'

'No.'

'It was in the papers,' said Keegan.

'I don't read the papers.'

'The details aren't important,' said Levin. 'Lester was – is – a career criminal. Last year he was convicted of murdering a rival. As it turned out, it was one of the few crimes he hadn't actually done. Last month, the conviction was quashed and he was released. During the course of the appeal, it emerged that there had been irregularities in the investigation. An investigation that was led by our friend Ben Sedge.' Levin paused as if he were waiting for Frieda to speak, then continued. 'You're probably wondering whether the murder was solved.'

'I wasn't.'

'It's not actually our concern. The fact is that when a case collapses it raises other issues. It's like –'

'A house of cards,' said Keegan.

'I was thinking more of dominoes,' said Levin. 'You know, one domino falls and it knocks over another and then another. I mean, not when you're playing dominoes. When you arrange them in a line. Hence the domino effect. Or cliché.'

'In what way?' said Frieda.

'As we speak,' said Levin, 'lawyers will be picking over Sedge's earlier cases. All of them. People may be released as a result. Guilty people.'

'Or innocent people,' said Frieda.

'Or innocent people. Which would, of course, be a good thing.'

'Why aren't the police doing this?'

'Because that's not what the police do. This is a quick preliminary check, just to see if any nasty surprises are coming.'

'Who wants to know?'

Levin looked puzzled. 'Everyone, I suppose. Or everyone who cares about doing the right thing.'

'So what do you want me to do?'

'Good,' said Levin. 'We've finally got to that. It's really very simple. We just want you to go and talk to someone, then tell us what you think.'

'I think I'm here under false pretences,' said Frieda. 'I've no special skills. I'm not a detective. I'm not an interrogator.'

'The woman in question is clinically insane,' said Levin. 'That's not a comment. That's her diagnosis. We sent someone to interview her.'

'Me.' Keegan leaned back and folded his arms. To Frieda he looked like an illustration in a psychology textbook: folding of arms demonstrating emotional withdrawal, self-defence bordering on hostility.

'He couldn't get any sense out of her,' said Levin.

'You can say that again.' Keegan gave a snort.

'Who is this woman?'

'It might be interesting if you come to her fresh, as it were,' said Levin.

'She killed her family,' said Keegan.

'Well, now she won't come to her fresh,' said Levin, mildly. 'They'll tell her at the gate. The warders will tell her.'

'Nurses, strictly speaking,' said Levin.

'Nurses with handcuffs. Anyway, Klein knows how to go online.'

'*Dr* Klein,' Levin corrected him.

'Klein is all right,' said Frieda. 'Is there something particular that you need to find out?'

'The woman is trouble,' said Keegan. 'And she's dangerous. What we want to know is whether she's going to be trouble to us. As far as I can tell, she's completely out of it. The question is whether she's going to start making sense and saying she's been wrongly convicted.'

'Which would be a bad thing?'

'You don't need to worry about that,' said Levin. 'As we agreed, you owe me a favour. All you need to do is go and see this woman and tell us what you think. Once you've talked to her, you might want to have a look at what we have about her case. Then we'll be all square.'

'As simple as that?'

'As simple as that.'

Frieda thought for a moment. 'What is all this?' she said. 'Who do you work for?'

'That's really a philosophical concept.'

'No, it isn't. Who pays the bills? Who owns this house?'

'I'm a sort of freelance consultant,' Levin said. 'Like so many people nowadays. And I'm hiring you – or at least talking to you – as another freelance consultant. And you owe me a favour. And we're all on the side of righteousness. And what harm, really, can it do for you to talk to this woman?'

'Where is she?'

'Chelsworth Hospital. Have you heard of it?'

'Of course I've heard of it. The whole country's heard of it. When can I go there?'

'Now, if you want,' said Levin. 'Or tomorrow. There'll be a pass waiting for you.'

'What do I ask?'

'Anything you like,' said Keegan. 'You won't understand the answer.'

'And who do I ask for?'

'Hannah Docherty.' He smiled. 'Yes. *The* Hannah Docherty. Now you'll understand why we're worried.'

Shay is the first to find out. She brings Dory's breakfast and Dory whispers a few words to her. 'My own knife,' she says. 'Hannah took my knife.'

'We'll get even.'

FIVE

Frieda, who had no patients until later in the day, said she would go at once and this time Levin insisted on a car. It wasn't a sleek black one, but a slightly shabby red Honda driven by Jude, who didn't respect speed limits and blithely shot through amber lights. Directed by a satnav with a stern woman's voice, they made their way out of London and were soon on the A3, going against the clogged traffic in the other direction. Jude gestured towards a flask of coffee, then chatted about her dog, a mongrel called Serena who, she was afraid, had moulted all over the car, and about her love of interior-design programmes on TV.

Frieda looked out of the window as the little car hurtled through the Surrey countryside. The heavy rain of the last few days had stopped and in its place was a fine drizzle that obscured everything in its soft grey film. Fields lay under water; fences ran across newly created lakes and little bridges stood useless.

They turned off the A3 and made their way past large houses with porches and well-tended lawns, through pretty villages where houses were thatched and there were tea-shops. It seemed another world from London, thought Frieda, as the car jolted over a speed bump and swerved to avoid a man walking a spaniel.

'Turn left in one mile,' instructed the satnav.

'Not far now,' said Jude.

The turning led to a smaller road with high wire fences, topped with razor wire, on either side. They came to a double gate with a hut beside it and Jude wound down the window and leaned out, waving a card. The gate swung open to let them through. As they rounded the corner a shape loomed out of the dank mist, dark and huge, more like a small, grim town than a single institution. It was flanked by Portakabins and trees bare of leaves, and had a low, modern building running off to the left. Behind was a dominating, solid mass of dark, stained brick, lined with rows of small, symmetrically spaced windows. Each window was barred. Some were lit and others were dark. Birds perched on the roof or rose circling above it, buffeted by gusts of wind.

Jude swung the car round on the gravel and parked beside a white van. Frieda took her phone and her keys from her coat pocket and put them on the seat. She left her bag as well. Empty-handed, she walked up to the main entrance.

Chelsworth Hospital was not a prison. Its inmates were patients and the doctors' job was to treat them and make them better. But as Frieda stepped through a series of reinforced doors, which clanged behind her, into a security capsule, where she was patted down and had to turn out her pockets, then walked along a blank narrow corridor in the wake of two bulky men, who had keys jangling on their belts, past gridded windows that looked out onto a tangle of barbed-wire fencing, it felt like all the other high-security prisons she'd been to over the course of her career. Its name marked it out, sending a special shiver of recognition through people when they heard it. A house of unquiet spirits.

They reached the back of the hospital, and another set of double doors was unlocked to take them out into a large area surrounded by a high, spiked wall. In the far corner, Frieda saw there was a greenhouse and she could make out shadowy figures inside, stooping as they worked. A man ambled past them, huge, smiling. His head was shaved and Frieda saw he had a livid scar running across his skull.

'The women's unit,' one of the nurses said, nodding towards a wing of the building that formed part of the courtyard.

'How many women are there here?'

'Oh, not so many. Maybe twenty-five, thirty.' He side-stepped another patient coming towards him, a nurse a few steps behind him. 'Half of them have murdered their kids. Sometimes at night you can't sleep for their screaming.'

'You wouldn't believe what some of them have done,' said the other nurse. He spoke with a kind of gloomy relish. 'We're meant to think of them as ill, not bad, but it makes you wonder.'

Frieda sat in a small room and waited. It was very hot, very quiet. Someone screamed in the rooms above her, but the scream died away. The old radiator in the corner gurgled. The door opened and a burly man in scrubs entered. He nodded at Frieda, then turned.

'Come on, Hannah,' he said. 'This is the doctor lady I was telling you about.'

Frieda stood up. Hannah Docherty came into the room.

Hannah Docherty: Frieda tried to put out of her mind everything she knew, or half knew or had overheard or glimpsed in newspaper headlines. She tried not to remember the photos she had seen all those years ago, and which still cropped up whenever a woman behaved in a way that no woman was ever supposed to behave, did something 'unnatural'. She tried simply to concentrate on the figure in front of her, as she limped into the room with an awkward, heavy-footed gait.

The first thing that struck Frieda was her size. Even

stooped as she was and draped in thick layers of clothing, Hannah Docherty was obviously tall and solid, with broad shoulders and large, almost mannish hands. At first it was impossible to see her face, because it was obscured by a coarse mane of thick, dark hair, with a single violent streak of white running down from the parting. Then Frieda saw that she was wearing handcuffs.

She lifted her head and Frieda saw her face: bruised, swollen, her full lip cut into a sneer and thick brows drawn down. Frieda met her eyes: almost black, but very bright, they seemed to glow at her out of the discoloured face, as if she were backlit. Frieda tried to make out Hannah's expression: was she scared, confused, sullen, angry? Perhaps she was all of these. Her dilated pupils and the slight drag of her mouth also indicated that she had been drugged. She raised her cuffed hands to her face and Frieda saw a swirl of tattoos, homemade, amateurish. They were on the backs of her hands, her lower arms, around her neck, like ink drawings on soft paper that had spread and become blurred and fuzzy.

'Hannah,' she said. 'I'm Frieda.'

Hannah stared at her but didn't move. Frieda took a few paces towards her and the woman flinched and stiffened; the nurse took hold of her arm.

'You want to be careful of her,' he said to Frieda. 'She can just go for people. She's even stronger than she looks.'

'Don't talk about Hannah as if she wasn't here. Please, take off her handcuffs.'

'She's just stabbed someone. Nearly killed them.'

'I'm assuming she doesn't have a knife on her now.'

'You never know.' He gave a low laugh.

'Take them off.'

He shrugged, then, removing the keys from his belt, unlocked the cuffs. Frieda saw red weals round Hannah's wrists. She drew out a chair and put it close to the woman. 'Here, sit down. You look like you've hurt your leg. I just want to talk to you.'

'She's not much of a talker,' said the nurse.

Frieda stared at him. 'I'd like to be alone with Hannah.'

The man looked doubtful.

'You can wait just outside.'

He looked from Frieda to Hannah. Then, muttering under his breath, he went out. Frieda shut the door and put her chair opposite Hannah's, but not too close. Hannah had wrapped her arms around herself and lowered her head once more, so that her hair hid her face. She rocked slightly, making tiny guttural noises.

'Do you understand what I'm saying?'

No reply. She went on rocking.

'I've come to talk to you and find out what you think about things that concern you.'

Nothing.

'I know you've been in here a long time. Perhaps it's hard to remember what happened before you were here. Do you remember?'

Hannah went on rocking, moaning.

'You might have things to say, things you couldn't say at the time about the way you were treated. You can talk to me, Hannah.'

Suddenly the woman sat up straighter. 'It's me,' she said, in a deep voice that sounded hoarse from disuse, almost rusty. 'It's me it's me it's me.'

'What is?'

'It's me.'

'Hannah, can you remember when your family died?'

'Me.' She lifted a hand and smashed it into the top of her head. 'Me.' Once more she struck herself.

'Don't hurt yourself,' said Frieda, resisting the impulse to take Hannah's large hand in her own to restrain her. 'Don't do that. Look at me.'

'No. No. Don't.' Then she said suddenly, in a voice that was quite calm and clear, 'I'm too hot.'

It was true: it was almost unbearably stuffy in the room and beads of sweat were running down Hannah's face. She pulled off her grey cardigan. Under it was another long-sleeved top that she grappled with, tugging its sleeves up her arms and trapping herself in its folds, fighting. Frieda could hear her heavy breathing.

'Shall I help?' asked Frieda. She rose, took the hem of the jumper, pulled it swiftly over Hannah's head, then sat down again. Hannah blinked at her. She was only wearing a dark blue singlet now, stained under the armpits. Her bare flesh was covered with tattoos, hardly any skin left unmarked by circles and geometric patterns, words and images, so that it was hard to know which to look at: the serpent, the rose, the crucifix, the swirling lines, the bird, the numbers and roman numerals, the web . . . She was like a violent manuscript in many colours.

'Your tattoos are amazing,' said Frieda. 'Have they all been done here?'

Hannah didn't reply, but she let her hands rest on her lap and was no longer rocking.

'What does that one mean?' asked Frieda, stretching out a hand but not quite touching what looked like an hourglass, or perhaps it was a crude drawing of a naked woman, surrounded by small oval shapes, perhaps raindrops or tears.

Hannah didn't speak; her black eyes burned.

'Do you have a favourite?'

There was no answer, but after a few moments, Hannah put a finger on the inside of her forearm where there were three tiny inked shapes that looked like wonky crosses with circles on top. She touched the middle one and made a noise.

'What is it?' asked Frieda. 'What does it mean?'

Hannah made another stifled sound. Frieda leaned forward, intent. Hannah touched the shapes softly again. Her breath came in little rasps.

'What is it?' asked Frieda. 'Hannah?'

'Me me me me,' she said. 'Me.'

She wrapped her arms around herself once more and her hair came down, like a curtain, between them. She rocked to and fro.

When Frieda left the room, she asked the nurse waiting outside how often Hannah was visited.

He looked at her as though she had cracked a joke. 'Her?'

'Yes. When did someone last come to see her?'

'I don't know. Before my time.'

'How long have you been here?'

'About seven years.'

'You're saying no one has visited her in seven years.'

'That's right. Or more.'

'Does she have no relatives?'

'Why would any relative want to see her?'

'So there's no one at all.'

'Why would there be?'

SIX

Back in the car, Frieda didn't speak for several minutes.

'You'll need to report back,' said Jude.

'There's nothing really to report.'

'Then they'll want to hear that.'

Frieda sighed. She didn't like talking on the phone, but Jude told her the number and Frieda dialled. Keegan answered. 'So?'

'I've seen her.'

'Did she confess?'

'We didn't get around to that.'

'Did you get any sense out of her?'

'I'll come and see you about it.'

There was no reply and Frieda realized that the line was dead. 'Wasn't he pleased?' said Jude.

'I don't know,' said Frieda. 'I can't tell whether we lost the signal or whether he just hung up.'

'He just hung up.'

'I suppose he's easier to work with when you get to know him.'

'I can't answer that,' said Jude. 'I've only known him for a year.'

Frieda's phone rang again. 'You were wrong,' said Frieda to Jude, as she answered it. 'So I'll see you tomorrow?'

'Who will?' said a woman's voice.

'Who is this?' said Frieda. 'Is Keegan there?'

'Who's Keegan? I wanted to talk to Frieda Klein.'

'Chloë?'

Chloë was Frieda's niece and they were even closer than that sounded. At times, Frieda had taught her, fed her, lived with her and, most recently, enlisted her in a break-in – committing a crime in order to solve one. She had once wanted to be a doctor – like her aunt – but was now living up in Walthamstow and training to be a carpenter.

'Who's Keegan?'

'Somebody I'm working with.'

'Is he a therapist?'

'He's an ex-policeman.'

'Oh, no.'

'It's just –'

'Frieda, you said you wouldn't.'

'Where are you? What are you doing?'

'You said to keep in touch,' Chloë said. 'I'm keeping in touch. It's my weekly call. It's just that I was expecting to leave you a message. It's almost the first time you've ever actually answered your phone.'

'It's because I'm doing this job.'

'I want to talk to you about that.'

'How about this evening?' said Frieda.

'This evening where?'

'My place?'

When Frieda had finished, Jude looked across at her suspiciously. 'You know you're not supposed to talk about this?'

'Who would I talk to?'

'Whoever you were talking to on the phone, for example.'

'That was my niece.'

'Like your niece.'

Frieda glanced back at Jude. Her lipstick was purple and her fingernails were blue, like the sky on a cold winter day.

She looked more like someone who would be working in a gallery or a bar in Shoreditch.

'How did you end up in a job like this?' Frieda asked.

Jude looked puzzled, as if she wasn't quite sure herself. 'After uni I had no idea what I was going to do. I did some travelling with different hopeless guys. I ended up living in Berlin for a couple of years. Then a friend of a friend asked if I wanted to do some research work.'

'Who for?'

'It was a bit vague.'

'What do you say when your friends ask you what you do?'

'I say I'm a researcher for a consultancy. That usually makes them change the subject.'

'Do you enjoy it?'

'It's all right for the moment. But at some point I'll go travelling again.'

'And now you know German.'

'Hardly a word,' said Jude. 'I told you. I was in Berlin. Everyone speaks English there.'

Frieda felt strange sitting in a car driven by a woman she barely knew. Jude had a casual, slightly detached way of speaking about her work that Frieda found disarming. But maybe that was the point. Was anything she had told her actually true or was it the sort of thing likely to appeal to Frieda, to get her to let her guard down? Or was she being too suspicious, if there was such a thing as being too suspicious?

'I'm a therapist,' said Frieda. 'Which means that I have a clear sense of what secrets need keeping.'

'I went to a therapist once,' said Jude. 'I had some issues when I was younger. I was in a bit of a mess. He didn't keep secrets. He'd tell me about his other patients. He'd say this one had done this and that one had said that.'

Frieda wondered if Jude was waiting for her to say: Yes, we've all done that. 'You should have left him,' she said.

'It didn't feel that easy.'

For the rest of the journey Frieda remained silent, through the blur of Wimbledon Common, Putney and Wandsworth, as London gradually came into focus.

Chloë stepped into Frieda's house wearing jeans, hoody, black boots and a grey woollen cap.

'You look like you've come straight from the workshop,' said Frieda.

Chloë looked down at herself. 'This is what I changed into.'

'Do you want some tea?'

'Have you got a beer?'

'We could go out and buy some.'

'Yes,' said Chloë. 'Let's go out.'

'When I said we could go out, you were meant to say, that's all right, tea will be fine.'

'But tea won't be fine. And you can't just sit in your house all day.'

'I've only just got back. Is it still raining?'

'No excuses,' said Chloë. 'You've got an umbrella.'

'I haven't.'

'Anyway, you never mind rain. And I've just been paid. I want a drink and it's on me.'

Chloë led Frieda through the rain to a new tapas bar, on Charlotte Street, that had been decorated to look like an ancient cellar, all brick floors and old barrels. She ordered a carafe of sherry, olives and bread. 'It's like being in Andalucía,' she said, taking a sip of her drink.

'Except for the weather.'

'When I went there, it rained the whole time. Every single minute.'

'So when are you going to make me a bench?' said Frieda.

'I've got through the fun bit, when it was all exciting and new. Now I'm discovering how hard it really is. I'm at the stage when either I give up or I spend the next five years trying to get any good at all. Then I'll make you a bench.'

'That's what it's like to do something difficult,' said Frieda.

'And I'm sleeping with one of the boys in the workshop.'

'Is that a good thing?'

'It's all right. So now you know everything about my life and I'm going to ask you about yours. For example, I thought you and me were going to end up sharing a cell together. And then you almost got killed. So when you said you were working for the police again, I half assumed – or hoped – you were making a really bad joke.'

'I'm not working for the police.'

'Oh, good.'

'I'm working with someone who used to be a detective and it's connected with the police. In a way. But it's just a one-off.'

'A one-off,' said Chloë.

'Yes.'

Chloë's expression had changed. Suddenly she looked like the troubled, chaotic teenager Frieda had known, years before, and had tried to help. 'I just thought of something,' she said.

'What?'

'"A burned child loves the fire." That's Oscar Wilde, isn't it?'

'I think so.'

'When I read it, I thought it was stupid. Saying the opposite of the truth as a way of being clever. But that's what you're like. You've been burned, and burned some more, and yet you always return to the fire. I don't understand it.

Are you going to keep doing this until you run into some-thing you can't walk away from?'

'It's not like that.'

'I can see that it's like an addiction. Sitting in a room lis-tening to people moan on about their silly little problems – that must get a bit boring after what you've been through.'

'I know what you're saying to me.'

'But . . . I can hear a "but" coming.'

Frieda couldn't stop herself smiling. She wasn't used to being questioned like this by someone she still thought of as a child. Wrongly. 'You may be right. When you do some-thing enough, maybe you should admit that it's what you do, that it's who you are. Even so, this is happening for a par-ticular reason. This man, the man I'm now helping, did me a favour when I was in trouble. More important, he did Karls-son a favour. I owe him one. And this is it.'

'Are you going to tell me about it?'

'I'm afraid I can't.'

'I'll probably read about it in the paper.'

'I hope not.'

'All right. Interrogation over. Now we can talk like nor-mal people. Which we haven't done for ages.'

'I was thinking about you this morning. I was going to get in touch.'

'What about?'

'You've got a tattoo, haven't you?'

Chloë looked incredulous. 'You were thinking about my tattoos? Are you considering getting one?'

'No,' said Frieda, then realized what Chloë had said. 'Tat-toos? Have you got more than one?'

'Certainly.'

'Show me.'

Chloë unzipped her hoody and took it off. Underneath

she had a black sweatshirt. She grappled with the collar and pulled it off her shoulder, exposing a flower, red with a black-thorned stalk.

'Is that a rose?' said Frieda.

'That's what I asked for.'

'Why?'

'Because I liked the look of it. And there's this one.' Chloë twisted round and pulled her shirt up. Up the side of her ribs a scaly snake was in a circle, about to swallow its own tail.

'Does that symbolize something?'

'Eternity,' said Chloë. 'That's what this guy in Thailand told me. Or endless desire. And I've got one more, but if I showed you that one in here, they'd throw us out. Or have us arrested.'

'Because of what it shows?'

'Because of where it is.'

'Oh. Why did you get them, Chloë?'

'If you pretend you didn't say that, I won't have to say that you sound like my mother.'

'What does Olivia think?'

'She had a fit. But she doesn't know about my secret one.'

'I wish *I* didn't know about it. So tell me why you get them.'

'I don't know. It was something to do.'

'I met a woman with tattoos this morning.'

'Were you in a prison?'

Frieda gave a start. 'What makes you say that?'

Chloe laughed. 'You're on a case.'

'It's not exactly a case.'

'If you're on a case and you meet someone tattooed, that means prison.'

'In fact, it wasn't a prison.'

'Was it Broadmoor?'

'It wasn't Broadmoor and stop trying to guess. I was talking – or trying to talk – to a woman who is a patient there. I didn't get any sense out of her. I was looking at her tattoos and wondering what they meant.'

'This boy I'm going out with has tattoos on his back and his chest and sleeves on both arms. He says they tell the story of his life. I told him he'd better not think of putting me on there.'

'That's interesting,' said Frieda, thoughtfully. 'I could see she was right-handed.'

'How could you see that?'

'It's to do with muscle development. And on her left fore-arm she had a tattoo that she might have done herself. It showed a woman's body in darkness and around her were six little almond shapes.'

'Almond shapes? What's that?'

'I don't think they're almonds. I think they're pomegranate seeds.'

'Why?'

'Don't you know the old Greek myth of Persephone?'

'Not exactly. Shall we get another carafe?'

Without waiting for an answer, Chloë waved the empty carafe at a waitress.

'Persephone was the daughter of the earth goddess, Demeter. One day she was seized by Hades and taken to the underworld. She was rescued, but not before she had eaten six seeds of a pomegranate. So for six months of every year she had to return to Hades. Which is why we have winter.'

'So what does that mean?'

'It could mean that this young woman is a prisoner.'

'I thought you knew that already.'

'And that she feels herself to be in Hell.'

'Who's she trying to tell?'

'Herself, perhaps. What do you think?'

Chloë had looked dubious but not as dubious as Keegan, when Frieda met him, Levin and Jude the next morning.

'Is that it?' he said.

'What do you mean "it"?'

'That's your report?'

'It's my account of what I saw yesterday.'

'You didn't get a statement but you looked at her tattoos.'

'It looked like a message. A message to herself.'

'You know that getting tattoos is what prisoners do?'

'I do, and I think it's possible that this tattoo is a message.'

'A message about being in some kind of Hell?'

'Yes.'

'And this is relevant – why?'

'I don't know if it is relevant.'

'Then I'll tell you. It isn't.'

'I didn't ask for this,' said Frieda. 'Levin asked me. Now I'm here.'

Levin hadn't spoken. He was leaning back on his chair, looking up at the ceiling. When he turned towards Frieda, he wore an expression of mild amusement. Frieda didn't know who it was directed at.

'You know the saying, "Don't get a dog and bark yourself"?' Levin asked. Nobody replied. 'My own version of that would be: don't get a dog, muzzle it and tie it up as soon as you've got it.'

'Who's the dog in this version?' asked Frieda.

'Well, you, I suppose,' said Levin. 'But I meant it in a respectful way. So what do you want?'

'You must have a file of some kind.'

'Yes,' said Keegan. 'We have a file of some kind.'

'I'd be interested in taking a look at it.'

'Do you know the full story of what this woman did?' asked Keegan.

'I know she was found guilty of murdering her entire family. I don't think there's anyone who doesn't know that. For a while she must have been the most reviled person in the country.'

'Yes, and with good reason. It was an abattoir. And let me tell you,' he leaned towards her, 'it's the most open-and-shut case I've ever seen.'

'Then there's no harm in me looking at the files.'

'We're looking at how the police handled the case, not the case itself.'

'I know that.'

Keegan turned to Levin. 'She's a therapist.'

'I'm in the room,' said Frieda.

He turned to her. 'You're a therapist.'

'That's why I brought her,' said Levin, the smile fading from his face. 'Give her the file.'

SEVEN

The files weren't files but boxes. Jude led her upstairs, past a closed door, and into a small room made even smaller by the bed at the end, covered with a brightly patterned quilt and with a hot-water bottle on the pillow. The only other furniture was the table and chair. There was an Anglepoise lamp on the table and under it were four boxes full of papers.

Jude switched on the lamp and pulled the boxes out. 'There you are,' she said. 'Plenty to keep you busy.'

'Yes.'

'Coffee?'

'I'd like that.'

'There's this Scandinavian place down the road that does amazing cardamom and cinnamon buns. I'm addicted. Do you want one?'

'Just coffee.'

'Your loss. Next time, perhaps.'

Frieda took a layer of papers from the first box and put it on the table. She took out her notebook and pen and put them beside the papers. Then she sat down and started to read. She read for six hours. She read through the three coffees that Jude brought her, and through the smoked salmon on rye bread. The stormy day outside darkened towards evening, rumbling with far-off thunder.

The papers were almost all photocopies and some were hard to decipher. They were in no particular order. Frieda spent the first half-hour sorting them into categories:

forensic reports, phone bills, police interviews, witness statements, court transcripts, psychological assessments and photographs.

She wanted to be as chronological as possible so she started with the police statements. Late on Saturday, 19 May, just before midnight, the police station had received an anonymous call, later traced to a nearby phone box, reporting the sound of a disturbance at 54 Oakley Road. Frieda checked the address on a map she carried in her bag. It was down in Dulwich, foreign territory to her, deep in south London. The police had arrived at twelve twenty on Sunday morning: DCI Sedge, who was at the station finishing up a report on a hit-and-run, and at the same time, in a patrol car, Constables Malik Gordon and Jane Farthing. The photographer and the forensic team had arrived a few minutes later. Signs of the disturbance were immediately visible through the front window: furniture was scattered, chairs lying on their sides. Sedge had knocked on the front door, and when there was no reply, they'd forced an entry. There they had discovered three bodies: Hannah's stepfather, Aidan Locke, fifty-three; her mother, Deborah Docherty, forty-seven; and her younger brother, Rory, aged thirteen. Deborah and Aidan were in their bedroom, but he was fully dressed and she was in her nightclothes. All three had been beaten to death with a claw hammer. Aidan was lying on his stomach, the other two on their backs. The hammer, wiped clean, was on the living-room floor. Hannah Docherty, aged eighteen, had identified the three bodies before they were taken to the morgue.

At first the assumption had been that it was a burglary gone terribly wrong. But later in the day Hannah had come into the picture as a suspect and then the case against her had seemed clear-cut and irrefutable. Frieda found a handwritten page of notes about Hannah: dysfunctional, reports of drug-taking from family and friends, anti-social behaviour, contact with police, warnings but no actual charges brought. She had quarrelled violently and publicly with her parents just weeks previously and moved out of the house to live in a squat. A few days before their death they had cut off her allowance. Her attempt at an alibi – that she had gone to meet her stepfather but he had never arrived and, in fact, it was her mother, Deborah, who had turned up – seemed nonsensical and was quickly proved to be impossible. The coroner's report showed that Deborah Docherty was already dead by the time Hannah claimed to have met her. Clothes belonging to her were found stuffed into a bag in a bin further along the street, covered with the blood of her murdered family. When interviewed by the police, she didn't confess, but became first hysterical and then catatonic.

Frieda turned to the forensic reports. Occasionally she made notes in her pad: that there was blood everywhere, not just in the bedrooms, but downstairs as well. That there was no sign of forced entry. That Deborah Docherty had been more savagely attacked than either her husband or child. That the hammer was so effectively wiped clean that it provided no evidence. That there was an apparent difference in the time between Aidan Locke's murder and that of Deborah and Rory. What had happened in that gap?

One piece of paper was a printed itemization of what was found on the bodies. Rory Docherty: pyjamas, *Lord of the Rings* motif. Aidan Locke: Karrimor suede walking boots, hooped blue and white socks, blue denim trousers, blue-and-white-checked shirt, watch (brown leather strap), frameless spectacles. Deborah Docherty: green-patterned nightgown, gold-coloured necklace with locket. The sparseness had its own sombre poetry.

She made notes, too, on the obvious inadequacies in the way the case had been handled, though she assumed Jock Keegan had already done this, and more thoroughly than she ever could. They had never established – or even tried to establish – where the hammer had come from and there was no evidence that Hannah owned such a tool. The crime scene seemed to have been carelessly handled. There was a memo from an officer noting that Deborah's first husband, Seamus Docherty, who had inherited their house and everything in it, had come to take away several bags of possessions. The memo called for this matter to be pursued but Frieda found no further mention of it.

Frieda made a note about the treatment of Hannah in the investigation. She had been made to identify the three bodies, in situ, she had been shown photographs and taken through the scene. 'To observe her reaction,' Sedge had written in his report.

Next she leafed through multiple statements from people who had known Aidan Locke and the Dochertys, trying to get an idea of what this family had been like. Locke: well known in the neighbourhood, entrepreneur, fingers in lots of pies, obviously wealthy, raised money for charity, a Santa in the local primary school, marathon runner, squash player, amateur dramatics. People talked of him in exclamations. Oh, Aidan! What energy! Adored his wife! Never stopped! Frieda felt tired even reading about him, and slightly relieved not to have known him.

Deborah Docherty was more private. She had been an accountant, part-time once she'd had children. Quiet, self-contained, organized, competent, someone to trust. Her first marriage had broken up when Hannah was twelve and Rory seven, and she had married Aidan the following year. Her second marriage had by all accounts been successful.

She was clever, sometimes fierce, and protective of her children – perhaps too protective. Friends spoke of her distress over Hannah's chaotic state.

There was less information on the brother, thirteen-year-old Rory: some friends but not that many, ups and downs at school. Hannah had seemed very fond of him, despite the age gap.

There was a lot of material on Hannah. Frieda read through it all: statements from her teachers, saying she had been an academically bright, diligent student until she was about thirteen (around the time of her mother's marriage to her stepfather Aidan), and by fifteen she was troubled – bad discipline, bad friends. Her GCSE results had been disappointing and then she had more or less dropped out of school, though she had still been entered for A levels, which she had been due to sit just days after the murders had taken place. In March, she had left home and for the next six weeks had slept in a squat. Friends and ex-friends had been interviewed and a picture emerged of someone who was going off the rails. Of course, by this time she was the main suspect for the murder of her family. Had this affected people's narratives? Frieda wrote down names in her notebook. There had been a boyfriend; she wrote him down too. A psychiatrist had found Hannah to be dysfunctional, self-destructive, largely unresponsive.

She laid down her pad and shut her eyes. Hannah reminded her of someone. Yes. She reminded her of herself at that age. She had the irrational feeling that she should have been there, thirteen years ago, to rescue her.

She opened her eyes again and wrote a question in her notebook: 'Why was she ever allowed to stand trial?'

Then she turned her attention to the court transcripts. These she just leafed through: there was too much for one sitting. She only looked closely at Hannah's evidence, what there was of it: she had been able to answer few of the defence's questions and none of the prosecution's. She had stuck to her inadequate alibi, repeating over and over again that she had gone to meet her stepfather but he had never arrived, although her mother later had (the prosecution had been derisive, asking why there was no corroboration of that phone call from her parents' phone records, and pointing out that her mother couldn't have been her alibi since she was in her house miles away being murdered). Apart from that, as far as Frieda could tell, she had stammered out broken phrases and mostly wept. Frieda couldn't begin to understand why her lawyers had allowed her to give evidence. She imagined Hannah, just eighteen, standing in the dock and crying and crying while men and women in wigs asked her questions that made no sense to her.

The last batch that Frieda looked at was the photographs. She had been putting them off, but now she lifted them onto the table, face down, and started to turn them, one by one. There were photographs of the house from the outside, and then of each of the family before the tragedy. Aidan was burly, bearded, smiling, exuding bonhomie even in a picture. Deborah was slim, perhaps even thin, with short dark hair and a guarded expression. Rory looked younger than thirteen – in the photo the police had chosen to represent him, he was small and pale, with a mop of pale red hair and a freckled, slightly anxious face. And Hannah – at first, Frieda could barely tell that the woman she had met in the hospital was the same person as this young creature. Hannah then had been tall and she looked sturdy and strong, but her dark hair was lustrous, her face glowed with health, her teeth were white, her clothes bright and stylish. She was smiling. Then there was one of Hannah just after she was charged, a headshot in which she had already started to become the woman Frieda had seen: her eyes were bloodshot, her hair a tangle, and on her face such an expression of bewilderment and fear that Frieda almost looked away, it felt so intimate.

She went quickly through the photos of evidence that had been collected and often bagged up: fingerprints, the blood splatters downstairs, the heavy claw hammer, the clothes belonging to Hannah that had been discovered a few houses down – a dress with a floral pattern and a cardigan, covered with her family's blood . . . Without warning, they became photos of the crime scene. The main bedroom: photo after photo from every angle and in close-up of Aidan and Deborah. Quickly she put them aside and found herself looking at a photo of Rory. He was wearing his *Lord of the Rings* pyjamas. One arm was flung out. He was lying face downwards so she didn't see his face, but she stared at the defenceless nape of his neck, with one little mole on it, his curled fingers and the small feet. At his skull, shattered, caved in.

She got up, went downstairs and stood in front of Levin, Keegan and Jude.

'You were right,' she said to Keegan. 'I'm just a therapist.' She turned to Levin. 'I can't do this any more.'

She sat in front of Thelma Scott, her therapist whom she saw only when she felt wrong, dislocated, unsure of what she was thinking. She put her hands on the armrests of her chair and looked into the old, clever face. A colleague had once said that Thelma looked like a frog but Frieda loved the way she looked, battered and calm and alert.

'I said I wasn't going to do this again,' she said. 'The

problem is that I made a deal. This man, Levin, did something for me and now I have to do something for him.'

'Is it something wrong?'

'I don't know. Not so far.'

'But you don't want to?'

'Chloë says I'm like the burned child who loves the fire.'

'What do *you* say?'

'I say that I don't know. I have a feeling of dread.'

'And you've told these people you won't do it any more?'

'Yes.'

'So?'

'I feel that I'm abandoning Hannah Docherty.'

'Frieda,' said Thelma, her voice stern. 'You're not God. Beware the rescue impulse.'

In spite of the rain and the wind, and the darkness that came rolling in over London, Frieda walked home from Thelma's house. She made herself a mug of tea and then she had a bath in the beautiful tub that Josef had installed for her. He was from the Ukraine and his English was still limited; he communicated through actions rather than words. She stayed in there a long time. She had meant to go round to her friend Sasha's that evening. Sasha was on her conscience – she was always on her conscience, since the previous year when events in her personal life had been the trigger for a crime whose reverberations Frieda and all her friends still felt – but she rang and rearranged to go the following day instead. She lit the fire and sat beside it with scrambled egg on toast, looking into the flames, hearing them crackle, hearing the wind outside. Then she played through a game of chess and went up to bed.

But she couldn't sleep. There were thoughts that pursued her, half-thoughts, faces in the darkness. At last she got up again and dressed and went out into the night. The rain had stopped but there were puddles everywhere, glinting under the streetlamps. Occasional cars passed. Frieda turned off down a small street. She was not thinking where she was going, but her feet were leading her along crooked byways towards the river. At first, she tried pushing away the impressions that were crowding in on her, but when she reached the road that covered the hidden Fleet River, she let them come to her.

What she had seen today in all the files was mad, but it wasn't mad in the right way: it wasn't a madness that made sense to her. It was both chaotic and organized. There was Hannah's risible alibi. There was a savage attack – but the bodies were all in their beds. Wouldn't at least one of the three have tried to run or fight, especially since the killer had waited between Aidan's death, and Deborah and Rory's? And Aidan was fully dressed, even wearing his shoes. So, presumably, his body must have been put on the bed next to his wife's by his killer. But that didn't fit with the apparent uncontrolled rage of the murders. There was the attempt to hide Hannah's clothes that were covered with blood. Why had they been put in such an obvious place, where the police were bound to find them? The prosecution lawyer had asked it as a rhetorical question in his summing-up and he had answered it. Because she was in a disordered state after killing her family. But was that right? She was ordered enough to try to hide her clothes but not ordered enough to hide them well.

She thought of Hannah, beaten by other inmates, cuffed and drugged by the nurses, unvisited for years on end, abandoned and alone. She had no one. She had Frieda. For a while.

*

She sent an email to Levin saying that she had changed her mind. She needed to visit Hannah Docherty again. She asked him to arrange it.

EIGHT

Frieda had a new client, a middle-aged woman who had been referred to her because she was suffering from acute, disabling panic attacks. She came into the room as if blown by the wind, surging forward, then stopping near the chair. Her dark hair was wet from the weather and plastered to her skull.

'Hello, Maria. I'm Frieda. Please, have a seat.'

The woman sat very upright, placing her hands on the arms of the chair as if it was about to speed off with her in it. 'This is like going to the dentist's,' she said. Her voice rasped and she gave a single cough to clear it. 'Just don't tell me to relax.'

'I won't.'

'Right, then.' Her eyes were deep in their sockets, and there were purple shadows under them. She had the look of someone who had lost a lot of weight in a short time. Her black jeans were loose on her and her grey turtleneck jumper was baggy. She turned her gaze on Frieda as though she was forcing herself. Frieda saw her hands clench the armrests. 'What now?'

'I know that you've been having panic attacks and you're probably feeling nervous about coming here, but today I'll just do an assessment, asking some general questions, getting a kind of picture of your situation before we start on our actual therapy sessions together. All right?'

Maria Dreyfus nodded. She wiped the back of one hand across her forehead, which Frieda saw was beaded with sweat.

'We'll start with basic things, like where you live, what you do, if you have a partner, children . . .'

So they began. Slowly, patiently, Frieda extracted information. Maria Dreyfus was fifty-four. She was a fund-raiser and events manager for a mental-health charity. She had been married for twenty-five years, and while there had been ups and downs, of course, she described the marriage as strong. She had two children – a daughter who was a lawyer and a son who was still at university. Her father was alive, but her mother had died of cancer eleven years ago. She herself had had breast cancer in her early forties. She had a sister to whom she was close and a wide circle of friends, although recently she had stopped seeing them, and some of them were offended by that.

'So I'm lucky,' she said. Her voice was low and attractive. 'I know I'm lucky. Nothing bad's ever really happened in my life, not compared to most people I know. My husband had an affair just after our son was born. That was painful, but it was ages ago and we got over it, though sometimes I can't believe I didn't just walk out of the door. My mother died. That was awful. But everyone's mother dies. I had breast cancer, but they got it early. I was scared, of course, but I didn't go to pieces or anything. I just dealt with it. I've always thought of myself as someone who deals with things. That's what my friends would say as well. I'm strong. I thought I was. Now I tell myself –' She stopped and frowned. 'I don't know what I was going to say. I don't know what I tell myself.'

'Tell *me*,' said Frieda.

'What should I say?'

'Tell me when it started. What happened? Describe it for me.'

She passed the back of her hand across her forehead once more, then put it against her throat briefly before replacing it on the chair arm. 'It's hard to say. For a long time now – a couple of months, anyway –' She stopped again. 'Does my voice sound weird to you?'

'Weird in what way?'

'Thin and dry and coming from far away.'

'No. But then I don't know what your voice normally sounds like. You're probably feeling self-conscious and removed from yourself and that's why it sounds strange to you – like hearing a recording of yourself.'

'What was I saying?'

'You were saying that for some time now – and then you stopped.'

'For some time I'd been having a peculiar and unpleasant feeling. Like a heaviness in my chest. I found it hard to swallow. And I had a nasty taste in my mouth and sometimes felt nauseous and short of breath. I lost my appetite. I thought maybe it was something physical. A bug I couldn't shake off. Then one night, I woke.' She took one hand off the armrest and put it on her stomach. Now she was looking away from Frieda, talking towards the window where the rain still streamed down the glass, obscuring the world. She'd had enough of making herself meet another person's gaze. Silence was thick in the room.

'You woke?'

'I woke and I couldn't breathe properly. I couldn't breathe, and there was such a pain in my chest, I couldn't move. I couldn't make myself move. It was quite dark. I could hear my husband breathing beside me, and I could hear myself trying to take a breath, but I sounded like an animal in a trap. I thought I was dying. I knew I was dying. This was it.'

Frieda waited.

Maria lifted her eyes. 'I didn't die. Obviously. I woke my husband and he called the emergency services and I was rushed to hospital with a suspected heart attack. But there was nothing wrong with me. Nothing physical. It was embarrassing, ridiculous.'

'You were having a panic attack.'

'Yes.'

'And they've continued.'

'Yes. Attack is the right word for it. I wake at night and I know it's coming. It's crouching and it's going to get me. I lie there, with a thundering heart and the blood pounding in my head, and I'm pinned to the bed and this thing is going to happen. It's like that man who has his liver pecked at by an eagle.'

'Prometheus.'

'Yes.'

'Is it just at night?'

'No. Nights are the worst. I used to love climbing into bed but now it's like climbing onto a torture rack. I lie awake, and I dread the small hours. I feel like an object, a *thing*, lying there staked out. I'm so tired.'

'You must be.'

'Have you ever had proper insomnia?' Frieda didn't answer. 'It's horrible. But it's not just at night. It happened at work a few times. It was ghastly. I knew I was making a spectacle of myself, but I couldn't help it. I'm on sick leave now, though I keep trying to go back. I'm not used to not working. I've worked all my life – I've always been the main breadwinner. When my children were born I went back after a few weeks. This is the first time in over thirty years I've had time off. I used to long to have a painless illness for a few weeks so I could read and rest, you know, but I don't do any of that. I lie in bed in the dark and listen to my heart banging. Or I just sit on the sofa, doing nothing. Me! I've never done nothing – it's a family joke. I can't see friends. I dread seeing anyone. I even dread seeing my children, the effort of talking to them. I don't want anyone looking at me. Into me.'

'What would they see?'

'I don't know. I just know this is not bearable.' She shifted abruptly in the chair. 'That's stupid. Of course it's bearable. I'm not dying of it. It's just . . .' She raised her palms in the air in a gesture of bewilderment. Her gaunt, intelligent face sagged. 'I don't understand it.'

'And you're used to understanding things.'

'Yes.'

'And to feeling in control.'

'Yes. This – it's meaningless. It's just dread. As if my time of reckoning has come.'

Leaving her office, half an hour after Maria Dreyfus had gone, Frieda found Jude, as arranged. She got into the car beside her.

'We need to pick up someone on the way,' Frieda said.

'What do you mean?' said Jude. 'Who?'

'Someone who can help.'

'Have you cleared this with Levin?'

'I only thought of it last night. He's round the corner.'

'That's not really the point.'

Frieda directed Jude across Tottenham Court Road. He was standing outside the back entrance of the hospital on the pavement reading a book. When he saw the car, he slipped it into a side pocket. Frieda got out and moved to the back seat. Even so, he had trouble fitting himself inside, his knees drawn up.

Jude pulled away. 'So who is this?' she asked.

'Ask him,' said Frieda.

'Is there a problem?' he asked.

'We didn't know anyone was coming along.'

'"We"? Frieda asked me.'

'I mean me. The people I work for.'

He looked round at Frieda with an amused expression. 'If this is something awkward, I can get out here.'

'This is Professor Andrew Berryman. He's . . . Well, what are you?'

'Neurology,' said Berryman. 'Brains.'

'Yes, I know what neurology means,' said Jude. 'But I thought that was what Levin was using *you* for.'

'I'm not really interested in the chemistry of the brain – in neurons and synapses,' said Frieda. 'I mean, I've studied it and read about it. I'm interested in how behaviour originates in experience, memory, trauma.'

Berryman laughed. 'And I'm the opposite. I chose a branch of medicine where you don't really have to deal with patients. Looking at people's brains when they go wrong turns out to be a neat way of understanding how they work. I'm quoting from my first year-one lecture.'

'So you think there's something wrong with Hannah Docherty's brain?'

'We all know there's something wrong with her brain – or her mind,' said Frieda. 'She's been in a psychiatric hospital for thirteen years.'

'You ought to have cleared this with Levin,' said Jude.

'If Levin doesn't trust me, then he can look him up. He was crucial in solving the Robert Poole case a few years ago.'

'"Crucial" is putting it a bit strongly,' said Berryman. 'But, then, I should warn you that the last time I saw Frieda, she'd been brought into A & E.' He looked round. Squeezed into the little car as he was, this took a considerable effort. 'You were a terrible sight. Are you all right?'

'As I said at the time, it wasn't my blood.'

'Not your blood?' said Jude. 'What the hell happened?'

'It's complicated,' said Frieda. 'You can ask Levin. He probably knows most of it. Actually, he probably knows more than I do. Anyway, the answer is, I'm fine. Other people came off worse.'

As they drove through London, Frieda gave an account of Hannah Docherty's case. At one point, Jude interrupted: 'You are going to be discreet about this?'

'Which one of us are you talking to?' asked Frieda.

'Both of you.'

'I could be pompous about it. And say I was a doctor.' Berryman looked out of the window. 'Of course, if it's particularly interesting I might have to write a paper about it.'

Jude turned and stared at him.

'Names disguised. And places.'

'Don't worry about it,' said Frieda. 'He doesn't have normal human reactions.'

'It may seem funny to you,' said Jude, 'but if it gets into the papers, I'll be the one in trouble.'

'I'll be discreet,' said Berryman. 'I promise. So we're going to talk to Hannah Docherty?'

'Not immediately,' said Frieda.

Dr Christian Mendoza was the clinical director of Chelsworth Hospital. His office was in the original, old part of the house, the faded Gothic construction that looked like the remnant of a stately home or a castle or a public school. Frieda and Berryman were led along murky corridors and up a winding staircase, but the office itself was spacious, with large windows looking out on lawns and woodland. Mendoza was about sixty years old, with thinning grey hair, so that his pink scalp was clearly visible across the top of his head. He was dressed in a grey suit with a dark blue bow-tie.

He wore very small round tortoiseshell spectacles. He waved them towards two chairs that had been placed in front of his wooden desk. Its surface was almost empty, except for a telephone, a mug full of pencils and pens, an open blank notebook and a small pile of files.

'Dr Frieda Klein and Dr Andrew Berryman,' said Mendoza. 'A psychotherapist and a neurologist.'

'That's us,' said Frieda.

'That's the benefit of modern technology. I was able to look you up and I was impressed with what I found. I only wish you'd given us more notice and I could have arranged a proper reception for you.'

'That's all right,' said Frieda. 'I only decided this yesterday evening.'

Mendoza took a handkerchief from his pocket, removed his spectacles and breathed on them, then carefully cleaned the lenses. 'So, my first question is why, after all these years, a psychotherapist and a neurologist should be interested in poor Hannah Docherty.'

'Isn't she interesting?' said Frieda.

'Everybody here is interesting. I'm curious about why she is of special interest to you.'

'I'm looking at the crime she was involved in.'

'The crime she *committed*.' Mendoza looked at Berryman. 'You're being very quiet.'

'Don't mind me,' said Berryman. 'I'm just the Dr Watson. Or the Sancho Panza, or whatever.'

'I'm sure that's not true.' Mendoza looked back at Frieda. 'I understand you've already met Hannah.'

'I talked to her, but she didn't talk back. So, before seeing her again, I thought it would be useful to get some kind of account of her time here.'

'What would you like to know?'

Frieda thought for a moment. There was so much. 'What was her condition when she arrived?'

'Of course, I wasn't here then. I came in 2007. But I've looked at her file. She was committed here in a floridly psychotic state.'

'Which was treated how?'

Mendoza shrugged. 'As you'd expect, with a regime of anti-psychotic drugs and therapy.'

'Anything else?'

'She received ECT from time to time.'

'I'd generally thought of ECT as a treatment for morbid depression,' said Frieda.

'Are you here to question our treatment?'

'I'm just trying to build up a picture of her state of health.'

'I can give you that in two words,' said Mendoza. 'Not good.'

'Over thirteen years.'

'Over thirteen years.'

'When she arrived,' said Frieda, 'she was a convicted killer of her parents and of her teenage brother. Did that make her a target?'

'You mean of other patients?'

'That's right.'

'As I said, I wasn't here then. But as I understand it, it was the other way round. You've met Hannah. She's a pretty formidable figure. She quickly acquired a reputation.'

'For violence.'

'That's right.'

'And how do you respond here to someone with a reputation for violence?'

'We're a hospital,' said Mendoza. 'Our first responsibility is to our patients, to maintain their well-being and their safety.'

'What does that mean?' asked Frieda. 'In practical terms?'

'For Hannah Docherty's safety and for the safety of others, her medication was increased, she was kept under restraint and, when necessary, she was kept in solitary confinement.'

'How often?' asked Berryman.

'How often what?'

'Was she kept in solitary confinement?'

'When it was necessary.'

'And her periods of solitary confinement, would these be a matter of hours or days?'

'Whatever was deemed necessary.'

'How many days?'

'I don't know. It's all in her files.'

Berryman pointed at the files on Mendoza's desk. 'Are those them?'

'Yes.'

'May I?'

Mendoza contemplated the files. 'You can look,' he said. 'But you can't take them away and you can't make copies.'

'I just want to look.'

'And you need to see it all in context. Hannah Docherty killed her whole family. While here, she has been consistently anti-social and lacks all self-control. She has committed serious acts of violence against nurses, doctors and fellow patients. The most recent was just a few days ago. She stabbed a woman with her own knife.'

'You mean the knife was in Hannah's possession, or was it the other woman who'd got hold of it?' said Frieda.

'It's not an important distinction.'

'I think it is.'

'It belonged to the other woman.'

'So Hannah was being threatened?'

'However hard we try,' said Mendoza, 'Chelsworth Hospital unfortunately has its share of violent incidents.'

'I've read about them.'

'We deal with the most difficult patients in the country, the ones people want to shut away and forget about. You should remember that.'

Meanwhile, Berryman had taken the file and was flicking quickly through the papers with a glare of concentration.

'Is she seeing a therapist at the moment?' Frieda asked.

'She's seeing Dr Styles. Julia Styles. I'm not sure how effective it is.'

'Can we talk to her?'

'I was hoping I could deal with any questions you had.'

'I would like to know about her therapy with Hannah Docherty.'

'All right,' said Mendoza. 'Wait here. I'll talk to my assistant.' He left the room.

Berryman got up and walked towards the window. 'Quite a place, isn't it?' he said. 'You half expect to see a bat or a headless monk.'

'What do you make of it?'

'I'm not surprised you didn't get anything out of Hannah Docherty.'

'ECT isn't as bad as they make out in the movies.'

Berryman smiled. 'Yes, I believe I may have read something about that.'

'I'm sorry.'

'That's not what I was thinking of. If you or I or an average person was put in solitary confinement, after about three or four days we'd be hearing voices. After a month most of us would be experiencing psychotic symptoms. Our brains aren't designed for isolation. It's like a plant being without light, except that we don't die, unless we kill ourselves. Instead the brain does strange things to fill the void.'

'And Hannah Docherty was often kept in solitary confinement?'

'You heard my question to the good doctor. At first I thought it was the equivalent of locking her in a cupboard for a few hours until she stopped screaming. That would have been bad enough. But looking through the file, I just stopped counting. For example, in 2003 she was in solitary for one continuous seven-month stretch. In 2005 she assaulted a warder and was in what they call "solitary-plus" for a year and a half.'

'That doesn't sound good.'

'It sounds like the sort of experiment on brain plasticity that we're unfortunately not allowed to carry out because it would be unethical. But I would make a hypothesis that after a year in solitary-plus the brain has become a different physical object.'

'So you don't think there's much point in talking to her.'

'No, no. I'm fascinated to meet her. Now someone's done the experiment, I might as well look at the results.'

Frieda frowned at him. 'You're not really like this, are you?'

'You think I might be nice underneath?'

Berryman had no interest in meeting Julia Styles. 'That's your territory,' he said, flapping his hand and barely looking up from the files. 'Since we can't take them away, I'm just making sure I have them in here.' He tapped his temple with a forefinger. 'Come and fetch me when you're done.'

Julia Styles's room was near Dr Mendoza's office, but her windows looked in the other direction, onto the courtyard where Frieda could see men walking, heads down against the strengthening wind.

'What can I do for you?' asked the woman, who had risen from her neat desk (one file, presumably Hannah's, one notebook turned to a blank page, one small pot plant with a single flower rising above the coppery leaves). She was small, neat, her blouse crisply ironed. Her tone was cool, her handshake firm but brief.

'I wanted to talk to you about Hannah Docherty.'

'I'm not sure what you want to know – and, of course, what Hannah says to me is in confidence. I can't divulge any details.'

Frieda took a seat opposite her. 'I don't want you to betray her confidences.'

'There aren't many of those.'

'She doesn't tell you much?'

'She hardly talks at all.'

'How long have you been seeing her?'

'On and off for the last nine years.'

'A long time. Has she changed a lot in those years?'

'She's got older. She's got tougher. She's got quieter. She's become more violent, more unhappy, more disturbed.' She met Frieda's gaze. 'She hates me.'

'Really?'

'Yes.' She gave a small, contained laugh. 'Not transference, don't go thinking that. She hates being in the same room. Very often she refuses to see me – and when a patient doesn't want to even see you, let alone say anything, well, there's not much you can do, is there?'

'I don't know if that's right.'

'Of course you don't know.' There was no mistaking the hostility in Julia Styles's voice now. 'You work at the Warehouse, don't you?'

'Sometimes.'

'And you have private patients as well.'

65

'Yes.'

'So you treat the discontents of the rich. Here, we deal with real madness, real despair, with dangerous rage, with minds that are so chaotic you can't penetrate them at all, or make any sense of what they're communicating.'

Frieda looked at Julia Styles curiously. Her cheeks were flushed; she was obviously angry. 'You think I don't understand what you have to deal with here.'

'Of course you don't. How could you? I gather from Dr Mendoza that you are here to establish whether Hannah Docherty is clinically insane or not.'

'Is she?'

'Look, Dr Klein. Hannah was a troubled and dysfunctional teenager who killed her mother, her brother, her stepfather. She is my patient, and my job is to help her recover. But ask yourself, what would that mean? It would mean she had gained insight into what she had done. She would have to confront the horror of it. She would have to acknowledge her guilt. Sometimes I think the kindest thing to do with people like Hannah is to leave them in their delusions.'

'I see.'

'You probably don't. I had a patient who killed his wife and his three young children while he was in a schizophrenic frenzy. A voice in his head was telling him that they were going to be brutally tortured, so he thought he was saving them. With medication and with therapy he came to understand what he had done. But is that such a good thing?'

'I don't know. And of course you're right that I can't understand what you face every day. But that's why I'm here: to learn from you.' She saw some of the tension go from Julia Styles's shoulders; her fist unclenched on the desk. 'Are you saying she has never acknowledged her guilt?'

'There's a phrase she repeats – the nursing staff tell me she does it in her room as well. They hear her howling it.'

'What?'

'She says, "It's me, it's me."'

'She said that to me as well.' Frieda considered this. 'Never "It *was* me"?'

'No. Always in the present.'

'It could be some kind of confession, of course – or it could be a way of asserting her identity.'

'It could be.' Julia Styles nodded.

A glimmer of understanding seemed to pass between them. Frieda nodded at her and smiled. 'You've been very helpful.'

'Have I?'

'Yes.'

Frieda stood up and the two women shook hands, for longer this time.

'She's one of my failures.'

'Because you can't help her at all?'

'Because I can't reach her.'

Andrew Berryman was no longer poring over Hannah's files. He was leaning back in his chair, his hands clasped beneath his head, and gazing at the ceiling as if something was written on it. 'Fruitful?' he asked, as Frieda came in.

'I don't know.'

'Shall we go and get that nice Dr Mendoza to take us to see Hannah?' He unlocked his hands and sat up. 'It should be interesting.'

But nice Dr Mendoza looked at them with a solemn expression.

'I'm afraid you can't see her today after all,' he said.

'Why not?'

He shook his head from side to side. 'She is unwell.'

'In what sense unwell?' asked Frieda. 'We've come all this way specifically to see her, as you know.'

He nodded sympathetically. 'It's a shame,' he said. 'A great inconvenience for you.'

Frieda clenched her jaw. 'We'd like to see her nevertheless.'

'I'm sorry, Dr Klein, but it's not going to work. Not today.'

'What I would like to know is whether it was ever going to work.' Berryman's tone was cheerful.

Mendoza didn't reply.

'Can we at least speak to her for a few minutes?' asked Frieda.

'She had a severe psychotic episode and has been heavily sedated. I'm sure you understand.'

'I understand very well,' said Frieda. 'Last time I was here, Hannah had been beaten up.'

'Last time you were here,' said Dr Mendoza, 'Hannah had just stabbed someone and nearly killed them.'

'And this time she has been drugged so heavily that we can't see her.'

'I'm not sure you understand the kind of patients we have to deal with here.'

'I understand that you want your job to be easy. You don't want trouble.'

'My dear Dr –'

'If you want my advice,' said Berryman, 'you shouldn't call her that.'

'But you should understand this – you've got trouble. And we will come back and we will see her.'

Mendoza looked at her, then suddenly stood up. He took off his glasses and, without them, his eyes were defenceless. 'You can see her,' he said. 'If that's what you want.'

*

68

An orderly took Frieda and Berryman up some stairs, through a room that was empty of people but contained several chairs, a sofa, a television, and through two sets of heavy doors. Now it felt like a prison, not a hospital. They walked along a corridor full of identical green doors with grilles in each one; their footsteps echoed. The orderly stopped at a door near the end and pulled a set of keys from his belt.

'You asked for it,' he said.

The room was small and bare: just a cell with a narrow bed beneath the high window that cast little light. He turned a switch and a garish brightness flooded the space. The shape in the bed didn't move. Frieda could see a greasy tangle of hair and one out-flung hand, a tattoo on its wrist.

'There she is,' he said.

Frieda went over to the bed and bent over the figure. 'Hannah,' she said softly.

There was no response. Very gently, she drew down the cover slightly to see Hannah's clammy, swollen face. There was blood around her nostrils and drool running from her mouth. Her neck was grimy with old dirt. She was breathing hoarsely and her lips puffed with each exhalation. Frieda put a hand on her shoulder and briefly rested it there, but Hannah was deeply asleep. Her eyes moved under their closed lids, and Frieda wondered if her dreams were nightmares or moments of freedom. She lifted a thick strand of hair away from Hannah's cheek and pulled the cover back over her.

'Well?' asked Levin. He was drinking peppermint tea from a huge mug and his tortoiseshell spectacles were steamed over. 'How was she?'

'Unavailable.'

'That's a pity.' Levin looked across at Keegan, who was on

his knees, pulling a large box out of a cupboard marginally too small for it. 'Isn't that a pity, Jock?'

An indistinguishable grunt came from the cupboard.

'The case is unsound,' said Frieda.

'Would you like some peppermint tea?'

'No.'

'Of course it's unsound. We know that. We just want to establish whether she is in any danger of knowing that and of making trouble.'

'No, she isn't. I'm certain of that at least.'

Keegan got up from the floor. He was perspiring. 'So that's that, then,' he said.

'No.'

'What?'

'It's precisely because she's in no danger of knowing that that we have to continue.'

'Continue?' Keegan frowned at her so that his forehead was corrugated with wrinkles. Levin put down his mug and leaned back in his chair. He took off his glasses and began scrupulously to polish them on his frayed orange tie. 'Continue with what?'

'With this investigation.'

'There is no investigation.'

'There is now.'

Keegan turned to Levin. 'Aren't you going to say something?'

'What would you like me to say?'

'That this is ridiculous. That this is *over*. Thank you and goodbye.'

Levin put his glasses back on and tapped them into position with his forefinger. 'What do you want?' he asked Frieda.

'Her doctor and her therapist have no doubt that Hannah is of unsound mind. But Andrew and I . . .'

'Andrew?'

'Professor Berryman.'

'Whoever he may be,' said Keegan. 'And I'm not going to ask what he was doing at Chelsworth Hospital with you.'

'We believe that her disordered state and her psychotic episodes are probably a result of profound psychological disturbance and prolonged bouts of solitary confinement, not to mention repeated sedation. Anyone would be mad. It only takes days, hours even, before people show the effects of solitary confinement. There have been numerous studies that demonstrate –'

Keegan sat on the edge of the table next to Levin. 'We don't need this,' he said. 'We've got enough on our plate without trying to . . .' He stopped and frowned. 'To what?' he continued, addressing his words to Frieda now. 'I don't even know what you want. You're saying that the case was improperly conducted. Well, thank you, but we know that already and it's why you were asked to assess her mental condition in the first place. You were meant to tick a box, not open bloody Pandora's. And then you're saying she's been sent mad by being locked up alone and heavily drugged. I'm sorry about that, of course, but it's way outside our remit.' He glared at Frieda. 'Don't look at me like that. I'm not here to solve the problems of the world. I'm trying to do a difficult job as well as I can. Whatever the reason, she's mad now. So what do you want?'

He stopped as though out of breath. Levin picked up his mug once more and peered into it with an air of interest. 'Yes,' he said. 'What do you want?'

'I just had this thought,' said Frieda. 'If the case is unsafe, and if Hannah Docherty was not of unsound mind, just deeply troubled, at the time, as so many teenagers are troubled, then we should start with a basic principle and see where that leads us.'

71

'What basic principle would that be?' Levin sounded genuinely interested.

'The presumption of innocence.'

Silence filled the room. Levin had taken off his glasses once more. Keegan stared at him. 'Tell her,' he said. 'Tell her it's out of the question.'

'Why is it?' asked Frieda.

'Because Hannah Docherty murdered her entire family and some arsehole copper screwing up the investigation doesn't alter that. You saw the files. She killed them and now she's in a hospital and she'll be there for the rest of her life because she's mad and she's a danger to herself and others. And anyway . . .' His voice rose in volume. 'It's not the point. The point is that we're looking into a senior police officer, Detective Chief Inspector Ben Sedge. It's a pile of shit and we're wading through it. That's our job. That's what we're being paid for. Hannah Docherty is just the small print.'

'A means to an end.'

'What's wrong with that?'

'Everything is wrong with that.'

'Walter.' Keegan turned to Levin. 'Tell her.'

'What shall I tell her?'

'Don't do this. Please don't do this.'

'It's OK, Jock.'

'It's not. Maybe you don't want to deal with the small, shitty, boring stuff. That's what I do. Hannah Docherty is a distraction.'

'It wouldn't be you. It wouldn't be us. It would be her.'

'Her.'

'Me,' said Frieda. 'Just me. And there's something else.'

'What?'

'If I'm going to talk to people, go to places, it may be a bit of a problem being just a psychotherapist.'

'That sounds right,' said Keegan.

'So what can we do about it?' asked Levin.

'It would be useful if someone could come with me. A policeman.'

'Did you have anyone in mind?' He gave a faint smile. 'Like Jock here?'

'There's somebody I'd like to try. But would they be allowed to do it?'

'Check them out and I'll get them seconded,' said Levin.

'You can do that?'

'This is just for a limited time. It can't be open-ended.'

'A few days,' said Frieda. 'A week or two at the most. If I haven't found anything by then, I'll walk away.'

'You talked about places you wanted to see,' said Keegan. 'What places?'

'The Oakley Road house, for a start,' said Frieda. 'Where the murders happened.'

'There are people living there. They probably won't be happy about you blundering around.'

'That's why I need someone with a badge.'

At group therapy, they sit in a semicircle and Tisha talks and talks about her little daughter and how she was taken away from her and how she still dreams about her, eight years later and five years into her sentence. But how can you dream about someone if you don't know what they look like? Shay leans across to her neighbour. 'Dory went for Hannah,' she whispers. 'Hannah got her with her own knife. Thirty stitches.'

'Shay?'

Shay doesn't notice Dr Styles is talking to her.

'Shay? Could I ask you to pay us some attention?'

Shay looks round at the doctor, who is sitting opposite the group.

'Is there something you'd like to share with us?' says Dr Styles.

'Not really.'

'Come on, Shay. We can say anything here, as long as it's nothing wilfully cruel or hurtful. Was it cruel or hurtful?'

'No.'

'Then share it with us.'

'It was about Dory. How she's been stabbed by Hannah Docherty.'

'It's not clear who was responsible.'

'No, Dr Styles.'

'But it's important to talk about it. We must talk about our feelings and what we can learn from this. Has anyone got anything to offer?'

There is a silence. The members of the group look down at the floor or up at the ceiling, anything so that they don't meet Dr Styles's gaze.

'You, Kelly,' says Dr Styles. 'Why don't you start us off?'

'How?'

'For example,' says Dr Styles, slowly and patiently, 'what can we learn from something like this?'

'That we shouldn't fight,' says Kelly. She speaks the words as if they are part of a lesson she has learned with difficulty. 'And that it's better to talk about things than . . . you know, than to fight.'

'That's right. That's a good start. But you look doubtful, Kelly. Is there some part of this that you don't understand?'

'But what if someone comes at you?' says Kelly.

'You tell me,' says Dr Styles. 'We're here to talk about things like that.'

'I just mean, if they come at you, you can't just talk.'

Shay leans across to her neighbour again, and speaks in a whisper. 'We'll see what Mary says about that.'

'Mary's in solitary. She won't know yet.'

'Mary'll know. Mary always knows. Mary'll see to Hannah. She'll show her who's boss in here.'

NINE

'I'm worried about identifying with her.' Frieda was once more sitting opposite Thelma Scott. 'She's an intelligent, energetic, self-sufficient woman. I get the impression her husband's always been dependent on her, as have her children, her friends as well. The word she uses for herself is "competent". She's having panic attacks. She feels unsafe in her world, which has come to seem like a hostile and even vindictive place.'

'You're describing a kind of paranoia.'

'For years she's controlled her feelings of vulnerability and fear. Now *they*'re controlling *her.*'

'Why would you identify with that?'

'I lie in bed at night, awake, full of dread. You're going to ask, dread of what?'

Thelma smiled. 'Let me ask the questions before you answer them.'

'Even if you aren't going to ask, I'll tell you. Dread that something is coming, that things are gathering to a head. Dread that there are enemies waiting in the shadows.' She remembered a word that Maria Dreyfus had used on her first visit. 'Dread of a reckoning,' she said.

Thelma nodded. She had the crabbed hands of an old woman but the voice of a young one. Her eyes were bright in the creases of her face. 'As I often do,' she said, 'I need to ask you how much of this is abstract and how much a more tangible fear. What kind of reckoning do you mean?'

'You mean, do I have real enemies in the shadows?'

'Or, at least, any that could really hurt you.'

'I'm not awake worrying that someone's going to break in.'

'But you have been attacked.'

'I have. And then, of course, there's Sandy. I can't get his face out of my mind. Or the knowledge that I was in part responsible for his death.'

'The person who killed him was responsible. Nobody else.'

'If it hadn't been for me, he wouldn't have died.'

'You haven't answered my question.'

Frieda nodded. 'I do have real enemies. Some I don't care about. Commissioner Crawford. Hal Bradshaw.'

'Remind me.'

'He's the profiler Crawford uses. He thinks I burned down his house.'

'That one.' Thelma's voice was dry.

'But, as you know, as you're waiting for me to say, my real enemy is Dean Reeve.'

Dean Reeve: the killer and child-abductor, the man the world believed to be dead but who had, Frieda was certain, killed his twin and was still out there somewhere. Out there and watching over her, protecting her, stalking her, loving her and hating her. Dean Reeve had come into her life five years ago, when his identical twin had been Frieda's client. He had killed a disturbed young woman who would otherwise have killed Frieda; he had murdered the man who had raped Frieda when she was a teenager; he had burned down Hal Bradshaw's house in revenge for Bradshaw's treatment of Frieda; he had tortured a psychotic patient who had threatened Frieda. He was the grotesque distortion of her protector. For many months now he had been absent from her life, but Frieda had no doubt that he was still there, somewhere, that he was watching her and that he would never go away.

'You still believe he's a danger?' asked Thelma.

'I *know* he is. I just don't know what form that danger will take.'

'So is this what you dread, when you like awake at night?'

'A part of what I dread. But I can't disentangle him from other feelings. Which is why I feel some kind of identification with my new patient.'

'So these other feelings . . .'

'There's something I think I should tell you.'

'Yes?'

'I seem to have got involved with the case I was telling you about.'

'*You* "seem to have got involved" – you talk as if you have no agency.'

'I have decided to become involved.'

'Last time we met you said you had decided against it. You were very clear why it was a bad idea.'

'I know.'

'This is why you're sitting here, not because you worry about identifying with Maria Dreyfus. She's your excuse. Even Dean Reeve is your excuse. You're here because of the new case, the one you know you should be wary of. That's where your feeling of dread is located.'

'Perhaps.'

'And the case?'

'It's about chaos,' said Frieda. 'Abandonment.'

Thelma looked at the clock.

'Chaos and abandonment,' she said. 'Something for us to talk about next time.'

Frieda walked from the Underground station to her house. Passing an electrical shop, she saw through its windows a succession of images on the row of flat-screen televisions: a footbridge stranded in an expanse of water; a line of half-submerged cars on a road that had turned into a river; a man in a yellow waterproof rowing along a street; waves surging along a sea-front. It wasn't raining any more, but the air was saturated and there were large puddles underfoot.

She reached her front door and unlocked it, stepping gratefully into the hallway where she hung her coat on the hook and unwound her scarf from her neck. For a moment she stood quite still. Something felt different. There was a faint smell in the air that didn't belong with the smell of wood and books and furniture polish that she was used to. She had noticed it before. She moved slowly through the house and into the kitchen. Everything seemed in place, her breakfast things washed up and on the draining-board, the herbs on the windowsill, the bunch of orange tulips in its vase on the wooden table. The cat-flap rattled and the tortoiseshell cat she had reluctantly inherited slid through it and stood before her, softly purring. She scratched its chin. There was a single spoon on the surface that looked as though it had stirred yoghurt or cream. She opened the fridge but everything was as she had left it.

In the living room, she lit the fire, setting a match to a tightly rolled ball of paper and watching until the kindling caught and a small flame was licking at the logs. She looked round the room. There had been a game of chess she had been playing through on the chess table by the window but the pieces had been put back in the box. Had she done that?

Her house – this narrow little house in a cobbled mews, squeezed between ugly lock-ups on one side and council flats on the other – had always been her refuge and her place of safety. She could shut the door on the world and be alone, in its dim light, its cleanliness and silence. Over the past few years some of its boundaries had been ruptured – she'd let the cat in, she'd let her chaotic niece Chloë in, and then Chloë's friends. Josef had taken it upon himself to install a whole new bathroom. Last year, suspected of murdering a man she'd once loved, she had had to flee from the house entirely and it had stood empty and neglected for weeks, gathering dust. But now she had a vague sense that someone had been here. She climbed the stairs to her bedroom and the bathroom, where Josef's beautiful tub stood, then the next flight of stairs to her garret study. The book she was reading was where she had left it, the marker in place; the charcoal and soft-leaded pencils were in the mug. She looked through the sketches in the pad. She vaguely remembered – or thought that she remembered – doing a quick drawing of the Hardy Tree, from memory, in preparation for a proper visit to St Pancras churchyard once the rains had stopped, but it wasn't there.

She called Josef, who was the only one with keys to her house.

'Yes? Frieda? Is me.'

'Have you been here recently, Josef?'

'Here?'

'In my house.'

'For the cat-flap.'

'I mean in the last few days.'

'No. You want that I come?'

'No. It's fine.'

'I can come this minute.'

'I was just wondering.' She ended the call and went downstairs to the fire, which was now burning steadily in the grate. She was imagining things, the atmosphere of Chelsworth Hospital seeping into her consciousness; the memory of Hannah there, drugged and bruised; the images she had seen in all those photographs of the murders of her family. That boy, Hannah's little brother, his smooth skull cracked open and blood everywhere. Her boundaries were crumbling.

TEN

'No,' said Karlsson.

'I haven't properly explained it yet,' said Frieda.

'You've explained enough. You want me to go around with you annoying people about an old case. Tempting as it may be – and it's not very tempting – there's no way I could do it. I can hardly get to the toilet.'

They were sitting in Karlsson's flat. There were windows looking out on the small garden. It was raining heavily again and there were pools of water on the muddy little lawn. Karlsson was sitting in an armchair. His plastered leg was resting on a wooden stool.

'I used to like the idea of a bit of sick leave,' he said. 'I could do some repainting. Get the garden sorted out.'

'The garden?'

'Look at that lawn. I've put seed on it, I've put fertilizer on it, I've stabbed it, I've rolled it, and it still looks like the day after a rock festival.'

'So you've given it your best shot.'

'Turf. Just roll it out like a carpet. Or I could have it paved.'

'You could hire Josef to do it.'

'This is my garden. I need to do it myself.'

'What you need is to get out there and do your job,' said Frieda. 'I could really use your help.'

'No.'

'We're not going to be running after villains. You could get round with a stick. Or in a wheelchair.'

'Look at me,' said Karlsson. 'Or, better still, read my doctor's letter, which explains why I'm not available for work.'

'I wasn't going to say this . . .' Frieda began.

'Then don't.'

'But the entire reason I'm doing this is because Levin arranged for your reinstatement.'

'All right,' said Karlsson. 'So the two of you got me out of the grave I'd dug for myself. Sometimes I wish you'd left me there. The fact is, I would be useful if your investigation was confined to bungalows and premises with wheelchair access.' He thought for a moment. 'If only there was someone who was available during my absence.'

'What?'

'If only there was a detective who was stuck in the office, while her boss was on sick leave.'

'No,' said Frieda. 'Absolutely not.'

'Was this your idea?' asked Detective Constable Yvette Long. She was sitting in the back seat. Frieda was in the front passenger seat. Josef Morozov was driving. Frieda wasn't sure who the car belonged to – Josef usually drove his battered van.

'Karlsson suggested it,' said Frieda. 'And I agreed.'

'Was it his idea of a joke?'

'What joke?' asked Josef.

'He thought you'd be the best for the job,' said Frieda. 'Anyway, if you didn't want to do it, all you had to do was refuse.'

'It was made clear to me that a refusal would be taken very seriously indeed.'

'I'm sorry about that.'

'You've got powerful friends, apparently.'

'They're not exactly friends. But it shouldn't be that bad.'

Frieda looked round at Yvette Long. Her cheeks were flushed and she was staring out of the window, avoiding eye contact.

'I made the call,' Yvette said. 'I spoke to the owner. Or the owner's wife. She's called Emma Travis. She didn't sound pleased.'

'But you persuaded her.'

'She probably doesn't want the whole murder business brought up. But I'm sure you've got a good reason for it.'

'I want to see where it all happened.'

'Why is Josef here?'

'Don't you want him?'

'This is a criminal investigation.'

'According to the file, the house was sold soon after the murder and there was substantial rebuilding. I thought Josef might help us get a sense of the previous layout.'

'How?'

'By being a builder.'

Yvette took a deep breath. Frieda couldn't quite tell whether it was a sigh of disapproval or just a breath. She turned round again and faced forward. Josef glanced at her. She thought she saw the faintest sign of a smile. She hoped and prayed that Yvette wouldn't notice.

'Before we begin,' said Yvette, abruptly, 'I want to clear the air about a few things.'

'What things?'

When Yvette spoke it was in a rush, as if it had been building up and she needed to say it all at once before she was stopped. 'First, I thought you had stopped working with the police. Second, I've got to admit that I'm puzzled by the fact that you seem to be reopening a case that was closed more than ten years ago. And third, you may think that everybody has forgotten how close you came to destroying DCI

84

Karlsson's career. But they haven't. Not everybody. Some people remember.'

'Yes.' Frieda spoke slowly and carefully. 'It's good to clear the air. As you know, the reasons behind all your questions make up a long and complicated story. But you also know that Karlsson is someone who takes responsibility for himself.'

'Which is why he needs people to look out for him.'

'And in a way all of this . . . this investigation, whatever it is we're doing, this is about getting Karlsson reinstated. Someone stepped in and helped and I owed him a favour.'

'That sounds like someone setting fire to a house and then wanting the credit for putting it out.'

Frieda looked round at Yvette once more. 'I don't want any credit,' she said. 'I'm trying to do the right thing. Isn't that what we're all doing?'

'It's just that people keep getting hurt. Don't you worry about that? I thought that therapists were supposed to make people better.'

'One day we should have a talk about what therapists are supposed to do.'

Yvette didn't reply and the rest of the journey was in silence, except when Frieda looked at her map and pointed out the directions to Josef. They drove through Peckham and then, suddenly and briefly, it was as if they were passing through a country park and a village before they were back in familiar-looking London streets. Frieda pointed out the turning and then they were in Oakley Road. Josef pulled up outside number fifty-four. The three got out and looked around. The cars and the front gardens and the immaculate façades all told the same story of comfort and prosperity.

'I was going to say that this doesn't look like somewhere where a family would be murdered,' said Frieda.

'Why didn't you?' asked Yvette.

'Because I don't know how a place like that is supposed to look.' She nodded at Yvette. 'You first. You're in charge.'

'You mean I'm your way in.'

'Are you going to argue about every single thing I say to you?'

'I'm just stating the truth as I see it.'

The small front garden was shielded by a hedge. Yvette rang the bell and the door was answered quickly. Emma Travis was in her early forties. She was dressed in a navy blue shirt and fawn-coloured trousers. She ushered them quickly inside as if she didn't want them to be seen. Yvette introduced them all. She described Frieda and Josef as consultants. Emma Travis looked suspiciously at them and Josef gave her a nod, his face assuming a serious professional expression.

'I have to say,' she said, in a wavering, emotional voice, 'that my husband was angry about this. The people we bought this house from sold it because they couldn't bear the bad publicity any more. I hope this isn't going to start up again. If the children got to hear about it, I don't know what would happen.'

'We're grateful for your cooperation,' said Frieda. 'Otherwise we would have had to obtain a search warrant. And then it becomes a public matter.'

'That would be terrible,' said Emma Travis.

'We'll be as discreet as possible.'

Emma Travis stood awkwardly, moving her weight from one leg to the other. 'Do you want me to show you around?'

'It might be best if you didn't,' said Frieda. 'We're going to be talking about things you may not want to hear.'

'Yes, yes, of course. That's right, I'm sure.' She looked at each of them. 'Can you tell me why you're here, after all this time?'

'We're checking one or two aspects of the case,' said Frieda.

'You probably think I'm just worried about property values. We did buy the house at a lower price than we would have otherwise. People were put off. But it's the idea of what happened here. Sometimes I wake up in the night and think about it.'

'That's understandable,' said Frieda.

'People come and look at the house. Can you imagine that? There are people who visit murder scenes as if they were tourist sites. They take pictures. Sometimes they've even knocked at the door and asked if they can look around.'

'My father visits battlefields,' said Yvette.

'That's different,' said Emma Travis. 'Battlefields are history. This is just . . . just horrible.'

'This is a sort of history,' said Frieda.

'Sometimes I think they should have knocked the house down and built a new one or a little park. They do that sometimes.' Emma Travis sighed. 'Can I make you some tea?'

'No, thanks,' said Frieda.

'For me, yes,' said Josef. 'With the one sugar.'

'And one for me too,' said Yvette. 'With just a tiny splash of milk.'

'Before you do that,' said Frieda. 'Can you tell us about the building work that was done?'

'It was done by the previous people. We've got the details in a file somewhere, I think. You'd have to ask my husband where it is.'

'Can we walk around on our own?' said Frieda.

'Will you be long?'

'We'll be as quick as we can.'

When Emma Travis had disappeared in the direction of the kitchen, Josef looked questioningly at Frieda.

'I was hoping you could give me an idea of how much the layout of the house has changed, down here and up on the first floor,' she said.

'I'll try.'

Josef raised his head and looked at the ceiling in the hallway. He gently touched a stretch of the wall. Then, one after another, he walked through the doors that led off the hall, to reception rooms on either side and down to the kitchen. Yvette and Frieda could hear him talking to Emma Travis. There was the sound of laughter.

'You should watch him,' said Yvette. 'Around a lonely housewife like that.'

Frieda was about to defend Josef but she stopped herself. Yvette could be right. Maybe she should have a word.

Josef returned, shaking his head. 'No big change down here. New conservatory at the back.'

'Rory's blood was found in the hallway here,' said Frieda. 'In the front room on the right.' She pushed the door open and they stepped in. It was a living room, the sort of living room that wasn't lived in. It reminded Frieda of a public area in an old-fashioned hotel, with carefully arranged chairs and some magazines piled on a low table.

Yvette walked to the window. 'The hedge shelters it from the street,' she said.

'I'm not sure,' said Frieda. 'It may have grown up since then. And then there was more of Rory's blood on the stairs.'

'How much blood?' asked Josef, distressed. Frieda knew he was imagining Rory's death and thinking of his own sons, far away in Ukraine.

'That's a good question,' she said. 'Yvette must know more about this than I do. But I suppose blood can be in pools, or spattered, or sprayed, or in drops. From the photographs of the scene it looked more like smears.'

'Oh, please.' Emma Travis had entered the room with two mugs of tea on a tray and a plate of biscuits. 'I couldn't help overhearing. Could someone help with the tray?'

Josef stepped forward and took it from her.

'I don't know how you can do this,' she said. 'I don't know how you can have it in your head.'

'It's difficult,' said Yvette. 'And we're just talking about it.'

'Don't even say that. I don't want to hear any more. I won't be able to forget it.' She looked at Josef and her face softened. 'Yours is the one with the deer on it. Do have a biscuit.'

She hurried out of the room. Josef and Yvette picked up their mugs and Josef took three biscuits.

Yvette sipped the tea. 'Smears. What does that mean?'

'I don't know,' said Frieda. 'There was more of his blood on the stairs and on the first floor outside his bedroom. And yet it appears he was killed in his bed, so it doesn't make obvious sense. There were also traces of his stepfather's blood downstairs and on the stairs. Less of it, I think. Let's go upstairs.'

Josef went first. He rapped on walls, stood on a chair to examine the ceiling, opened doors. 'Is all different here. All rooms changed.'

'This is where the bodies were found,' said Yvette. 'They probably wanted to make it like it had never happened.'

Josef stood at the top of the stairs, his back to them and to the street.

'There was one room here.' He pointed to the right.

'That was Rory's bedroom,' said Frieda.

'Ah,' he said, on a drawn-out sigh. 'The boy. And one here.' He pointed to the left.

'Spare bedroom,' said Frieda.

'Bathroom between.' Josef turned and walked along the corridor beside the stairs. He pointed enquiringly up another flight of stairs.

Frieda shook her head. 'Nothing happened up there. It was all here.'

He gestured ahead, in the direction of the front of the house. 'Big room there.'

'The main bedroom,' Frieda said. 'This was where Deborah Docherty and Aidan Locke were found, Deborah in a nightdress, Aidan in his clothes.'

'I couldn't live here,' said Yvette. 'It gives me the creeps even walking around. Don't you feel it?'

'Houses know,' agreed Josef.

'There are places like that,' said Frieda, 'where bad things have happened, terrible things have been done over and over again. I don't feel it here, though. One awful, tragic thing happened. I don't think I'd like to live here, but not because of the murders.' She looked around. 'It's strange, though.'

'It's not so strange,' said Yvette. 'There are lots of possibilities.'

'Such as?'

Yvette thought for a moment. 'Deborah and Rory are in bed. Aidan and Hannah have a row downstairs, she beats him with a hammer. Realizes what she's done and decides to make it look like a robbery gone wrong. Or she's angry at the whole family. Goes up and kills her sleeping mother. Aidan isn't entirely dead, crawls up, leaving traces of blood, gets to the bedroom and Hannah finishes him off. Then kills her brother, gets blood on her, some of which she leaves traces of as she goes downstairs.'

'That's good,' said Frieda. 'But it can't be true.'

'Why?'

'When they found the bodies, the pooling of the blood in them showed that Aidan Locke had died earlier than Rory or Deborah.'

'That was just one possibility,' said Yvette. 'I only had a moment to think about it.'

'Let's not come up with scenarios too quickly,' said Frieda. 'Let's hang on to the oddity. The bits don't seem to fit together. Deborah and Aidan are together, but he died earlier. And she's dressed for bed and he isn't. And then those two bodies are found together, and yet it's the blood of Aidan and Rory that is found downstairs. Not hers. And why is only Rory's blood found in the front room?'

'Maybe she killed him there.'

'No. As I said, the evidence points to him being killed where he was found, in his bed. And, anyway, there would have been more blood there. Much more. You should see the photos of the bedrooms.'

'She could have killed him downstairs and cleaned up some of the blood. People don't act logically when they commit a murder.'

'They don't,' said Frieda, 'but the laws of biology and physics still apply.' She sank into a reverie, then suddenly realized where she was. 'Time to go, I suppose.'

Downstairs, they returned the mugs to Emma Travis and she led them to the door.

'We may need to come back at some point,' said Frieda.

'As long as there aren't uniforms and police cars.'

Emma Travis opened the door but Frieda held back. 'Your neighbours – have they been here long?'

'Are you going to bring it all up with *them*?'

'I was wondering if they'd been here when it happened.'

'The ones that side' – she gestured to the left – 'only arrived a year or so ago. But the ones on the other side, they've been here for ever.' She raised her eyebrows. 'They're the ones who organize the street party every year.'

'What are their names?'

'Sebastian Tait and Flora Goffin. They're married but she kept her own name. They're perfectly nice, a bit eccentric.'

Frieda turned to Yvette and Josef. 'Why don't you two wait in the car?'

ELEVEN

Sebastian Tait was tall and bony and pale, and he was wearing a long striped apron and slippers. There was a cotton scarf wrapped around his neck, and very thin glasses perched on the end of his aquiline nose. He seemed to think that Frieda was there to service the boiler.

'No,' said Frieda. 'I don't know anything about boilers.'

'I've taken the morning off.'

'Even so, I can't repair your boiler. I'm here about the murders of the Dochertys in 2001. I think you lived here then?'

His expression changed. 'If you're a journalist, I'm afraid I'm going to have to ask you to leave.'

'I'm not a journalist. I'm part of an inquiry into the way that case was conducted.'

'Are you a police officer?'

Frieda paused. 'I'm a consultant working with the police.'

'Do you have identification?'

'Wait,' said Frieda.

She walked out of the house and returned a minute later with a glowering Yvette, who showed her own badge, mumbled an explanation and left.

'I know who you are,' said Tait.

'DC Long just told you.'

'No, I mean I know who you are. I've heard of you. I know what you do. You should have said so before.'

Frieda started to answer but Tait wasn't paying attention.

'I can't give you long. I've promised to be at work soon.

It's a bit of a mess, I'm afraid. Flora's away and the cleaner's had a baby.'

Frieda looked around. It was indeed a mess, but not of dirty plates or scattered papers. There were scraps of material everywhere, small bright heaps of silk.

'I make things,' Tait said. 'In my spare time, of course. At the moment, I make ties, but not many people want ties any more. I sometimes make hats as well. You look surprised.'

'I wasn't really.'

'The kind that ladies wear at Ascot. It's great fun. It's like being an engineer really – you have to construct that kind of hat. Do you wear hats?'

'No.'

'A pity. In my day job, I'm a tailor. Bespoke suits for men and women. We're a dying breed. You may have heard of us – Taits of Piccadilly?'

Frieda hadn't heard of them but didn't reply. He gestured for her to sit, then lowered himself into the sofa, his long legs crossed in front of him.

'I'm not quite sure what I want to ask. But I was hoping to find out more about the Dochertys as a family, get some sense of what they were like.'

'You've come to the right house, then.'

'You knew them?'

'Oh, yes. We arrived here in 1995 and they came the year after. We became friends. It doesn't always happen in London, does it? Not with neighbours. Sometimes it's still hard to believe. When I look at their house, I still think of what it was like when they were there. We had such fun. When it all happened . . .' He seemed to be struggling for words and not finding them. 'And Rory, that was beyond anything. Just thirteen. Rick took it very badly.'

'Rick?'

'Our son. He was the same age as Rory. They were thick as thieves, always round at each other's houses. Though I'm afraid at school Rory was bullied and Rick didn't step in. That made it all worse, of course, when it happened. He felt terribly guilty, probably still does.'

'Have you just the one child?'

'Two. Saul was just six months older than Hannah.' He pulled a face. 'Is, I should say. Hannah's still alive. Though she might as well be dead.'

'So the two families were close.'

'Yes. We even went on holiday together a few times. Corsica. The South of France. The best was Greece – we went on a dinghy sailing course. Hannah was the best by far. She was a natural athlete. I was hopeless, of course. I could hardly fit myself into the boat, knees up to my chin, and I kept getting hit by that thing the sails attached to.'

'The boom?' suggested Frieda.

'It's so odd to think of those times now. I can't work out if it's the past or the present that seems unreal. They just don't connect.'

Frieda didn't respond. What did she want to know from this man?

'I can show you photos if you want – or, at least, I could if everything wasn't such a mess. Flora would know where they all are. But do you want coffee? I should have offered you some.'

'No, thank you. You knew them well. Does what happened make any kind of sense, in retrospect?'

'How could it make sense?'

'I mean, does it feel plausible that Hannah killed her entire family?'

'Why does it need to feel plausible? She did it. She was a pretty weird kid by the end.'

'In what way?'

'She and Saul used to get on really well. Saul was a bit of a shy, nerdy kind of kid, and Hannah took him under her wing when they were younger – even though he was older than her. She was protective of him, just like she was of Rory. She was never angry with Rory. I remember she once got into a fight with a boy who was bullying Saul, really went for him. But then she hit adolescence, and that fierceness turned into something scarier. Crikey, she was wild. I remember once looking out of the window and seeing into their garden, and she was tearing up the flowers Deborah had just planted. I can still see the look on her face, a kind of lit-up fury, as if electricity was running through her. Sometimes we could hear her shouting. Saul was the good boy doing his homework in his bedroom, and she was out getting drunk and throwing things through windows and taking God knows what drugs. Then, of course, she went off the rails, dropped out of school pretty much, left home. Poor Deborah.'

'How did Deborah take it?'

'Badly, I think. But it was hard to know. She was always so controlled. People thought she was reserved or even shy, but I don't think she was, really, more watchful. She had a kind of steely detachment from things.'

'That's an interesting thing to say.'

Sebastian Tait re-crossed his long legs. 'It just popped out. Flora's always telling me to think before I speak.'

'What about Aidan?'

'Aidan? He was great.' Frieda waited. 'He was the opposite of Debs. He talked a lot, was extrovert and sociable to a fault, full of enthusiasms, every week a new thing. I used to play tennis with him. Keen on wine. So am I. I should show you my cellar. Had a very loud voice and a very loud laugh. Very charming.' He nodded thoughtfully. 'Very charming,' he repeated, lingering on the words. 'But a good guy in the end.'

'Did he get on with Hannah?'

'He tried. She ran circles round him. I think she was a bit contemptuous of him, really.'

'Why was that?'

'You're the therapist. Because he was a man. Because he was her stepfather. Because he was what she called a reactionary. Poor sod, he wasn't a reactionary, just a bit clueless about politics and what-not. Me too. I just like making suits and ties and hats, and the rest of the world can do what it likes.' He looked at the watch on his bony wrist. 'Really,' he said apologetically, untangling his legs and levering himself out of the sofa. 'I don't think the boiler person is coming and I have to go.'

'Thank you.'

'I wish you could have met Flora. She's better at remembering things.'

'Perhaps another time.'

'Then you could have coffee and look at those photos.'

Frieda took his number and keyed it into her phone. 'And your sons,' she asked. 'Would they mind me getting in touch with them?'

'I'll give you their emails. They're both in London. Rick's a doctor. Saul's in IT. They've both got beards, of course. They think I'm some kind of relic.' He gave a small whoop of laughter, then reached into his apron pocket and drew out a vivid tie made of interwoven strips of silk. 'Can I offer you one? One of my mosaic ties. I'm rather proud of them, if I say so myself.'

'I don't really wear ties.'

'For your husband, then.' His eyes flitted to her ringless fourth finger.

'You keep it.'

He wrapped it round his thin neck, over the top of the cotton scarf.

'I've enjoyed meeting you,' he said. 'It's been too long since I talked about the Dochertys. We don't mention it in the family any more.'

'Because it's too painful?'

'Too painful. Too strange. Too long ago.'

'Goodbye.'

'I haven't asked,' he said, laying a hand on her forearm. 'Do you know how Hannah is?'

'She's not in a good state.'

'Has she ever confessed?'

'No.'

'Poor girl,' he said, and smiled. 'Poor everyone.'

As Frieda approached the car, Emma Travis came hurrying out of her house. She knocked on Josef's window and he wound it down.

'Are you a builder?' she asked.

'I am a builder.'

'Could you give me your card? It's so hard to find anyone good in Dulwich.'

Frieda looked suspiciously at Josef as he steered the car back northwards. 'Are you going to work for her?' she said.

'Is difficult with the work now.' Josef looked at her with a smile she didn't quite trust. 'All the Romanians coming here. And the Bulgarians.'

Frieda heard a disapproving sound behind her from Yvette: something between a sigh and a grunt. She looked round. 'Have you heard of Detective Chief Inspector Ben Sedge?'

'No.' Her eyes narrowed. 'Actually, his name does ring a bell. Why would that be?'

'He's been in the news lately. He led the original investigation. I think I should talk to him.'

Yvette gave a shake of her head and her expression turned to something like alarm. 'You don't understand,' she said. 'When police start investigating other police, it becomes delicate. It's like family. People don't like it.'

'You mean they close ranks.'

'It's easy for you to say that.'

'I'm not asking you to talk to him.'

'Which would be completely out of the question.'

'Which is why I'm not asking you. I just want to get a number. Or someone who can put me in touch with him. Can you do that? Discreetly?'

'I'll see. Maybe.'

TWELVE

When Frieda arrived home she wanted a bath, she wanted tea, she wanted to pull the curtains on the world, but first she knew she had to call Levin. She had to tell him what she wanted to do.

'What do you expect from him?'

'I'm not exactly sure. But DCI Sedge ran the inquiry. Maybe he had some doubts.'

'Even if he does, he probably won't admit them to you.'

'I wanted to make sure that you were all right with it.'

'I trust you to do what you think is right,' said Levin. 'Until it all goes wrong.'

'That's a joke, I hope.'

'You're a psychotherapist,' said Levin. 'You know that there's no such thing as a joke.'

Frieda took the Overground through east London, though it felt more like the train was flying over it. When she had first moved to London she had lived out in Dalston and the area had felt as if the city had turned its back on it, left it for dead. Now the abandoned warehouses were studios and apartments. What had been lock-ups under the railway arches were now coffee shops and artisan bakeries. She got off at Shadwell and walked down towards the river. The Bear was easy to miss, the narrow façade of a pub in a small cobbled street. She pushed the door open. It was late morning and the interior was deserted, except for a young, dark-haired woman behind the bar, drying glasses.

'I'm looking for –' Frieda began, but the woman interrupted her.

'Upstairs.' She gave a nod at a doorway. Even in that single word, Frieda heard her accent and smiled to herself. Probably one of those Romanians or Bulgarians that Josef was worrying about. She walked up a creaking narrow wooden staircase that wound round to the left. On the walls were engravings of ancient prize fights, men in breeches holding up their bare knuckles. When she reached the first floor she looked around. There were several closed doors.

'In here,' said a voice.

She opened the door in front of her and stepped inside. The worn old carpet on the floor, the old brown wooden panelling made the room look smaller than it was. She could see only the silhouette of a man, seated at a wooden table by the large window. He stood up.

'I thought we'd meet in your office,' said Frieda.

'This is my office.' The man held out his hand. Frieda shook it cautiously.

'We met once before. Frieda Klein.'

'*Dr* Frieda Klein.'

'You don't have to call me that. And this isn't really your office, is it?'

'A friend of mine owns this place. They use this room for functions – weddings, wakes. It's a useful place for meeting people who might not be comfortable in a police station. Coffee?' Frieda nodded and Sedge poured some into a mug from a flask on the table. She took it and walked across to the window. She'd been expecting a view but even so she almost gasped. On the street side, the Bear was small and overshadowed, but the rear looked out on the river, over to Rotherhithe on the other side, and along the north bank towards Limehouse and the curve of the Isle of Dogs. Sedge walked over and stood beside her. She could sense the bulk of him. She smelt his aftershave: tea and lavender.

'I live in Romford now,' he said, 'but this is where my family comes from. There were people called Sedge living in Poplar a hundred years ago.'

'London's like that,' said Frieda.

'My grandfather told me you could walk east from Greenwich and you'd see ships queuing along the river as far as the eye could see. My great-grandfather worked in the docks. My granddad said a crate fell on his dad's head once. When he was in a good mood he'd let the kids feel the hole. At least, that's what my granddad said.'

'I'd be comfortable in a police station,' said Frieda.

'But I wouldn't.' He turned and looked at her. 'I checked up on you. I found it hard to establish your exact role in the Met.'

'I don't have an exact role. And I'm not in the Met.'

'But you've found a way of getting involved. As far as I can see, when you're not on the run, you've been effective.'

'It doesn't always feel like that. There's generally been a downside.'

'But people are starting to know you, to talk about you. When you met me at that fuck-awful auction, I was on show. Ever since the Geoff Lester case went south, I've not exactly been the flavour of the month.'

'Do people blame you for it?'

He smiled at her. 'I've heard about your problems with the commissioner,' he said. 'Half the game in the Met is politics. I was the one left standing when the music stopped.' He gave a little nod. 'If you come in and start asking questions in front of everyone, people will feel there's a bad smell about me. Hence, my office here. Anyway, it's nicer than the station in Stepney.'

'I want to talk about Hannah Docherty.'

'Yes, I know.'

'Do you think she should have been found guilty?'

Ben Sedge laughed, though it sounded slightly forced to Frieda, a piece of bravado. 'You don't waste time, do you? I can see why you and the commissioner didn't hit it off. We're talking about a young woman I put away, almost certainly for the rest of her life.'

'It's a simple question.'

'Oh, yes?' Sedge banged his mug down on the table. His brows were drawn together and his eyes glared at her. 'It might be simple from where you're sitting but it's not so fucking simple for me, excuse my language. This is my career, my whole bloody life, you're asking about. I don't see why I have to defend myself to someone like you.'

'You don't have to, of course.'

There was a silence in the room. Sedge's face slowly relaxed. He turned away from Frieda, looking out at the river.

'It was my first big case. I'd never seen anything like it. Nobody had. What they can't prepare you for is the smell of it. I can't describe it.'

'You don't need to.'

He glanced at Frieda again. 'Yes,' he said. 'I heard about that too. Well, we thought at first it was a burglary gone wrong or a really evil burglary gone right. But it never could have been that. As soon as we found out about Hannah, it fell into place. She'd fallen out with her family, she'd threatened them. She didn't have an alibi.'

'She *did* have an alibi.'

'Not an alibi that made any kind of sense.'

'You constructed the case. Did anything about it make you uneasy?'

'Like what?'

'The murderer used a claw hammer, which was found at the scene. There were no prints on it and no evidence about where

103

Hannah would have got it from. Hannah's stepfather was killed earlier than the other two. And he was wearing his clothes. They were dressed for bed. What did you make of that?'

Sedge shook his head. 'You ask if I'm uneasy. I'm always uneasy. That's why I'm good at my job, and I *am* good, whatever mistakes I've made along the way. What we do is turn up when something terrible has happened and we try to make sense of it, and mostly we do, but there are always bits left over, things that are inexplicable. All I can say is that the case stood up. You're right, there were pieces in the puzzle that were missing, or that didn't quite fit. But, still, everything led to Hannah Docherty. There wasn't even a sniff of another suspect.'

He poured himself another coffee. 'It's cold,' he said. 'Shall I get us some more?'

'I'm going soon,' said Frieda. She found it hard to tear herself away from that view, the slow, heavy flow of the river. It brought back memories and longings and fears. 'One last thing. I was surprised that the defence didn't make more of some irregularities.'

'Like what?'

'Confronting Hannah with the crime scene before she was interviewed. And, from what I read, the scene wasn't properly secured. People were allowed to take objects away, evidence was lost.'

Sedge stared at her; she could see his jaw clenching and unclenching. 'You've got a nerve. I've been trying to help. I know I've made mistakes and I want to do what's right. I don't know what more you want me to say.'

'It was just a comment. From an amateur.'

'We're not perfect,' Sedge said. 'We're just people, like builders and plumbers. We cut corners. We make mistakes. But we try. I don't remember that about Hannah and the crime scene. It was probably a way of getting her to talk, making her face up to what she had done.'

'Or face up to the brutal murder of her family.'

'The jury heard the evidence,' said Sedge. 'They were out for less than an hour.'

Frieda looked away from the window, up at Sedge. 'An hour, and Hannah Docherty's been shut away now for thirteen years. I hope they were right.'

'I thought you could go and see the officer he was working with,' Frieda said to Yvette. 'Malik Gordon.'

'Did you?'

'Yes.'

'To what end?'

'To find out what he thought about the investigation, to ask him for his impressions, to see what he thought about Hannah, if he was anxious that any leads were missed – I don't have to spell it all out.'

'That's certainly true. I know him.'

'You know Malik Gordon?'

'Yes. It's not surprising. I'm in the Met, so is he. I'm in my thirties, so is he. I'm a detective constable, so is he. OK?'

'OK,' said Frieda, mildly. 'So that's a good thing, isn't it?'

'How can it be a good thing?'

'You can talk to him more easily.'

'Really? It's easier to accuse someone you know of handling a case badly, and even charging the wrong person, than a stranger? That's encouraging to know.'

Frieda stood up. 'You're not accusing him of anything, Yvette. You're asking for his help. I'm sure you can do it tactfully. And tomorrow we're going to see Hannah's father, Seamus Docherty.'

She left before Yvette could reply.

THIRTEEN

The next morning, Frieda met Yvette at Hackney station. It had been raining all night and was raining still, and Yvette was struggling with a vast red umbrella whose fabric was coming away from its spokes. She walked towards Frieda, the umbrella dangerously near the tops of other people's heads; her blue coat was streaked with water and her expression was grim.

'Good morning,' said Frieda.

'Hmm.'

'We don't have to be there until half past so I thought we could have coffee. There's a place just up the road that looks fine. And dry,' she added.

She led the way to a small café. Yvette battled the umbrella shut and followed Frieda inside. They ordered coffee and sat at a wooden table near the window, where they could watch people hurrying past through the gusts of rain, heads down.

'So,' said Frieda. 'Malik Gordon.'

'Yes.' Yvette took a sip of her cappuccino, leaving froth on her upper lip. 'I saw him.'

'And?'

'And I hope you know what you're doing with this case.'

Frieda kept her expression neutral. There had been a time, not so long ago, when Yvette, appalled at what had happened to Frieda and guilty for her own part in it, had set aside her hostility, acknowledging her jealousy and insecurity. She had helped Frieda and become for a while almost as fiercely protective of her as she was of Karlsson, whom she revered. It had even seemed possible that the two women could become friends of a sort. The terrible events of the previous year and Karlsson's temporary suspension and disgrace had swept that away, and Yvette was as opposed to Frieda as she had been when they'd first met, over five years ago. What was more, she wanted Frieda to understand that.

'If I don't know,' Frieda said, 'I'm hoping you can advise me.'

'Well.' Yvette took another sip. The steam rose into her face and moisture appeared on her flushed cheeks. 'He was quite forthcoming, which was nice of him in the circumstances.'

'Yes.'

'It was his first big case and he was very upset by it. He says that when he saw the bodies he threw up. People often do, the first time. He says it's still the most gruesome thing he's ever seen. One of the other officers on the case couldn't cope at all and left the force.'

'What was his name?'

Yvette frowned. 'I don't remember – it must be in the files. Except it wasn't a he. Malik said she's working in a shop on Mare Street in Hackney.'

'What sort of shop?'

'Flowers.' She gave a small snort. 'That's a serious career change.'

'Go on.'

'He was especially upset by the boy.'

'Rory.'

'Yes.'

'Did he say much about Hannah?'

'He says that when they interviewed her the first time, she was out of it.'

'In what way?'

'Like a wild animal. They had to forcibly restrain her.'

Frieda thought of Hannah now, still wild, still being forcibly restrained. She nodded.

'He told me stuff you already know – like she'd fallen out with her mother and stepfather, that she was living in a kind of squat. It was obviously pretty squalid. There was a creepy boyfriend.'

'Did he say "creepy"?'

'I don't know.' Yvette looked surprised. 'Maybe that's my interpretation. There were drugs, mixed-up relationships.'

'Mixed-up in what way?'

'Everyone sleeping with everyone else, I think. He says that from the moment they met her, there was never any doubt in his mind that it was Hannah. Sedge bent over backwards to consider other possibilities, I gather – but there weren't any. She was the only real suspect. She was the only person there was evidence against – and there was a lot of it. Blood and DNA and fingerprints and no alibi.'

'She said she went to meet her stepfather, but it was her mother who met her.'

'It wasn't much of an alibi. There was no record of a phone call from him to her, no one saw her that evening, and her mother certainly didn't, because she was lying dead in Dulwich. We may not know much but we know that.'

'Did he think the case was solid?'

Yvette looked at Frieda with a stony expression. 'He thought the conviction was one hundred per cent the right one.'

'But not the case?'

'You don't know how things work on the ground. He may have cut corners, and that's not right, I'm not defending it – and God knows I've stuck my neck out when I've seen officers do that, and I've been through shit because of it. I'm just saying that sometimes it's what happens. Malik was fierce in his defence of Sedge. Sometimes good, honest, idealistic, clever detectives don't tick all the boxes and fill out all the forms. That's all.'

'So Ben Sedge cut corners but he got the right person.'

'That's right. And what Malik asked me – and what I'm asking you – is what the fuck are we doing stirring it up now, all these years later? What if you make enough noise and find enough shit to overturn the conviction, even though she obviously did it? What then? Do you want to take responsibility for having a crazy murderer released because of bureaucratic irregularities?'

Frieda smiled at Yvette. 'It's not often that I'm accused of following rules too rigidly.'

Yvette almost smiled back. Frieda saw the muscles in her face relax. Then she remembered herself. 'I'm just saying, you have to think about it,' she muttered.

'I will. Now, let's go and visit the father.'

Brenda Docherty led them into a high-ceilinged sitting room. She must have been about the same age as her husband, whom Frieda knew to be in his early fifties. She had greying brown hair cut quite short and wore a flecked turtle-neck jumper over corduroy trousers. There was a pen tucked behind one ear and glasses hung around her neck on a cord. Her manner was cordial but guarded. Behind her, Frieda saw a dog, rough-haired and floppy-eared, with a beseeching expression in its brown eyes. It looked old. When it saw Frieda it produced a single, experimental bark, then gave up.

'I'll fetch Seamus. Do you want any coffee?'

'We've just had some, thank you.'

'He'll be with you in a minute.' Brenda Docherty turned in the doorway, visibly hesitating. 'He's not happy about your visit,' she said.

'I'll be as quick as I can.'

'When I heard you were coming, I took the day off work. I must say, I don't quite understand why you have to rake it up again, after all these years.'

Frieda felt Yvette's gaze on her. She didn't answer, just waited until Brenda left the room, and they heard her voice calling from the bottom of the stairs. Frieda's eye was caught by a photo on the mantelpiece above the fireplace. She rose to look at it: three people sitting on a hay bale in a stubble field. On the left was Brenda Docherty, slimmer, with her hair long and tied back in a colourful bandanna. On the right was a man Frieda took to be Seamus Docherty. And in the middle sat Rory, leaning into his father, whose arm was round his thin shoulders. Judging by other photos that she had seen of him, Frieda thought it must have been taken not many months before he was killed – probably the autumn of the previous year. He was wearing shorts and a blue T-shirt, and his face was freckled from the sun. He was smiling widely, but still had the anxious look about him that Frieda had noticed in other pictures. She looked at the other photos along the mantelpiece, but there were no others of his previous family. No Rory or Deborah. Of course, no Hannah.

'I don't know how I can help.'

Seamus Docherty sat in the armchair facing them. He had a quiet voice and a thin face, an air of forced calm. His hair was receding and Frieda could see the bones of his skull, the shape of the sockets round his grey eyes. He looked very different from Aidan Locke, Deborah Docherty's genial, larger-than-life second husband.

'I know this must be difficult, Mr Docherty.'

He didn't speak, just inclined his head slightly.

'I don't know if you're aware of the questions that have been raised about the investigation into the three murders.'

'I am not aware.' Was there a touch of irony in his voice? 'What kind of questions?'

'Just procedural ones.' This from Yvette, loudly.

'So why has that anything to do with me?'

'I just wanted to ask you a few things,' said Frieda. She leaned forward slightly. 'Mainly about Hannah.'

'Hannah.' He repeated the name as though it had a nasty taste.

'Perhaps you could start off by telling me her state of mind at the time of the murders.'

'I can't say anything that I haven't already said before.' Frieda waited. 'She was angry.' His grimace was almost a smirk, as if he would suddenly burst into laughter. 'Obviously.'

'Who was she angry with?'

'Who *wasn't* she angry with? She was angry with her mother. That above all. She'd always had a difficult relationship with Debs. Deborah.' Frieda saw him flush as he corrected himself. 'She was angry with her stepfather. She was angry with her teachers. I think, or thought, she was angry with her boyfriend, though she never told me anything about that. She was angry with her friends. She was angry with politicians. She was angry with journalists. She was angry with people in business. She was angry with anyone who was rich – which takes us back to her mother and step-father, I guess.'

'Was she angry with her brother?'

Seamus Docherty gave a small grunt and twisted his face away from them. He passed a hand – long-fingered and delicate – across the back of his head, as if checking the hair was still there. 'Rory. I don't know. I didn't think so. But –'

He stopped talking. They heard a radio playing from somewhere in the house.

'And you?' asked Frieda. 'Was she angry with you?'

'Yes.'

'Very?'

'Yes.'

'And with your new wife?'

'Yes. Poor Brenda.'

'Was she so angry with all these people that she was murderous?'

Seamus Docherty stared at Frieda. She saw his jaw muscles tighten. 'Clearly, I didn't think so at the time or I would have done something.'

'Why was she so angry?'

'Do you have children?'

'No,' said Frieda.

'No,' said Yvette. Her voice was still too loud.

'She was a teenager. A clever, difficult, prickly, tempestuous teenager.' At these words, Frieda thought of Chloë. 'Her parents were separated, God help us both. She was very devoted, almost clingy when she was little. Very protective of me.' He blinked fiercely. 'When I left, she took it hard. It was a difficult age. She was just approaching her teens. I tried to see her regularly but Deborah and Aidan made that quite difficult. Her boyfriend at the end was bad news. She mixed with drug addicts and layabouts. She read books telling her the world was a bad place. And one day she –' He stopped, swallowed so that they could see his Adam's apple bobbing in his throat. 'You know what she did.'

'So it makes a kind of sense to you?' asked Frieda.

'Of course it doesn't make sense. We thought it was a phase, something lots of teenagers go through, except she just did it more wholeheartedly because she was a wholehearted kind of person, always had been. Then she killed my son.' He gave a dry cough and repeated, 'My son.'

'What did you feel when you discovered that you had inherited everything?' asked Yvette, into the silence.

He turned his grey eyes to her. 'I don't know what to say to that,' he answered, after a pause. 'My son was dead. My ex-wife was dead. My daughter was a murderer and locked away in a hospital for the criminally insane. Everywhere I turned there were journalists asking me what it was like to be the father of a monster. Asking me how she'd become like that, what we'd done to her as parents or what we hadn't done. What I got out of it hardly seemed relevant. Not when it was set against what I'd lost.'

'It was a lot of money,' said Yvette.

He regarded her stonily. 'I felt – Well, it was unsettling. We were divorced. The money was to go to the children, and then to *their* children.'

'What was your own financial situation at the time?' Yvette asked.

'I don't understand why you're asking these questions.'

'Because someone cut corners,' said Yvette. She darted a bright, hostile glance at Frieda. 'And now we have to go through certain things again.'

'I'm sure you know all of this already. I wasn't well off. They were. Deborah's money came from Aidan. He was the high-flying businessman.'

'But now you're well off.' Yvette looked around the large room.

'Better off.'

'As a matter of interest, can you tell us how much the estate was worth?'

'I don't see why it's a matter of interest, so I'd prefer not to. If you don't mind.'

'I understand,' continued Yvette, the colour high in her cheeks, 'that you collected some things from the house while the investigation was still in progress.'

Frieda watched the two of them. She realized Yvette, in spite of her distrust and her reluctance, had been doing her homework.

'Did I?' asked Seamus Docherty.

'Yes.'

'I might have done.'

'Why?'

'Because they were mine.'

'What were they?'

'I can't remember.' He pinched the top of his nose between thumb and forefinger. 'Brenda said I was too soft-hearted, a bit of a pushover – not that she's much better. A pair of fools, that's us – that's why I married her. She's kind. We make each other safe. What was I saying?'

'What you took from the house.'

'Yes. When Deborah and I separated, I didn't insist on taking things that were mine – well, because mostly they weren't mine, they were ours, and I didn't want to make a fuss, but there were a few things. Some books, a picture, a box of photos, stuff like that. So I went and got them. Or some of them, anyway.'

'There were papers too,' said Frieda.

'My solicitor was asking questions about the accounts so I thought it best just to gather everything up and give it to him.'

'In the middle of the investigation?'

'They weren't relevant. Just bit and pieces. I told them that when they came to retrieve them. Anyway, there was nothing useful there, nothing about legacies or anything, and I chucked everything away. I couldn't bear to keep it all. Kids' reports. Stories they'd written. I didn't want to read them . . . You can't imagine what it felt like seeing them. Rory's back-to-front handwriting. Pictures. Photos – you know, happy families.' He glared at them both. 'Old letters. Even a few from me to her, from the old days. I thought I wanted them but it turned out I didn't. I couldn't keep them in the house.'

'So you threw everything away?'

'Pretty much. Not the teapot or the picture. Almost everything else. Sometimes now I wish I hadn't. The bin men must have come early the next morning because when the police arrived it had already gone.'

'Can I ask you about your ex-wife?' asked Frieda.

'What about her?'

'What kind of terms were you on with her?'

Suddenly he looked more wary. 'We didn't have much to do with each other. She lived in her world and I lived in mine.'

'But you had two children. Did you talk about Hannah and her problems?'

'Not really. Deborah gave me instructions sometimes – she was always very good at that, very certain she knew best.'

'How else would you describe her?'

'Who, Debs?' This time he didn't correct the name.

'Yes.'

Seamus Docherty stood up and went to the window. With his back to them, he said, 'She was clever, stubborn, a woman of few words but with deep feelings. She spoke her mind. You'd want her on your side. She was determined, organized, ambitious for her children. And for me, once,' he added.

'Until you left her,' said Yvette.

He turned. 'We left each other.' His voice was soft, uninflected. Frieda couldn't tell if he was angry or sad.

'Was it because you'd found someone else?' Yvette persevered.

'There was no ill will.'

'Easy for you to say that.' Yvette looked surprised at what she had said, and her face flushed.

Seamus Docherty looked away again, back out of the window where the rain fell. 'No one can understand a marriage from the outside. There were good times once, and then they weren't good any longer. It was painful, distressing, too prolonged. We both let the other down. Now she's dead and nothing can be changed.'

'She left you, didn't she?' said Frieda, suddenly certain. 'Not the other way round.'

Seamus Docherty slowly turned to face her. 'Have you ever been divorced?'

'I've never been married.'

'No children, no marriage, no divorce. You've had a sheltered life.' Frieda didn't say anything. 'There's always mess when a marriage ends – never believe anyone who tells you different.'

'So she had an affair with Aidan, who was richer and more successful than you,' said Frieda. 'And she left you. Did you feel bitter?'

'I'm not saying that's what happened. And, no, I didn't feel bitter.'

'Or angry?' asked Yvette. 'You must have been furiously angry and humiliated.'

'No.'

'Did Hannah know it was her mother who had ended the marriage? Is that why she was so angry with her?'

'I haven't said that it was. You're making assumptions. I don't know what Hannah knew or thought or decided. She usually knew everything that was going on. She wasn't someone you could hide things from. She was always on the look-out, always listening in to conversations, picking up secrets. Little Pig with Big Ears – that's what we used to call her when she was small.'

'You talk about her in the past tense,' said Frieda, softly.

'Because she is in the past for me. She killed my son.'

'She's still your daughter.'

'I have no daughter. I have no children.'

'You've never visited her?'

'I went once, just to look her in the face. She's a monster.'

'She's still a human being.'

'Easy for you to say that. Easy for you to stand there and talk about what happened. I try not to think about the past.'

'She's all alone. You're the only person she has.'

'She doesn't have me. I'll never see her again. She's dead to me.'

'I'm going to find out how much the estate was worth,' said Yvette, as they walked back down the street towards the Overground station.

'Good.'

'Though it's a wild goose chase.' She snapped her umbrella open. 'And, also, you want to know about Hannah's life before the murders.'

'Yes?'

'There's a woman who's made herself the Hannah Docherty expert. Look on Google. It's her life's work. She's completely obsessed. She'll know things about Hannah that even Hannah never knew.'

'What's her name?'

'She's called Erin Brack.'

'She thinks Hannah's innocent?'

'I don't know. But, innocent or guilty, she thinks she's a freedom fighter.'

FOURTEEN

Maria Dreyfus arrived late. Her coat was wrongly buttoned and her dark hair was scraped back in an asymmetrical bun. 'Sorry,' she said.

'That's all right.'

'I was going to say it was the public transport, but it wasn't.' Frieda smiled. 'Then I'm glad you didn't say it.'

'It was me. I didn't know whether to come. I had a row with my husband. He thinks I should snap out of it.'

'Is that what he said?'

'Not quite. He said that sometimes talking cures make things worse, not better – that dwelling on what's wrong can make it seem more real, more solid. Suffering becomes who you are. If that makes sense.'

'It does.'

'I'm not saying I agree.'

'It would be fine if you did. Because, of course, it's something that therapists have to consider carefully. But you aren't here to embrace your suffering. You're here to work out why you're feeling the way that you do, and by understanding it you may be able to have some power over it.'

'He also said I should go back to work and maybe think about taking up some form of exercise. Running, he suggested.'

'Right.'

'And he was angry because we haven't had sex for weeks. Months, actually.'

'How did that make you feel?'

'Guilty. But then angry too. Very. Like a gale howling through me. I felt like punching him. It was like he was telling me to be a good wife: good at work, good in bed. Compliant. Of course that's unfair. He only wants to help. Or mostly he only wants to help. He's a bit aggrieved too. I probably should start running and having sex and working and behaving like a normal person. Whatever that means. It's just –' She stopped and passed both her hands over her face.

'Yes?'

'I've had enough.'

'Enough of what?'

'Enough of everything. Of working and cleaning and shopping and cooking and talking and attending to the needs of my husband, my father, my children, my friends, my work colleagues, generally making an effort. It takes all my energy to – I don't know – pick up a dirty sock from the floor, open my mouth and make the right words come out. Smile. Push a trolley round the supermarket. You know. Stuff. I want –' Again she stopped, frowning.

'You want?'

'I don't know. I want this feeling to go away. I want to be someone else.' She leaned forward in her chair. 'Can you help me?'

'To be someone else? No. But to find yourself? That's what we're going to do, together.'

'I'm not sure if finding myself is going to make me very happy.' Maria gave a short, derisive laugh.

'Oh, happiness,' said Frieda. 'That's not what this is about.'

Frieda had the rest of the afternoon to herself, and the evening. It lay ahead of her, beautifully empty and quiet. She went up the road to the greengrocer's and bought herself some aubergines and red peppers: she would light her fire, take a long bath, have roasted vegetables with a glass of red wine.

As she was putting the food away in the kitchen there was a knocking at the front door.

'Chloë.'

Her niece was soaked through, and she was laden with shopping bags. When she stepped over the threshold, her shoes squelched. 'Frieda, I would have called but my mobile's out of battery so I thought I'd come round instead. I'm so glad you're in.'

'Come and sit by the fire and get dry. Aren't you working today?'

'Half-day off.'

Frieda looked at the bags. 'Where are you on your way to?'

'Here, if that's all right with you.'

'Here?'

'I thought it would be nice to have dinner together. I've already bought the food. You're not going anywhere, are you?'

'I hadn't been planning to.' Frieda tried to feel glad. 'That looks like a lot of food for two.'

'I thought we could ask other people round too.'

'Other people?'

'Reuben and Josef.'

'Oh.'

'And then there are a couple of people I've met recently and I thought I could invite them as well.'

'Here?'

'If that's all right.'

'This evening?'

'Yes. Last-minute thing, you know. It'll be fun.'

'I'm not sure.'

'Frieda!'

'Why can't you do it in your own house?'

'Mum's got some new man coming round so I couldn't do it there. Don't you want me here?' Chloë's face assumed a look of comical dismay. Her mascara had run and water still dripped from her hair, running down her cheeks like tears.

'You and four others? I was planning a quiet evening.'

'Seven, actually. And us as well. Why do you want a quiet evening?'

'Seven.'

'They've all said yes.'

'You've already asked them?'

'I knew you wouldn't mind. Jack's coming too.'

'Chloë, you can't just ask seven people round to my house without telling me.'

'I am telling you.'

'That's not what I mean.'

'Will you help me cook?'

'I was about to have a bath.'

'I'd love a bath at some point too. I'm wet through and so cold. Don't worry, I've got a change of clothes with me.'

Frieda sighed. 'I wasn't worrying. Do you want one now?'

'That would be great. Just a quick one. You could peel the onions while you're waiting. Someone told me that if you don't cut off the root end, your eyes won't water so much.'

There were nine of them, and not enough chairs – they had to fetch the stool from the garret and the chair from her room. There was too much food: an assortment of salads and dips and breads that barely fitted onto Frieda's small table, among the candles. Chloë's face was red from cooking and anxiety. Frieda hadn't had time for a bath. Josef arrived with a whole spiced chicken, even though Chloë had told him that her friends were all vegetarian and Dee a vegan, who didn't like to be anywhere near meat. He also brought his honey cake, which reminded him of his homeland, and two bottles of vodka. Reuben came with red wine and runny cheese. He was wearing his favourite waistcoat, as if this were a party. Jack arrived late, empty-handed, and perhaps, thought Frieda, already slightly drunk. He was wearing tight, canary-yellow trousers and two scarves around his thin neck. His hair was cut shorter than usual but as if to compensate he had grown a beard; it was a brighter orange than his hair and he stroked it occasionally. He perched on the stool, between and slightly behind Frieda and Josef, and had to lean forward to spear his food. Frieda had been his supervisor and he had revered her; he had also helped her in previous cases. When he and Chloë had been involved with each other, it had felt strange and complicated.

At the far end of the table, they were talking about travel. Chloë was anxiously over-animated. Every so often she darted a gaze in Jack's direction – ever since they had broken up there had been an uneasy relationship between them, sometimes charged with possibility, at others with hostility.

'Did you read that finding,' said Jack, suddenly, to Frieda, 'about how women are more likely to have a faith than men?'

'No. That's interesting.'

'I have faith,' said Josef. He tapped his chest. 'We all must have meaning in our life.' He raised his voice. 'You agree, Chloë?'

'What?'

'You have faith?'

'I have *chicken*,' said Reuben. 'Who wants some down that end? Chicken is a vegetable, really.'

'Sorry, Josef,' said Chloë. She beamed at him: she'd always had a soft spot for Josef. 'I'm an infidel.'

'Do you know how they keep chickens?' asked the young

man next to Chloë; he had a shaved head and close-set beautiful brown eyes.

'Faith is such an odd thing,' said Jack. 'People say they just know things, but you can't know what can't be proved. You can only believe.'

'I'd eat road kill, though.'

'You're quiet, Frieda,' said Reuben. 'How's it going with that mad girl?'

'She's not a girl any more – and I'm not entirely sure she's mad. Or not mad in the way you mean.'

'Chloë told me about what you do,' said the young man with the shaved head. 'It sounds really interesting. You're looking into the Hannah Docherty case, is that right?'

'I'm not sure that's for general publication,' said Frieda.

'There are lots of Anglican vicars who lose their faith after decades,' said Jack. He drank some of Josef's vodka, then poured wine into his empty glass. 'Wouldn't that be painful, all of your life built on something you don't believe in any more?'

'Frieda,' said Chloë. 'Surely you can tell us a bit. We're not going to talk about it.'

Frieda looked at her niece. She seemed hectic and slightly tense. 'I'm going to see one of her fans tomorrow,' she said. 'To get a better sense of Hannah as she used to be. Erin Brack. Yvette came across her on the internet.'

'Erin Brack.' One of Chloë's friends, a woman called Myla, who hadn't talked for most of the evening, had pulled out her laptop from the duffel bag slung on her chair and was already typing into it. 'There can't be many of them around. Let's see.'

'I pray,' said Josef to Jack, pouring more vodka into their glasses. 'If I doubt, I pray more. Now is time for honey cake. Please, everyone.'

'And what is prayer,' asked Reuben, 'but talking to yourself?' He smiled round the table and stood up. 'I'm going to have a cigarette out back. Anyone coming?'

Josef and Dee, the vegan, joined him. Jack picked up a slice of cake and looked at it. 'Talking to yourself,' he muttered, and bit into it, spraying crumbs. 'That's not enough.'

'Here we are. Erin Brack. Look. She's got a blog.'

Chloë and the young man leaned towards the screen.

'She's crazy,' said Chloë, after a few seconds. 'You want to be careful, Frieda.'

'She certainly writes a lot,' said the young man, scrolling down. 'She seems to write her blog almost every day.'

'What about?' asked Frieda.

'Conspiracies, I think,' he answered. 'Here's one: chemicals in the water deliberately causing infertility.'

'It says here she has a collection,' said Chloë.

'What kind of collection?'

'No idea. She just keeps referring to "my collection".'

'She calls it "archive" sometimes,' said Chloë, and turned away to answer her buzzing mobile.

'And "murderabilia",' said Myla.

Reuben, Josef and Dee reappeared, their hair damp from the rain. 'Time to go,' said Reuben.

'We've only just been given cake.'

'That was Mum,' said Chloë, sliding her phone back into her pocket. 'She was very upset. She wants to know why you didn't invite her as well.'

'I didn't invite anyone. You did.'

'She doesn't see it like that.'

'What would you do, Frieda?' asked Jack, standing up and pulling on his coat.

'Sorry?'

'What would you do if you were a vicar who'd lost their faith?'

Frieda looked at him. She gave him a small nod. 'I'd stop being a vicar.'

'Even if your congregation believed? You might still be helping them.'

'I know what you're driving at, Jack. This isn't about Anglican vicars.'

Colour flared into his cheeks. 'Why do you say that?'

'If you no longer believe in what you're doing, you don't have to do it.'

'Can I come and talk to you?'

'You don't need my permission.'

'I've got myself in a muddle.'

'We're all in a muddle,' said Reuben, who was in his jacket and finishing off Frieda's wine. 'It's part of being human.'

Frieda closed the door on the last of her visitors and started clearing up. She thought about Erin Brack's collection. Murderabilia. And she wondered what was in it.

FIFTEEN

Frieda looked at the address and the map and decided to go the long way. She took the train east to Erith. From the station she walked across a main road and through a housing estate to the south bank of the Thames. To the right, across scrubby marshland, she could see the Dartford bridge, like a geometry drawing on a grey watercolour. The distant cars and lorries moved across, north to south, silent and slow, as if she were watching them from a great height. Directly across the river, she could see a jumble of warehouses with containers piled, as if in a children's game, parked cars, and then along the bank, land that had been scraped clean, scoured grey, and brown earth, ready for something: a factory, storage, housing. Beyond that was heathland and fields and on the horizon a church spire. These were London's edgelands, a half-abandoned industrial landscape, a half-ruined rural space. Frieda liked it.

She turned left and started to walk along the riverbank away from the sea towards London. Fifty miles to the west, there were parts of the Thames Path that were quietly rural, green, tree-shaded riverbanks, quaint little towns, millionaires' mansions with trimmed lawns, Henley and Windsor. Here it was different. This was the Thames downstream from London, which veered from being forgotten to being abused, heedlessly built on, demolished and dumped on. It was a place Frieda came to from time to time, usually on bright cold winter days when she needed the wind to clear her head. There were patches of wildness, heathlands, sometimes bird sanctuaries, but even the green havens felt post-industrial, almost post-apocalyptic, riven with ditches and dykes, precariously reclaimed from the sea or the river or swamps or somewhere in between.

Developers and politicians had called the area the Thames Gateway but the name itself was ambiguous and troubling. Was it a gateway in or a gateway out? From time to time Frieda had struck up conversations with bikers or hikers, old couples, young girls pushing buggies, residents of Greenhithe, Dartford, Purfleet, Belvedere. They could be welcoming or wary, suspicious, even hostile. There was a feeling that they had been pushed out from somewhere or that people from somewhere had been pushed onto them: immigrants, London's rejects. Even the giant industrial buildings – cement works, sewage treatment facilities – served London but weren't wanted there. This was one of the places Frieda came when she wanted to think about London. This was what London wanted to forget about, to expel, to suppress.

Frieda walked past a vast supermarket car park and a half-demolished warehouse and a patch of land that was being cleared and flattened by three bulldozers. She reached the sewage works, turned away from the river and walked along the side of it. Gorse bushes and brambles made the path almost impassable. At the other end she emerged on to a newly constructed road. She looked at the rough map she had drawn for herself, turned right, and after a few minutes she had arrived at Oldbourne Drive. It was like a square with one side missing. The houses couldn't be more than five years old, but already they looked battered without being weathered. There were slates missing on the roofs and the window frames were peeling. The façades looked as if they had been drawn by a small child: a door and a car port on the ground floor, two windows on the first floor, one larger window on the second. The drive framed a small and very basic children's playground with a see-saw and bright red metal benches. Frieda made her way to number sixty-three and rang the bell.

The house looked abandoned. It had one of the only driveways without a car on it. But there was a rustling sound and the door opened.

'Frieda Klein.'

It was said so loudly and enthusiastically that Frieda felt self-conscious and looked around to see if anyone could have heard. There was no one. There were houses, cars, a playground. But still it felt deserted.

Erin Brack was taller than Frieda and large, without being fat, just solid and imposing. She had dark curly hair and brown-framed glasses. She was dressed in a white-and-brown-hooped sweater, black jeans and white training shoes.

'It was good of you to make time,' said Frieda, cautiously.

'Come in, come in.'

Erin Brack almost hustled Frieda inside. There was a stale smell in the house of dampness, old cooking, as well as cleaning fluid and air-freshener, which somehow made it worse rather than better. She gestured around her at the piles of newspapers that were on the floor, the stairs and every visible surface wide enough to support them. Frieda followed her into a living room at the back of the house.

'Sorry for the mess,' said Erin Brack. 'Cleaner's day off. That's a joke by the way. I don't have a cleaner. Take a seat.'

Frieda looked around. She could see that Erin Brack didn't have a cleaner. There was a chair and a sofa and a wooden kitchen chair but there was nowhere to sit. Every surface was covered with papers, magazines, newspapers. There were plates and mugs and glasses. Even the wall space was covered.

The flowery wallpaper was almost completely obscured by pages ripped out from newspapers, maps, photographs. There were portraits of smiling boys and girls. For a moment Frieda hoped they might be family photos, a precarious trace of normality, of social ties, but Erin Brack followed her gaze and identified them one by one. They were the smiling faces of people who hadn't known what Fate was preparing for them.

'I thought you might be at work,' said Frieda.

'I'm on sick leave.'

'I'm sorry to hear that.'

'For four years.'

'That sounds serious.'

'The doctors find it difficult to pin down,' said Erin Brack. 'It's a constellation of symptoms. I've had back problems for years. And breathing difficulties. I have a mood disorder as well. It's hard to put a simple label on. But you know all about that.'

Frieda didn't reply.

'Enough about me. Can I get you some tea? I can go out and buy some biscuits.' Frieda looked around warily. 'Don't worry, I'll wash some mugs up for us. You've got to have tea with me. There's so much I want to talk about.'

'Of course,' said Frieda. 'Tea would be good. No biscuits. I just want to talk to you about Hannah Docherty.'

'And I want to talk to you about other things as well. I know about you. I want to talk to you about the Robert Poole case. I've got a whole scrapbook on that one upstairs. Follow me while I make the tea.'

Frieda stepped into Erin Brack's kitchen, then stepped back out again. She was unsure which was worse: what she had seen or what she had smelt. 'I'll stay in the living room.'

As she waited, she received a text from Yvette, saying she

had managed to track down three of the people who'd lived in the squat where Hannah had been in the weeks leading up to the murders: she would pick Frieda up the following morning and they would see each in turn. Frieda had just sent a reply when Erin Brack came through holding two mugs. Was it long enough to have actually boiled the water? She gave Frieda a mug with a drawing of a skull on it. 'I thought that would appeal to your sense of humour.'

'About Hannah Docherty,' said Frieda.

'Completely,' said Erin Brack. 'I couldn't be more excited. But first let me find you a space.' She lifted a pile of papers from the sofa and threw them onto another pile. 'It may look disorganized . . .' Frieda murmured something polite '. . . but I know where everything is. It's my own system.'

Frieda sat on the sofa. There was a low table in front of her. She pushed the piles of paper apart so that she could put the mug down. She tapped the mug and ran a finger around the rim. She did everything except drink from it. 'I've heard that you're a collector,' she said.

'In a small way. When there's a crime that interests me, I want to know everything about it. As much as the police know. More sometimes.' Erin Brack pushed more papers aside, so that she could sit next to Frieda. She moved close up against her and addressed her in a conspiratorial tone: 'The police just wanted to put Hannah Docherty away. They didn't care what really happened. I'm so excited to hear that you're involved. You feel the same as I do, don't you?'

'Have you collected things that belonged to the Dochertys?'

'I think of myself as a curator.'

Frieda had suspected and now she felt certain. 'Yes. Did you perhaps go to Seamus Docherty's house in Hampstead shortly after the murders and remove bin bags that he had taken from his ex-wife's house?'

'I did. Three whole bags, and he just threw them away. They didn't care about what had really happened.'

'"They"?'

'Everybody. The police, the family, even her so-called friends. They just wanted to shove Hannah into prison and forget about her. I wasn't taking things. I was rescuing them. You know, you can learn a lot about people from what they throw away.'

'What did you get?'

'All sorts of stuff. Letters, bits from the house, photos, school reports, bits and pieces. I got other things later as well, from the actual house in Dulwich.'

'What kind of things?'

'Oh, whatever they were chucking. My prized possession is a teddy bear that I think belonged to Hannah. Imagine that. I wrote to her about it but she never wrote back. They must have intercepted it.'

Frieda paused. This was the important bit. 'Would you let me look at them?'

'Totally,' said Erin Brack, cheerfully. 'I'd be honoured.'

'Could I do it now?'

'There's a bit of a problem with that.'

Uh-oh, Frieda thought. 'What sort of problem?'

'I said I've got my own way of arranging things. This house is like my own museum. It's like a cross between a museum and a library and a warehouse and a few other things, and I have to live here as well.'

'Could you at least show me?'

'No problem.'

'Now?'

'As soon as you've finished your tea.'

Frieda looked down at her mug. Something was floating in it. It might have been a tea leaf but it might not. 'Maybe straight away?'

'All right,' said Erin Brack. 'I've got two rooms upstairs where I keep things.'

Frieda looked around her. 'Aren't you keeping things here?'

'Sort of. Some of them. But this is also where things are kept while waiting to be arranged.'

Frieda followed her up the stairs. Erin Brack turned the handle of a door on the first floor, then leaned against it, pushing.

'Is something wrong?' asked Frieda.

'It's a bit full.'

'What is?'

'The room.' She was breathing heavily. 'Sometimes the piles tip over against the door. Can you give me a hand?'

Frieda pushed at the door as well. It moved a couple of centimetres and then stopped.

'It needs a sharp heave,' said Erin Brack. 'We'll do it together. On three. One, two, *three*.' They both shoved the door hard and it shifted forward. From inside there was a clatter and something shattered. There was enough of a gap now for Erin Brack to squeeze through into the room. Frieda followed her. At first it was hard to make anything out because the curtains were drawn. Frieda could just see shapes.

'There's a light by the door.'

Frieda felt on the wall and found the switch. The sudden bright light made her blink. It was difficult to say how high the piles were because the floor was out of sight. As on the ground floor, there were papers and magazines, but more of them, some in piles, others just lying where they had been thrown or dropped. There were also objects. It looked like a car-boot sale, and there was almost too much to take in. Frieda saw a bird cage in a tin bath; there was a pile of electrical devices, a radio, a clock, a food mixer, a bicycle wheel with no tyre, and much, much more.

'Is all this from the Docherty case?' said Frieda, with a feeling of despair.

'No. This is stuff that is from the first half of the alphabet. But I'm not completely consistent. Sometimes I go by the first name and sometimes by the second, then forget which I've done.'

'Are they all murder cases?'

'Mainly. There are some others I'd like you to look at.'

'Not just now.'

'As you can see, it might be a bit of challenge at first for you.' Frieda nodded. 'What I'll do, now that we've got to know each other, is go through it and dig things out for you.'

'All right.' Frieda turned and forced her way back out through the door. This was going to be more difficult than she had anticipated. She walked down the stairs and stood by the front door. There wasn't much more to be done.

Erin Brack was behind her. 'Do you ever want an assistant?' she asked.

'How do you mean?'

'I've always wanted to do what you do.'

'This is a one-off,' said Frieda, quickly. 'The real help you can give is by showing me anything that might be useful.'

'You're going to be surprised,' said Erin Brack. 'There are things the police never knew.'

'Why didn't you tell anyone?'

'Nobody wanted to know. I'm telling you.'

'Like what?'

'I told you. I'm going to go through it all. Get it arranged. Then you can come and see it.'

'All right,' said Frieda. She didn't know whether to be pleased or dismayed. 'Let me know whenever you're ready.'

She took a card from her pocket, wrote her number on it and handed it across.

Erin Brack looked at it and smiled. 'I read about the Dean Reeve case,' she said.

'Yes, it was in the papers.'

'I think you're right.'

'In what way?'

'I don't think he really died. I think he's still out there. I know that nobody believes you. I know what it's like not to be believed. But I believe you. That may be some comfort.'

'Thank you.'

Frieda turned and left. She walked back down towards the river. When she got there she leaned on the railings and stared at the water that, an hour earlier, had been flowing through London.

SIXTEEN

Jason Brenner was the first on their list; he lived in Forest Hill. Yvette turned off a roundabout into a cul-de-sac. The two women got out of the car and looked around. There was a row of six little pebble-dashed houses. Frieda imagined them when they were first built as neat, smart cottages on the edge of fields or woodland. They might have felt like an escape from London. Even now, the road wasn't paved. There were just patches of concrete and gravel. But Fern Close was thoroughly, brutally surrounded. Opposite the line of houses was the wall of a warehouse. At the end of the road there was a chain-link fence and, on the other side, a timber yard. Of the houses, the first was bricked up with breezeblocks. The furthest along had a decrepit caravan in its front yard and next to it a rusted car with no tyres. Brenner lived in the second house from the end. It looked abandoned, except that where two windowpanes had been broken, someone had taken the trouble to block the gap with cardboard.

It was half past nine in the morning and Jason Brenner looked as if they had woken him up. He was wearing jeans and nothing else. It was a grey, rainy day, but even so the light seemed to hurt his eyes. He was resistant at first, but Yvette showed her badge and Frieda talked of taking him to the police station and having his place searched, so he led them inside and up the stairs. They went into a back room where there was nothing more than a couple of old arm-chairs and a low glass table. There were dirty plates, glasses and beer cans scattered about, but still the room didn't feel like anyone lived there.

'I'll be back in a minute,' Brenner said.

He padded out of the room and they heard the sound of running water and coughing. Frieda and Yvette looked at the chairs and remained standing. Frieda stared out of the window. The house backed onto a car showroom selling a brand of car she didn't recognize.

'This is five minutes away from where the Dochertys lived,' she said. 'It feels like a different world.'

'You've got to stop doing that,' Yvette said.

'What?'

'Talking about bringing people into the station for questioning. One day someone is going to call your bluff or get a lawyer.'

'I didn't mean to embarrass you.'

'I'm not talking about being embarrassed. I'm talking about being disciplined or fired.'

Brenner came back into the room and Frieda was able to look at him properly. She could guess that he had been handsome once, but it needed some imagination. He was so thin that his sharp cheekbones looked as if they might break through his papery, pallid skin. His dark hair was long and matted. He had a beard that wasn't quite a beard. Too much skin showed through. He had dressed only by putting on a dusty brown zip-up cardigan and a pair of black workman's boots, unlaced and with no socks. He picked up a coat from the floor, rummaged in the pockets and found a packet of cigarettes and a lighter. He lit a cigarette.

'You knew Hannah Docherty,' said Frieda.

'A long time ago.'

'Obviously. She's been locked up for a long time,' said Yvette.

'Shall we go somewhere?' said Frieda. 'Get a coffee or a tea?'

Brenner took a phone from his trouser pocket and looked at it. Frieda found the sight almost comical. This man had nothing, but he had a smartphone. He shook his head. 'I'm meeting someone.'

'Then we'll try to be quick.' Yvette had taken up a position that Frieda was becoming familiar with, her feet slightly apart, her hands on her hips, her chin lifted and her brows drawn into a frown. 'You were an associate of Hannah's.'

He gave a slight smile. 'Associate?'

'Friend,' Frieda amended. 'Boyfriend even.'

'We hung out.'

'You didn't give evidence at the trial,' said Frieda.

'I wasn't asked.'

'A close friend of yours was accused of murder. You might have wanted to help.'

'I'm not a character-witness sort of person.'

'Can you tell me anything about Hannah's relationship with her family?'

'What can I say? It wasn't good. She'd moved out. She was staying with us at this friend's place.'

'That was Thomas Morell.'

'Tom. Yeah, that's right.'

'Do you know where to find him?'

'We lost touch.'

'I know,' said Yvette.

'And Shelley Walsh,' Frieda continued.

Brenner gave a slow smile that made Frieda feel uncomfortable.

'Shelley. That's right. We lost touch as well.'

'That's a pity,' said Yvette. 'Old friends are important.'

'We drifted apart.'

137

'Because of the murder?' asked Frieda.

'It happens.'

'Well, when *this* happened, this murder of a family that became a national story, did you think that Hannah had done it?'

'What does it matter what I think?'

'You were spending time with her. You were her friend. You were sexually involved with her. And now she's been locked up for thirteen years. Don't you have an opinion about that?'

His expression changed and he stepped forward. 'What the fuck are you doing here? If you want to look into this, then look into it, just don't ask what I fucking think about it.'

'All right, then,' said Frieda. 'Let's be specific. She was getting on badly with her family. Do you know why they were getting on so badly?'

'Because she was a teenager. Because they were trying to control her. Because she was spending time with people like me.'

'Anything else?'

'There was some argument just after she left. Her mum or her stepdad said she'd been taking money from them.'

'And had she?'

'I don't know.'

'You were living with her. You were sleeping with her. She must have told you.'

'She may have helped herself once or twice.' He gave a shrug. 'We didn't have food to eat.'

'*We*,' said Frieda. 'So she was stealing on behalf of you all.'

'I didn't say that.'

'And you said she helped herself. That suggests there was money available in the house.'

'Of course it fucking suggests it.'

'Substantial amounts of money.'

'I didn't say that.'

'And that's you all knew about it.'

'That's rubbish.'

'Were you in trouble with the police during this period?'

'Trouble?' He raised his eyebrows exaggeratedly. 'They were always round our place on one pretext or another.'

Frieda was standing by the window, looking outside. 'There's something about this street,' she said.

'There's a few things,' said Jason. 'None of them good.'

'No, I mean the shape of it, the direction, it reminds me of something.'

'That's the river.'

'What river?' said Yvette. 'There's no river.'

'You can't see it,' said Jason. 'It runs underneath, along this street and under the car park.'

'That's right,' said Frieda. 'I should have realized.'

'It's funny. I've only met one other person who was interested in this bloody river that you can't see and nobody knows about.'

'Hannah?'

'She used to talk about it. She knew all about it. She couldn't believe there was a river underground that went all the way from Upper Norwood to the Thames and nobody knew about it. It never seemed much of a big deal to me.'

'What's it called?' asked Yvette.

'The Effra.'

'You know the name,' said Frieda. 'You must be a little interested.'

He shook his head. 'We used to go up to Effra Road in Brixton and she said it was because of the river. That's how I know.'

'Do you miss her?'

'I don't think about the past.'

'You look as if you've been through a difficult time, these last years. Almost as bad as Hannah, in its own way.'

'You don't know anything about my life.'

'You don't think that the way someone lives says something about their life? Also, you shouldn't be injecting drugs, and if you've got hepatitis, you definitely shouldn't be injecting drugs, or taking drugs in any form, or drinking alcohol.'

Brenner lifted his right hand and Yvette took a step forward but he just pointed at Frieda. 'You don't come in here and say things like that. Something might happen if you keep doing things like that.'

'Careful,' said Yvette.

'Or what?' said Brenner.

'Are you serious? We can turn this place over. I'm sure we can find something.'

'And then? I've been in prison. I can handle that.'

Frieda looked at Yvette. 'Have you got a card? With your number.'

Yvette handed one across to her, with a disapproving sigh. Frieda scribbled her own email and mobile onto it as well and handed it to Brenner. 'What was it like to see that happen to a friend of yours?' she asked. 'And to do nothing. Just stand by.'

Brenner looked down at the card. 'It didn't feel like anything,' he said.

'It's all a bit late,' said Frieda. 'But if you remember anything, ring that number.'

Back in the car, Yvette paused before starting it.

'What a bastard,' she said.

'You think?'

'He knew about the money. He has no morals of any kind – he doesn't care about some young girl he was sleeping with.'

'So which is it?' said Frieda. 'Is he indifferent or did he do the crime himself? Or did he do it with her? Or is it none of the above?'

'He's obviously gone downhill since then. If there was any money, he didn't get his hands on it or he spent it quickly.'

'At any rate, he's not got any money now.'

'He didn't show any concern at all about Hannah Docherty,' said Yvette. She seemed angry.

'Maybe he thinks she did it and doesn't deserve any concern. Anyway, why does he need to perform for two strangers who pop in thirteen years after it all happened? I wonder if he told us in another way.'

'How do you mean?'

'By the look of him, by the life he's led. By what he's done to himself.'

'Why did you say that about hepatitis? About injecting drugs? Was it in the file?'

'You saw the puncture marks on his arm when he let us in,' said Frieda.

'I didn't, actually.'

'And then his emaciated state and the yellowness of his eyes. It was pretty obvious.'

'You see, that's not remorse for his girlfriend. That's what people who do that when they're twenty look like when they're thirty.'

'Let's go and see what the others look like now.'

Tom Morell was nothing like Jason Brenner and it was hard to imagine the two men ever being friends. He was quite short, plump, with a mop of dark brown hair and a broad face. He was dressed in a pair of dark trousers and a grey jacket, with a bright-checked shirt underneath. They met him at the housing association he worked for in Peckham and he offered them both coffee, seeming disappointed when they refused. Frieda noticed a photo on his overflowing desk of a beaming woman holding a baby, who was unmistakably his.

'Thanks for seeing us,' she said, taking a seat opposite him.

'It's the least I can do. I had quite a shock when you said it was about Hannah.'

'Why?'

'I haven't talked about her in ages. When it first happened, I couldn't talk about anything else. I went over and over it, on a loop. I remember once getting drunk in a bar and telling the whole story to a total stranger, who was wasted too. It was like I couldn't believe it until I'd talked it out of my system.'

'And then you stopped.'

'One day I realized I was enjoying telling the story. Like I was some kind of hero for having lived alongside this girl who became a mass murderer. It was almost my party piece, the thing that made me interesting, gave me a kind of status. So that was when I shut up a bit. I still talk to Trudi sometimes – my wife.' He gave a nod to the woman in the photo. 'She knew Hannah as well and was in and out of the house. But less and less. It's become more like a dream. Not misty, too clear, unreal. But I'm going on about myself. What's happened?'

'There have been concerns about how the inquiry was conducted,' said Yvette.

'Well, I don't know what I can tell you about that. I only met the police once – no, twice. The first time was a junior officer – a young woman who seemed in rather a state, actually, not like how I thought a police officer would be. And once the man in charge – what was his name?'

'DCI Sedge?'

'That's the one. He was a bit stern with me. I gave a statement, but I don't think it was particularly helpful, one way or the other. I was out of town on the night of the murders.'

'It was more a general context that we were after,' said Frieda.

'What kind of thing?'

'Tell us about the house first of all.'

Tom Morell looked rueful. 'By the time Hannah joined us, it was pretty dreadful. Not at all what I'd had in mind when we started out. I had this idea of a commune, where everyone was welcome and everyone equal, where we all contributed what we could and helped those in trouble. You know the kind of thing. But it didn't really work out like that, though the first year or so was all right. We were in this house that had been abandoned for ages so it was pretty run-down. Then the woman I moved there with had a fling with one of the others and they both left together. By that time Jason and Shelley were there. Have you met them yet?'

'We've talked to Jason Brenner.'

'How is he?'

'Not in the best of health,' said Yvette.

'He wasn't a very easy housemate,' said Tom Morell. He looked from Yvette to Frieda. 'This won't be used in any way?'

'We're not interested in his drug habit, if that's what you mean.'

'Right. He was injecting heroin and drinking as well. Stealing to pay for it. He was an odd mixture of apathetic and aggressive. Funny, women seemed to like him in spite of that, though he never seemed bothered.' He gave a little shrug. 'I was always polite and reasonable and attentive and they never looked at me, but Jason – he just had to crook his little finger. He was good-looking, I guess.'

'I understand he was involved with Hannah.'

'I guess she was involved with him. He didn't have relationships. He just fucked women. Sorry.'

'It's fine.'

'He had a thing going on with Hannah, who deserved better, and with other women he brought back to the house, and with Shelley, who was off her head most of the time. She was rather shrill about it all, not that I blame her.'

'Shelley?'

'Yes. She yelled a lot. And Jason couldn't give a toss. And Hannah . . . oh, I don't know.'

'You liked her.'

'It's hard to remember what I made of her now, because of what happened. That gets in the way. But I did like her. So did Trudi.'

'So when she was charged with murdering her family, you must have been devastated.'

'I couldn't believe it. I mean, I accepted it had happened but I couldn't square it with the woman I knew. She was nice. That's a stupid word, but she was.'

'Everyone we've spoken to has talked about her being wild and troubled.'

'Maybe. But no more than Jason or Shelley or any number of people who came through our doors. She was just a lost kid.'

'She stole,' said Yvette.

'Did she?'

'According to Jason Brenner, she stole from her family.'

'Maybe she did.' He leaned forward suddenly. 'I went to the trial,' he said. 'To the public gallery.'

'What was it like?' asked Frieda.

'She looked so helpless. Half of me was horrified by her and the other half felt sorry for her.'

'When you said you talked about it obsessively after it had happened,' said Frieda, 'were there things you didn't ever say?'

Tom Morell looked at her, colour rising in his face. 'Why do you ask that?'

'Sometimes we feel compelled to repeat a story until it has become our fixed version of reality. I'm interested in what we need to leave out.'

He stared at her for a few moments, then said abruptly: 'I had sex with her.'

'Hannah?'

'Yes. When she was upset because of bloody Jason Brenner. A few nights before it happened.'

'And why had you left that out of your story?'

'I told myself it was a way of trying to comfort her. But I'd wanted it to be more than that.'

'And she didn't?'

'Not at all. I was just this overweight man who cooked spaghetti for everyone. It gives me a shivery feeling even now. I had sex with her and she cried in my arms and I held her, and then not many hours later she murdered her family.' He looked at Frieda. 'I never even told Trudi. It seemed some kind of taboo.'

'What happened to the squat?' asked Yvette, into the silence.

'It broke up. I don't know how long it took because I never went back there. I couldn't face it. It had started out as my experiment in how to lead a good life – and look what happened. Maybe I was partly to blame.'

'Hardly,' said Yvette.

'I've a little daughter now.' He looked towards the photograph on his desk.

'She's lovely.'

'I tell myself that I'll protect her. But Hannah's parents weren't unloving. Maybe they even protected her too much, so that she felt trapped. How does a kind young woman turn into a brutal murderer?'

'That's the question,' said Frieda.

There are many different ways of visiting patients in Chelsworth Hospital. The more privileged can stroll across the lawns, supervised or unsupervised. More usually, there is the visiting room, where visitors are liable to be searched. Visitor and patient face each other across a table and any physical contact is closely monitored. In special circumstances, relatives may visit a patient's bedside.

None of these is judged appropriate for Professor Hal Bradshaw. At the front desk, he surrenders his mobile phone, his wallet, his watch, his keys, two pens and a small notebook.

'As per the agreement,' says the male nurse, who has the bulk, the tattoos and the demeanour of a nightclub bouncer.

'Don't I need a pass?' asks Bradshaw.

The nurse shakes his head. 'You're only going to one place. I'll take you there and then I'll bring you back here.'

Bradshaw is led through the part of the building that is like the country house it had once been, and through the part that is like a hospital with bars and locks, and beyond that along corridors and finally to a room with no windows and grey linoleum, nothing on the pale green walls and just four moulded plastic chairs. He sits down and the nurse picks up one of the other chairs and puts it down next to the wall. He sits on the chair and it seems too small for him, like a chair used by children playing at being adults. They sit in silence and Bradshaw looks at his wrist but his watch isn't there. Normally at such a time he would take out his phone and check his mail but he doesn't have it and he feels almost undressed without it.

Finally the door opens and Mary Hoyle comes in with another male nurse. He gestures towards a chair and Mary Hoyle sits down. The nurse sits just behind her and to one side, but close, so that he can reach out and touch her. Or stop her. Hal Bradshaw looks at her. He has seen the photographs. A couple of blurry ones when she was a little girl. The iconic mugshot after her arrest. The sensational ones showing her looking blissed-out that were taken during the time of her killing spree and that all the newspapers carried; they still get used every time a journalist writes about 'unnatural' female killers. But he has been writing and negotiating and bargaining for this opportunity to see her face to face.

She looks like a primary-school teacher.

She is wearing grey slacks and a pale green T-shirt. Her hair is cut short, boyishly, and her eyes are as blue as precious stones, startlingly so. Bradshaw thinks of the old superstition, that the eyes of a dead person register the last image that the person saw. He wonders for a moment what those eyes have seen. She smiles at him, as if she's sharing a joke with him, as if they are both aware of the absurdity of it all.

'So, are you going to help me to get out?'

'I've looked at your case,' Bradshaw says. 'It looks promising. Obviously I need to assess you.'

Her smile turns slightly sad. 'People keep wanting to assess me and examine me and prod me.'

'I'm sure we can help each other.'

'How could I possibly help you, Dr Bradshaw?'

'Please, call me Hal.'

'Like the song?'

'What song?'

'It doesn't matter. Hal. How could I help you?'

'Your case is interesting. Millions of words have been written about it and yet nobody's ever written about it properly. In my opinion. If I can do that, that will help you. It will show that you have gained insight. That you've grown. That you're safe to release.'

'It was Davy,' says Mary Hoyle. She gives him her best smile. 'I was only a teenager when I met him. I fell under his spell.'

Bradshaw smiles reassuringly at her but at the same time he remembers the reports of the trial, how each had blamed the other. But he has also read the court psychiatric report. He remembers a phrase: 'Without her, he was nothing.'

'So what I'd like to do is to come and see you regularly, and if we make progress, that can only help you with the board.'

'I'm sure we can make progress,' says Mary Hoyle. 'That's what we're meant to do here, isn't it? Make progress.'

'Yes.'

'I'd be happy to see you.'

'That's great, Mary. Really positive.'

'Can I ask you one question, though?'

'Anything.'

'Do you know a woman called Frieda Klein?'

Bradshaw is so surprised that for a moment he can't speak. 'How do you know about Frieda Klein?' he asks.

She smiles again. There is something captivating about that smile, promising secrecy, intimacy.

'We have a wonderful library here. We can read anything, literature, history, porn.' Hoyle looks amused by Bradshaw's expression. 'True crime. The only books we can't have are books about crimes committed by people who are actually in the hospital. So the books about me aren't here. I imagine you've read them.'

'I've looked at them,' says Bradshaw, uneasily.

'There are one or two about Hannah Docherty, and they're not here either.'

'Who's Hannah Docherty?'

'I've read about Frieda Klein in several books. There was the one about the little girl who was kidnapped.'

'So what?' says Bradshaw, not liking the change of subject.

'And now she's taken an interest in Hannah Docherty.'

Bradshaw looks at Mary Hoyle in disbelief. 'You mean Frieda Klein is meddling with someone in this hospital?'

'She's been here. That's all I know.'

'What's that about? Why is she interested?'

'I don't know,' says Hoyle. 'I don't know about any of this. Look.' She holds her arms out. 'What do you see?'

'I don't know,' says Bradshaw, warily. 'What am I meant to see?'

'Nothing. No tattoos. And look at my face. No piercings. I don't take sides. I don't get sucked in. But a place like this is like a family, a family whose well-being I do my best to contribute to. People know they can turn to me here. But Hannah Docherty killed her family. And now she's doing damage to the family in here. And some people don't like it.'

Bradshaw thinks for a moment. 'That sounds like Frieda's sort of person. There's usually plenty of damage wherever Frieda Klein goes. She burned my house down once.'

'She burned your house down?'

'It wasn't exactly her. But she had a responsibility.'

'Interesting,' says Mary Hoyle.

'It's not interesting at all,' says Bradshaw, standing up.

He holds his hand out to her but the nurse behind her shakes his head. 'No touching,' he says.

SEVENTEEN

The next morning Frieda's final patient was Maria Dreyfus. Things had got worse with her. Her anxiety had spilled over into the session itself, about the whole idea of having therapy.

'I've been talking to friends,' she said.

'That's always good,' said Frieda.

'No, it isn't. It's like having ten clocks and each of them shows a different time. I told you that my husband, Rob, says I should be doing exercise. Which I do. I go for walks when I can. Some people say I should change my diet, cut out gluten or carbs. One friend says we should see a marriage guidance counsellor. Another one says that Prozac saved her life. Another said it's just about being in our mid-fifties. That's what it's like and it'll pass, like the weather. I just need to wait. So what do you think?'

'I think we can use these sessions to decide what *you* think is best for you.'

'I'm against the whole idea of pills. I used to think I didn't want to put chemicals into my brain to make me a different person. But sometimes at the moment I feel like I'd rather be anyone but me.'

'Medication can work for some people. But it's not a quick fix.'

'I believe in therapy for other people. I think other people can find the causes of their pain or their bad patterns. I just don't believe in it for myself.'

'Why?'

'Because *I*'m the problem.'

'Go on.'

'I don't know what else to say or how to describe what I mean. I guess I can't imagine not feeling like this. Take the feeling away and I wouldn't be me.'

'Who would you be?'

'I don't know.'

'You're saying you don't want to change.'

'I just can't imagine it. It would be like taking the salt out of the sea, blood out of a body.'

'You're letting dread define you.'

'Dread *is* me.'

Frieda phoned Erin Brack.

'Hey, Frieda, how's it going?'

Talking to Erin Brack, Frieda felt as if she was meeting a cheerfully drunk person while grimly sober. She was also aware that she mustn't offend her. 'I'm fine,' she said. 'I was just wondering if it was still all right to borrow the Docherty material.'

'Totally fine. But you're going to need a van, I can tell you.'

'I can get a van.'

'And a strong pair of arms.'

'That too. So when can I come?'

'I'm almost ready for you. What about next week? Thursday?'

'Fine,' said Frieda.

'I'm really looking forward to talking to you about it.'

'Good.'

'I've got some ideas.'

'I look forward to hearing them.'

'I can't imagine how I can help you!' said Shelley Walsh, as she opened the door of her Wimbledon semi and whisked Frieda and Yvette inside before anyone could glimpse them.

'Detective Constable Long has explained why we're here?' asked Frieda.

'Please, would you mind taking off your shoes. I know you'll think I'm fussy, but I've only just cleaned the floor and it's so wet outside.'

Frieda bent and took off her shoes. Yvette stared at Shelley Walsh incredulously. 'My shoes?'

'If you wouldn't mind. And coats hang on those hooks there.'

They waited while Yvette laboriously untied the double-knotted laces on her boots.

'Shall we go into the kitchen? I have to warn you that I can't give you long. A few minutes. I might not have a job but that doesn't mean I'm not a busy woman. My husband complains that I never stop!' Shelley Walsh gave a bright, sudden smile.

'That's fine,' said Frieda. 'Just a few minutes.'

The kitchen was like a laboratory that hadn't yet been used for conducting experiments. The copper pans that hung in descending order of size above the hob gleamed; the food mixer looked brand new; the wooden spoons in the pink jug were like a flower arrangement. And Shelley Walsh was equally immaculate. She was small and slender. Her dark blonde hair was tied tightly back; she was dressed in spotlessly clean and unfaded blue jeans, with a navy blue jumper over a white shirt. Her nails, Frieda saw, were manicured and pale pink; her lips were glossy and her eyebrows plucked into a neat arch that gave her a faintly enquiring look.

'What can I do for you?' She folded her hands together and placed them on the table in front of her. She arranged her face into an expression of neutral helpfulness.

'As you know, we're revisiting the Hannah Docherty case,' said Frieda, carefully.

'How strange.'

'We just wanted to ask a few questions about Hannah when you knew her, at the time of the murders.'

'I hardly *knew* her.'

'You were friends.'

'I wouldn't say that.'

'What would you say?'

'I met her,' suggested Shelley Walsh. 'Yes. I did meet her.' As if even this were in doubt.

Beside her, Frieda heard Yvette give strange half-snort.

'You met each other when you were fifteen.'

'If you say so. It was so long ago.'

'According to the files I've seen, you remained in close contact for the next three years.'

'That seems an exaggeration. Hannah knew people I knew. I don't see any of them now,' she added hastily. She twisted her hands together briefly. 'I was just a girl.'

'You lived together.'

She stared at Frieda, then at Yvette. She gave a small, tight laugh. 'I really think that's misleading.'

'When Hannah fell out with her mother and stepfather and left home, she came and stayed in the house you were living in. With Jason Brenner and Thomas Morell, among others.'

'Well, very briefly.'

'Until she was charged with the murder of her family.'

'And found guilty. Found guilty of the murders.'

'Indeed. So you were friends with her for three years, and in the final weeks of her life prior to her arrest you shared a house.'

'Lived under the same roof is a better way of putting it.'

'What were you doing at this time?' asked Yvette.

'Me?'

'Yes.'

'I don't see why – but, well, I was . . .' She stopped for a moment, stumped. Frieda saw her hands writhe again. 'I was between things.'

'Between what things?'

'Between school and, well, *this*.' She unwound her hands and gestured to the bare surfaces, the glinting utensils, the room where she scrubbed and scoured her time away.

'This between-time was quite chaotic, wasn't it?' asked Frieda, gently.

Shelley Walsh stared at her. 'I don't know why it matters to you.'

'It doesn't. Not in the way you mean. Most people have times when they don't know what to do or who they are.'

'I gather there were lots of drugs,' said Yvette. She seemed to be taking a grim pleasure in the interview.

'I don't see why you're asking me these unpleasant questions.'

'It was an unpleasant business,' said Yvette.

'Which is why I want nothing to do with it. Nothing.' She turned to Frieda. 'It was a long time ago and I've put everything behind me. Everything.'

'That's hard to do.'

'It's quite easy, really.'

'We want to know about Hannah,' said Frieda. 'That's why we're here. You were all young and at an uncertain time in your lives. What was it like, that house?'

'Messy.'

'You mean, emotionally messy?'

'Oh, no, I mean *messy*, as in mess everywhere. No one washed anything up or cleaned anything or threw anything away. You should have seen the bathroom.' She gave a shudder and then a high peal of laughter. 'I don't know how I put up with it.'

'So. It was rather chaotic and I assume there were a lot of drugs.' Shelley didn't reply, just looked at her hands, once more twisted together on the table. 'And probably not much money.'

'Not much,' she murmured.

'You, Hannah, Thomas Morell and Jason Brenner lived there, and there were other people who came and went. And the police took an interest in what was going on.'

'There's nothing else to say. I left after, you know, and I worked in a leisure centre and I met my husband and we courted for three years and married five years ago and here I am. Here I am,' she repeated. 'We're planning to have a child. Very soon.'

'When Hannah was living with you, what was her state of mind?' asked Frieda.

Shelley Walsh wrinkled her nose. 'What do you mean?'

'What was her mood?'

'She was trouble.'

'Troubled?'

'No. Trouble.' For a moment, it was as if a mask had slipped. Shelley Walsh's eyes glittered at them.

'Go on.'

'Nothing else, really. She was angry.'

'With her parents?'

'With everyone.' Frieda remembered that Hannah's father had also called his daughter angry, as had Sebastian Tait, the tie-making neighbour of the Dochertys. 'She rampaged around the house. That's what she did. Rampaged.'

'She was sexually involved with Jason Brenner, I believe.'

'I couldn't say.'

'As were you,' continued Frieda.

'Oh!' It was an involuntary cry of protest and disgust. Frieda thought of that stringy, unwashed man with his dirty fingernails in his squalid home, and compared him with this germ-free, panic-stricken pretty woman.

'Did he leave you for Hannah?'

'No. Don't.'

'Or perhaps it was at the same time. I imagine that either would have been painful for you.'

'I don't want to talk about it.' She blinked several times. 'I'm not the same person. I have a good, decent life. I don't want to think of him. Or her. Or any of it. I can't. It's not right to ask me.'

'I know it's hard to revisit things like this,' said Frieda.

'I think it really is time for you to go now. Really. I haven't anything more to say. I don't even know what you're doing, digging it all up again.'

'You used to go to Hannah's house.'

'What?'

'Brenner told us,' said Yvette. 'When no one was there.'

'I don't remember.'

'And take things.'

'What do you want? Why does this matter? It was when I was still a kid, and now Hannah's mad and shut away, like she should be, and I've put all that behind me and got on with my life. It wasn't easy. I didn't have anyone to turn to. You could say Hannah had it easy compared to me, and I didn't go and kill anyone.'

'You didn't have family?'

'My mum – she wasn't any good at looking after herself, let alone a child. Why do you think I was living in that crappy house? And when it all fell apart, she just disappeared on me, was nowhere to be found. I had to do it all by myself. ' She lifted her hands and tugged her ponytail tighter. 'That's not the kind of mother I'm going to be.'

'Good for you. But you did go to Hannah's house.'

'Sometimes. Sometimes. So what? It was Hannah's, after all. It wasn't as if we broke in. And if we took stuff, it was just what they wouldn't miss because they were so rich and entitled and had more things than they knew what to do with. What they spent in a month on designer clothes and wine was more than we got in a year. They left cash lying around as if they were asking to be robbed.' For a moment, she seemed to be thirteen years younger and spouting words that had probably come from Jason Brenner. Then she said to Frieda, her voice quieter, 'Do you know what? I dream about that house sometimes. I dream about it and I wake up feeling sick. And dirty. I have to go into the bathroom and take a shower. In the middle of the night. To wash it all away.'

'What do you dream?'

'I don't know. You can't imagine what it was like.'

'You mean, finding out that the person who you were living with had killed her family?'

'She's an animal. That's the kindest thing I can say about her. An animal.'

'Did you think at the time that she was capable of such a thing?'

'Well, she hated her mother and her stepdad.'

'That's not the same.'

'I don't know. I don't know what I thought. I don't know anything about it.'

'Did she hate her brother as well?'

'Rory?' For the second time, Frieda had the impression that she was looking at a different, less hysterically defensive Shelley Walsh. 'Hannah loved Rory and he loved her. He was very cute, young for his age. Poor little thing.' Her tone hardened again. 'So she must have been mad, mustn't she, to do what she did?'

'I take it you haven't been to see her,' said Frieda.

'Why on earth would I do that?'

'You haven't been in contact with her at all?'

'I don't ever want to see her or hear about her again.'

'Do you ever see Jason Brenner or Thomas Morell?'

'That part of my life is done with. Though Tom was nice. He was kind. I don't know what he was doing in that house.' Her eyes flickered to the clock on the wall. 'I think you should go now. I mean, Jerry might come back early. He does sometimes.'

'Your husband doesn't know about that part of your life?'

'Of course he doesn't, and I hope he never will. Why would I tell him something like that? That's not who I am. That was someone else entirely.'

She stood up and so did Frieda and Yvette. At the door, while Yvette painstakingly retied her laces, she said, 'I'm sorry I didn't offer you coffee. I'm not drinking caffeine at the moment, or alcohol. In case I fall pregnant.' She laid her hand with its manicured and polished nails on her flat stomach. 'You don't want to harm your unborn baby, do you? You can't be too careful.'

EIGHTEEN

'I've been reading about you,' said Chloë.

'Oh, God,' said Frieda. 'Is there something in the papers?'

Once or twice in her career, Frieda had found herself becoming part of a story, targeted by a newspaper, photographed, speculated about, commented on. She had hated every moment of it.

Chloë didn't answer at first. She leaned across the table and poured herself another mug of tea. 'Do you want some more?' she asked.

'I'm all right.'

Chloë took a sip. 'It's nothing to worry about,' she said.

'It's when people say that that I start worrying.'

'No, really, it's nothing to get in a state about. I've been reading about you on that woman's blog.'

For a moment Frieda couldn't remember, and then suddenly she could.

'Oh, right,' she said, in a weary voice. 'Erin Brack.'

'She keeps mentioning you.'

'I only met her once.'

'But you're working with her.'

'I wouldn't put it like that,' said Frieda. 'I need her. She's a collector, a bin-raider.'

'It's so creepy.'

'I've been to her house. It was strange.'

'So she's an obsessive, but you're not like that at all. You're a scientist.'

'That sounds like a criticism.'

'You keep saying you're going to stop all this,' said Chloë. 'And then you do it again. Well, we've talked about this already.'

Frieda was about to reply when she saw that Chloë was looking past her, at something over her shoulder.

'Didn't they used to be the other way round?'

Frieda turned her head. Chloë was looking at the mantelpiece. 'What?'

'Wasn't the bottle on the left of the mirror and the vase on the right?'

'Maybe.'

'I'm sure there's something different. It's funny how you remember things without knowing you've remembered them.'

'You might be right. The mind is odd like that,' said Frieda. 'When you know things without knowing them, remember things without remembering.'

'Maybe it was your cleaner.'

'I don't have a cleaner.'

'Or a friend. Or a lover.'

Frieda gave Chloë a sharp look, and Chloë pulled a face, defiantly refusing to apologize. But the mood had changed and Chloë finished her tea and said she was meeting someone.

As soon as she had gone, Frieda switched on her laptop and did a search: 'Erin Brack. Frieda Klein'. In a couple of seconds she was on a website called Crimescene. Across the page was a graphic based on police tape, with the words 'Crime Scene: Enter Here'. Frieda clicked on it, then clicked on the blog. The latest entry was dated the previous day:

For anyone who's interested (only kidding! I know you all are), Frieda Klein is now fully on board with the Hannah Docherty case. (See what else I've written about Frieda here, here and here.) As not everybody knows, I've got my own Docherty archive, which has got some fascinating stuff in there. I've been a bit of a voice crying in the wilderness for years where Hannah is concerned but that's all about to change. I'm just getting things in order so that Frieda can apply her very special branch of skills to the archive. We'll be good to go in exactly one week, I'll hand it over and then things will start to get exciting.

I'm so excited and humbled to be working with Frieda. I promise you'll all be the first to know what transpires as the plot thickens. Watch this space! ☺ ☺

Frieda started muttering to herself. She picked up her phone, then stopped herself. She waited a full minute, willing herself to calm down. She wanted to strangle Erin Brack. She made the call.

'It's so great to hear from you again!'

'I read your blog.'

'Great.'

'I've been thinking,' said Frieda. 'What if I came today? With a van?'

'We arranged it for next week.'

'We're all under pressure. I'll take what I can.'

'It won't be properly arranged.'

'That's fine. So I'll come this afternoon.'

'All right.'

Frieda was about to say goodbye when she remembered something. She caught a glimpse of her own reflection in the mirror on the wall. She had read that workers in call centres had to look at themselves in mirrors and smile as they talked. She couldn't go that far, but she tried at least to sound amicable. 'It was kind of you to write what you did,' she said.

'It was nothing.'

'No, no, it's good what you've done all these years, saving the material. But I'd be grateful if you'd avoid writing about what's happening, as it happens.'

'Have I done something wrong?'

'No, no, not at all,' said Frieda, trying to sound soothing. She felt as if she was trying to calm a toddler who might burst into a tantrum at any moment. 'I'm not an expert but . . .'

'You are.'

'I'm really not, but I think if we're going to do something like this, then it's good to be discreet. We shouldn't tip everyone off in advance. Does that make sense?'

'Yes, Frieda. I understand completely.'

'You understand that I'm paying you for this,' said Frieda.

'I do *not* understand,' said Josef.

'I'm hiring you and I'm hiring your van.'

'Today I am free.'

'I can charge it on expenses. It's not my money.'

Josef looked doubtful. 'We see.'

They had driven down through the Blackwall Tunnel, through Woolwich and now Thamesmead.

'Much building,' said Josef, shaking his head. They passed a house whose entire façade had been painted with a flag of St George.

'How are things back home?' asked Frieda.

Josef shook his head again. He didn't speak.

'Are you in touch with your wife? Your sons?'

'I try to.'

'How are they?'

'Sometime up, sometime down.'

'You could bring them over.'

'Is difficult.'

The only voice for the rest of the journey was the satnav,

directing Josef past Plumstead, Abbey Wood and Belvedere. Suddenly seeing it on a sign, Frieda thought that Belvedere must once have been a beautiful view. It still was, in a way, but whoever had given it the name originally probably wouldn't agree.

As soon as Josef pulled up outside 63 Oldbourne Drive, the door opened, as if Erin Brack had been looking out of the window, waiting for them. 'I don't think you need that big a van,' she said. 'You're not moving house.'

'This is the only van I know,' said Frieda.

'No worries,' said Erin Brack. 'I've boiled the kettle.'

'I'm afraid we're in a hurry.'

They stepped inside and she heard Josef's intake of breath, then he said something to himself in Ukrainian. They exchanged glances.

'I'm in purdah,' said Erin Brack.

'What?'

'I'm offline. Like a Trappist nun.'

'I just meant not to talk about *this* case.'

'But people will be curious about what's going on, why I'm not saying anything.'

'The best answer to that is just not to say anything.'

'That might be easy for *you*. My readers expect things from me.'

Erin Brack led them to the room upstairs. To Frieda's eyes it seemed unchanged from before. Perhaps it was a little easier to open the door.

'You just point at things,' said Frieda. 'And we'll carry them away.'

There was a lot but it was mainly papers and notebooks and photographs that Erin Brack had piled into bin-bags, one of which was splitting at the side. There were clothes, a pencil case and some shoes that fitted into two more bin-bags.

There was also an old brown suitcase. Frieda picked it up. It was full. 'How did you get it?'

'It was left out for the bin men. I just got to it first.'

'How did you know?'

'It's like birdwatching,' said Erin Brack. 'Or astronomy. Or fishing.'

'Is it legal?'

'Basically,' said Erin Brack. 'But it can be a grey area. It depends where it's left.'

'Where was this left?'

'I can't remember.'

'What's inside?'

'I don't know. It's locked. I'm sure it's easy to break open. I never got around to it. Exciting, isn't it? It might be the clue you need.'

Frieda looked at the case and wondered who had closed it, who had locked it. It felt wrong. Even being in Erin Brack's house. But was it really so different? Frieda herself had done worse things than helping herself to rubbish before the bin men arrived. She handed the case to Josef.

There were some things she didn't take: a desk lamp, a stapler.

'And then there's this,' said Erin Brack. She reached into a corner, breathing heavily, and re-emerged holding a teddy bear. One of its eyes was missing and it was battered in the way a toy animal gets battered from being held and dragged around, slept with and slept on for year after year. 'Why would someone throw that away?' said Erin Brack. 'Doesn't that seem suspicious to you?'

Frieda stepped back. She didn't even want to touch it. 'Perhaps it was too painful,' she said. 'Sometimes it's important to throw things away. It's a way of staying sane.'

'Lucky for me, then,' said Erin Brack.

NINETEEN

Frieda didn't look through any of the things they had collected at once. There was so much. She and Josef carried everything upstairs to her garret study and left it for later. The following day, she saw four patients and went to a meeting at the Warehouse. When she returned home it was late afternoon and already nearly dark.

She took off her coat and scarf and hung them on the hook in the hall, unlaced her boots, bent to stroke the cat. The answering machine was blinking in the hall, but she didn't listen to it immediately. She went into the kitchen where she fed the cat and put the kettle on. Only when she had a mug of tea in her hand did she listen to the messages. There were five, and three were from Erin Brack.

In the first, she breathed heavily for several seconds before saying, in a conspiratorial whisper, 'Frieda? Frieda? It's me.' There was a long pause, as if she was waiting for Frieda to pick up. 'Frieda? Just calling about our mutual friend.' The second began halfway through a sentence already – 'I just thought I should say . . .' and ended with the sound of something being dropped and a muffled shout. 'Sorry about that,' she said in the third. 'I was just saying, you should look at the boy's geography teacher. That's all. I'm naming no names, but *geography teacher*! OK?'

Geography teacher. Which geography teacher? But not now. She finished her tea, then went upstairs to her study. The bin-bags full of clothes had been pushed into the corner with the suitcase, and the boxes were on her desk. She lifted out sheaves of papers, notebooks and bills. Later, she knew she would have to go through everything properly, but for now she was looking for things from Rory's school. She found his maths graph book, a third full, and a blue soft-backed notebook with stories in it, in messy blue biro with lots of crossings-out. Again, it was only half full. Even the last story hadn't been completed. She put it to one side, trying not to think of the photograph of Rory in his bed, his head, his skull. A bit further through the box, she came across a report from the previous term, just two printed green pages stapled together. The section for geography was towards the bottom of the first page: 'Rory has worked hard this term, and he has understood the concept of sustainability very well. His diagrams can be careless.' She looked at the name: Guy Fiske.

There were not many people called Guy Fiske on Google, and when she added 'geography teacher' and 'UK' there was only one. In 2013, Guy Fiske, sixty-one, had been convicted of historic child abuse and been given a ten-year sentence. Frieda read through the multiple accounts of his offences against the students who had been under his care and her mood grew increasingly grim; her heart felt heavy. For more than two decades he had abused minors, one apparently as young as eleven, the others between thirteen and fifteen. They were all boys. Five of them, now grown men, had given evidence against him. There was a photograph of Fiske, sandy-haired, with a high forehead and a small chin, innocuous-looking – but, then, what is a paedophile supposed to look like?

Frieda noticed that one of the men – Jem Green, twenty-seven, a local-radio DJ – had waived his right to anonymity. There was a clip of him standing outside Preston Crown Court, a burly man, with dark hair slicked back and a close-shaved beard, who spoke very calmly about the events leading up to trial. He said he had decided to go public to encourage others who had been through similar experiences to come forward and speak out. 'This is a good day in my life,' he said. He gave a slight grimace, a downward turn of his mouth, as if to control his emotions. 'I feel something has at last been laid to rest.'

That had been a year ago. If Jem Green was now twenty-eight, it was almost certain he had been at school at the same time as Rory, who would have been twenty-six if he were still alive. In fact, he must have been there at the same time as Hannah as well. Frieda followed the links. With three clicks, she had his email address at work. She sat for a long time in her garret study before she wrote him a short, careful message. Then she called Yvette. She didn't seem happy to hear from Frieda.

'Am I interrupting something?'

'Just say what you have to say.'

'I need to find out where a man called Guy Fiske is in prison and I need to see him as soon as possible.'

'Is that all?'

'Is it straightforward?'

'I was being sarcastic.'

'If it's a problem, just say it's a problem.'

'Obviously it's a problem. What's it about?'

'He was Rory's geography teacher. He's serving a ten-year sentence for child abuse.'

There was a long pause.

'I hate these cases.'

'I know.'

'So you're wondering if Rory was abused.'

'Yes.'

'Why? I mean, why does it make any difference, apart from being horribly distressing? A kid who might have been abused by his teacher and who was then killed by his sister. Where does it get you?'

'It clearly has to be followed up.'

'OK. I'll arrange it.' The hostility seemed to have gone out of her and she just sounded subdued.

'I appreciate it, Yvette.'

Frieda had a long bath, then made herself a Greek salad and poured a glass of red wine. She sat at the kitchen table with the cat at her feet and the rain dashing itself against the windows, but she couldn't settle. At last, just before eleven o'clock, she pulled on her walking boots and her coat and left her house. She walked on deserted side-streets, avoiding the thoroughfares that were always busy until she crossed City Road and came to Bunhill Fields Burial Ground. It had once been a Saxon burial ground, a refuse tip, a dumping ground for bones from the charnel house and for animal bones from Smithfield, a plague pit, and then become the unhallowed site for religious outsiders and nonconformists. John Bunyan lay here, and Blake. All those restless lives now old bones under the damp earth.

The rain pulsed down as Frieda walked through the cramped headstones, jammed together and leaning in different directions, like a toppling forest, a crumbling city. In the distance was the sound of traffic; here it was silent, except for the patter of rain in the trees above her and a rustle in the bushes. She stopped by a large stone, looming towards her in the darkness. She was wet and cold and thoughts swarmed through her. Images. Rory lying in his *Lord of the Rings* pyjamas with his caved-in skull. Hannah, with her bruised face and dark, glittering eyes. In the corner of her vision she saw a shape: a fox winding its way through the headstones, low to the ground and quite silent. She watched it go, then turned.

*

Back at home, she rubbed her hair dry and pulled on a dressing-gown. She still wasn't tired, and went upstairs to her study. It felt like the whole world was asleep but her. There were new messages in her inbox and she saw that one was from Jem Green. She clicked on it. *Hi Frieda. Always happy to talk. Give me a call.* He had included his mobile number. She looked at the time his message was sent and saw it was at 02.27, just a few minutes ago, so she picked up the phone.

'Jem here.' There was an echo on the phone; his voice boomed.

'It's Frieda Klein. Is this a bad time?'

'That was quick. Not bad at all. I'm a night owl. You must be too.'

'Sometimes.'

'So, what do you want?'

'Are you comfortable talking about your past?'

'I went through all of that years ago. Just tell me what you're after.'

'I don't know how you can help. Perhaps you can't. I need to find out what I can about the Dochertys, Rory and Hannah.'

'Oh, yes, that. I remember them.'

'You were at school with them both?'

'Am I to assume that you think Fiske might have targeted Rory? Or Hannah?'

'It's something to consider.'

'Why? I mean, what's this for?'

'We want to make sure that Hannah's conviction is sound.'

'Are you fucking serious?'

'I'm looking at the case. That's all.'

'And what's Fiske got to do with it?'

'Maybe nothing.'

'Rory and Hannah Docherty.' There was a pause. When he spoke again, his voice was quieter. Frieda imagined him somewhere, settling back in his chair, listening to the rain outside. 'I was two years above Rory, and three below Hannah, so I didn't really know them. She was quite famous in the school – I mean, famous before she became famous. She was good at sport and kept getting prizes. And then she was famous because she was such a public mess.'

'Mess?'

'She went from being the good student to being the really bad one. I remember she turned up at assembly once out of her head.'

'Drunk?'

'Whatever. It wasn't just self-destructive, it was like she had to display it. But I'm pretty sure Fiske didn't have anything to do with what happened to her. As far as I know, it was only boys he went for.'

'And Rory?'

'I don't know. He was the kind of kid he might have picked on.'

'What do you mean by that?'

'Quiet. Anxious. Afterwards, people said he'd been bullied.'

'After he'd been killed?'

'That's right. Fiske targeted boys who wouldn't make a fuss.'

'You don't fit that.'

'I did then, believe me. What you're hearing is my new self, the one I've been working on for years. How am I doing?'

'You have to tell me that: how *are* you doing?'

'Mostly I'm fine but sometimes I think I'll always be that scared, humiliated little boy hiding behind the bold exterior I've made for myself.'

'I hope you've had help.'

'I have. But the best thing I did for myself was to give up the booze, and to give evidence against him.'

'It was brave.'

'It stopped me feeling so ashamed. What went on at that school, it was terrible. Nobody daring to say anything. I hope Rory Docherty wasn't one of the victims. That wouldn't be fair, would it?'

'Nothing about any of it was fair.'

Guy Fiske sat opposite Frieda. He laid his hands on the table; they were smooth and pink and the nails were neatly cut. He was small, with sparse grey hair and a pouched face. His eyes were brown and sad. His air was polite and apologetic.

'Nobody visits me,' he said.

'I'm here to ask you about a boy who was your pupil from 1999 to 2001, when he was in years seven, eight and nine.'

'I would like to be of help,' said Guy Fiske, cautiously. He blinked several times; his eyes were red-rimmed. 'I don't know if I can remember that far back.'

'I think you'll remember this particular boy. Rory Docherty.'

'Oh, *Rory*! Poor Rory. That was a terrible, terrible thing.'

'We're re-examining the Docherty case. There may have been some irregularities.' Frieda heard her vague, glib words slip from her.

'I see.'

'What do you see?'

'You want to know if . . .' He stopped. His brown eyes stared at her. Frieda waited. 'With Rory,' he said. 'Rory Docherty. He had reddish hair.'

'Yes.'

'What do you think prison is for?' he asked. 'I mean, what's it doing?'

'Could we perhaps stay with Rory Docherty?'

'Is it just for punishment? Or do you think people can be redeemed?'

'Did you assault Rory in any way?'

'Because even nice, liberal people who believe you go to prison and serve your time – atone, that's the word – even they draw the line at people like me. No redemption for me. It's not very Christian, is it?'

'Mr Fiske . . .'

'Guy. Call me Guy. Or can't you bring yourself to call a paedophile by his first name? You probably wouldn't want to shake my hand, would you?' He sat back in his chair and looked away from her at last and Frieda found she was relieved to be released from his soft brown gaze. 'You want to know what happened with Rory?'

'Yes.'

'Nothing. But why would I tell you anyway? That's what you're thinking. Why should you believe me?'

'And why should I?'

'What have I got to lose?'

'I don't know. It can be very hard to acknowledge even to oneself the things one's done. The mind refuses.'

'I never touched him,' he said slowly, and Frieda couldn't stop herself wondering if he was imagining touching him. Or remembering. 'I don't understand why you're even asking. What does it matter now? He's dead.'

'It still matters.'

'Do you believe me?'

'It's not that simple. Did you ever teach Hannah?'

'No.'

'You're sure?'

'It's not something you would forget. I'd know if I'd taught a girl who murdered her entire family.'

Frieda thought they were done but he spoke again.

'He seemed young for his age. He was a bit of a mummy's boy – and I always thought his mother was more than she seemed at first glance.'

'Deborah Docherty? Why?'

'Still waters run deep.'

'What do you mean by that?'

'Rory adored her.'

'She was his mother.'

'*Adored* her.'

'You make that sound sinister.'

'I'm just saying.'

'You've got a visitor.'

Hannah Docherty opened her eyes at the voice and turned her head. Her neck hurt. Her throat. Her head was making a faint humming sound. There was a shape in front of her; she squinted in the harsh light.

'You've got a visitor.' The voice was loud, grating against her ears. 'It's like buses, isn't it? No one comes to see you for years and years, and then several arrive at once. Why all this interest?'

Hannah allowed herself to be led down the corridor, down the stairs. One foot in front of the other, and her body was unsteady, tipping from side to side. The strip-lights flickered; windows passed her – brief frames of wet greenness and, in the distance, a wood with bare branches. Grass. Trees. Sky. Rain. She used to like rain. Soft and clean, washing the world. Once upon a time.

Someone bumped heavily against her, sending her staggering. She heard a snicker of laughter, curling into the air.

'Oi,' said the orderly, his voice bouncing off the walls. 'Watch your step, matey.' He steered her round to the left. 'We're going in here. Sit down, will you? Are you going to behave nicely?'

Then there was the sound of a door opening, closing, footsteps and a violent scrape of a chair being pulled back. And there was a man sitting in the chair opposite her. His forearms were on the table and he was leaning forward. His face stretched and grimaced; his mouth made strange shapes. He was saying her name.

'Hannah,' he said. 'Hannah, do you remember me?'

Hannah stared at him. He came in and out of focus. He lifted a hand and let it fall. He was talking too quickly: his words ran into each other and she could make no sense of the stream of sound.

'Hannah,' he repeated. 'It's Tom. Tom Morell. Do you remember me? You lived in that house with me. Before. I'm sorry I haven't come before.'

Hannah didn't answer. Her expression was dazed.

'I was scared,' he said. 'That's the truth of it. But I haven't forgotten about you. I just wanted to say that I'm sorry about everything. So sorry.'

There was water on his cheek. Raining outside, raining inside. She put out a finger to touch it.

'Careful now,' said a voice from behind her.

'Can you understand what I'm saying? Hannah? Can you hear? Do you remember?'

Remember? His words bounced inside her skull. His face worked. She closed her eyes. Remember.

The next time Hal Bradshaw meets Mary Hoyle it feels like they're old friends, slipping into their usual intimacy. By contrast, the two nurses look bored and resentful and tense. One sits close by her, constantly observant.

'So, what do you make of me?' Hoyle asks.

'I was hoping we could work together. People are fascinated by you. I thought you and I might be able to collaborate on a book.'

'I could do that.'

'Really? That would be terrific.'

'After I get out.'

'I was hoping we could do it straight away. It could be helpful to your case.'

'It could be helpful. Or it could be unhelpful. You never know.' There is a new firmness in her tone, but then her expression relaxes. 'You didn't answer my question.'

'I've talked to Dr Styles. She says you're making excellent progress.'

There is a pause.

'But?' says Hoyle.

'People have strong feelings about you, both outside and inside. I mean . . .' Bradshaw hesitates. He isn't quite sure how to put this. 'Killing those children. And recording it. You know.'

'I feel like I'm not the person who did that. Obviously I was found unfit to plead. But in my sessions with Dr Styles I've taken responsibility for what was done.'

'Yes, yes, of course,' says Bradshaw. 'But there are naysayers. For example, you mentioned this young woman, Hannah Docherty.'

'Did I? I don't remember that.'

'She was recently involved in a violent incident.'

'I'm in solitary. I don't hear about things like that.'

There is a snorting sound from behind her. It comes from the burly nurse sitting by the wall.

'What's that?' asks Bradshaw.

'You hear things,' says the nurse.

'Someone told me,' says Bradshaw, 'there was a feeling that this Hannah Docherty had made an enemy of you in some way. That you were out to get her.'

'Why would I have an enemy?' says Mary Hoyle.

'It's about respect,' says the nurse. 'And disrespect.'

'I'm the one who needs protection. That's why I'm on my own right now, meeting nobody. What can I do if Moss says things like that about me?'

'It's just one man's opinion,' says Bradshaw.

'Ah! So it was Moss.'

'I didn't say that,' says Bradshaw. 'And it doesn't matter.'

'Moss. He shouldn't be saying things like that.'

TWENTY

Frieda tried to see her friend Sasha once a week. She had been suffering from severe depression. She was vulnerable. Frieda had been concerned about her. But Sasha couldn't always manage it, and Frieda felt she couldn't impose herself. This Saturday morning, when they were sitting in Frieda's living room drinking tea, was the first they had seen of each other for almost a month. Six months earlier she had been briefly in a psychiatric ward, heavily medicated. Frieda tried not to make her feel she was being scrutinized, spied on, but she couldn't help checking her out. It had been an assessment she had been used to making in her early days as a doctor. Look at the condition of the hair, fingernails, state of cleanliness and neatness, signs of agitation.

Sasha wouldn't have looked well to someone meeting her for the first time. Her long blonde hair was unkempt, her eyes were dark with tiredness. She fidgeted constantly, rotating the mug of tea on the table, pushing her hand through her hair. Outside it was rainy and windy, and every time the water gusted against the window, Sasha flinched as if it hurt her. But Frieda was reassured. Sasha was better than she had been. More responsive, more alert.

'You should have brought Ethan,' said Frieda.

'Oh, you don't want a four-year-old running around your house smashing things up.'

'One of the main rules in life,' said Frieda, 'is that you should never own anything that you would mind a four-year-old smashing up.'

'He'd find something,' said Sasha. 'But it's not that. I'm doing well with him. Except sometimes I can feel people looking at me: is she safe with him? Is she going to lash out at him or forget to feed him? And I'm back at work, for a couple of days a week.'

'That's good.'

'It's tiring. And Ethan's tiring. So to sit here and be just us . . .' She looked up. 'It's all right, you know.'

'What's all right?'

'I haven't left Ethan home alone. I've hired this woman, Mariana. I hand over almost my entire salary to her and she helps with Ethan. And things. So you don't need to worry about him.'

'I wasn't worried. How are your therapy sessions going with Thelma, by the way?'

'I think she disapproves of me.'

'I'm sure that's not true.'

'I would if I were her. What I wish is that it was like the old days, that I could just talk to you.'

'You can talk to me,' said Frieda. 'You're talking to me now.'

Sasha put both her hands on the table and drummed her fingers, as if she were playing it, like a piano. 'I suppose you can't go to a therapist if one of your problems is that you almost destroyed their life and got them killed.'

'You never did anything wrong,' said Frieda. 'Nothing at all. It wasn't you who nearly killed me. The reason I'm not your therapist is because I'm your friend. It's good to see someone from outside your life. You look better, Sasha, you really do.'

'I don't know whether it's me or the pills. I feel out of my head.'

'What are you taking?'

Sasha rummaged in her pocket and produced a brown plastic bottle and handed it to Frieda. 'It's funny,' she said. 'I studied SSRIs when I was a post-grad. I was always a bit dubious about them. I never know whether they're working or whether it's a placebo effect. Whatever it is, after the last terrible year, I'll take it. I'll take anything.'

As Frieda started to reply, she was interrupted by the doorbell. The two women looked at each other.

'If you've organized a surprise party,' said Sasha, 'I'm not really in the mood.'

Frieda got up. 'That's another good thing,' she said. 'You're getting your sarcasm back.'

She opened the door. A shock hit her like a dull throbbing. Two uniformed police officers and a man in a suit were standing in the doorway.

'Dr Frieda Klein?' said the man in the suit.

'Yes,' she said slowly. 'Yes, I am.'

'My name's Detective Chief Inspector Waite.'

'Do I know you?'

'Know me? Why would you ask that?'

'I've met a lot of policemen,' said Frieda. 'Over the years.'

'You're a doctor,' Waite began.

'I trained as a doctor. I'm a psychotherapist.'

'You're a psychotherapist,' said Waite. 'And you see so many police officers that you have trouble keeping track of them?'

'That's right.'

'We'll probably get to that in due course.'

'I'm sorry,' said Frieda. 'Has something happened?'

'Can we come in?'

'If there's something you want to tell me, I'd rather you just told me.'

'We want to talk to you. It would be better inside.'

'I don't know why you're being mysterious.'

'Please,' said the detective, and stepped forward, so he was almost against her.

Frieda felt as if he was trying to physically intimidate her and her instinctive impulse was to push back. But she didn't. She knew it would probably just lead to more trouble. 'All right.'

She stepped aside and the three officers walked down the hall and into the living room, which they seemed to fill. Sasha looked up in alarm. 'What's going on?'

'I don't know.'

Waite looked at Sasha. 'Could you give us a moment?'

'It's all right.' Sasha stood up. 'I was just going.'

'You don't need to go,' said Frieda.

'It's probably best,' said Waite.

'What do you mean?' said Frieda. 'What's all this about?'

'Shall I call Karlsson?' asked Sasha.

'Who's Karlsson?'

'Why do you need to know?' asked Frieda.

'He's a detective,' said Sasha. 'And he's a friend of Frieda's.'

'It's all right.' Frieda put a hand on her arm. 'Don't worry. I'll ring you later.'

Frieda looked at Sasha with concern as she put on her jacket, fumbling with the zip as if it was an unfamiliar design. When she was done, she came over and hugged Frieda. 'Are you involved with something?'

'I don't know,' said Frieda.

'I thought you were done with all this.'

'It keeps coming back.'

Sasha let herself out, looking small and vulnerable.

'Is something up with your friend?' asked Waite.

'Yes.'

'Mind if we sit down?'

The two uniformed officers took two of the chairs and put them against the wall, side by side, and sat on them. Waite sat at the table and gestured for Frieda to sit opposite him.

'Pretty house,' he said. 'Psychiatrists must be richer than policemen.'

'Fifteen years ago this street was derelict.'

'Nice one. Prime central London location. Good call.'

'You had something to say.' Frieda was making an effort to sound calm.

'I looked your name up. I thought there might be a speeding fine, a court appearance. But you've been a busy lady.'

'I think you've got this the wrong way around. If you've got something to tell me, then tell me. If you've got a question, then ask it.'

Waite leaned forward, his elbows on her table. She could see his face in high definition. His dark hair was pushed back against his head, but it was thin over his scalp. It was really time for him to cut it short, to stop pretending he wasn't going bald. 'You know a woman called Erin Brack.'

Frieda paused. She hadn't been expecting this. 'Was that a statement or a question?'

Waite frowned, looked across at the two officers, then back at Frieda. 'You know, usually when I meet respectable members of the public, such as yourself, they're eager to cooperate. They want to be good citizens. All right. Put a question mark at the end of the sentence. Do you know a woman called Erin Brack?'

'I've met her twice.'

'In what context?'

'I'm sorry. I don't want to be a bad citizen, or whatever it is you call it, but this isn't how it works. If you're

182

investigating a crime, you need to tell me what it is. You can't just ask vague questions.'

'Because of what? Because you might give yourself away?'

'Because it's how the legal system works.'

'You seem to know a lot about it.'

'Force of circumstances,' said Frieda. 'It wasn't my own choice.'

'You mean when you were on the run?' said Waite. 'Or the various crime scenes you've been found at?'

'Yes. Those. So if you want me to answer questions, you need to tell me what this is about.'

'All right, Dr Klein. Yesterday there was a fire at the house owned by Erin Brack.'

'What kind of fire?'

Waite continued as if she hadn't spoken. 'When the fire was put out, a body was found. It was the owner, Erin Brack.'

Frieda stared at Waite. 'She's dead?'

'Oh, yes.'

She put both her hands on the table in front of her and looked down at them for a few moments before asking, 'Was the fire an accident?'

'Investigations are in progress, but we don't think so. And when we looked at her phone records, there were calls – repeated and of some duration – over the last few days.'

'Yes, she called me.'

'What about?'

For a moment Frieda couldn't even speak. She thought of poor, clumsy, hopeless, obsessed Erin Brack. What was it she had wanted from life? And what had happened to her? Frieda forced herself to answer. 'She kept a blog. You can read what she said there.'

'We know about her blog. That was the first place we

looked. But we want to hear it from you. What did you talk about during those calls?'

Frieda found it difficult to think clearly about this, although she didn't quite understand why. She had barely known Erin Brack, and she had found her troubling and irritating. The idea that anything could happen to her had never occurred to her.

'I don't think I can answer any of your questions,' she said slowly.

'What?'

'You heard me.' Frieda looked at Waite's changed expression with a detached sort of interest. She could see that it might have appeared frightening, if she had cared about it at all.

'This isn't like . . .' Waite stopped. He seemed to have trouble searching for what it was that it wasn't like. 'Like something optional. We're police. We're questioning you.'

Frieda took a small notebook from her pocket. She wrote on a page, ripped it out and handed it to Waite. He looked at it. 'Who's this?'

'Call him,' said Frieda. 'He'll explain.'

'What's this? Phone a friend?'

'Just call that number.'

'If you don't answer our questions, I'm going to arrest you.'

'What for?'

'Perverting the course of justice. We can add that to your file.'

'Just call the number. Then you can decide if you want to arrest me.'

Waite stood up and glared down at her. The other two officers stood up as well.

'I've got a better idea. We'll put you in a cell. Then I'll think about calling this number.' He nodded at the officers. 'Take her. If she does anything, cuff her. We'll call it resisting arrest.'

Jimmy Moss is in ward four, one of the 'safe' wards, preparing a bed. He's bent over, pulling a stubborn, tight sheet over a corner of the mattress. He doesn't hear them and he doesn't see them. A blow to the back of the head and he sinks to his knees, a blow to the kidney and he folds over on the floor. Something strikes his knee and he hears it as well as feels it, a splintering sound. It doesn't seem connected to him. His face is next, blackness and blood and fragments in his mouth. Then silence and pain rolling towards him, like black storm clouds.

TWENTY-ONE

There was a clattering of bolts. Even the white cell door sounded angry as it opened. Frieda was lying on the bed, her back against the brick wall. Jock Keegan stepped into the cell. He looked around as if he was appraising it, comparing it with other cells he had known.

'I'm sorry,' said Frieda. 'I asked them to phone Levin.'

'If you think I'm going to be amused somehow by all of this, then you're wrong.'

'I don't find it amusing in any way. And I'm sorry. As I said, I asked them to ring Levin.'

'They did ring Levin. But I didn't think it was the best use of his time to come all the way down to wherever the hell this is.'

'Thamesmead,' said Frieda.

'Whatever it's called, it took me an hour to get here.'

'I hoped it would just take a phone call to sort out.'

'Just a phone call?' He gestured helplessly, throwing out his hands. 'I said from the start that I didn't know what it was all about. "She's got a gift," Levin said. "It'll be discreet," Levin said. "She can do a bit of work for us on the quiet."'

'I didn't ask for this.'

'I've read your file. There are career criminals I've dealt with who've spent less time in police custody than you have.'

'I asked for Levin because I thought he could sort this out. If you can't, just say so and I'll think of something.'

'I don't know why you're not wanting to cooperate in a murder investigation.'

Frieda looked around. 'Is there surveillance in here?'

'I wouldn't know,' said Keegan. But he walked forward, sat on the bed next to Frieda, and when he spoke to her it was in a whisper, their faces just a couple of inches apart. 'What?'

'Erin Brack had material on the case,' said Frieda. 'I think that's why she was killed.'

'That sounds important,' said Keegan. 'The sort of thing the police need to know.'

'I've got it.'

'What do you mean?'

'I collected it from her the day before she died.'

'What is it, this material?'

'It's just stuff she raided from bins. I haven't gone through it properly.'

Keegan looked cross and thoughtful at the same time. 'How do you know that there's any important evidence there?'

'I thought there was a small chance there might be. I wasn't sure. But I am now.'

'How come?'

'Because Erin Brack was killed. She wrote in her blog that I had got in touch with her. She said she had evidence that she was giving me. And then she was killed and her house set on fire.'

'So tell the police.'

Frieda shook her head. 'Right now, it looks as if all Erin Brack's evidence has been destroyed. I was going to collect it in a few days' time, and she made that clear in her blog. No one knows I've got it. That's good. If I tell the police, it will get out. It always does. In two days it'll be in the newspapers.'

'That sounds very cynical.'

'It's happened to me before. I just need some time,' said Frieda. 'A few days. I need the police off my back. So what should I do?'

Keegan stood up and walked around the cell. Then he visibly made up his mind. 'All right,' he said.

DCI Waite sat opposite Frieda. Between them, to her left, was the digital recording device. On its fascia was a little screen. On it, Frieda saw herself, filmed over Waite's shoulder, looking at the screen.

'Don't worry about it,' said Waite. 'It's for your own protection.'

'It's not a problem.'

'So, I understand that you are now willing to make a statement.'

'Yes.'

'Why the change of mind?'

'I'm sorry. I was shocked to hear of Erin Brack's death. I wasn't thinking clearly.'

'Like post-traumatic stress?' He didn't disguise his sarcasm.

'Something like that.'

'What was the nature of your relationship with Erin Brack?'

'Murder investigations were a sort of hobby with her. She knew that I was interested in the Hannah Docherty case.'

'Interested in what way?'

'I'm a psychotherapist. I went to see Hannah to assess her psychological state.'

'Which was?'

'Poor. She's spent extended periods in solitary confinement.'

'What happened between you and Erin Brack?'

'Not much. She wanted to talk about the case. There was little I could say.'

'She wrote on her blog that she was working with you.'

'That was an exaggeration. I met her twice. Briefly.'

'She rang you repeatedly. What did you talk about?'

'There's a glamour about these big murder cases. People want to be a part of it. It's almost like celebrity.'

'Did she tell you anything significant?'

'No.'

'Did she give you anything significant?'

'She talked about doing so. And then she died.'

'She was murdered. Do you know of any reason why anyone would want to do that?'

'No.'

'You were both involved in a murder investigation.'

'Neither of us was. And we weren't involved with each other. Poor Erin Brack was obsessed, eccentric, a bit lonely, and she wasn't a threat to anyone at all.'

There was a long pause. Then Waite leaned forward and pressed a button on the recorder. Frieda saw her own face on the screen. It looked remote, passive, detached.

'So we're done,' said Waite.

'Good.'

'What I don't understand is why you wouldn't answer questions, and then you phone your friend – a man who turns out to know people who know people – and he comes all the way down here and then you change your mind and answer my questions and really say nothing much at all. That's what I don't understand.'

'As I said, I was confused.'

'That's the thing. You don't seem like the sort of person who gets confused and shocked. What's this about?'

'I thought the interview was over.'

'You know that interfering with a police inquiry is a serious criminal offence?'

'I've told you everything I know.' Frieda stood up.

'This isn't one of your games,' said Waite. 'A woman is dead.'

'Then why are you talking to me?'

Before she turned and walked away, the expression on Waite's face almost frightened her.

'That nurse,' says Hal Bradshaw.

'What nurse?' asks Mary Hoyle.

'James Moss. He was attacked. He's badly hurt.'

'There are dangerous people here. Sometimes I'm glad I'm in solitary.'

'It's just that you mentioned him last time.'

'Did I?'

'Yes.'

'I suppose that if Moss said things about me, he probably said things about other people as well.'

'How does it make you feel, hearing about what happened to him?'

'My therapy has helped me. I realize now that violence is never an answer.'

'And Hannah Docherty?'

'What about her?'

'Is she safe now?'

When Hal Bradshaw thinks of Mary Hoyle, it's her blue eyes he sees, those expressive, beautiful, confiding blue eyes. Now she turns them on him.

'I can only speak for myself,' she says. 'I don't know what other people might think she deserves.'

TWENTY-TWO

Keegan said his orders were to take her straight to Levin, but Frieda insisted on being dropped at her house. Without stopping to remove her coat, she went straight up to her study. First of all, she opened up the small brown case. It was packed full of women's clothes, the smell of age and decay in their folds. She looked through their layers and saw nothing suspicious. She closed it and pushed it under the desk, then picked up a splitting bin-bag and up-ended it so that all its contents spilled out onto the floor with a rustle and a clatter: folders and papers and knick-knacks, even a few pieces of jewellery. She did the same to the next one, objects and scraps of paper tumbling onto the floor, but left the third, softly bulging, which appeared only to contain clothes. She stood back and surveyed the heap in front of her: it looked like rubbish and reminded her of the times she had seen Chloë trying to sort out the chaos in her room, tossing old essays, fliers, letters, torn tights and scrunched-up tissues into a discard pile. But Erin Brack might have been killed for a clue that was buried here, among the cast-offs of a family's life.

She sat on the floor and picked up an eyeshadow palette, greens merging into brown. Her mobile buzzed: it was Levin. She ignored it and started to pick things out at random: bills, torn photos, old postcards, spiral-bound notebooks. She opened a cardboard folder and saw car-insurance details. Her mobile buzzed again. There was a battered paperback of *Catcher in the Rye*. The pages were damp and mouldy. A bobble hat. A wristband. Swimming certificates. Guarantees for the boiler and the dishwasher. A wall calendar with nothing written on it. Frieda pushed her hand into the pile and pulled out a handful of paper: a birthday card from Hannah to her mother, a Valentine card with a large question mark inside and the inscription 'From your secret admirer', a shrivelled conker on a string, a four-leafed clover stuck with yellowing brittle Sellotape to a piece of stiff white paper. Perhaps one of these things contained the clue that Erin Brack had died for – but, if so, it was like having a key but no lock, not even a door.

A text pinged onto her screen. It was from Levin. 'Come at once.' She sighed and pushed everything back into the bags.

'So.' Levin took off his glasses and laid them on the table in front of him. He didn't give his usual vague smile; everything about him seemed different today. 'Erin Brack.'

'Yes.'

'I've just looked at her website.'

'So you have an idea of what she was like.'

'I have an idea of what she believed.'

'Every conspiracy going.'

'And yet perhaps in this case . . .' Levin didn't finish the sentence. 'What are you thinking?'

'Before Erin's death, I believed that the sheer incompetence of the original investigation meant they might have convicted the wrong person. Now that Erin has been killed – and I'm certain it was murder – I feel sure of it. I believe that Hannah Docherty has spent thirteen years in a hospital for the criminally insane, often in solitary confinement, for a crime she didn't commit. I don't believe she was psychologically ill at the time her family was murdered, just angry and troubled, then traumatized by grief and suspicion. The insanity came later.'

As she spoke, Frieda thought of Hannah – or, rather, Hannah's image rose up in her mind. A dark shadow.

Levin nodded. 'And someone else got away?'

'Yes.'

'And they've killed Erin Brack because she might inadvertently have in her collection something to incriminate them.'

'Yes.'

'Which they know about because she wrote publicly about it.'

'That's right. She even gave the date I would take it away.'

'But you arrived early.'

'Yes.'

'So whoever torched Erin Brack's house, with her inside, believes they've destroyed the evidence.'

'Yes.'

'So you know why I was anxious to see you and what you need to do at once.'

'Look through everything more carefully.'

Levin shook his head reprovingly at her. 'You need to get those things out of your house immediately. I assume that's where they are?'

'You think –'

'Of course. Someone killed Erin Brack for them.' He paused, softly tapping his fingers on the table. 'It will make the collection safer – but it won't necessarily make you safer, since we can't exactly make a public announcement about the removal.'

'I don't think anyone knows I have them.'

'Someone always knows.'

'You're right. I'll take the stuff somewhere else.'

'We could do that for you.'

'I'll do it. I need access to it. There must be something there.'

Levin looked dissatisfied. 'You're sure about this?'

'Yes.'

He put his glasses back on. 'I feel there's something wrong with this plan.'

'Well, if there is, say sorry to Keegan from me.'

'You're sure no one comes in here?' asked Frieda.

'Well, obviously, people *come* in here.' They were standing in a yard with the workshop Chloë worked in behind them. Chloë was tussling with a key and a large, rusty padlock. 'Like us, now. If I can open the door.'

'But they don't spend time here, or work here.'

'It's a storeroom. It's full of old planks and weird stuff that no one wants but never gets round to throwing away. You're being a bit odd, if you don't mind me saying. What's in those bags anyway?'

With a wrench, the key turned and the padlock sprang open. Chloë took it off the metal hoop and pulled at the double wooden doors. They swung outwards to reveal a large, cement-floored space, shed more than room, with light glimmering through the high windows onto piles of wood and old tools. There was a large saw with a broken handle and something that looked like an ancient mangle. Chloë pressed the light switch. Long fluorescent bars flickered for several seconds before steadying. Corners came into view, a pram without wheels and a porcelain sink, a crooked column of stacked cardboard boxes. On a high shelf there were two empty bird nests.

'Perfect,' said Frieda. 'It's much bigger than I expected.'

'Welcome to Walthamstow.'

'So that's where you work.' Frieda gestured towards the workshop.

'Not so different from a hospital, really.'

Frieda looked at her niece. She was wearing old canvas trousers held up with a broad belt, and a long-sleeved T-shirt that looked suspiciously like one Frieda used to own until it had disappeared. On her feet were stout scuffed boots. Her hair was cut short. There was a smudge of dirt on her cheek. She looked strong and contented, as if she was standing on her own ground at last.

'One day you can make me that bench. Or maybe a stool.'

'I might start with a chopping board. I'm good at those.'

'Olivia still unhappy about your career choice?'

'It's just the way she is. There always has to be a drama. It's Dad who's really cross. You know how he is.' Frieda did know. 'That's all right, though. It's my life, not his.'

'Good.'

They carried the bags and the case inside and piled them against a wall.

'So, are you going to tell me what's in them?' asked Chloë.

'I don't really know myself.'

'That means you're not going to tell me.'

'It means I don't know.'

'Whose are they?'

'They belonged to someone who's died and, for reasons that are too complicated to explain, I've inherited them. So I've got to make sure there's nothing important before I throw them away. I didn't want them cluttering up my study.'

'You were never very tolerant of mess, were you? Anyway, I'll leave you to it.'

She handed over the chunky key and left.

*

Alone, Frieda stared inside the bags that she had so recently emptied and stuffed full again. It was clear that the only way she was going to find anything was to put all of this in some kind of order – but what kind of order? What was the structure she was going to impose on mess? There was so much, and she didn't know where to start because she didn't know what she was looking for. She went across to the stacked cardboard boxes and lifted off the top ones. Then she knelt on the floor and took each item from the bin-bags and inspected it before dropping it into a box. Some of it she had already seen when she had riffled through the pile in her study; the rest seemed more of the same, a reminder of all the things people collect through the years: bills, receipts, school reports, certificates, notebooks, a couple of old passports with their corners snipped off, quotations for repairs to subsidence, Aidan's birth certificate, a small plastic photo album with holiday snaps in it, dozens of bank statements, none showing an overdraft or any large, inexplicable sums of money going out of the bank or into it, although Frieda didn't put them into a particular order or look through them properly, birthday cards, half a pack of envelopes, a sheaf of recipes. One by one she transferred them from bag to box. It took a long time, and the light outside faded. She heard splatters of rain on the corrugated-iron roof and then they gathered in force, hammering down. Would the rain ever stop?

Two of the boxes were full. She pulled the clothes from the next bag, shook each garment out and folded it before laying it in the third box. Just a random assortment, from the look of it: a strappy top, a pair of grey men's trousers, a flecked jersey, boy's trainers, their laces still knotted, a sweatshirt, a colourful patterned scarf, a checked shirt with a grubby collar, several ties. The moths had got at some of them and there was a musty, unwashed odour.

Finally Frieda turned to the case. The clothes she had glanced at earlier were smarter than the ones in the bag and presumably had belonged to Deborah. They were neatly folded: two thin shirts, one white and one pale blue, a black skirt, a black bra and matching knickers, a cardigan, a leather belt, several pairs of sheer tights rolled into a ball, a pack of Kleenex. That was all. Frieda closed the lid and pushed the case against the wall, then sat back on her heels. It just seemed like a few leftovers from an ordinary kind of family, made extraordinary by the manner of their deaths. If there was something here, she couldn't see it, or not yet.

At two in the morning, Frieda woke. She lay open-eyed in the darkness while the rain fell outside. Something was troubling her. She realized she was thinking not of the case but of Shelley Walsh, so brittle and bright and respectable, so full of a repressed sense of abandonment. She was like a small child playing at being a grown-up, scrubbing her house as though her life depended on it. She might not be able to help Hannah, but she could perhaps help Shelley. She could hear Thelma Scott's stern voice cautioning her: beware the rescue impulse.

The next day, when Shelley Walsh opened the door and saw Frieda, her face fell. 'We've already talked,' she said.

'I want to talk to you again.'

Shelley looked at her watch. 'My husband will be home soon.'

'Then we'd better be quick.'

'You're a woman,' Shelley said. 'Don't you understand what I've been through? I put it behind me. I made myself a new life. I became a new person.'

'Hannah Docherty didn't escape.'

'Not everybody is strong enough.'

'Are you going to let me in?'

Shelley looked at her watch once more. 'Ten minutes. And I really shouldn't be doing this at all. You'll have to talk to me while I cook.'

She led Frieda through to the kitchen where a complicated meal was in progress, vegetables, chopping boards, pans in different stages of use. Shelley started slicing an onion. 'Don't ask me what I'm cooking. Just say what you have to say. You probably want to hear more about boyfriends and drugs.'

'No, I don't.'

Shelley paused in her chopping. She lifted her left hand and looked at it. Suddenly the tip of her index finger bloomed red and blood dripped from it.

Frieda looked around, saw some kitchen roll, tore off a piece and handed it to her. 'Are you all right?'

'Don't say anything.' She wrapped the paper round her finger.

'I often do that,' said Frieda, although she didn't.

'I wouldn't have done it if you weren't here. I'm trying to think of too many things at the same time.'

'I'll go in a minute. I just need to ask you a couple of questions.'

Shelley didn't look at Frieda. She started chopping the onion again. 'There'll probably be blood all over them.'

'You know what I've found, over the years?'

'No, I don't, and I don't want you to tell me.'

'If there's an easy, quick way of settling a case, then that's the way it gets solved. Even if there are things left over, bits that don't fit. But those bits are what interest me. That's what I can't let go of.'

Still Shelley didn't look up. Chop, chop, chop.

'I keep thinking about the house you and Hannah were in,' Frieda continued. 'I want to get a clearer picture of it.'

'I thought you said it wasn't about boyfriends and drugs.'

'Tell me about Tom Morell.'

'Tom Morell?'

'You lived with him.'

'I know who you mean, but what do you want me to say? He was just – well, just there. Always there.'

'What was he like?'

'Nice.'

'That word has always worried me.'

'What's wrong? Can't somebody just be nice?'

'It can be an evasion. It's not very illuminating.'

'Sorry about that.' Shelley's voice was high and sarcastic. 'What do you want me to say? He was polite and overweight and always kind of hovering in the background. Better?'

'Much better. How did he get on with Hannah?'

Shelley made a clicking sound with her tongue. 'How would I know?'

'Because you were there.'

'I wasn't thinking about Tom Morell.'

'But if you think about him now.'

'He liked her. He probably had a thing for her.'

'A thing.'

'You know. And he was the kind of man who liked to rescue people. Perhaps he thought he could rescue her.' Shelley had stopped chopping. Now she put down the knife and wiped a wrist against her eyes. 'I don't know why Hannah needed rescuing more than me.'

'What do you mean?'

'Hannah had a home she could go back to. She was just slumming it. I didn't. Why didn't someone want to rescue me?' Shelley blinked rapidly several times. She had a little smile on her face, which twitched as she tried to keep it in position.

'Did your mother never want to?' Frieda asked her gently. 'I mean, before she went missing from your life.'

'She didn't "go missing". She left, she moved away. You know what? Good riddance.'

Frieda was about to return to the subject of Hannah, but the sight of Shelley trying not to cry as she scraped the onions into the pan, the stiffness of her thin shoulders and her bright, angry smile, stopped her. 'How was your relationship with your mother?'

'I left home when I was fifteen. You can work it out for yourself.'

'Tell me about her.'

'Tell you about my mother? My mother who left and never told me she was going, never bothered to say goodbye? Why? What is there to say? I'm not going to be a mother like that. I'm going to look after my child and protect it and keep it safe.'

'She didn't keep you safe?'

'I ended up living in a squat and taking drugs.'

'What was she like? Describe her for me.'

'She was a mess. She had no self-control. She was irresponsible, that's the word.'

Shelley put the pan on the hob and lit the flame under it. She tipped in some oil and stirred the onions vigorously with a wooden spoon.

'In what way?'

Shelley picked up an aubergine and turned it in her hands. Her small neat face wore a look of distaste. 'She drank,' she said.

'She was an alcoholic?'

'Even when she wasn't on one of her binges, she often

couldn't get out of bed. She would lie there, curtains closed, all day long. I'd leave for school in the morning and she would be this huddled shape under the covers. I'd come back and she would still be there. Everything was a mess. Everything smelt bad.' Shelley wrinkled her nose.

'She was depressed?'

'She was something.'

'When you were little as well?'

'I forgot the garlic. I've got out of order with everything. It'll be spoiled.'

'Shelley?'

'She was different when I was at primary school. She'd wait for me at the school gates and she held my hand on the way home and sometimes we'd have bread and jam and she'd read me stories. I remember that.' For a moment her immaculately made-up face softened.

'But then she changed.'

'Yes, well, that's all in the past.'

She picked up a flat garlic clove and a smaller sharp knife and tried clumsily to peel it, but her tissue-bandage kept getting in the way.

'Can I help you?' asked Frieda.

'No.'

'What about your father?'

'What about him?'

'Was he around?'

'I know his name and that's about it. They weren't together long – just long enough to have me and then he left. There were other men, on and off. None who stayed. None I wanted to stay. You can peel the garlic, if you want. I don't crush it, I chop it very finely.'

Frieda took the knife and the clove. 'So it was just you and your mother?'

'Just the two of us.' Shelley gave a sudden high trill of laughter. 'Happy families.'

'It sounds painful.'

'So why ask me about it?' Shelley jabbed at the onions. 'Why poke round and stir up memories?'

'I don't mean to distress you unnecessarily.'

'Then don't do it. Put the garlic in with the onions. Please.'

'You moved out when you were fifteen.'

'I suddenly thought, I don't have to put up with this any more. It wasn't as if she was going to miss me, was it?'

'Did she miss you?'

Shelley swept a plate of diced courgettes and peppers into the pan. Her back was very straight. Her ponytail swung when she turned to look at Frieda. 'It was too late.'

'Did she try to get you back?'

'She tried to make me feel guilty.'

'Did you?'

'Why should I? She was a bad mother. She cried and said she would be different, but she'd said that before, and she said she couldn't help herself, but I don't believe that. Look at me. I went through terrible times but then I pulled myself together. I got a job. I married a good man and I try to make him happy. I work hard.' She gestured at the sparkling kitchen, everything in its proper place.

'But she was concerned about you?'

'You should ask her about that. If you can find her.'

'When did you last see her?'

'I wasn't living with her. I don't know.'

'Was she ever reported missing?'

'She wasn't missing. She just wasn't around. Anyway, I don't know because I wasn't around either, was I?'

'But someone must have been worried about her.'

'Why? She didn't have many friends left.'

'Did you ever try to find her?'

'It's not supposed to work like that. She never tried to find me, her daughter. Why should I think of her? Anyway, that was another life. I was another person. I want nothing to do with it all. Nothing. If she came knocking at the door, I wouldn't open it.'

'All right.'

'And if I did open it, I would be very cold and polite and pretend I didn't even recognize her.'

'How would you feel if I tried to find her, or at least to –'

'If she apologized, I wouldn't accept her apology. I'd say, "It's too late to pretend to care. Too little, too late."'

'Do you think she'll ever come knocking at your door?'

'Of course not.' Again she gave a trill of unnatural laughter, as if someone were tapping a knife on the rim of a glass. 'I'm only her daughter.'

She peeled the tissue away from her finger. 'It's still bleeding,' she said, as if it were an accusation.

'I'm sorry,' said Frieda.

Shelley walked with her to the door, not like a hostess, but more as if she were making sure Frieda was really going. As Frieda stepped out of the front door, Shelley touched her on the shoulder. 'You saw Jason,' she said. 'He was my boyfriend. When I was with him we took drugs and we stole and we lived in a squalid squat. I escaped from all of that. Is that something to feel bad about?'

'You feel bad about something,' said Frieda. 'And, by the way, keep that finger clean. The cut looks nasty.'

TWENTY-THREE

Joe Franklin had gone, with his new haircut, his clean white shirt and the precarious sense of recovery that made Frieda more than usually gentle with him. Now it was Maria Dreyfus's turn. She came into the room as though a wind was blowing her.

'I wish I believed in God,' she said, before she was fully seated.

'Why do you wish that?'

'Because then I could pray.'

'What would you say in your prayers?'

'Please. Please please please.'

'Please help?'

'I don't know. Just please.'

'Please rescue me?'

'Maybe.'

'Rescue you from what?'

'From myself, of course.' She glared at Frieda. 'Which no one can do. I know. I'm no fool. My brain hurts. I had such a bad night. I can't shake it off. You know, sometimes I actually hit myself to get rid of the feelings. Like this.' Abruptly, she lifted her hand and slapped the top of her head, then gave a small snort of what might have been laughter.

'Don't do that,' Frieda said.

'Why?'

'You're here to talk, not hurt yourself.'

'Talking hurts the way hurting doesn't.'

'Nevertheless, in here you talk, or choose to remain silent. You do not hit yourself.'

'Sorry. I don't know why I did that – it was stupidly theatrical.' There was a silence. She stared at Frieda, unblinking. 'I don't know why I don't mind meeting your eyes. Recently I've hated that. When friends look at me I feel like squirming, screaming at them. I can't bear their eyes on me. Maybe I'd do better on a couch, where I don't feel your eyes going into me.'

'I don't have a couch.'

'I'd probably hate it anyway. I'd feel like I was acting a part. And I'd only fall asleep. I'm so tired. I talk to you in my head, you know. I tell you things I'll probably never tell you in person.'

'What kind of things?'

'You're trying to trick me.' She pushed both hands through her hair. 'Why not? OK. For instance, sometimes I feel so angry with my husband that it's like being on fire. Or feeling sick – I can feel sick with rage.'

'Go on.'

'It's physical, like a kind of huge, burning disgust. I don't know why. Even when he had his affair, I didn't feel like this. It's like he's done something to me, betrayed me in some deep way. Perhaps it's connected to the affair, perhaps I buried the anger and now it's finally expressing itself. But that doesn't feel quite it. That seems too easy, too glib, an explanation.'

Maria Dreyfus was talking in a way that she hadn't done before, freely, not weighing up the consequences of what she was saying or censoring herself before the words were out of her mouth.

'When I was young,' she continued, 'I thought I could do anything I wanted. I was bold. I was full of hope. I took risks. Men fell in love with me – I don't mean great crowds of them, but enough to make me understand that I was desirable. I felt powerful then. It's as if I've gradually lost that power, without even realizing it. Now here I am, middle-aged, my hair turning grey, my children gone, my husband a bit bewildered by me, and I don't understand how that young woman has turned into this one. Compromised. I think that's the word.' She rubbed a hand over her clever face. 'It's like my fineness has gone. All chipped and whittled away. I'm just a blunt instrument now. I didn't think this was how it was going to be – my life.'

For a few moments, Frieda let the words settle in the room. Then she said, 'And you blame your husband for this?'

'Maybe. It's not fair, of course. It's just a marriage. Quite a good marriage, if my friends' marriages are anything to go by. I love him, I guess. I think he loves me – he would certainly say he does. But I don't think he *sees* me any more. I don't see myself.'

'You feel invisible.'

'Unrecognized. Perhaps everyone feels this. Perhaps this is what growing older means. Perhaps my panic is just me getting used to something that, in a few months' time, will feel quite natural, quite OK. That's what people say: this, too, will pass. I say it to other people. But maybe –' She stopped.

'Maybe?'

'Maybe I don't want it to pass because that would mean an acceptance that life is like this: just a gradual process of loss.'

She started to weep, making no sound or any attempt to stop or to wipe away the tears. They flowed down her face,

207

like a stream down a steep hill, and she sat there, looking at Frieda, while Frieda looked steadily back at her. At last, she leaned forward and took a tissue from the box on the low table between them and wiped her face carefully.

'Well.' She smiled. 'That was unexpected.'

When Frieda had phoned Flora Goffin, the neighbour of the Dochertys whose husband she had met a few days previously, she had said she would prefer them to meet on neutral territory. 'I'd feel more comfortable.'

'All right.'

'The Corner Bar. It's a stone's throw from our house. We'll both be there. I'll make sure to leave the office early for once. And I've asked the boys to come half an hour later. Four birds with one stone.'

Frieda arrived early and secured a large table near the window. She asked for a glass of tap water and drank it looking out of the window. A familiar white van passed and she blinked. Surely that was Josef's van. What was he doing here? She remembered that he'd said he was going to do some work for Emma Travis but it was rather late for that. She frowned.

She saw Sebastian Tait drift past the window, tall and gangly; his wife was tiny beside him, walking with brisk steps to keep up. They passed out of her field of vision. In a few seconds they reappeared beside her. Flora Goffin had a freckled triangular face and a head of curls. When she took off her mac she was wearing a linen suit that looked expensive and dangling earrings that swung as she talked. Sebastian hovered behind her. Frieda thought he must be at least a foot taller than his wife.

'Nasty weather,' Flora Goffin said. She had a husky voice and a Scottish accent.

'Now then,' said Sebastian, putting a large leather bag on the floor, taking off his coat and shaking the raindrops from it. 'What can we get you?'

'It's on me,' said Frieda. 'I'll get a bottle of wine. Red or white?'

It took a minute or so to persuade Sebastian Tait she was buying, and then he insisted on choosing the wine. Flora Goffin watched him with a humorous expression as he leaned over the bar, talking earnestly to the waiter, then turned to Frieda. 'You'll understand how strange it is for us to be revisiting the past like this.'

'Of course.'

'I don't know what kind of help it is you need, or what you're doing at all. Perhaps you can start off by explaining that.'

Flora Goffin leaned forward slightly, as if she were an interviewer, and looked at Frieda shrewdly as Frieda began to give her brief account of what she was doing. When she started to identify herself, Flora interrupted her.

'I know who you are. I've been looking through everything online about you. There's quite a lot. My PA knows all about you.'

'It's not very accurate.'

'I thought of going to see Hannah,' Flora said, so suddenly that Frieda was taken aback.

'But you never did.'

'I didn't know why I'd be going. I didn't know what I'd say. Anyway, I'm still a bit in the dark here. What could we have to say that would be any help?' There was a faint edge to her voice.

Sebastian returned and pulled out a chair, arranging his long limbs in sharp angles. 'It's on its way,' he said. 'A nice Soave.'

'I was asking Dr Klein what use we can be.'

Frieda hesitated, looking between the two of them. 'It's not just that the case was badly conducted. I don't believe Hannah Docherty is guilty.'

Sebastian re-crossed his legs. Frieda saw that he was wearing one of his ties. Above it, his bony face was pale, cadaverous. 'What?'

There was an awkward interruption as the waiter put a bottle of white wine and three glasses on the table, with a bowl of large green olives. They watched in silence as he wound a corkscrew down, then pulled out the cork. He held it an inch above a glass.

'I'll pour it myself.' Sebastian Tait's voice was hoarse. He looked shocked. 'Just leave it on the table.'

'Why?' asked Flora, as soon as the waiter had turned away; her gaze was fierce. 'What makes you believe that?'

'It's hard to explain.'

'Nobody else has ever expressed any doubt. No doubt at all.'

'I'm expressing it now.'

'Just yours?' asked Flora. 'Or other people's?'

'I'm the one pursuing it.'

'On your own?' She gave Frieda a sharp nod. 'I've read about you, remember.'

'Largely alone,' said Frieda. 'But there are significant question marks over the whole case, and the point is this: your neighbours, your close friends, people you went on holiday with, were killed and perhaps their daughter Hannah – whom you also knew well – has been in a hospital for the criminally insane for thirteen years for a crime she may not have committed.'

'Really? I mean, really?' This was Sebastian, cradling his wine glass in his long, thin hands and speaking in a half-whisper.

'I'm trying to find out,' said Frieda. She looked from one to the other. 'Is there anything you can tell me, anything at all, about Aidan and Deborah, or Hannah, or even Rory that you think I should know – that the police never discovered all those years ago? Anything at all.'

She looked at them in turn and they looked back. She saw Sebastian's eyes slide to his wife, then away again. The rain dripped down the window and the wine bar filled with people taking shelter.

'They were our friends,' said Flora at last. 'But, you know, people are mysterious. They were mysterious, and after they died they became even more so. Deborah in particular.'

'In what way?'

'She withheld herself.'

Out of the corner of her eye, Frieda saw Sebastian smile.

'What would she withhold?'

'If I discovered she'd been a spy, that wouldn't surprise me.'

'You were always rather hostile to her,' observed Sebastian, mildly, looking out of the window as he spoke.

'Rubbish. She was my friend.'

'Friends can be rivalrous.' Sebastian looked at Frieda. 'Don't you agree?'

'Men like to think that about women,' said Flora.

'You had reason,' said Sebastian. 'Let's not be forgetting.'

The air was suddenly thick with unspoken thoughts. Frieda sat still and quiet, waiting.

'Shall we get back to the point?' said Flora.

'What is the point?' Sebastian drank some of his wine, then leaned forward to take an olive that he pushed into his mouth.

'Hannah is the point,' said Frieda.

'Whenever we speak of her, which isn't often,' said Flora, 'it's as if she's dead. We use the past tense about her. Have you noticed?' She looked at Sebastian.

'Perhaps that's the easiest way to deal with it,' said Frieda. 'Now, can we return to my original question? Can you tell me anything that you think the police might have overlooked?'

'Flora?' Sebastian raised his eyebrows at his wife.

'Oh, for goodness' sake.' She clipped her glass down on the small table. 'Stop it.'

'What?'

'Just stop it.' She turned to Frieda. 'What my dear husband is hinting at, jabbing at, prodding at, is that I had a thing –' She stopped suddenly and Frieda saw a tide of red spread over her face and neck. 'With Aidan.'

'When?'

'I can't remember the exact dates.'

'July 1999 to January 2000,' said Sebastian. 'Which is rather a long time. For a thing.'

'Don't try to take the moral high ground,' said Flora. 'It doesn't suit you.' She glared at him angrily. The flush had dwindled to a small red patch on either cheek.

'You're right,' said Sebastian, holding up his hands in mock surrender. 'You're quite right, of course.'

Frieda had the strange sense that he was enjoying this public disclosure. 'Why did it end?' she asked Flora.

'It just did. It was always going to.' She shook her head. 'No, that's not quite right. Aidan was always so cheerful, so energetic, but all of a sudden he became lethargic, even depressed.'

'Who knew?'

'About him being depressed?'

'No. About your . . .' Frieda hesitated. The word felt so wrong. '. . . thing.'

'I did.' Sebastian gave that strange smile again.

'Did Deborah?'

'Probably,' said Flora. 'I'm almost sure she did. She never

212

said and was always very friendly. I just always thought somehow she would know.'

'Hannah?'

'No. Definitely not. She couldn't have.'

'Rory?'

'No.'

'Was it acrimonious?'

'It was embarrassingly civilized. We all kept on seeing
each other. There were still drinks in each other's gardens
and conversations over the fence, that sort of thing. The
children kept on being friends, or at least Rick and Rory did.
Hannah was in her own world by then.'

'Do you have any idea if Aidan had another affair after
you?'

Flora looked at her in bewilderment. 'It never occurred to
me. I didn't see him much and, in fact, I thought he seemed
under the weather, or perhaps unhappy, but I never had the
sense there was another woman.'

'Perhaps he didn't tell you,' said Sebastian, a small smile
twitching his mouth.

'I never saw anything, did you, Sebastian?'

'Me? No.'

'Or with Deborah?'

'We weren't looking for anything.'

'So you don't know much about their personal lives in that
last year?'

'Not really.'

Flora gave a muted exclamation as two young men passed
the window. There was a strange hiatus as they noticed their
parents through the glass and raised their hands in exaggerated and self-conscious gestures of greeting.

'Saul and Rick,' said Sebastian. He stood up. 'I'll order
some more wine, shall I?'

'I'm fine,' said Frieda.

'Red this time, I think. And some more of those olives. And then we'll leave you to it. Hard to talk about things like this in a group.'

Flora's face brightened as her sons came towards the table. Frieda shook hands first with Saul, who was tall and thin, like his father, and had a long, clever face; then with Rick, the doctor, who was small and dark and full of restless energy. He pulled an extra chair over and they sat down next to each other. Flora went over to Sebastian at the bar and Frieda saw him put a hand on the small of her back, in apology, perhaps, or reconciliation.

'The Dochertys,' said Rick, coming straight to the point. 'This is so weird. You can't imagine how weird. Isn't it weird, Saul?'

Saul nodded.

'Were you close to them?'

'I was really close to Rory when we were little. We did everything together. I got him into all sorts of trouble. I once persuaded him to nick some sweets from the shop down the road. When he died, I wanted to move house. I couldn't stand being next door to where it had all happened. It was like I couldn't escape it.'

'I wanted to ask something rather painful and grim,' Frieda said. 'Do you remember Guy Fiske?'

Rick lifted both hands as if to ward off the suggestion. 'No,' he said. 'I know what you're going to say. Fiske did lots of awful things. But not that. Surely not.'

'I'm sorry,' said Frieda. 'But I'm wondering how you could possibly know that. He did teach Rory.'

'He never came anywhere near me,' Rick said. 'Really. I'd have known if he'd done anything to Rory. Wouldn't I?'

'I don't know.'

'Or Rory would have said something. At least to his mother.'

Saul was listening closely. He looked nervous and sad. Frieda remembered his father describing him as the good schoolboy, the nerd, whom Hannah had protected.

'What was Hannah's relationship with Rory like?' She was asking Saul but it was Rick who answered.

'Rory adored her. He was a shy boy. He didn't have the easiest time at school. I didn't help him either. I was his best friend at home, but at school I looked the other way. Some mate, eh? That's one of those things I can never make right, but at least nowadays I can face up to it. But Hannah, she was his protector. You wouldn't want to cross her. I've met people like her in hospital. She didn't have a safety valve or a thermostat – she didn't know when to stop, or how to stop. I guess that's what happened that night. She didn't stop.' He rubbed the side of his face. 'It's really hard to think about it,' he said. 'It's something that didn't happen to us and yet it marked us all for ever, if that makes sense.'

Frieda nodded. Sebastian returned with two extra glasses and a bottle of red wine that he put carefully on the table. He patted Saul on the shoulder, then left again. Frieda looked at Saul, meeting his eyes.

'She was the nicest person I've ever met,' he said at last.

'Was she?'

'She hated cruelty. She hated bullies.'

'She was found guilty of murdering her entire family.'

'They said she was mad.'

'Did you ever think, towards the end, that she was?'

'Unhappy. Angry. All over the place. Not mad. I must have been wrong. It's the only thing that makes sense.' He paused; Frieda could see him swallowing. She knew he was preparing to ask her something. 'Have you seen her?'

'Yes.'

'Is she coping?'

'No.'

She saw his nervous face twist.

'I should have gone myself. Will you see her again?'

'I will.'

'Can you tell her that Saul is thinking of her? That he hasn't forgotten about her?'

'You again.' It was the younger nurse, bulky and sullen and beetle-browed, with a smell of tobacco and sweat about him.

'That's right.'

'You didn't say you were coming.'

'I don't need to say. I've got clearance.'

'She's not in the right frame of mind for visitors.'

'Let me be the judge of that. I know what's happening here.'

'You should be careful of what you say.'

'And you should know – everyone here who has a duty of care towards Hannah should know – that I am keeping an eye on her.'

Later that evening, when Frieda was in bed reading, her mobile rang.

'Hello?' There was a sniggering, snuffling sound at the other end. In the background she could hear laughter. 'Who is this?'

'Jason. Jason Brenner. Hannah's old mate.' He sounded drunk or stoned, his voice slurred.

'What is it? Is there something you want to tell me about her?'

'Yeah. You told me if there was something important I remembered, I should call you.'

'Tell me.'

'I remembered I used to make her suck my dick.' The laughter in the background grew louder. 'Are you still there? She wasn't keen but she did it. That's what. A mass murderess sucked my dick.'

Frieda hung up.

It took her many hours to get to sleep and then before it was light she woke again suddenly and sat up in bed, alert and with a feeling of excitement. It was as if someone had shaken her, or a sound had disturbed her. But she was alone and the room was quiet, just the sound of wind outside and in the distance the faint hum of traffic. And yet she knew that something had woken her. A thought, an idea, a memory.

She pulled her duvet up to her chin and closed her eyes, thinking, concentrating, trying to remember, trying to hold on to the shape that was just at the edge of her vision, sliding back into the shadows. And then, like a flash of brightness, she had it. She looked at the clock by her bed and saw it was nearly three. She told herself that it made no sense to go now: nothing was going to change in the few hours before daylight, but she knew that she wouldn't go back to sleep, not with this shimmer in her brain.

So at half past three Frieda walked out of her house. She emerged from her little hidden mews and headed west. As she walked towards Marylebone, she didn't notice the blocks of flats, the hotels, the town houses. As always there were people around, taxis, the rumble of traffic from Euston Road. By ten to four she was on the night bus, which was empty save for one young woman in a headscarf sitting at the front. By half past four she was in Walthamstow and inserting the key into the heavy lock of the workshop, pulling open the door. She felt for the light switch and then blinked in its sudden dazzle. Behind her the wet yard gleamed; occasional spots of rain still fell.

Frieda went inside and clanged the door shut. She crossed to the boxes and pulled the one filled with clothes into the centre of the shed, directly under the light. She took out the sweatshirt, the strappy top, the flecked jersey and the men's trousers, and there it was. A brightly patterned coil of material: not a scarf, after all, but a bandanna.

At a quarter past six, she was standing outside Seamus Docherty's house. No lights were on and all the curtains were closed, but she rang the doorbell and then, after a minute or so, rapped the knocker assertively as well. Their dog was barking now. Upstairs, a light went on and then she heard shuffling feet.

'What the hell?' Seamus Docherty was wearing pyjama bottoms and a towelling robe that he held closed with one hand. His face was creased with sleep. The dog was beside him, making a gruff noise in its throat as if a bark was forming.

'When you threw away all of the things you took from Deborah's house, did you put anything in with it?'

'What are you doing here? I was asleep.'

'I need to know: did you throw away anything of your own at the same time?'

'What? What are you on about?'

'All the things you collected and then threw away.'

'Yes. I heard what you said, I just didn't understand it. What time is it?'

'Did you throw away things that were yours as well?'

'What? Why would I do that? I wasn't exactly in the mood for a spring-clean. But this is ridiculous. Why are you standing on my doorstep in the middle of the night asking me what I might have thrown away thirteen years ago? Is there something wrong with you?'

'It's gone six.'

'Oh, so that's all right, then. Perfectly reasonable.'

'Can I come in?'

'Why?'

'There's something I want to show you.'

Seamus Docherty stared at her. There were bags under his pale grey eyes and lines bracketing his mouth; his neck was thin and sinewy.

'OK,' he said at last. 'Come in and show me whatever it is. Be quiet – I don't want Brenda being woken. I don't think you'd find her as reasonable as me.'

In the kitchen he filled a kettle, then splashed water over his face.

'Right,' he said. 'What is it that brings you knocking at my door in the dark?'

Frieda put her hand into her pocket and pulled out the bandanna. 'This.'

Seamus Docherty looked at it, his eyes narrowed. Then he looked at her. 'So you've come here with a scarf. Why has that got anything to do with me or Deborah or the whole fucking history or anything at all, except –' He stopped. Frieda saw his hands were trembling.

'Because it's Brenda's.'

'Brenda's,' he said.

'Yes.'

'And so bloody what?'

'It was with all the stuff you threw away.'

'And you know this how?'

'You mean how do I know it belonged to Brenda?'

'Yes. That. And how do you happen to know what I threw away thirteen years ago, after my son and ex-wife had been slaughtered by my daughter.'

'She's wearing it in the photo in your living room.'

'Photo?'

'Of you and Brenda and Rory sitting on a hay bale.'

'This is unbelievable.'

'So I need to find out –'

'How do you know what I threw away?' He thumped his hand on the kitchen table hard. Behind him the kettle was boiling.

'That's not the point here. The point is that, among all the things you took away from the house, or that my, um, source tells me were later thrown away there, there was this bandanna.'

'And this is relevant how?'

'That's what I want to establish.'

'Seamus, what's going on?' Brenda Docherty stood in the doorway in her plaid dressing-gown. Then she saw Frieda and, for a second or so, her face was blank. Then it hardened into an expression of hostility. 'What are you doing in our house?'

'She's got a bandanna,' said Seamus. He lowered himself into a chair by the table and propped his head on a hand. 'She says it's yours.'

'It is, isn't it?' said Frieda. She held it up.

'How did you get that?' asked Brenda.

'It was with everything that came from Deborah and Aidan's house after the murders.'

'I don't understand any of this,' said Brenda. 'Not how you came by it, not why it matters, not why you're here. But, yes, it used to belong to me. I gave it to Hannah.'

'Really?'

'Yes, really. She liked it and I gave it to her.'

'When?'

'Why on earth would I remember that?'

'Shortly before her family was killed?'

'I don't know.'

'It must have been after the photo was taken that I saw, in which you're wearing it. I think that must have been taken in the autumn of 2000. So after that.'

'If you say so. Now, I think Seamus and I need to have showers.'

'Odd.'

'What do you mean, *odd*?'

'In the year before the tragedy, I'm told that Hannah was wearing only black clothes. Goth. This doesn't really fit in.'

'What are you implying?'

'Nothing. Thinking aloud.' A wave of tiredness came over Frieda. 'I'll go now, but if you remember anything more about it, please tell me.'

'Can I ask you a question?' Brenda Docherty pulled the belt tighter on her dressing-gown.

'Of course.'

'What do you want?'

'Want?'

'Yes. Going around stirring up old pain and grief, poking into terrible things that should be left alone. What do you want to get from it?'

'I want to find out what happened in that house thirteen years ago.'

'What happened is that a sick and dangerous girl murdered her entire family. That's what happened. What you're doing, in the name of truth or justice or whatever you want to call it, it's cruel.'

There was an edge to her voice, of panic or rage. Frieda nodded at her. 'I'm sorry I woke you both,' she said. She picked up the bandanna from the table. 'I hope it's all right if I take this with me.'

TWENTY-FOUR

Frieda leaned towards Hannah without touching her. 'I'm Frieda. I visited you before. Do you remember?'

Hannah Docherty looked at her. Her face was bruised, one eye closed to a slit. Her hair was greasy. Her neck, above the shapeless navy sweatshirt, was still grimy. There was a cold sore at the corner of her mouth.

'Hannah. You don't need to say anything. I'm your friend.'

'No one. No one.'

'You've been alone for a very long time.' Frieda kept her voice low and clear, enunciating each word carefully. She couldn't tell if Hannah was following her. 'I know that. You've had no one to talk to. But I am here and you can talk to me if you want to, or stay silent if you want to.'

Hannah did not respond, except for the trace of a frown crinkling her forehead. Frieda remembered the photos she had seen of her as a teenager, strong and full of life, with clear skin, bright eyes and glossy dark hair.

'I've brought you some fruit. Even the security guards couldn't find anything sinister with it.'

She lifted the satsumas and grapes out of the plastic bag and placed them on the table. Hannah stared and licked her lips. Then she put out a hand and touched a satsuma cautiously.

'Have something now if you want.'

Hannah's one good eye flickered towards her and then back at the fruit. Suddenly, she lifted the bunch of grapes and pushed it into her mouth, chewing frantically. Juice dripped down her chin. After a few seconds she took the mangled bunch away from her face and held it out to Frieda. 'You?' she said, in her hoarse, rusty voice, the voice she never used, or that she used only to cry out with.

'That's kind of you. But it's all for you, Hannah.' She pulled the bandanna out of her pocket. 'Did you used to wear this?'

Hannah gazed at it, then touched it with a forefinger. 'Blue,' she said. 'Green.'

'But did you wear it?'

Hannah didn't answer. They sat awhile in silence. Then Frieda said, 'Saul Tait said he's thinking of you.'

Hannah made a sound. Frieda thought maybe it was a sob.

'He said you were the nicest person he'd ever met.' She waited. 'I know you didn't kill your family.'

Hannah put a hand up and covered half of her discoloured face. 'Sssh,' she said.

'I know that you didn't kill your mother or your stepfather. Or Rory,' she added.

Hannah spread her fingers wide over her face.

'A terrible thing has been done to your family and to you.'

Hannah moaned and bent over, her hair falling over her face.

'If you can say anything to me about that time, it would help,' continued Frieda. 'Because I'm going to find out who did it.' She waited and put a tentative hand on Hannah's shoulder. 'It wasn't you. Do you understand?'

'Rory?'

'You didn't kill Rory.'

Hannah put her arms round herself and started to rock back and forward, back and forward, a large, battered creature with matted, unwashed hair, making a faint keening noise. There was a kind of transcendental homelessness about her. Frieda kept the hand on her shoulder. She wondered when Hannah had last been physically touched out of friendship and comfort.

'I tell you what,' she said. 'Why don't I wash your hair for you?'

Hannah lifted her swollen face. 'Hair?'

'Yes.'

'Me?'

'Yes.' She took her hand away and stood. 'Wait here. They can't say no.' She thought how quickly she had started using a language of alienation – the staff had become 'they', anonymous and hostile.

They could say no, and they did, but half an hour later, Hannah and Frieda were in a small bathroom on the first floor. Hannah sat in a metal chair with its back against the basin, a coarse towel over her shoulders, her head tipped back. Frieda had managed to get hold of shampoo in an industrial-sized bottle and a black comb, missing several of its teeth. She also had a plastic jug. She turned on both taps and filled the jug.

'Tell me if it's too hot.'

She poured jug after jug of water over the heavy tangle of hair, running her fingers through it to separate out the knots. A small moan came from Hannah.

'Too hot or cold?'

'No.' The word was almost a wail. 'Please.'

'Close your eyes. I don't want you to get soap in them.'

Hannah shut her good eye. Frieda squirted shampoo on to her scalp and massaged it in, bringing thick coils of hair up into the lather. She felt the bones of Hannah's skull and she watched her bruised face soften and her heavy body relax. She was thirty-one years old. All of her adult life had been lived in this place where she had been bullied, ostracized, drugged, beaten, shut into a cell, abandoned to the torment of her own mind.

'I talked to Jason Brenner,' Frieda said. She could feel Hannah flinch and tense under her fingers. 'He mentioned the River Effra. He said you loved the idea of it. Do you remember that?'

Frieda felt a slight movement under her hands. Was Hannah shaking her head? Was it a denial?

'It's something I share with you,' said Frieda. 'The idea of a river like the Effra, hidden, covered up, forgotten, but still flowing under the streets and pavements.'

Frieda wasn't sure if Hannah was even listening to her. Was she just talking to herself? She rinsed off the shampoo and then repeated the process, then slid a hand under the back of Hannah's head to lift her into an upright position. She rubbed her hair dry. Then, starting with the last few inches of the thick hair, she began to tease out the knots, pulling clumps of loose hair from the comb every few seconds. She remembered how she used to wash Chloë's hair for her and how her niece had shouted and wriggled. Hannah sat quite still and Frieda couldn't tell if she was enjoying or enduring the experience. Gradually the hair became smooth and sleek.

'I think your face suits a side parting,' said Frieda, remembering how Hannah looked in photos of her as a teenager. 'There.'

She gathered Hannah's hair in a thick, damp ponytail and tugged off the band tying her own hair back to secure it.

'Do you want to see?' she said. She gave Hannah a hand and pulled her to her feet, then turned her to face her reflection. The two women looked at Hannah in the mirror, taller and bulkier than Frieda, utterly shabby in her sweatshirt and her grubby drawstring trousers, with a discoloured face. She stared at herself, then with a surprising delicacy lifted a hand and touched her cheek softly, her split lip.

'Me,' she whispered.

'You, Hannah.'

Frieda sat by her fire with a tumbler of whisky. The wind blew in gusts against the window, and the flames threw strange shadows round the dimly lit room.

She thought about Shelley Walsh, her turbulent past and her ordered present, and in the background the mother who had never mothered her. She thought about Hannah Docherty, bruised and bowed over, and all the years she'd spent in a kind of Hell. And then other images came into her mind as she looked into the fire: those missing girls; Mary Orton, the old woman she had been unable to save; that fierce old journalist, Jim Fearby, who had died in his obsessive quest for the truth; Sandy, the man she had once loved, whom she had left, and who had been murdered. So many people she would never see again.

The cat came into the room and wound itself round her legs. Frieda bent down to scratch its chin and felt something missing under her fingers. She lifted the cat onto her lap: the thin leather collar was no longer there. She put the cat onto the floor and went to the front and then the back door, drawing the bolts shut, standing for a moment in the quietness of the hall, listening to the wind blow.

Hannah Docherty lies and stares up into the darkness. In Westow Park, children running around, little Rory, her mother, a blanket on the grass. Her mother leans in close, smelling of perfume, spices, roses.

'Under here,' says her mother, 'there is a hidden river. It begins here in this park. When it rains, the park gets wet, down there at the bottom. It's the river trying to get back to the surface.'

'No,' says Hannah.

'Yes,' says her mother. 'Long ago it was a stream and people could walk by it and children could paddle in it but it was covered up. But it's still here and it flows from here to the River Thames, miles and miles away.'

'Why was it covered?' says Hannah.

'I don't know,' says her mother. 'Maybe it was in the way.'

'What's it called?'

'Effra,' says her mother. 'It's called the River Effra.'

Ever since, Hannah had thought about where the river went and how it knew where to go. Later, as a teenager walking through Brixton, smoking weed with friends, she had looked up as if in a dream and seen the street sign: Effra Road. She felt as if the river had hidden and survived, then secretly followed her down the hill from Norwood.

Once she had been at a party in a squat in Vauxhall. It was the last days of the squat. They were going to be evicted. It was like a wake. She had mentioned the Effra and a shy young man with glasses and a long thin scarf and dark clever eyes had said, 'It's here.'

She'd said, 'What do you mean, it's here?'

And he'd said, 'It runs under this building. It comes out into the Thames at Vauxhall Bridge, just over the road.'

So, as the sun came up, she and the boy had left the party and walked over the nightmarish junctions of Wandsworth Road and leaned over the railings and couldn't see where it came out. And they smoked and looked at barges passing on the river and up at the MI6 building above them, and Hannah never saw the boy again and never saw the River Effra.

TWENTY-FIVE

Frieda announced her name at the front desk. A young officer led her through the police station, upstairs, along a corridor that passed an open-plan office, round a corner to an office on the far side. He knocked and pushed it open. A woman was sitting at a desk, typing on a keyboard. She looked up with a frown. The officer announced Frieda's name.

'All right, all right,' she said. 'You'd better sit down.'

Detective Chief Inspector Isobel Sharpe didn't look like Frieda's idea of a detective. With her dark-framed glasses, her curly hair tied up in a bun, she looked more like the forbidding head of a girls' school.

'I hope you're expecting me,' said Frieda.

'Karlsson rang me from his sick bed,' Sharpe said.

'He said you were the person to talk to about missing persons. He said it was your special subject.'

'I was on a Royal Commission about them.'

'That sounds like a good thing.'

'It was like most commissions. It took two years and we made recommendations and nothing changed. What can I do for you?'

'You sound a bit senior to do this. I'm interested in finding a woman. That's probably not the sort of thing you do.'

'I almost certainly can't help you.'

'Oh.'

'But now that you're here you might as well sit down and tell me about it.'

So Frieda sat down at the desk opposite her and said everything she knew about Justine Walsh, which was very little. When she was finished, DCI Sharpe didn't speak for a moment. Then she tapped on her keyboard.

'What are you doing?'

'The national database.'

'Are you allowed to do that?'

DCI Sharpe looked puzzled. 'I'm a police detective.'

'This isn't an official police inquiry.'

'Karlsson vouched for you. Just so long as you aren't planning to commit a criminal offence.' She paused, then looked at Frieda with a sharper expression. 'You're not, are you?'

'Of course not.'

'It's just that I've heard about you.' She looked at the screen with more attention. 'There's four Justine Walshes. A victim of domestic abuse in Stockport in 2012. Born in 1978. Another charged with fourteen counts of shoplifting in 1999.'

'Where?'

'Norwich.'

'That doesn't sound right.'

'One more who was robbed in the street in Stockwell. She's too old: eighty-three. And the other entry is from the early nineties in Birmingham. So there's nothing useful.'

'I didn't expect anything like that,' said Frieda. 'She led a rackety sort of life and then she suddenly went missing. Her daughter hasn't seen her since. I wanted to talk to you about that. Isn't it almost impossible for people to disappear nowadays, with credit cards and mobile phones?'

DCI Sharpe pushed her chair back from her desk. She seemed almost amused. 'That's what people think,' she said. 'People ask why we don't have a proper register of missing people, with everyone on it. Just build a bigger computer and plug it into Facebook and Twitter. Get better identity cards, more CCTV cameras. The problem is that going missing is a bit of a philosophical problem. There are people who run away, who move away, who escape, who get bored, who go on holiday and stay there. They fall in love and run off with someone, they fall out of love and run off to escape someone. They are abused teenagers or persecuted gays or girls forced into marriage. They're men having mid-life crises or wives tired of the husbands' mid-life crises. They are going abroad on a gap year or they are going abroad to join an Islamist army or they are just emigrating.'

'I get the point.'

'I could go on and on.'

'You don't need to.'

'And somewhere in all that, there are a few real missing people: people in danger, criminals on the run, Alzheimer's patients gone wandering, lost children. That's the problem. We used to have the National Missing Persons Bureau. Then, for reasons I never quite understood, we changed it to the UK Missing Persons Bureau. The name may have changed and the software may look different but the problem remains the same. We've got lots and lots of information and not much knowledge.'

'It seems strange to me,' said Frieda, 'that a grown woman, a mother, with a troubled daughter, just suddenly goes missing and there's no police investigation, no nationwide search.'

'Because everything that you've told me about her, her circumstances and her family history, indicates that she's the sort of person likely to move away, to leave her old life behind. The police might make some brief enquiries but it would quickly be designated a lost-contact case. They wouldn't even give it a case number.'

Frieda thought for a moment. It felt like there was nothing more to be done. 'Karlsson told me you were the expert on finding people. It sounds more like you're the expert on *not* finding people.'

'Yes, Karlsson told me about you as well.'

'You mean that I'm rude and badly behaved.'

'He put it more gently than that.'

'But what you're really saying is that you can't help me.'

'What I'm trying to say is, first, that missing people aren't a simple category; second, as you say, it's harder to disappear than it used to be, so the people who manage it are really hard to find.'

Frieda stood up. 'Thank you for giving me your time.'

'If there's anything else I can do, just call me.'

Frieda looked at DCI Sharpe, who was peering at her screen. Her attention was already elsewhere. 'What if she's dead?'

DCI Sharpe glanced up, as if it was an effort to engage with Frieda once more. 'What?'

'You're right. Justine Walsh was the kind of woman who would walk out on her life. But just for that reason, she wasn't the kind of woman who could have sustained it. She would have turned up somewhere, or run out of money and come back. Also, she was worried about her daughter. She would have checked on her.'

'I don't know anything about that. What I know is that people run out on their families and often they don't look back.'

'But what if she died?'

'You mean if she disappeared and died and was never found?'

'Yes.'

'If Justine Walsh died and her body hasn't been found after all these years then it probably never will be.'

'There's another category. What if she disappeared and was found but wasn't identified?'

'The overwhelming majority of people who are found are identified.'

'We know that Justine Walsh isn't in that category. And you've told me there's a whole group we can't investigate. So why not try the group we *can* investigate?'

DCI Sharpe smiled, almost reluctantly. 'We should have had you on our commission.'

'You wouldn't want me on a commission. So what about it? The bodies of women that are found and not identified. Is that another group that's too big to investigate?'

DCI Sharpe shook her head slowly. 'No. It's not a big group at all. You don't even need the police database for it. Pull the chair around to this side of the desk.'

Frieda did as she was told and sat next to the detective as she tapped at the keyboard.

'So what was the date she was last seen?'

'I don't know. Some time in 2001, I think.'

More tapping.

'There we are,' said DCI Sharpe.

Frieda looked at her screen. A collection of boxes had appeared. It looked like a social media site that might have been created in the Soviet Union. There were portraits in different styles – some looked like drawings done by teenagers or by talentless street artists. Two looked like tailors' dummies with no features. One had just a few objects, an earring, a brooch, a belt; another contained a piece of fabric.

'What am I looking at?' asked Frieda. 'Are these bodies found in London? Was that at the time she disappeared?'

'You don't understand,' said DCI Sharpe. 'This is all of them.'

'What do you mean, all of them?'

'These are the unidentified female bodies found since 2001.'

'In south London?'

'In the whole of the United Kingdom.'

Frieda looked more closely and counted the boxes on screen. 'But there are only thirteen. I thought there'd be hundreds.'

'I told you. It's very rare. Take a look. If one of them interests you, click on it. Or her.'

Frieda scanned the details. Four were identified as Afro-Caribbean, one as Oriental. 'Oriental,' she said. 'I didn't know that was still a thing.'

'We probably need to look at some of our terminology.'

Of the rest, one body had been found in Leeds, one in Scotland and one in Birmingham. That left three in Greater London, one in Essex and one with no identifying place at all. Frieda took the mouse and clicked on the last. It had been washed up on a beach in the north-east of Scotland. Probably too far away. One London body was identified as aged eighteen to thirty: too young. Frieda clicked on the Essex body. Found in a car park in 2010. Not decomposed. Of the two remaining bodies, one was described as thirty-five to fifty and 'dark European'; the other was twenty-five to fifty and 'light European'. Frieda clicked on the dark European. She saw what looked like a passport photograph of a round-faced woman. Below it were the words 'Show Sensitive Images'. Frieda clicked on the words, confirmed that she was over eighteen and two more photographs appeared. The same woman, but with her eyes closed, as if she were asleep on a white pillow. Frieda looked at the text. She had been found under a road bridge in 2012. Too late to be Justine Walsh.

'She must have come over from Romania,' said Frieda. 'Or Bulgaria. Or Poland. Or Ukraine. And it didn't work out. And then she ended it and nobody came for her.'

'As I said, it's very rare.'

'They were all somebody's child once,' said Frieda. 'Which leaves us with one.'

Frieda clicked on 'light European', twenty-five to fifty. She had been found by a dog, in a shallow grave in Denton Woods, south London in April 2010. Body severely decomposed.

'How do they know she was light European?' Frieda asked.

'Hair colour.'

The particulars were vague: Marks & Spencer underwear, dark trousers, light-coloured shirt. Flat leather shoes. No jewellery, no watch, nothing.

'This one,' said Frieda.

'There's no guarantee it's her,' said DCI Sharpe. 'It's a hundred to one. A thousand to one.'

'No. This feels right. If you were in Dulwich, with a dead body, and you needed somewhere you knew you'd be undisturbed, that would be a good choice.'

DCI Sharpe looked at Frieda curiously. 'It's not good to dwell on these things,' she said.

Frieda shook her head. 'These remains. Can I get access to them?'

'What for?'

'We need a DNA sample. Then maybe someone can say goodbye to their mother.'

Frieda took a photograph of the bandanna with her mobile and emailed it to Saul Tait. 'Do you remember Hannah ever wearing this?'

Karlsson was trying to read a novel. He usually read non-fiction – biographies, histories, books about science – and was finding it a bit of an effort. He kept having to go back a few pages. When the phone rang he was almost pleased to be interrupted, but this quickly changed.

'Mal,' the voice roared. 'Is that you?'

'Of course it's me.'

'It's Crawford here. What the fuck is going on?'

Karlsson held the phone away from his ear slightly. 'I can't really help you,' he said, as politely as he could manage – his relations with the commissioner had been strained since he'd resigned before he was sacked, and then been reinstated because of Levin's intervention. 'I'm still at home with a cast. It will be a few weeks before I can return to work.'

'I'm not talking about your leg. I'm talking about that bloody woman.'

'I don't know what you mean.' Karlsson did know what Crawford meant. When he talked in that tone, he meant Frieda, but he was trying to gather his thoughts.

'Your Dr Klein. What's she up to?'

'In what sense?'

'What's she doing with that prankster?'

'You mean Levin?'

'Don't play dumb. I know what's going on. She's been per-verting the course of justice down in Thamesmead. She's got hold of your Yvonne woman . . .'

'Yvette. And I'm sure it's authorized. But I'm not the per-son to ask: I'm on sick leave.'

'I know what's going on, Mal, that's all I'm going to say. And tell Dr Klein from me that I've got my eye on her.'

'This,' said Shelley Walsh, in a whispering hiss, 'is getting very irritating.' She separated the last word out into its four syllables. 'Why are you here a*gain*? I told you to let every-thing be.'

'I know, but –'

'And who's *she*? Who's *he*?'

'This is my colleague Sasha Wells. And this is her son, Ethan.'

'Your colleague?' Shelley opened her eyes very wide; she raised her immaculate eyebrows. 'And her son? Why is her son here? One of you is bad enough. What will everyone think?' She glanced around wildly, as if there would be neighbours staring from every window.

'Could we come in?' asked Frieda.

'No! I've said everything I wanted to say. I've said more than I wanted to say. I want you to leave. Now. Or I'll call the police. And that little boy is standing on my flowerbed.'

'The police know we're here,' said Frieda.

'I beg your pardon?'

'Please. If we could just come in.'

'This has gone too far,' said Shelley, standing back from the door so that they could file into the house. 'Wipe your feet,' she said to Ethan. He stared up at her with his dark, serious eyes, then shuffled his muddy shoes on the doormat.

It was eleven in the morning and the kitchen was filled with the smell of baking.

'I won't offer you coffee,' said Shelley, 'because you won't be staying that long.'

'Can I have milk?' asked Ethan.

'Milk?' Shelley looked at the little boy as if he was speaking a foreign language.

'We'll get some later,' said Sasha to Ethan, laying a hand on his head.

'If you say "please",' said Shelley.

'Please.'

She poured milk into a tumbler, almost up to the brim,

and handed it to Ethan, who drank it with his eyes fixed on her over the rim.

'Thank you,' said Sasha, in her soft, clear voice. 'What a lovely kitchen. I wish I could keep things as neat as this.'

'I consider it my job.'

'I think we may have found your mother,' said Frieda.

Shelley put her hand against her chest, then her throat. 'What do you mean, found? I don't want her to be found. I don't care. I told you. How dare you go around finding people?'

'Shelley, listen. If it is your mother, then she is dead.'

'My mother?'

'Perhaps.'

'Why are you telling me this?'

'Because you need to know. The body of a woman was discovered in a shallow grave in south London, and we think it may be Justine Walsh's. Which is why we are here now.'

'When was it discovered?'

'In April 2010.'

'That's four years ago. It could be anyone. Why should it be her?'

'We need a sample of your DNA,' said Frieda. 'Then we can test it against hers.'

'Why should I care anyway? 2010 means that there were nine years when she didn't bother to try and find me.'

'It had been there for many years.'

'How many?'

'I don't know?'

'Nine?'

'It's possible.'

'I don't understand.'

The oven started to make a pinging sound.

'Shall I look at your cake?' asked Sasha.

'They're biscuits. She just went missing.'

'Until we know if it's your mother, we can't work out what actually happened,' said Frieda. 'Sasha is a geneticist. She has come to take a DNA sample, if you'll consent to that.'

Sasha put a tray of biscuits she had taken from the oven on the surface and nodded at Shelley. 'It will take about five seconds,' she said. 'It's very simple. It's just a swab I wipe inside your mouth. I have a consent form for you to sign.' She opened up her leather case and drew out a form.

Shelley stared at it. 'Then you'll know if it's her?'

'Yes.'

'How long will it take?'

'A few days,' said Sasha.

'What if I don't want to know?'

'Can I have a biscuit?' asked Ethan.

'Don't you want to know?' asked Frieda.

'I don't know.'

'You might find it helps you to know at last,' said Frieda.

'I'm doing well,' said Shelley. 'In my life. My husband doesn't know anything about that time.'

'Have you thought he might want to know and to help?'

'I'm not that person any more.'

She picked up the pen and stood poised above the form. Then, as if in a great hurry, she wrote her signature across the bottom and handed it to Sasha. 'Have a biscuit,' she said to Ethan. 'Have as many as you like. Take them all. We never eat them. I don't know why I make them.'

Sasha drew on a pair of thin plastic gloves. She took a small sealed bag from her case and took out a swab. 'I'm just going to wipe the inside of your cheek and under your tongue and above your teeth,' she said to Shelley. 'OK?'

Shelley nodded. She squeezed her eyes shut and opened her mouth wide, looking suddenly like a small child.

'Done,' said Sasha, after a few seconds. 'Thank you.' She put the swab into a transparent container, then pulled off her gloves.

'That's it?'

'That's it.'

'Good. Now go away.'

'I'll phone Yvette and see what she can do,' said Frieda, as they left.

An email from Saul Tait arrived: *This is weird, but, yes, I do remember Hannah wearing it. She used it to tie her hair back when she went for runs. I remember clearly.*

So that was that. She was back to square one with the collection.

TWENTY-SIX

Frieda spent the following afternoon at the Warehouse, seeing patients, then attending a meeting to discuss outreach projects. She had arranged to meet Jack afterwards, and he put his head round the door at exactly five o'clock. 'Am I too early?'

'You're exactly on time.'

'You're not busy?'

'Come in, Jack.'

He was wearing a red duffel coat, with a stripy scarf, and had a bad cold; his voice was husky and he kept pulling out tissues from his pocket to blow his nose. 'I'm taking an unpaid sabbatical,' he announced.

'To do anything particular?'

'To think.'

'About whether you want to continue as a therapist?'

'Are you angry?'

'Why would I be angry?'

'Or disappointed?'

'I'm not your mother, Jack.'

'You're nothing like my mother.'

'So you're going to think?'

'I need to think about whether the problem is being a therapist or being *me*. And then there's the problem of what else I could possibly do. ' He ran his fingers through his wild hair. 'I could be a gardener, I suppose.'

'Do you like gardening?'

'I've never tried it, except that time when your mother made me pull up the weeds in her garden.'

'Which didn't work out so well.'

'Gardeners make the world a better place.'

'Some gardeners do.'

'Anyway.' His face brightened. 'I'll have six weeks free so I can help you.'

'Help with what?'

'Your case.'

'That's very kind of you but . . .'

'Give me a task.'

Frieda thought for a moment. 'It's complicated. And I'm not sure it's safe.'

'I don't mind that.'

'Then you're a fool.'

There was a knock at the door, and this time it was Reuben putting his head round. 'Can anyone join in?' He pulled a chair up to the desk and settled himself into it. 'What are you talking about?'

'Jack's taking a sabbatical,' said Frieda.

'Frieda's case,' said Jack.

'Yes.' Reuben's eyes gleamed. 'Irresistible, isn't it? Almost too perfect.'

Frieda looked at him sharply. 'What do you mean?'

'Just that: an angry teenage daughter, a controlling mother, an absent father, a charming stepfather, who's taken his place in the bed. And the little brother – like a lamb to the slaughter. I can imagine giving a lecture on it.'

'Yes,' said Frieda, thoughtfully. 'It is. Too much so.'

'What do you mean?'

'I'm thinking about the things that don't add up – or that do add up too neatly.'

Reuben leaned across the desk and found a blank sheet of paper. He took a pen out of his jacket pocket. 'What are these things?'

'You really want this?'

'Absolutely.'

'OK. Number one, the layout of the house makes no sense. Or, rather, the order of the deaths. The murderer would have gone past Rory's room, killed Aidan but not Deborah, waited at least an hour, then killed Rory and his mother. Why would anyone do that?'

'Because they were cruel, and wanted to watch them suffer?' Jack suggested.

'Maybe.'

'Two?' said Reuben.

'Two: Rory was found in bed, in his pyjamas. But his blood was also in the hallway and on the stairs. If he wasn't killed in his bed, what is the staging for? If he was, why is his blood also downstairs?'

Reuben and Jack looked at each other but didn't speak.

'Three: all the deaths feel different. Incoherent. Rory was lying on his face with the back of his skull caved in. Horrible. Aidan was quite cleanly killed, if that's the right word for it. It looked calculated and deliberate. Deborah had been savagely beaten.'

'It could be an expression of anger,' said Jack. 'Or hatred.'

'It's the obvious explanation. Four: why were Hannah's bloodstained clothes so easy to find? Five: why was her alibi so peculiar?'

'What was it?'

'She said she was going to meet her stepfather. But then she changed that to meeting her mother.'

'When people are traumatized they get confused,' said Reuben.

'I know. But it feels odd.'

'Anything else?'

'Seamus Docherty. He's Hannah's father, Deborah's first

husband. There was something wrong with his tone, I thought. I want to go back and see him, though. More obviously, Justine Walsh, the mother of Hannah's housemate Shelley, went missing at the same time and that seems a large, strange coincidence. I think we've just found her body and that makes a fourth murder. And a fifth, with Erin Brack's death, of course. Poor woman.' She looked at Reuben, who had stopped writing. 'She was killed because someone believed she had a piece of evidence that would incriminate them.'

'What?'

'I don't know. But if she did, then I have it now. ' She turned to Jack, 'Which brings me to how you could help me.'

'Good.'

'It won't be very exciting and it may take a long time. I need someone to help me go through everything I collected from Erin Brack and sort it all into categories.'

'I could do that. What categories?'

'We – I mean, you – could first of all divide the objects between the family members, things that refer or belong to Hannah, Rory, Deborah and Aidan. Obviously there'll be an overlap.'

'And then?'

'We could make a timeline for each of them, construct a narrative of their last weeks or months. Maybe something will come of it or maybe it'll amount to nothing at all.'

'But you'll be there too?'

'Some of the time. There's one more thing. It's in a building in Walthamstow, in the yard where Chloë works. Is that a problem?'

Jack flushed. 'Why should it be?'

'I'll make sure it's good with Chloë as well.'

TWENTY-SEVEN

Frieda was in her consulting room, writing up her notes on a session, when her phone rang. She looked at it and saw Yvette's name on the screen.

'Yes?'

'Hello? Hello? Is that Frieda?'

'Of course it's me. So?'

'I've got the result back.'

'Yes?'

'I don't know whether it's good news or bad. I'm not clear whether you expected –'

'Just tell me.'

'It's not a match.'

There was a long pause. Frieda didn't know what to say.

'Hello? Frieda? Are you still there?'

'I'll call you back later, Yvette. I need to think.'

'I don't know what you mean.'

'Later.' Frieda hung up. Suddenly she felt stifled and trapped by being indoors. She got up, put on her jacket and left the building. She headed north towards Regent's Park. She needed to clear her head, to see grass and trees. But when she got to Euston Road she stopped on the south side and watched the traffic, the buses and the lorries that made the pavement tremble beneath her feet. What a terrible road it was. She watched a young woman on a bicycle coming from the east, impossibly vulnerable. A huge cement truck passed her and it looked as if she might be blown over by it. But she wasn't. Frieda turned and walked back to her house. She let herself in and went up the stairs to her little study. She opened a drawer and quickly found what she was looking for: an envelope. She opened the envelope and checked that the comb – the comb she had used on Hannah Docherty – was still there.

She took out her phone. 'Yvette. I've got another sample.'

'I can't just keep doing this.'

'Just one more and then I'm done.'

'I'll see what I can do.'

'I'll bring it over now.'

The next day was Saturday and Frieda spent the weekend in a sort of suspension. She had planned to go to Walthamstow to take another look at Erin Brack's collection but couldn't face it. Not today. She met Sasha, as she did every weekend, and they walked with Ethan to Clissold Park and kicked a ball around with him. And they went and drank coffee. Sasha asked what had happened with the DNA sample and Frieda said to wait. She wasn't sure yet. Sasha looked at her curiously and didn't pursue it. The rest of the weekend Frieda spent mostly alone. She felt as if she was in a dream. She had started a process, and until she discovered what was going to happen, nothing really mattered. On the Sunday she met Reuben and they walked across Hampstead Heath, into the wild part where it felt like you weren't in London at all – you couldn't see any buildings, not even the Shard. You couldn't hear traffic. There were just the jet trails in the sky. Reuben asked what was happening and Frieda just said, 'Wait.'

On Monday afternoon, just after four, there was a ring at Malcolm Karlsson's front door. Getting out of his chair was awkward and his walking was still slow, so the bell rang again.

'I'm coming, I'm coming,' he shouted. When he opened

the door, Frieda and Yvette were standing outside. 'What is it?' he said.

'How's the leg?' said Frieda.

'Still broken. Now, what's up?'

'We wanted to tell you first,' said Frieda.

'It doesn't make any sense,' said Yvette.

Frieda tried to take Karlsson's arm to help him back to his chair but he shook it off and toppled. Yvette caught him and the two of them almost fell over. Finally he managed to lower himself back into his chair.

'You're clearly getting more mobile,' said Frieda.

'All right,' said Karlsson. 'What have you got to tell me?'

'It's about the Docherty inquiry,' Frieda began.

'Frieda had this idea,' said Yvette. 'She checked the bodies of women who had been found but not identified in the past thirteen years.'

'What for?'

'Justine Walsh, the mother of Shelley Walsh, disappeared at the time of the Docherty murders.'

'Who's Shelley Walsh?'

'She was a friend, or associate, of Hannah Docherty's. A body was found a few years later in some woods in south London, fairly nearby. We checked the DNA to see if was Justine Walsh. It wasn't.'

'Was that worth coming here to tell me?'

'It was Deborah Docherty.'

Karlsson looked at the two women. Yvette's eyes were bright with excitement. Frieda was looking at him with a kind of curiosity. 'I don't understand.'

'Frieda got a DNA sample from Hannah Docherty. It matched with the body.'

'But Deborah Docherty's body was found in the house,' said Karlsson. 'With her husband and son.'

248

'No,' said Frieda. 'Deborah Docherty's body was found nine years later, severely decomposed in Denton Woods.'

'But what about the body in the house?'

'The police are investigating that,' said Yvette. 'They're doing another DNA test.'

'But we know what they'll find,' said Frieda.

'That girl's mother?' said Karlsson.

'That's right. Justine Walsh.'

Karlsson had been leaning forward in his chair. Now he sank back. 'So what does that mean?'

'What it really means,' said Frieda, 'is that the Hannah Docherty inquiry has been reopened. Now the police can do what they should have done in the first place. I'm through with it.'

There was a pause. Karlsson and Yvette exchanged glances.

'What?' said Frieda.

'It's just I've never heard that from you,' Karlsson said. 'The idea of letting the police get on with their job.'

'What do you want me to do? Start interviewing witnesses on my own?'

Karlsson managed a smile. 'That's what you do, isn't it? But maybe the team on the investigation won't be receptive to your peculiar talents. Not like me. Besides, don't you want to know what actually happened?'

Frieda shook her head. 'What I want is for Hannah Docherty to get out. Nothing else matters. I've done all I can do.'

Karlsson looked at Yvette. 'Do you know who's leading the investigation?'

'I can find out.'

'Good. And keep Frieda in the loop.' He looked back at Frieda. 'So, you can get back to your job, Yvette can get back to her job, and I can get back to learning to walk again. All's right with the world.'

Frieda went straight from Karlsson to see Levin and Keegan. It was early evening and Keegan poured three glasses of whisky. The two men sat in silence as Frieda told them what had happened.

'I thought I owed it to you to tell you,' she said, when she had finished.

Neither man responded. Levin looked down into his whisky, which he hadn't touched. Keegan drained his own glass and poured himself another.

'So that's basically it,' said Frieda.

Keegan took another sip of his drink. 'Good. That's very good.'

'What? The drink?'

'Checking the unidentified bodies. That was very good.'

'It seemed pretty obvious.'

'Only afterwards. It took some sharp thinking to bring it all together.'

'That's good of you to say, because I know we've had our differences.'

'I'm just trying to get my head around it,' said Keegan, as if Frieda hadn't spoken. 'Deborah Docherty isn't at the murder scene she should be. She's at another one.'

'Yes, it's very strange.'

'And this other woman, Justine Walsh, is in Deborah Docherty's house. In Deborah Docherty's bedroom. And she's identified by Hannah Docherty as her mother.'

'That's right. But you saw the state of the body. Hannah Docherty identified her, at the scene, in what must have been a state of shock. If you see a woman in your mother's bed, wearing your mother's nightgown, you're going to see it as your mother.'

'So how did it happen?'

'That's why we have police forces,' said Frieda. 'To answer questions like that.'

'They didn't manage it the first time.'

'Well, now they have a second chance.' Frieda stood up. 'I'm not one for goodbyes, but this feels like a goodbye.'

Keegan stood up and held out his hand. Frieda shook it.

'Maybe we'll meet again.'

'I can't imagine where,' said Frieda.

'You never know.'

Frieda put her untouched whisky on the table. Then she turned to Levin. 'You haven't said anything.'

He looked up at her. 'I thought you would find this harder to walk away from.'

'What do you mean, "walk away from"?'

'The investigation hasn't even begun. Hannah Docherty isn't out yet.'

'We'll see.'

As Frieda left the house, she felt as if she was escaping. Even though it was raining, she walked home. When she got in she took her clothes off, had a bath and felt purified, free of it all.

She had two days of hard work. She saw patients, she went to the Warehouse and talked to Reuben about expanding her role there. She told Chloë that she would be coming to the shed soon to take away all the things she had left there. She dealt with a backlog of letters. She cleared up the house. She threw out some old clothes. On the Thursday morning, after a session with Maria Dreyfus, she switched on her phone.

There was a missed call from Yvette and she rang the number.

'I'm on my way to see you,' Yvette said. Even in those few words her tone sounded strange.

'It's bad news.'

'I'll be outside.'

'Go to the coffee shop round the corner,' Frieda said.

She gave Yvette the address of Number Nine, then walked there herself. She ordered two coffees, and just as they were being placed in front of her, Yvette came in, looking flustered, her cheeks red. She sat down opposite Frieda. 'I'll have tea,' she said, then noticed the coffee. 'Coffee's fine.'

'They're not proceeding with the case,' Frieda said.

Yvette looked surprised. 'How did you hear?'

'Is there any other bad news you could be ringing about?'

Yvette shifted awkwardly in her seat. 'There could be.'

'Who's the detective in charge of the investigation?'

'It doesn't matter. He's not someone you know.'

'What's his name?'

'I'm not going to tell you.'

'Why not?'

'You might do something. You might go and shout at him or hit him. It's happened before.'

Frieda stared past Yvette out into the street. She certainly felt like doing something. Hitting someone was a possibility. She forced herself to speak calmly. 'How could they possibly not proceed with the case? After finding the body?'

'He . . .' Yvette stopped herself. 'Or she. Well, it's actually a he. He said that nothing had really changed.'

'How can he say that? What about the body?'

'It's not me. I'm just reporting what was said. I was only able to have a brief conversation and that was just because Karlsson asked him as a favour. He said Hannah Docherty's prints were at the scene. Her statement was still inconsistent. She still had the motive.'

'But it wasn't her mother who was dead at the scene. It was Justine Walsh. Her mother was in the shallow grave in the woods.'

'DCI – I mean *he* said that was the really key bit of evidence. It was Hannah Docherty who identified Justine Walsh as her mother. And you have to see he has a point, Frieda – there's a way in which what you found only makes things worse for Hannah, if they could be worse. Why would she make a false identification if she wasn't the murderer?'

'Because she was in shock. Because her mother is who she would have expected the damaged corpse to be.'

'I'm not the one who's arguing this.'

'Then tell me his name and I'll go and argue it with him.'

'It doesn't matter. The inquiry's over.'

'Why was Justine Walsh in the Docherty house?' said Frieda.

'Is that a question I'm supposed to answer?'

'It's a question the police are supposed to answer. Why was she killed in the Docherty house, while the woman who actually lived in the house was killed somewhere else?'

'There are always loose threads,' said Yvette. 'Unanswered questions.'

'That's just like giving a verbal shrug.'

'No. It's the way it goes. There are things we'll never know.'

'Speak for yourself,' said Frieda.

She felt an intense weariness. It was starting all over again.

TWENTY-EIGHT

'You again.' Levin twinkled at her in his sinister way.

'Me. You knew, didn't you?'

'Knew what?'

'Knew they'd never reopen the inquiry.'

'Let's say I'm not entirely surprised.'

'How can you be so calm?'

'Am I calm?' He settled back more comfortably in his chair. 'Well, I probably am.'

'Are you just going to let this happen?'

'The real question is: are *you*? But I know the answer already.'

'Which is?'

'No, of course you're not.'

'Do you feel no responsibility?'

'That's an interesting question.' He frowned, reached his hand into his jacket pocket, drew out a bag and looked at it with an air of surprise. 'Would you like a toffee?'

'No.'

'Bad for the teeth, I suppose. No, I don't feel responsibility for this case. You choose what you're responsible for, and you've chosen Hannah.'

'I hardly think I had a choice.'

'Really?'

'I can't just let her rot in that hospital.'

'I understand.' He sounded gentle and vaguely sad.

'It's impossible.'

'But you're on your own now. You see that, don't you?'

'Yes.'

'We could let you keep DC Long for a bit longer, if it would be helpful.'

Frieda considered. 'She deserves a bit of a break from me.'

He popped a toffee into his mouth. 'Just you, then.'

Her mobile rang.

'Hello, Frieda here.'

'Is that Frieda Klein?' A woman's voice, one that Frieda felt she recognized but couldn't place.

'Yes.'

'This is Emma Travis, from fifty-four Oakley Road. The Dochertys' old house,' she added unnecessarily.

'Of course.' There was a pause. 'Was there something you were wanting to speak to me about?'

'Oh, well, not really.'

'Something you thought might be helpful, perhaps?'

'Oh, no.' Emma Travis sounded flustered. 'Nothing like that.'

'I'm sorry. How can I help you?'

'I just wondered – well, I need to get hold of Josef.'

'Ah.' Frieda remembered the white van she'd seen driving past the bar the evening she'd met Flora Goffin and Sebastian Tait for a drink. Her suspicion hardened into certainty and she grimaced at the phone. 'Do you need his number?'

'I have it. As a matter of fact I've seen him once or twice. He came to look at the repairs needed,' she added hastily.

'So how can I help?'

'He's not answering his phone.'

'I see.'

'So I wondered if you could tell him to call me.'

'I can tell him you asked me.'

255

'Thank you. Gutters, you know. Gutters and things that need patching.'

'Yes.'

'Tell him to call.'

This time Frieda didn't see Sedge in the Bear, with the broad brown sweep of the Thames behind him, but at his home in Romford. He was on annual leave – 'Which is a polite way of saying gardening leave,' he'd said on the phone, with a laugh that wasn't quite convincing. His house was a thirties build that stood back from the road. Through the front window she could see the conservatory at the back and beyond that a long lawn. When he opened the door, she smelt furniture polish and lilies. Everything was neater than she'd expected. Coats hung in an orderly line in the hall above paired shoes; next to them was a bag of golf clubs and two tennis racquets.

Sedge himself didn't look quite so neat and well tended. He had thick stubble on his cheeks and his checked shirt was buttoned wrongly. But he held out a hand and shook hers with a firm grip.

He had made coffee and they sat in the conservatory looking out onto the lawn, which was thick with fallen leaves. 'Just because I'm on gardening leave doesn't mean I'm looking after the garden,' he said.

'What are you doing?'

'My wife, Laurie, says I should get out, play a few rounds of golf, meet friends, paint a room, maybe.'

'But you don't want to.'

He cradled his coffee between his large hands and stared gloomily out of the window. 'We don't have kids. My mother's my only family, apart from Laurie. My work's my life and always has been. Whatever mistakes I've made, I've always been a worker. Ask anyone. I expect my team to work hard but I work harder.'

'So you haven't played golf and you haven't done the garden. What have you been doing?'

He rested his gaze on her for a few moments. 'Well, obviously, I've been thinking about the mess I've made. Which is one reason I can't go and play golf and hobnob with my mates in the bar. There's no avoiding it. For the rest of my life I'll be DCI Sedge who got the bodies muddled up.'

'It's good of you to see me, in the circumstances.'

'You mean because you're the one who figured it out?'

'Yes.'

'You're pretty much the only person I want to see. I feel I can talk to you about it without having to defend myself. Strange, isn't it?' He took a sip of his coffee. 'So. What are you wanting from me?'

Frieda had a list of questions in the small notebook in her coat pocket, but she didn't want to take it out and lay it in front of her. It felt like too much of a reminder of what he'd lost. 'First of all, just tell me what you thought when you were told that the woman who was murdered in the Docherty house wasn't Deborah Docherty.'

'What did I think?' Sedge gave a short bark of laughter. 'That's easy. I thought, Holy shit. I thought, Oh, no, please, God, no, don't let this be happening to me. And, That's the end of me. And, How will I face the guys after this?' He looked up at Frieda, his eyes glittering.

'But what did you think about the case?'

'Oh. Sorry. You think I'm being self-involved. What did I think? I guess I thought it wasn't possible, there must be some wild mistake. Because of course it was Deborah Docherty. I mean, there she was, lying in her bed, with her murdered husband, and her murdered son in the next room, and her daughter identified her. Hannah Docherty *identified* her. How could she not be Deborah Docherty?'

'But she isn't.'

'No. She isn't. I honestly don't know what to make of it. I mean, it makes a horrible kind of sense that Hannah Docherty would murder her family. We know she was angry and troubled and had got in with a bad lot. But why would she murder this other woman?' He shook his head.

'Do you know anything about Justine Walsh?'

'Nothing, apart from what I've learned in the last few hours.'

'You know her daughter Shelley Walsh shared a house with Hannah?'

'Yes.'

'But you never met Shelley?'

'I suppose I must have done. I mean, I went to their house. I remember that. God, what a tip. The police already had their eye on it. But I can't remember her, though it would be strange if I hadn't talked to her during the investigation.'

'Records show that you did talk to her, just the once.'

'There you are, then.'

'Did you know that her mother disappeared at the same time as Deborah Docherty?'

'I don't think so,' Sedge said slowly, his brow furrowed with the effort of remembering. 'Though I might be wrong. It was a long time ago.' He took another small sip. 'I talked to the boyfriend. What was his name?'

'Jason Brenner.'

'I talked to him at least twice. He was a creep.'

'That's what Deborah Docherty's ex-husband called him as well.'

The front door slammed and there was a clatter as something was dropped on the floor. 'Ben?'

'In here,' he called. 'I've got a visitor.'

Laurie Sedge was tall and very striking, with a dramatic fall of blonde hair and exuberant clothes.

'I've just been to the market. What a crush.' She held out her hand to Frieda. 'I'm Laurie, by the way. I'm glad Ben has company.'

For a moment, Frieda thought Laurie would bend down and give her a kiss. 'I'm Frieda Klein.'

The woman's brow creased and her mouth pursed. 'Oh, my God. I know who you are.'

'Please,' said Sedge. 'Don't.'

'You're the one who got him into all this trouble and now you're sitting calmly in our house drinking coffee.'

'We're discussing the case,' said Sedge. 'I thought you were going straight from the market to work.'

'What's there to discuss?' She turned to Frieda. 'My husband is the best detective in the country. He's won awards for bravery. He's a good man. He's made one mistake, and now look. What kind of justice is that?'

'Laurie. It's OK.'

'How can it be OK?'

'I know it's hard,' said Frieda, who was rather taken with Laurie Sedge's passionate defence of her husband. 'I'm not here to rake over mistakes.'

'Why are you here, then?' Her voice wavered and, for a moment, Frieda thought she might cry.

'We're reviewing the case,' said Sedge.

His wife pulled a tissue out of her pocket and blew her nose. 'This has been horrible,' she said to Frieda.

'I'll see you later,' said Sedge to her. She nodded and walked forlornly from the room. 'Sorry about that.' He picked up his coffee mug.

'I don't blame her.'

'Where were we?'

'We were talking about Jason Brenner.'

'That's right. He'd been in trouble with the police. Drugs mainly.'

'You asked a few minutes ago why Hannah would murder Justine Walsh. Doesn't this make you wonder if Hannah did murder her?'

Ben Sedge stared at Frieda, his mug lifted halfway to his mouth. 'What?'

'Perhaps it wasn't Hannah.'

'You mean she murdered Aidan and Rory and someone else murdered Justine?'

'Maybe she didn't murder anyone.'

The look on his face was almost comical. 'Let's get this clear. You're saying not only did I get the wrong body, I got the wrong murderer.'

'Is it impossible?'

He stood up and went to the window, then laid his forehead against the glass. They heard the front door open and shut once more.

'Well?'

'Of course it's impossible. More than impossible. It's crazy.'

'Why?'

'What are you trying to do? Look at me. You've already ruined my career, but you can't let it rest. You've got to drag me through the mud.'

'This isn't about you.'

'Really? That's not how it seems from where I'm standing.'

'It's about Hannah.'

'Who killed her whole family.'

'You're sure about that?'

'Of course I'm fucking sure.' He wiped a hand across his brow. 'Jesus,' he muttered, under his breath. 'Don't you see that it makes even less sense?'

'Why?'

His face tightened. As he looked at her, Frieda could see him coming to a decision. Then his whole body seemed to sag slightly and he gave a shrug. 'OK. If you really want to know what I think. Hannah was violent and angry. She had fallen out with her mother and stepfather. Her alibi was farcical. There was blood all over her clothes. Just because it wasn't her mother she killed doesn't mean it wasn't her doing the killing. She was the one who identified the body. Why would she do that if she was innocent?'

'I wanted to ask you about that. You were the one who took her to identify the bodies.'

'That's right.'

'Why would you take a traumatized young woman to look at the corpses of her family?'

'She was the closest relative. Also, it's useful to look at their reactions.'

'In case they did it, you mean?'

'Exactly.'

'So how did Hannah react?'

'She just stared. She seemed bizarrely calm, though later she was wild.'

'How did you interpret it? Grief? Pain? Shock?'

'I don't know.'

'And then she said the woman in the bed was her mother.'

'As clear as anything.'

'And you took her word for it.'

Ben Sedge gave her a tight smile. 'As you say, I took her word for it. In my defence, I think most people would have done the same. Because why lie?'

'Because she was in shock?'

'Look. It doesn't really make a difference, does it? She clearly killed her mother later as well. Or earlier. Who knows?'

'You mean, killed her mother and drove her somewhere and buried her. Did she have a driving licence?'

'Hannah? I don't know. She was eighteen so she might have had. It would be easy to find out. But that's something you can ask the investigating officer.'

'As I'm sure you already know, they're not reopening the inquiry.'

'So I was informed, though I haven't been told to come back to work yet. I'm a case that's still pending. They're not pursuing this because what would be the point? This only makes things worse for Hannah, doesn't it? A fourth murder, and she's already locked up for life.'

It was what Yvette had said as well. Frieda nodded. 'They're not opening the inquiry, but I am.'

'You?'

'Yes.'

'Why?'

'Because I don't think she killed anyone.'

'In spite of all the evidence.'

'In spite of that.'

'Why?'

She couldn't tell him about Erin Brack, so she simply said, 'I have a feeling.'

'A feeling,' he repeated.

'Yes.'

'So you're sitting there saying you have a *feeling* I didn't just make a cock-up, that I'm responsible for a wrongful conviction.'

'I suppose I am.'

Ben Sedge stared at her for several seconds. Frieda tried to read the expression on his face: she didn't think it was anger. It looked more like curiosity, or perhaps a grudging respect. He turned back to the window, where drizzle blurred the glass. 'It's going to rain again,' he said. 'Won't the sky run out of rain eventually? It's like people crying. I've seen people cry so much you can't believe there's enough water in their tear ducts. What the fuck do you want from me?'

Frieda joined him at the window. 'Perhaps you can help me.'

'You've a nerve.' Sedge sounded more admiring than hostile.

'If you were starting the case afresh, with this new evidence, what would you do?'

'Why ask me? I should be the last person you'd turn to.'

'You were there. You know what it looked like, smelt like, felt like.'

'As I say, it was a long time ago.'

'But you must remember some things vividly. It wasn't an ordinary case.'

'No.' He sounded sombre. 'It was an appalling case. Some of my team had to have counselling.'

'But not you.'

'What's strange is that I remember the reactions of my team more than my own. I remember one of the team being sick. I felt I had to be strong to keep everyone going, you know?'

'What would you do now, if you were me? Where would you look?'

'You're serious, aren't you? You're seriously asking me to help you ruin my own reputation.'

'That's not how I'm thinking about it.'

'For truth and justice, you mean?'

'Something like that.'

Sedge rubbed his hand against his stubbly cheek. 'Obviously, the first thing that springs to mind is that Justine Walsh and Aidan Locke were probably having an affair. Otherwise why would she be in bed with him?'

Frieda nodded.

'So I'd need to find out if this was true. If it was, then I'd ask who would be angry enough about that to kill them.'

'And Rory.'

'Perhaps he was collateral damage. He was just there.'

'And Deborah too.'

'It's odd, I'll give you that. But you know what? There are odd things in every case, things that don't make sense.'

'This isn't just odd, this is an additional murdered woman.'

'I know. What I mean is that you're staring at a mess and seeing a pattern there. But maybe it's just a mess. My mess, I grant you. Anyway, I would begin by talking to people who knew Aidan Locke and Justine Walsh.'

'Thank you. Anything else?'

'Yes.' They had both been talking staring out of the window, but now he turned to look at her and she turned as well. 'I would say this, of course. Keep an open mind.' He held up a hand to prevent her speaking. 'Keep an open mind about Hannah Docherty. I like your spirit and your tenacity. But does it occur to you that you might be wrong?'

'You are certain Hannah is guilty?'

Sedge pushed his hands deep into his pockets and hunched his shoulders. 'You talk about your gut feeling,' he said eventually. 'I know about those. I have them too. They can be dangerous for detectives. You have to both put them to one side and yet hold them there, at the edge of your vision, if you see what I mean.'

'And your gut feeling is that Hannah did it?'

He nodded. 'I got a sense of danger from her,' he said. 'It was almost like a smell.'

'It could have been the smell of great pain.'

He smiled at her suddenly, his blue eyes crinkling. He appeared both amused and yet in a state of distress. 'Well, of course. You can interpret these things any which way. You're the therapist. But keep an open mind. Because she killed them, you know.'

There was a message from Reuben on her voicemail, asking her to call him as soon as she could.

'Reuben?' she said.

'I thought we could meet.'

Something about his voice stopped her asking why, or making an excuse. 'Of course. Where?'

'We could walk somewhere.'

It was raining and he hated walking.

'Are you at the Warehouse?'

'No. I'm on the Heath.'

'I'll meet you near the bandstand.'

'Right.'

'Give me half an hour.'

There were very few people around. A few dog-walkers and some joggers running through the steady drizzle. She saw Reuben at once, in his dandyish coat, his grey hair damp.

She put a hand on his arm.

'What is it?'

'I have a lump in my neck.'

'Show me where.'

He unwrapped his soft scarf and put two fingers gently on the skin just below his ear. 'There.'

'Let me feel.'

She laid her fingers where his had been. 'Does it hurt?'

'No.'

'You should go to your doctor, Reuben.'

'You think it's serious?'

'You should get it checked out.'

'You think I've got cancer?'

'It's a lump. It doesn't feel like a gland. You know as well as I do that it could be nothing or it could be something. You need to get it checked out.'

He nodded and looked away at the lowering sky.

'Why don't you make an appointment with your GP now?'

'It's probably nothing.'

'Do you have the number on your phone?'

He nodded.

'Make an appointment. And if they can see you at once, we can walk there together. Or we can go and have coffee somewhere.'

She turned away as he called, looked at the dogs and the runners and the rain falling.

'I'm going tomorrow morning,' he said, sliding his mobile back into his pocket.

'Good.' She linked an arm through his. 'Let's go and get that coffee, then.'

'I've got a lump under my arm as well.'

'It's good you're going to the doctor.'

'I guess.' He nodded glumly, water dripping from his hair.

'I'm glad you told me. Come on now.'

TWENTY-NINE

Frieda had become used to being greeted by Shelley Walsh with a look of irritation or even horror. Not this time. As she.opened the door, Frieda saw the face of a woman who had lost her mother for a second time. She was as well groomed as ever, but she was so pale that her skin was almost white.

'Why wasn't it you who told me?'

'I'm sorry,' said Frieda. 'I gave the police your address.'

'You should have been the one to come.' But Shelley didn't seem angry, more sad and defeated.

'Can I come in?'

Shelley didn't speak, just stepped aside. By now Frieda knew where everything was: the teapot in the cupboard, the mugs hanging from hooks, the teaspoons in a drawer next to the cooker. She poured the tea and she and Shelley sat in the conservatory, looking out at the garden that was as neatly ordered as the house. Frieda sipped her tea and waited for Shelley to speak.

'So why didn't you?' she said finally. 'Was it easier to get someone else to do it for you?'

'You never seemed very pleased to see me,' said Frieda. 'Also, it was the police's job. I thought they'd need to ask you questions.'

'They seemed embarrassed,' said Shelley. 'There was a young policeman and a young policewoman and I think they wanted to leave as soon as they could. But when they told me what had happened, I started crying and asking questions

267

and saying that it didn't make any sense. That just made things worse. For them, I mean.'

'What did they ask you?'

'Nothing. They waited for me to stop crying and then they left.'

'I'm sorry.'

'What for?' said Shelley, with some of her old sharpness. 'You already explained it. You left it to the police. It wasn't your responsibility.'

'I'm sorry about your mother. I'm sorry about the way you heard it.'

'You're welcome.' Shelley paused for a moment. 'No. That's what you say when someone says "thank you". What do you say when someone says sorry to you? I suppose I should say, "That's all right. It doesn't matter."'

'Have you talked to your husband about it?'

'I told him the body had been found. I had to. I had the crazy thought of not telling him at all, but it wasn't possible.'

'You can have a funeral now,' said Frieda. 'It can be a good thing. We need to say goodbye.'

'It's not so simple. The police told me about that. There already was a funeral, although they didn't know it was my mother. And the body was cremated. And the ashes were scattered.'

'You can still have a service or a memorial of some kind.'

'I said goodbye a long time ago. How many goodbyes can one person say?'

'She was an absence. That can be difficult. Now you have something real.'

Shelley was looking down at her tea, fiddling with the mug. Frieda saw she was plucking up courage to say something.

'Do people talk to you about things like this? I mean, in your job.'

'Things like what?'

'You know. Losing a parent.'

'Yes, of course. Often.'

'Do you think it would help? For someone like me?'

'Do you have friends you can talk to?'

'I've got friends. Obviously. I'm not sure they're the kind to talk about this sort of thing with.'

'Then yes. You ought to talk to someone.'

Now Shelley looked up and faced Frieda directly. 'I was thinking of you.'

'There are two reasons why I couldn't do that for you. The first is that we have a personal connection now. When you see someone in that way it needs to be someone outside your life. Talking to a therapist isn't like talking to a friend. It's quite different. But I could have a preliminary talk with you. We could decide between us what you need and then I could find the right person for you.'

Shelley seemed cast down. 'I know it's because I wasn't very welcoming when you first came here.'

'It's not because of that. I've told you why.'

'You said there were two reasons.'

Frieda hesitated. She wasn't quite sure how to put this. 'The police told you that they weren't proceeding with an investigation.'

'They didn't tell me anything.'

'As you know, Hannah was convicted of all the murders. With your mother being found at the scene, and Hannah's mother being found elsewhere, it looks rather different now. But the police still believe that Hannah Docherty did it. That she killed her mother and your mother as well.'

269

'And you don't?'

'It's complicated. I want to look into it. And while I was doing that, I couldn't be talking to you as a therapist.'

'I'm confused. You think that Hannah killed her family but that someone else killed my mother.'

'No. That doesn't sound right. I'm not sure what happened, but it needs looking at.'

'Hannah was a difficult girl.'

'I've known lots of difficult girls.'

'But you think you know better than the police.'

'The thing is, Shelley, you'll need to talk to someone who can help you work through the feelings you had as a girl, with all that happened between you and your mother, and also your feelings now that you know she's dead.'

'And you can't do that?'

'No. Because a therapist will need to ask you one kind of question while I want to ask you another kind.'

'What kind?'

Frieda looked out of the window. A squirrel was running along the top of the wooden fence at the back of the lawn. It disappeared into the next garden. 'For the moment, I want to ask you just one or two questions. But they may be painful for you, and if they are, you only have to say so.'

'What sort of questions?'

'Did the police tell you where your mother's body was found?'

'In the Docherty house.'

'In the *bedroom* of the Docherty house.'

'They told me that.'

'And what did you think?'

'What I thought was that it was terrible that my mother hadn't just disappeared but that she had been murdered and that it hadn't been known about.'

'That's not what you thought, that's what you felt. Why do you think your mother was there?'

Shelley took a deep breath as if she'd been stung. 'Is that the sort of question you ask your patients?'

'I told you. I can try to help you but you can't be my patient. Why do you think your mother was in the Dochertys' bedroom?'

'How should I know? She didn't talk to me about things like that.'

'Things like what?'

'You're trying to get me to say that my mother was having an affair.'

'Well, was she?'

'What's the point of even asking me?'

'Because you're her daughter.'

'All right, the answer is no. I don't think my mother was having an affair with Hannah's father.'

'Hannah's stepfather.'

'Either of them.'

'You don't think your mother was the sort of woman who had affairs.'

Shelley looked tired now. Frieda wondered if she had pushed her too far.

'You don't understand what my mother was like.'

'So tell me.'

'It's not just that her life was a mess. You know that. It's that I can't believe she would have had the energy to have an affair, the sense of purpose or whatever you want to call it. Not at that period of her life.' Shelley wrinkled her nose. 'I can imagine her letting herself be fucked –' she looked taken aback at the word she'd used, her eyes blinking rapidly '– but not doing anything that needed planning or commitment. If I try to remember my mother, I think of her lying on the sofa

271

with her legs splayed out and a bleary look on her face. Or tottering around screaming at me with her hair all matted, looking like a madwoman. Or crying and saying she was sorry, with mascara running down her cheeks. Or having a good day, and that felt even worse than the bad days because it made me hopeful, but at the same time I knew it didn't mean anything. That was my mother.' Shelley's voice wobbled. 'Useless. Of course she couldn't have had an affair. '

'And yet she ended up dead in the Dochertys' bed, beside Aidan.'

'It doesn't make sense. I don't think she even knew the Dochertys. I'd knocked around with Hannah but there wasn't much chance of the two families socializing, I can tell you that.'

'So what was she doing there?'

'You ask me as if I'm somehow responsible. Maybe she came round and confronted Hannah and Hannah snapped. As someone who knows Hannah – or knew Hannah – that sounds more likely.'

'So Hannah killed your mother,' said Frieda. 'And then killed her own family.'

'That's enough. You said I should tell you if I didn't want to answer questions. I'm telling you. I don't want to answer questions.'

Frieda stood up. 'It was courageous of you to talk to me at all. I promise you, Shelley, if I learn anything new about your mother, I'll let you know.'

Shelley looked up at Frieda. 'Why would I want to know?'

As Frieda approached Seamus Docherty's house, the door opened and Docherty emerged, with his dog on a lead.

'You,' he said. 'It's like having a stalker. I'm afraid I'm going out.'

'It's all right,' said Frieda. 'I can come with you.'

'I'm not sure that's a good idea. I'm being polite, by the way. I mean, no.'

'I can always come back with a police officer.'

'I've seen a police officer. They told me about Deborah being found. I've said what I have to say.'

'I know different police officers. And that would be boring. It would mean going into a police station and making a statement. Have you ever given a statement? Do you know how long it takes?'

'All right. At least it's not a dawn visit this time. If you can keep up.'

'It won't take long.'

They walked up the road and Seamus talked about his dog, about how it was a mongrel mixed with another kind of mongrel. It was the healthiest kind, apparently, he said. And it forced him to get exercise. They reached the end of the road that led on to the Heath. Then they walked up Kite Hill. When they reached the top, they stopped and looked across London.

'It's changed even since I've lived here.' He pointed at the tall buildings. 'None of them were there. In ten years' time there'll be fifty more.'

'You bought at the right time,' said Frieda.

'I don't know if that's some kind of accusation.'

'Just a statement.'

'Well, we couldn't afford the house now. It's all bankers and gangsters. At least, I assume they're gangsters.'

'You probably could still afford the house. I know how much money you inherited when Deborah and Rory were killed.'

Yvette had found out for her: the estate had been worth over two and a half million pounds, and that was thirteen years ago.

273

Seamus turned towards her. 'Yes,' he said softly. 'My ex-wife and my son died. My daughter was put into a hospital for the criminally insane for life. And I became rich. And I would give every pound I got to see my son again. What are you trying to say to me and why are you here? Nothing about a bandanna this time?'

'It must have been a surprise,' said Frieda.

'What?'

'That your ex-wife didn't die in the house. That her body has only just been found.'

'I am trying very, very hard not to think about it.'

'You were married to her.'

'That's why.'

'Justine Walsh's body was found in the bedroom of your ex-wife's husband. Is that something you're trying not to think about?'

'I never knew Justine Walsh. This was the first time I'd even heard her name.'

'She was the mother of a friend of Hannah's.'

'The police told me that.'

'Some people might assume that Justine Walsh was having an affair with Aidan Locke.'

Docherty bent down and unfastened the lead. The dog ran off and immediately started barking at a black Labrador, backing away as he did so. 'Sammy's a wuss,' he said.

'Tell me more about Deborah. Describe her.'

'Debs was . . .' Seamus gazed into the distance, searching for a word. 'Different,' he said at last.

'Different in what way?'

'Different from most women. She was extraordinary, really. She didn't look it, but she was.' He stopped and gave a little nod to himself, as if in confirmation of his words. Frieda waited for him to continue, and at last he said, 'She had an impersonal quality about her. Cool. She stood back and looked at people. If Aidan had had an affair, I think she would have been contemptuous, perhaps, or even a bit amused, in a scornful kind of way.'

'But not threatened or jealous?'

Seamus shook his head slowly from side to side. He seemed weighed down with thoughts. 'I don't think so.'

'Did she love him?'

'Aidan? Probably. She was very ambitious for him. But she would never have killed someone out of jealousy.'

His phrasing struck Frieda as strange. 'Could you imagine her killing someone for *any* reason?'

'She was very unsentimental.'

Frieda looked around. The top of the hill was almost crowded. There were runners and people with dogs. Especially people with dogs. Some had six or seven, with leads radiating out from them. 'It must have been complicated for you, when the murders happened. Who would kill a whole family?'

'Someone like Hannah, obviously.'

'Or a person who would stand to gain if the whole family died, or as good as died, in Hannah's case. I mean you, of course.' Frieda paused. 'I'm just trying to see it from the police's point of view.'

Frieda thought that Docherty might be angry at the suggestion, or even break off the conversation. But he answered calmly enough. 'The police interviewed me. Clearly they saw that I wouldn't do something like that.'

'But it must look different now. Your wife having being killed somewhere else. And buried.'

'Different? She was dead either way.'

'Did Hannah know about you and Deborah sleeping together?'

'I don't think children ever like to think about their parents' sex lives.'

'I don't mean when you were married. I mean later. When you were separated. When you were both with other people.'

Docherty looked round at her. His air of calm had gone and he blinked rapidly. Frieda could see that he was thinking fast.

'Why would you say that?'

'You seemed to know quite a lot about what your ex-wife was thinking, what she would have done. It's common for people to sleep with their ex-partners. It can be comforting, or reassuring, or just a temptation.' Docherty didn't answer. 'I'm right, aren't I?'

He swallowed before he spoke. When he did so, his voice had lost its ironic inflection. 'It was the year after we separated and was quite unexpected. Like a fire suddenly bursting into flames when we both thought it was just ash. I was with Brenda and she was with Aidan. Nobody ever found out. No one knew. Our last farewell.'

'Just once?'

'No. But only a few times, over the space of one crazy month when I thought I was going a bit mad. Then we stopped and we never talked about it again. It died away and it was like it never happened.'

'And you chose not to tell the police.'

'It wasn't relevant.'

'You don't get to decide that.'

'Perhaps I was wrong. It felt too intimate. And I thought, once they knew, it was inevitable Brenda would find out as well.'

'Did you still love her?'

He hesitated, his eyes scanning the horizon. 'I don't know

if there's a proper answer to that. Even when I hated her, I never managed to feel distant from her. She was the woman I'd been married to for years. She was the mother of my children. That doesn't mean I wanted her back or that I didn't love Brenda as well. Debs never made me happy like Brenda does. She was too harsh, too unyielding. She was always critical of me, kept wanting me to be someone different.'

'You say no one knew.'

'They didn't.'

'Hannah?'

'No. Why would she?'

'Because she was your daughter.'

Seamus gave a shrug. 'If she'd known, she wouldn't have kept it to herself.'

'Brenda?'

'No!'

'One other thing. Rory's geography teacher was Guy Fiske.'

'And?'

'You know what I'm saying.'

'Stop this. My son was killed. Are you suggesting he was abused as well?'

'I'm just trying to find out what happened.'

'What happened is that Hannah killed my son and ex-wife. And now some other woman as well.'

'I'm not sure that's true.'

'Who else could have done it?' He hesitated. 'Are you thinking, even as a theory, even for a moment, that I could have killed Debs, killed my little boy?'

'I've got no theories. I'm just asking questions. For instance, what kind of clothes was Hannah wearing in the last few months before the crime?'

'What does that matter?'

'Bear with me.'

'I can't remember exactly, but they were kind of grungy and torn, ugly really. Like a demonstration of something.'

'What colours?'

'Black. Always black or dark brown. But you know that already – you mentioned it last time you accosted me with that bandanna, if you remember.'

'Yes. And yet the clothes she apparently wore when she killed three people, or now four, and that were found covered with blood, were a flowery dress and a cardigan. Doesn't that sound strange to you?'

'I don't know. When you decide to kill your family, maybe you put on special clothes to do it.'

'What was the last contact you had with them?'

'I told the police about that at the time. Debs called me a couple of nights before she died and said she had something she wanted to talk to me about.'

'You've no idea what?'

'It was probably about holiday arrangements. It was that time of year. I was going to take Rory to Cornwall, Hannah, too, if she agreed to come.'

'You're sure that's what it was about.'

'It was years ago. Of course I'm not sure.'

Frieda left him there, at the top of the hill, and walked away from the Hampstead side. Every road she went down seemed to be blocked or wind round on itself, leading her back to the beginning. She took out her phone. Jack answered.

'Meet me at the yard,' she said. 'There must be something.'

THIRTY

In the dim light of late afternoon, with rain gushing down from a low brown sky, the joiner's yard was a depressing place. Frieda and Jack made their way round the large puddles that had formed to the door of the shed. Frieda inserted the key into the rusty padlock and pulled at the double doors; they swung open with a creak. She found the lights and turned them on, seeing once more the objects stacked against the walls and on shelves come into view under the flickering fluorescent lights. The cement floor was damp in patches where rain had seeped through, but the Docherty collection was untouched.

'Wow,' said Jack, stepping into the shed. The rain drummed on the corrugated roof above them, and dripped from a leak onto an old pram, making a metallic ping. Water dripped off him and his wet hair lay flat against his skull. He looked younger than usual, thinner. 'It's cold in here. I'll have to bring extra jumpers. And a Thermos flask.'

'I'll show you what we've got,' said Frieda, 'and we can make a plan.'

She pulled the three cardboard boxes and the suitcase away from the wall and opened them. They squatted on the floor. She could barely bring herself to look once again at the piles of papers, receipts, bills, notebooks, dog-eared photos, certificates, reports, old passports, medical cards and bank statements; at the old clothes with their smell of decay; at the flotsam and jetsam of long-ago lives.

'Wow,' said Jack, again, but this time he sounded

uncertain, dismayed. He picked up an empty crisps packet, a single sock with a balding heel. 'It's not in any order at all.'

Wherever possible, I'd like you to separate things into four individual piles: Deborah, Aidan, Hannah, Rory. And I guess a fifth pile for everything that doesn't fit into that.'

'Like this.' Jack held up the sock.

'It will get easier as you go. That sock, for instance: it's probably Rory's because of its size.'

'What am I looking for?'

'I'm not sure. I suppose for something that feels wrong, that doesn't fit. Once everything is sorted into piles, you need to go through them and try to get a kind of chronology.'

'Right.'

'And there might be nothing to find, Jack.'

'I get that.'

They heard a sound and looked round. Chloë was standing in the doorway, the steady sheets of rain behind her. She was wearing a leather jacket, heavy boots and a hat pulled down low. Jack gave a small grunt and bobbed his head.

'I was leaving. How's it going here?'

Frieda stood up. 'We've just started. Jack's got some time off and he's going to help me sort this.'

Chloë looked down at the collection. 'The stuff that belonged to someone who died?'

'Yes.'

'That you said you were just going to go through to make sure there was nothing valuable?'

'That's right.'

'Well, I can tell you straight away: there's nothing valuable. Unless, of course, you're looking for evidence of some kind. This is about Hannah Docherty, right?'

'Chloë.'

'I know that tone of voice. I'm an adult now, remember?'

'Of course.'

Chloë squatted down beside Jack and gazed at the pile of clothes. 'What are you searching for anyway?'

'We don't know,' said Jack. He looked skinny and pale beside her.

'So how will you know if you find it?'

'We don't know that, either.'

'Fun way to spend your time off.'

'I'm doing it to help Frieda,' said Jack.

'These clothes are better.' Chloë was looking into the suitcase. She lifted out the pale blue silk shirt. 'I wonder where she was going.'

'Or who the "she" was,' said Frieda. 'I don't think these clothes belonged to Hannah's mother.'

She looked at the label on the black bra: 34C. She knew from the files she'd read through at Levin's house that Deborah Docherty was a 32B. These clothes belonged to Justine Walsh, she thought.

'I could help.' Chloë sat back on her heels. She was talking to Jack now.

He turned to her. 'You?'

'Since I'm just across the yard.'

'What about your work?'

'I have lunch hours. And I often finish early. It'd be nice.' Her voice was amiable, but perhaps sarcastic. Frieda tried to make out her expression. Chloë patted Jack playfully on the shoulder so he nearly toppled. 'Like the old days.'

That evening, Josef came to her house with a bottle of vodka. Frieda poured herself a tumbler of whisky instead. They sat beside her fire, shutters closed against the weather.

'I had a phone call,' she said.

'Please?'

'From Emma Travis.'

'Ah.' He tipped the vodka down his throat and wiped the back of his wrist against his mouth. His brown eyes shone softly.

'Josef . . .'

'Lonely woman, Frieda.'

'Exactly. Lonely and vulnerable.'

'What to do?' Josef shook his head sadly.

'She wants you to get in touch. Gutters, is what she said.'

Josef looked at her solemnly, then poured himself another shot. He rubbed the back of his hand against his chin so that Frieda heard the rasp of stubble. 'I show you picture of my sons?' he said.

'I'd like that.'

'From their mother.' Josef pulled out his mobile and tapped its screen a couple of times, then handed it to Frieda.

She looked at the two boys, who were tall, dark, smiling for the camera, one with his arm slung round the other's shoulders. 'They're very handsome,' she said. 'And they look happy, in spite of everything that's going on.'

'Going on?' said Josef, looking concerned.

'I mean in the country, in Ukraine.'

'All right, yes, happy.' Josef dispatched the vodka. 'Happy far from me.'

'Is that what's troubling you?'

'Bad, bad times. Frieda. This is not right. I am their father.'

'I know.'

'I am scared for them.'

'Of course you must be. Are they still in Kiev?'

'Yes.'

'Do you want them to come here?'

Josef shook his head slowly from side to side, his large brown eyes deep and mournful. 'They have new father.'

'Stepfather. You're their father.'

'Look like men now,' he said. 'Not boys. Grown.'

'So you feel you've missed their childhood?'

'Is too sudden,' he said, coming over to her chair and taking the phone from her hand. 'Look. I show you them a year ago.'

He started to scroll through the photos with his stubby forefinger. Frieda watched the stream of images. And then she felt a pinching of her attention, as though something were trying to force its way into her mind; something too large and sharp to get through.

'There,' said Josef. 'One year. Boys then. Now men.'

'It must be painful,' said Frieda, softly, trying to keep her thoughts on Josef and his sons. 'Do you talk to them?'

'Skype. But is bad. They bored. I am far away. Just a memory, while they live in land of fighting.'

'Have you asked them if they want to come here?'

Something. Something she had seen. A door opened in her mind; a door into darkness.

'Every time. Every time I ask.'

He returned to his chair and poured more vodka. 'Life is hard,' he said, with a sigh, but then his face brightened. 'I help Reuben make shed in garden.'

'Reuben wants a *shed*?'

'He says.'

'That's difficult to imagine. Josef, there was a photograph I saw just now, when you were scrolling through.'

'Yes?'

'It reminded me of someone.'

'Which?' He picked up the mobile and turned to the photos again.

'There were pictures of that house you were working on last year.'

'When you were running away?'

'Yes.'

Frieda thought back to that terrible summer, when Sandy's body had been fished from the Thames, his throat cut, and Frieda had been the main suspect. She had gone into hiding in order to find out the real murderer, living in strange rooms among a community of the dispossessed in abandoned parts of London. The truth, when she finally found it, was intimate and dark, like a deep trap.

'In Belsize Park,' he said. 'People with too much money.'

'Can I see the photos?'

Josef seemed puzzled but he tapped on his phone, then handed it over.

Frieda was looking at a long garden that had been turned into a building site, with three figures in the distance, by the kitchen door, one in a hard hat. They had their backs to her, but still . . . It was the set of the shoulders. Her guts coiled and her throat thickened.

She drew her finger across the screen. A wall with a hole torn through it. Again, and a section of a loft conversion. Then a group of builders drinking tea. There. Was it? Was it?

'Frieda,' Josef was saying. 'Frieda.'

She drew her finger once more across the screen for the next photo, and now he slid into view, full on, unmistakable. She sat very still, staring at the image she held in her hand. Solid and strong, with broad shoulders. Hair clipped right down and greying now. Brown eyes with those small pupils. That amused half-smile. Yes, she remembered the smile. And she was absolutely certain that he was smiling at her, imagining the day when she would see this photograph. He had posed for her. Dean Reeve, her ghost.

At last she put the phone on the table, screen up so the figure was visible. 'This man.'

'Marty? He was my mate on the site. He helped me.'

Frieda remembered Josef talking of Marty, how he had worked alongside him; how he had covered for him when he was helping her; how he had been there when the police had interviewed him in the garden and, putting two and two together, had understood Josef knew Frieda. And she remembered, too, how this Marty had spent time with Sasha's little boy, Ethan, when Sasha was ill. Ethan had taken a shine to him. Marty. She felt the blood coursing through her body, pulsing in her wrists, drumming in her heart.

'Where is he now?' she asked.

Josef held his hands out, palms up. 'Gone away.'

'Where?'

'I not know, Frieda. Frieda? What?'

'You have no idea where he is?'

'He say he is free always. Finish job, then off again.'

Frieda reached out and turned the phone upside down. She made herself look Josef in the eyes, although she didn't want to see his expression. 'This isn't Marty,' she said. 'This is Dean.'

Josef's mouth opened but he made no sound.

'Dean Reeve,' continued Frieda.

'No,' said Josef. 'No. Big mistake, Frieda.'

'It's not your fault.'

'This is Marty. He say.'

'It's Dean.' Now Frieda looked away from Josef and into the flames. She was talking to herself, not Josef. 'The man who abducted Joanna Teale when she was a tiny child and turned her into his brainwashed wife, who abducted Matthew Faraday and would have killed him, who murdered the research student Kathy Ripon, who killed his own twin

285

brother and who slept with the dead man's wife, who killed Beth Kersey to save me, who burned down Hal Bradshaw's house to avenge me, who tortured and killed the man who raped me to avenge me, who is stalking me and protecting me and trying to control my life. Who the world thinks dead. This is Dean.'

Josef stood up. 'He trap me, pretend to be my friend,' he said. 'Tell me. I do anything.'

'He's been in my house, Josef.'

'Your house? Here? When?'

'I've had a feeling that someone's been here, changing things around a bit. He wants me to know, or suspect.'

'But how?'

'He could have taken my keys from your jacket and got spares cut.' Josef didn't reply. 'He could, couldn't he?'

'This fucking bad, Frieda.'

'Yes.'

'You must not be here.'

'I'm not going to run away again. But I have to change every lock in the house. Do you know a good locksmith who would come out at once, even though it's late?'

'Yes. My friend Dritan from Poland. He has shop on Mare Street but I know him. He come if I ask.'

At the mention of Mare Street, Frieda felt a flicker of memory, but she pushed it away for later.

'Good. And send me that photograph, please. I'll talk to Karlsson about what we should do.'

'We get him,' said Josef. He held up the vodka bottle in a kind of pledge, then drank.

'You think so?' Frieda took a sip of her whisky and waited for its burn to fade. She felt oddly disconnected, as if all of this was happening at a distance. Hadn't she known all along it was Dean, stealing into her house, putting his fingers on all of her possessions, drinking from her mugs and creeping upstairs to riffle through her drawings that she let no one see, to look at her bed, touch her sheets, run his hands through her clothes? She shuddered. How could you protect yourself against someone who wasn't really there, or catch someone if he was already a ghost?

Dritan arrived with two huge canvas bags. He and Josef shook hands and clapped each other on the back before he turned to Frieda. He was small and dark, with thin fingers, weathered skin and eyes that were almost black.

'Thank you for coming out so late,' said Frieda.

He shrugged. 'Josef asked me. I mean, told me.'

'I want every lock changed, on the windows as well as the doors.'

'How secure do you want them to be?'

'What do you recommend?'

'The double-format Avocet ABS cylinder, front and back.'

'Is that good?'

'It prevents the snap and bump key attack.'

'And that's important?'

'What people don't understand is that most cylinders have sacrificial leads that can be snapped, but the Avocet is designed to snap twice and –'

'I'll take them.'

'How many keys?'

'Two.' One for her; one to leave with Karlsson, she thought. No one else must have one.

'Rods for windows and fixing points top and bottom. Are you happy with that?'

'Look, I don't know about locks. Just make this house as secure as possible. I should have done it before.'

'It won't be cheap.'

'But will it be quick?'

'Josef will help me. We will be done by midnight.'

Frieda made them both tea, then called Karlsson but got his voicemail. She left no message. She went up to her bedroom and stood for a while, looking around her. What had he touched? What had he done in here? This house was her safe place, her bolthole against the world, where she came to be alone, and Dean Reeve had been here. She went to the bed, pulled off the duvet, the sheets and pillowcases and threw them into the corner of the room. She could put on clean sheets, but she didn't want to use the duvet or the pillows. They were contaminated. She took the sleeping bag Chloë used sometimes from the top of her cupboard and unrolled it, laying it on the bare mattress. She looked at all of her clothes hanging from the rail. He knew what she owned, what she wore. She went into the kitchen and collected a roll of bin-bags, returning to the bedroom with them. She pulled all the clothes off their hangers and stacked them on top of the bed linen, not looking at any of them. She opened the top drawer of her chest and removed all her underwear, then her T-shirts from the second drawer, then her jerseys. She swept every bottle or tub of lotion into a bag. Her perfume. Her scarves. She took the dressing-gown from the back of the door and threw that away as well, and her slippers. She took the towels from the bathroom, her toothbrush, her flannel.

In the kitchen, paying no attention to a bewildered Dritan and Josef, she took all the food from the fridge and tipped it into the bin. She poured the milk down the sink. She put every mug and cup and glass into the dishwasher and turned it on. She went up to her garret. Tomorrow she'd have to get her laptop looked at to make sure he hadn't hacked into it.

She picked up her sketchpad and leafed through it. Had he seen these? She remembered her drawing of the Hardy Tree, whose roots grew among a huddle of gravestones in St Pancras churchyard. A few days ago she'd found it was no longer there. Dean had taken it. At last she felt anger burn through her. He might have found her out, but she was going to find him.

While they were still hard at work and the house vibrated with the noise of drills and hammers – though the midnight deadline had gone – Frieda walked through the rain to the twenty-four-hour supermarket in Holborn and bought underwear, a toothbrush and toothpaste, towels, a pair of jogging trousers and a long-sleeved running top from the limited sportswear section. That would have to do until tomorrow. She also bought milk, bread, butter and a jar of marmalade; a large bottle of whisky. She saw only two other people in the shop, drifting up and down the aisles. Their footsteps echoed.

When she got back, she took a tumbler from the dishwasher, opened the whisky and poured in a couple of inches, adding a small amount of water. She took it into her living room, but couldn't make herself sit down. Energy coursed through her. The cat was lying asleep in the armchair. She drank the whisky slowly, peat and disinfectant, but still felt icily clear.

'Done,' said Josef in the doorway.

'Thank you both very much. How much do I owe you?'

'I'll send the bill,' said Dritan. 'Special discount for Josef's friend.'

'And it's secure?'

'They are good locks, the best.'

'So nobody can get in?'

'If someone really wants to get in, nothing's going to stop them. These locks will slow them down. That's the best I can promise.'

'I see.'

'Tomorrow I can organize alarms for you, if you want. Cameras in every room.'

'You think that would make a difference?'

'It would make some difference. But you know yourself, alarms go off when they shouldn't, especially when you have a cat, and the police often don't respond anyway. It's your choice. It depends on how worried you are.'

'All are worried,' said Josef.

'All I'm saying is that there's good security and bad security, but no absolute security. Every lock can be broken, every house entered in the end.'

'No alarms,' said Frieda. 'No cameras.' She wasn't going to give Dean any more power over her.

THIRTY-ONE

At half past seven the next morning, Frieda knocked at Karlsson's door and waited, wondering if he was still in bed. But then she heard the tapping sound of his crutches, a crash as something fell to the floor, a curse. The door opened.

'Frieda!'

'Sorry it's so early.'

'No. It's fine. Come in. Coffee?'

'Please, if that's OK.' She had been up all night scrubbing surfaces, scouring her bath and her fridge, washing china and cutlery.

Karlsson made his way into the kitchen and she followed him. 'Shall I make it?'

'No. I'm getting used to doing everything propped up on these bloody things. I haven't fallen over in ages.' He took in her jogging trousers and top. 'You look unusually sporty. Have you run here?'

'I threw away my clothes.'

'A spring-clean. But without spring.' He gestured through the window to the sodden garden.

'All of them.'

'Why?'

'And all my sheets and towels.'

'Hang on a minute.' There was a roar from the coffee grinder. 'There. What's going on?'

She watched him as he poured boiling water over the coffee, then heated some milk and poured it into a small jug. He did everything meticulously, taking a cloth to wipe up spilled drops on the surface. For some reason, this carefulness made her feel sad for him. He handed over her coffee, then lowered himself onto a chair, his leg stretched out.

Frieda took her mobile from her pocket and pulled up the image Josef had sent her. She passed it to Karlsson, who stared at it without expression, his mouth a hard line.

'Is this who I think it is?' he said at last.

'It's Dean, yes.'

He laid the phone face up on the table between them. 'You're absolutely sure?'

'Yes.'

'Not his brother?'

'It's Dean.'

'When was it taken?'

'Eight or nine months ago.'

'How did you get this?'

'He worked with Josef last summer on that house in Belsize Park. He went under the name of Marty. He was Josef's friend, his mate. He and Josef looked after Ethan when Sasha had her collapse.'

'I was there,' said Karlsson, very softly, under his breath.

'In the house?'

'In the garden. I was there. I think I saw him.'

'It's not your fault.' The words she had used to Josef.

Karlsson laid his hand over the phone, then lifted it up again, as though the image would have disappeared, like a magic trick.

'Josef had a set of my keys with him. He must have taken them and got them cut.'

'He has your keys?'

'It doesn't matter. I got a locksmith round last night and had all the locks changed. But he did. I knew someone had been in my house, rearranging things. He wants me to know.'

'Right,' said Karlsson. 'Right.'

'That smile. It's for me. He's smiling for me.'

'We've got to do something.'

'What?' said Frieda. 'He's officially dead. Nobody will believe me. They'll just think it's another symptom of my paranoia.' She stopped abruptly. 'You do, don't you?'

'Yes, I do.'

'Good. But who can I turn to? Who can stop this?'

Karlsson closed his eyes for a moment. 'If I didn't have this bloody cast on,' he said at last. 'We know he's in London, anyway.'

'Or has been.'

'You have to move out of your house, Frieda.'

'You think he wouldn't find me? I'm as safe there as anywhere. And, anyway, I'm done with all of that. I'm not going on the run again.'

'We've got to get the case reopened.'

'You think Crawford's going to allow that?'

'He'll have to. And you should tell Levin about it.'

'I thought of that.'

'He's got the kind of power I don't. He can make things happen.'

Levin was sitting in his shirtsleeves and braces at a desk piled with files. There was a fire in the small grate, a carafe of red wine on the mantelpiece. He managed, thought Frieda, to turn everywhere into a gentlemen's club, and he was apparently too polite to notice she was wearing running clothes and walking boots.

'I want your help.'

'That wasn't the agreement.'

'This isn't about the Dochertys.'

'Tell me.'

293

Frieda told him. The expression on his face was inscrutable. Every so often he took off his glasses and turned them over in his hands, then replaced them, delicately tapping them back onto his nose. She showed him the photograph of Dean.

'Wait here a moment,' he said.

He went out of the room, and when he returned, it was with Keegan. He looked exhausted.

'Frieda has a problem,' said Levin. 'Tell him, Frieda.'

She did. Keegan glowered at her throughout, pacing about the room. One day, she thought, he would have a heart attack out of pent-up anger, or perhaps it was only with her that he was so angry. But when she finished, he didn't argue with her. He stared intently at the photograph on her phone and then at the multiple images of Dean Reeve that Levin pulled up on his computer.

'Don't ask me if I'm sure,' said Frieda.

'I can tell you're sure. That doesn't mean you're right, of course.'

'I am.'

'I've a friend.'

'What does that mean?'

'He used to be in the Met with me. He finds people.'

'People like Dean?'

'Anyone. He's a bit like you.'

'I don't know what you mean by that.'

'Like a dog with a bone.'

'Thank you.'

'I can ask him to take a look.'

'Thank you.'

Keegan grunted and gave a dismissive shrug.

'I mean it. Thank you. After all our differences.'

'We can still have those.'

*

294

Frieda went to a department store and bought a pair of black trousers, three shirts, a thin grey jersey and some underwear. There was a thought that she had stowed away and now she pulled it out. Mare Street. What seemed like a long time ago, Yvette had told her that, according to Malik Gordon, Ben Sedge's sidekick on the Docherty case, one of the police officers, had been so distressed by the murders that she had left the Met and opened a florist's on Mare Street.

Frieda took a bus there, getting off at Dalston Lane and walking south along the canal. A few years ago, it had been a run-down area; now it was full of young men with beards and round glasses, young women in bright clothes, bars selling vegan food. After five minutes, she came to a flower shop, Jane's Blooms, and walked into the cool, damp green of its interior. There were buckets of flowers everywhere, bright and perfumed. The bell jingled as she closed the door and a young woman looked up from the counter, where she was counting long-stemmed roses.

'Can I help?'

'Is this the only florist on Mare Street?'

'As far as I know.'

'I'm looking for the woman who started it.' She forced her memory back to the police reports she had read, sitting in the small office in Levin's house. It seemed like years ago. 'Jane Farthing. Is she here?'

'Yes, she's doing flowers for a funeral. Is she expecting you?'

'No. But I won't take long.'

Jane Farthing came out from the back, wiping her hands on a large apron. She had curly brown hair, freckles on the bridge of her nose and a professionally friendly smile. 'Yes?'

'My name is Frieda Klein. I was hoping to talk to you about something that happened a long time ago, when you were a police officer.' She saw the colour spread over Jane Farthing's face and down her smooth neck. 'It's all right. There's nothing at all to be alarmed about. I'm looking into the Docherty case again and someone mentioned that you'd been involved.'

'The Dochertys, yes.' She frowned. 'Are you a journalist?'

'I'm a consultant working with the police.'

'A consultant? What does that mean?'

'It means I'm asking questions about the inquiry.'

'I'm done with all of that.' She looked at the young woman standing near them.

'I know you are.'

'Now I sell flowers. The police station's a few yards away. I see police cars racing along the road with their lights and their sirens and I'm just so glad I'm out of it. I don't want to talk about the Dochertys. I don't want to think about them.'

Frieda hesitated. 'I believe Hannah Docherty is innocent.'

Jane Farthing stared at her. Then she said, 'Come out back. I can do the arrangements while we talk.' She nodded at the young woman. 'Keep an eye on everything.'

She led Frieda into the neighbouring room. It, too, was full of flowers and greenery, and pots and vases in various sizes. A basin ran along the length of one wall, and a long table stood in the middle, with scissors and twine. Jane positioned herself at it. She picked up several thistles and laid them in front of her, then some lilies. 'I hate lilies,' she said. 'But people always want them at funerals.'

'I hate them too,' said Frieda, thinking of the time that Dean had sent her lilies.

'Why do you think she's innocent?' Jane snipped at a stem. 'There was never any doubt.'

'That's what everyone keeps saying.'

'I'm not the one to ask about it.'

'Why's that?'

'Don't you know? All my life I'd wanted to join the police, and on my very first murder case, I couldn't hack it. I was so determined not to let it get to me. If you're a woman, you'd better be as tough as anyone, tougher. But I discovered I wasn't tough. I went to pieces. I kept having flashbacks and being sick and crying.'

'It was an extreme case.'

'You've no idea.'

'Can you tell me?'

'What? So that I can have nightmares again?'

'Did you have therapy?'

'One session of counselling. It was useless. I think he was rather religious and he kept talking about evil and I don't believe in evil. Or I didn't until then. Do you?'

'No.'

'I don't remember it the way you probably want me to remember it. I don't remember it chronologically. It doesn't have a shape. It has a smell, that horrible sweet stench you can't get out of your nostrils. Rotten, foul, but almost like food. It's a smell you taste and then you feel poisoned. And it has a colour. Dark red, nearly black. Blood everywhere. There was blood on the ceiling and up the walls. Sticky dark blood.' She snipped more stems. Frieda saw her hands were shaking slightly. 'With bits in it. Bits of body. Do you understand? Little pieces of them spread around like some foul stew. And that boy in his pyjamas. And her. She was the worst. I never ever want to see anything like that again: what hate can do. The father and the brother were recognizable. But her – God. There was an eye but not in its right place and then nothing, just a mess of bone and flesh and you could hardly tell she had been a person. Hannah must have hated her mother. Except you think it wasn't Hannah.'

Frieda was surprised by her shock at Jane Farthing's account. Her memories seemed entirely unprocessed. It was like she had just stepped out of the room and was reporting what she had seen and felt. And smelt.

'I was unlucky in a way,' the woman said now, still snipping.

'In what way?'

'We arrived at the house and the front door was open. I just felt something was wrong and I was the first in the bedroom.' Jane Farthing's eyes had gone unfocused, unseeing, like someone in a waking dream. Frieda didn't know if all this was good for her but at the same time she didn't want her to stop. 'Just for a minute my training kicked in. It's funny that way. I took out my phone and called it in and then I just stood there. They got there so quickly. The photographer had been doing another job in the area. He was there in a few minutes. I think it was a few minutes. Sedge was furious.'

'Why was he furious?'

'Messing up the scene. Contaminating it. It was my own fault. You need to do the forensics first, then the photographs. Preserve the scene. I just wasn't thinking straight. It was like I was under water and everything was happening slowly and far away. For weeks, I kept thinking it had got onto me. The smell, the blood. We were all just blundering around in shock.'

'Did you meet Hannah?'

'When she identified the bodies. I'll never forget her.'

'Tell me.'

'She didn't look real. She was tall and strong and had this long, wild hair, and a glassy, glittering look to her. But, then, nothing about it seemed real.'

'What do you mean by that?'

'You read about crime in books and see it on TV and that's what comes to seem real – something you can solve and understand and sort away. This was like being in Hell.'

'And that was why you had to leave.'

'Yes.' Jane Farthing moved to the basin, turning on the tap to rinse her hands. 'And that's why I can't help you understand anything, because I didn't understand anything myself. I just felt like I was looking into a pit that went down and down, and if I didn't stop looking I'd fall into it myself.'

'I'm glad you opened your shop.'

'A bit of a cliché, perhaps.' She smiled suddenly. 'Trying to cure myself with all of this. But I couldn't think what else to do.'

When Frieda left she bought a tub of early hyacinths, several bunches of daffodils and a paper windmill for Ethan. She walked back down Mare Street carrying them, the little windmill turning, thinking of what Jane Farthing had said and of what she had seen. Who had hated Justine Walsh so much they had obliterated her face? Why had she been lying beside Aidan, in Deborah Docherty's nightgown? Where had Deborah Docherty been? And Hannah? And she thought of Ben Sedge's last words to her: *Keep an open mind. Because she killed them, you know.*

There was a message on her voicemail from Tom Morell. He sounded furtive, his voice a half-whisper.

'There was something. It probably means nothing. But that night I told you about, Hannah said something.' There was the sound of a woman calling to him and he broke off, saying Frieda should call him.

In the car park, Hal Bradshaw meets Dr Julia Styles. She is standing near his car, as if she is waiting for him.

'What do you make of her?' she asks.

'Impressive. Interesting.'

'Are you on her side now?'

'I'm a scientist. I don't take sides.'

'But you want to write a book with her.'

'With her. About her.'

'And you'll be speaking on her behalf at the hearing.'

'I'll present my findings. Is that a problem?' He waits, his car key in his hand. 'Look, the question we all face is whether we allow redemption to women like Mary Hoyle.'

Styles shakes her head. 'The problem is whether she might do it again.'

THIRTY-TWO

'Mal!' Commissioner Crawford's voice was hearty; his eyes were cold. 'Take a seat. Rest that leg of yours. Tell me what it is that's so urgent it couldn't wait.' He lifted his wrist and ostentatiously looked at his watch. 'I can give you five minutes.'

Karlsson took a deep breath. 'Dean Reeve has surfaced. I have the evidence for it.'

He looked away from Crawford's outraged face and took the folder out of his briefcase, pulling out the photostats of the photographs from Josef's phone.

'Stop right there,' said Crawford, holding up a hand like a traffic warden. 'Right there, Mal. I'm warning you.'

'This is important, sir.'

'Stop. I'm warning you, Mal. This has gone too far.'

'This is Dean Reeve.' Karlsson held the paper in front of Crawford.

'She's put you up to this. I can't believe it. After everything else she's made you go through.'

'I thought it my duty to tell you.'

'And it's my duty to tell you that you are out of order. Get out of my office.'

'If you're wrong, and it was discovered that you'd dismissed the evidence, you might not be –'

'Are you *threatening* me?'

'I'm just pointing out that there would be serious consequences.'

'Jesus, Mal.' Crawford picked up the photo and peered at it. 'Dean Reeve had an identical twin, right?'

'Right.'

'Who ran out on his wife.'

'That's what we're meant to think.'

'Listen to yourself. You'll be telling me no one actually landed on the moon next. He ran out on his wife. Here you are, then. This is him. Or just another poor fucker who looks a little bit like the man who used to be Dean Reeve but is now just ash.'

'But –'

'That's all. Time's up. Go home. Before I stop being in a good mood.'

Frieda opened the door to a man she didn't recognize. He looked about forty, short brown hair, dark eyes, a wary expression. He was wearing a blue windcheater, dark trousers and trainers. Ex-sportsman, Frieda thought. Or ex-army.

'I'm Stringer,' he said. 'Bruce Stringer.'

'I'm sorry,' said Frieda. 'What's this about?'

'Keegan sent me.'

Frieda poured herself coffee. Stringer wouldn't take anything more than a glass of water. He placed it on the table next to his chair and didn't touch it again. He took a notebook from his pocket and a pen. 'I'm not totally clear,' he said. 'Keegan said you'd tell me. Someone's bothering you. And you want to find them. Have I got that right?'

'It's a little difficult to explain.'

'I need whatever you know. A name or two. An address. The question is: what is it you want?'

Frieda paused. She remembered that difficult moment in therapy. Something, some fear or anxiety or depression, had been a part of the patient's life. Suddenly they had to give it a name, say it aloud, give it a shape, turn it into a narrative. Where to begin?

'I got involved with the police over the kidnapping of a boy called Matthew Faraday. It was done by a man called Dean Reeve. It turned out that years before he had also taken a little girl called Joanna Vine.'

'I read the file.'

'If you've read it, you'll have seen that the police believe he's dead.'

'He hanged himself.'

'And you'll probably have read somewhere in the same report that there's a mad psychotherapist who claims that Dean Reeve staged it and that he's still alive.'

'And you think he's out to get you?'

'It's a bit more complicated than that.'

'I saw that in the file as well. You were found almost dead at a murder scene involving two women.'

'They've got names. They were called Mary Orton and Beth Kersey.'

'You were alleged to have killed Beth Kersey in self-defence. But you claimed it wasn't you. You said it was Dean Reeve.'

'That's right.'

'Which seems like a strange way of getting revenge.'

'As I said, it's complicated. But, look, if you don't believe me, I can find someone else.'

'No, you can't. Or you'd have tried.'

'All right. I'll accept you at your valuation. But, still, you don't have to do this.'

'Keegan asked me. That's all I need to know. Well, not quite all. I've been around. I was in the force for fifteen years. People get caught and put away, or they're not caught and they're not put away. And sometimes they forgive and forget and some- times they don't. But this feels different. What is it with this man? Do you feel threatened by him? Do you want him caught? Do you want to meet him? What does he want with you?'

'I know what I want – to find him, apprehend him, stop him doing more harm. I don't know what he wants. He feels like something in my head, something only I can see. Sometimes he does things to me, sometimes for me. It's like he's sending me messages I can't read. It's like he's haunting me.'

'Do you believe in ghosts?'

'No, I don't. And sometimes I really used to wonder if I could be imagining it all. I've seen enough patients who believed there were enemies out there, enemies that only they could recognize. Lying awake at night, once or twice, I asked myself if this was what it was like to be mad.'

'And?'

'Well, that's the kind of question you ask yourself in the middle of the night. I was sure anyway, but then I saw this.' She took out her phone, found the photograph and showed it to Stringer.

He looked at it and shrugged. 'It's not exactly proof.'

'I don't care about proof. It's him. And he wanted me to see that.'

'Why? To mess with your head?'

'I don't know. That's why I talked to Keegan. And it's escalating. He's been here.' Frieda gave Stringer an account of the previous few weeks, the evidence that Reeve had been in the house. 'So,' she said, when she had finished. 'Can you find him?'

'I need names.'

'What names?'

'Anyone who's met him. And places he's been.'

'That's difficult. Most of the people who met him are dead or they didn't know who he was when they met him.'

'Just the names. Leave the rest to me.'

'There's Matthew Faraday, the boy he kidnapped. He

barely even saw Reeve and he was very young at the time. And there's Joanna Vine, the girl he kidnapped. She lived with him for almost twenty years, collaborated in the kidnap of Matthew. But I'm not sure she'll talk to anyone.'

Stringer was writing on his pad; Frieda saw he was using shorthand.

'Don't worry about that. I just need the names.'

'Some of it's a bit complicated. He met my sister-in-law, Olivia Klein.'

Stringer looked up from his notebook. 'Met? How?'

'He kind of befriended her when she was drunk and took her back to her house. I don't think anything happened. But I made her change her locks.'

'He sounds like an animal to me.'

'What do you mean?' said Frieda. 'What kind of animal?'

'Marking his territory.'

'Please don't say that to Olivia.'

'You've got a number for her?'

'Would you like me to talk to her for you?'

'It's better if I do it.'

Frieda gave Olivia's number to Stringer. She gave him Josef's number, and the last address she had for Joanna Vine. 'She might be rather aggressive.'

'Don't worry.'

'She's probably moved.'

'It doesn't matter. I need places as well.'

'What sort of places?'

'Where he lived, where people he knew lived.'

Frieda had to hunt through some old notebooks until she found the address of where he had lived in Canning Town. She also gave Stringer the name of the old people's home where Reeve's mother had lived and died.

'He used to visit her,' Frieda said. 'But the people there

won't know anything. And it's years ago now. The staff have probably all changed.'

'We'll see. Is that all?'

Frieda thought for a moment. It wasn't all. There was another name that she could hardly bear to say. But she had to. 'Caroline Dekker,' she said.

'Who's that?'

'Dean Reeve had a brother. Alan Dekker. They didn't know about each other. Well, not at first. The body found hanging. That was Alan.'

'Allegedly.'

'It was Alan.' Frieda felt suddenly nauseous. 'You saw my statement in the file, didn't you?'

'Yes, now that you mention it, I think I did.'

'Carrie had a terrible time after Alan was killed. She thought Dean was her husband. She had lived with him as her husband for a day or so.' She paused.

Stringer looked up from his notebook. 'Are you saying what I think?'

'I don't know what you think. But she lived intimately with the man who killed her husband.'

Frieda thought Stringer would express shock or say something sympathetic but he just carried on writing in his notebook. 'So she might not be very welcoming, but treat her gently.'

He closed his notebook. 'I'll see what I can do,' he said.

'I don't have your phone number or email.'

'I'll contact *you*.'

'I suppose it's easier to find people than it used to be, what with the internet and mobile phones and credit cards.'

'It depends how much people want to stay hidden. Usually the old way is the best, talking to people, following leads.'

'You know that he's killed several people, don't you?'

'I just find them,' said Stringer. 'What happens next is up to you.'

'That's not what I meant.'

Jack took a gulp of beer directly from the bottle. 'Can I get you one?' he asked.

'Not at the moment,' said Frieda.

They gazed at the different piles of paper scattered around on the floor of the shed.

'It's not like looking for a needle in a haystack,' he said. 'It's just like a haystack with lots and lots of hay. And it's felt like we've just arranged the hay in different heaps.'

'You've done very well,' said Frieda.

'I was imagining it like what they do after plane crashes. A plane hits the ground and explodes and it looks like nothing at all, just bits of fuselage and wires and whatever. And they bring it all to some giant hangar and put everything where it belongs and gradually the whole plane takes shape and you can see where it broke apart, where the fault lines were.'

'That's what I was hoping for.'

'Yes, but lives don't have a shape like a plane. You can order them in as many shapes as you like. It just depends on the story you want to tell.'

'That sounds a bit like therapy,' said Frieda.

'It sounds like the dangers of therapy. That's always been my problem. It's easy to create a narrative. The problem is working out the authentic, true narrative, or the useful narrative.'

'So where are we so far?'

'Follow me and I'll give you the guided tour.' Jack walked around the shed pointing at the different piles. 'This is Deborah Docherty. This is Hannah. This little pile is Rory. This is Aidan Locke. Now it gets a bit fuzzy. That pile is general family stuff. And that pile is stuff that didn't seem interesting at all. It was just stuff, brochures, programmes, minicab ads. It was the kind of thing you find at the bottom of a drawer because you forgot to throw it away.'

'We'll need to check everything,' said Frieda.

'I think I've looked at every single bit of paper. I even dreamed about it last night. I dreamed that you came to check through the papers and asked me how I'd arranged them but I couldn't remember and couldn't explain.'

'Talk me through one of the piles,' said Frieda. 'Just to give me an idea. Try that one.' She pointed at random.

Jack knelt down and lifted a printed card. 'This is the Aidan Locke pile. I think what we have here is mainly the sort of thing you put in a drawer and keep because about once every three years you might need to refer to it. Here's his NHS medical card, and there's a P60 for a job he had.'

'What job?' asked Frieda.

Jack looked at the form. 'I don't know. It just gives the name of an employer: Benson Harcourt. But it was in 1995, so it probably doesn't matter. There's his paper driving licence, which reveals that his middle name was Charles. There's a vaccination certificate for a cat from 1997. Only one, so I'm deducing that the cat is no longer alive. There's Locke and Docherty's marriage certificate. There's a pile of certificates thanking him for giving blood. He kept them with all his other documents, so he was clearly proud of them, and rightly so. There's his National Insurance card and a certificate for his ownership of Premium Bonds, which I didn't think were still a thing. And finally there's an Enduring Power of Attorney form for Ronald Locke and Jennifer Locke, who I'm guessing are Locke's aged parents.' He stood up. 'And so, Aidan Locke, that was your life. Not much to show for it.'

Frieda crouched down and started leafing through the pile. 'He got married, he gave blood, he had a cat. That's something.' She paused at the blood-donor forms and leafed through them. 'He stopped,' she said.

'Stopped what?'

'Giving blood. Two years before he died. I wonder why.'

'Are you serious? What does it matter?'

Frieda stood up and looked at him. 'Have I taught you nothing? I don't mean about crime. I mean about therapy, about life. Everything matters.'

'That's your problem,' said Jack, his face flushed. 'You're incapable of seeing something as unimportant. Not everything is symbolic. Even Freud said sometimes a cigar is just a cigar.'

Frieda smiled. 'No, he didn't.'

'Everybody knows that. It's his most famous saying.'

'Everybody may know that but they're wrong. If Freud had said it, he would have been wrong. But he didn't say it.'

'You want to bet?'

'I never bet. Especially when I'm right.'

Jack took out his phone, walked to the corner of the room and tapped at it energetically. Frieda continued leafing through the papers. She heard a grunt from behind her. She turned to Jack. 'Well?' she said.

'All right. Maybe Locke stopped giving blood because he moved.'

'No. Locke and Deborah Docherty moved in together in 1996. He gave blood for three years after that.'

'Maybe he got tired of it. Maybe he didn't have time.'

'It's something to consider.'

'Frieda, what could Aidan Locke stopping giving blood

possibly have to do with him being murdered two years later?'

'Good.'

'What do you mean good?'

'Finally you're asking a question we might be able to answer.'

Nobody seems quite sure how the Stanley knife got into Chelsworth. It may have been brought in by a visitor, passed across during a familial hug. Or brought by a nurse. Or hidden in a parcel. Or forgotten by a builder. The carving knife is from the kitchen. The scalpel was taken from the dispensary and has been hidden in a mattress for the past month. And the flick knife? Aggie Stretton brought it in herself. How? She looks at the others and laughs.

'How do you fucking think?' she says.

'Didn't they search you?'

'Yeah, they searched me.'

It took cigarettes, bags of weed, the calling-in of favours, to assemble the four weapons. They look at them spread out on the blanket almost with awe.

'That'll be enough,' says Aggie. 'Even for fucking Hannah Docherty.'

THIRTY-THREE

'I thought you were done with me,' said Yvette, on the phone.

'I thought so too. But I was hoping you could do one more thing.'

'What?'

'Get hold of Aidan Locke's medical records.'

'That shouldn't be a problem.' She sounded remarkably compliant.

'Thank you.'

'What am I looking for?'

'I'm not sure. But Aidan Locke gave blood almost all of his adult life. Regular as clockwork. Then, two years before he died, he suddenly stopped, so I'm wondering if there was a reason.'

'OK.'

'I'm grateful.'

'Hang on,' said Yvette, before Frieda could end the call. 'Tell me how it's going.'

'We're a bit stuck,' said Frieda. 'But I've got Jack sorting through all the things I collected from Erin Brack, to see if there's anything there. She was killed for a reason.'

'And you're still convinced Hannah didn't kill her family?'

'I'm convinced that it's not proven. I'm convinced there was a miscarriage of justice thirteen years ago, which has now, with the refusal to reopen the case, been repeated. I'm convinced that Hannah was not clinically insane at the time, but has been profoundly psychologically damaged in hospital. She's been in Hell. And, yes, I believe she did not do it.'

'But no ideas who did it if she didn't?'

'Not yet.'

Olivia's voice on the phone was loud and shrill. 'There's a man here.'

'What sort of man?'

'He says he knows you.'

'Is his name Bruce Stringer?'

'That's the one. He says he wants to ask about Dean Reeve. I don't know why he's come to me. I mean, I don't even know if I met him. You say I did, but let's face it, he is a bit of an obsession with you.'

'You met him, Olivia.'

'Even if I did, I can't remember much about it. I wasn't entirely sober.'

'Tell this to him, not me.'

'Yes, but he asked an *extraordinary* question.'

'What was that?'

'He asked . . .' Olivia lowered her voice. 'I don't even want to say the words.'

'Whether you'd slept with him.'

'In a word, yes.'

'Just tell him anything you remember. You don't need to tell me.'

'Of course I didn't! I would remember something like that. What have you been saying?'

'I just gave him your name.'

'Why are you dragging everything up again, Frieda? It's all in the past. Just let it go. Get on with your life.'

Frieda thought of the smiling face she'd seen on Josef's phone, the eyes looking into hers. 'You don't need to worry,' she said. 'Tell Bruce Stringer whatever you can remember and that will be that.'

Frieda was shocked by Hannah's appearance when she shambled into the room, her gait heavy and lopsided. She tried to think what Hannah suddenly reminded her of and then she had it: as a child, she had come across a dying badger hobbling across the path, dragging its bloody hindquarters, and had been shocked by how different it looked from the handsome animal in children's books. It was big, cumbersome, its coarse yellowy hair matted with blood and its eyes glaring but somehow defeated. That was what Hannah looked like now: a wounded animal in its end game. Her face looked dirty with old bruises. She lowered herself into the chair that Frieda held out for her, and winced as she did so.

'Where do you hurt?' asked Frieda. Then she addressed the nurse at the door. 'What happened to her?'

'She fell.' The nurse stared at her, barely bothering to make it sound plausible.

'Was she badly injured?'

'Bruises. She's a tough one.'

'You can leave us.' Frieda turned back to Hannah. 'Where does it hurt?'

Hannah didn't make a sound but she put her hand against her ribs.

'Can I look?' Hannah didn't respond. Very slowly, to give her time to reject her, Frieda lifted up the grubby T-shirt and looked at the mottled bruises that spread over her torso, purples and yellows and browns. She smelt sour, like a cellar where old apples have been kept. Frieda touched her where her hand had been and a groan came from Hannah. She pulled the T-shirt down again. 'You might have broken a rib,' she said. 'I'll make sure you're properly bandaged up. And these bruises must be very painful. Have you had painkillers?'

'Pain?'

'Did you fall – or were you pushed?'

'Doesn't matter,' said Hannah. Frieda was startled to hear her speak clear words. 'Everyone's gone.'

'What do you mean, Hannah? Who's gone?'

'All.'

'Your family?'

'Just me.'

Frieda paused. She didn't know if Hannah's words made any kind of sense, or if she had any real understanding of what Frieda had asked her. 'Can you tell me anything about your family? About where you were that night? The night that they died. Do you remember?'

'Do I remember.' It wasn't a question, just a dull reiteration.

'You said you met your mother.'

'I can't,' said Hannah. She looked at Frieda; her eyes were dark and fierce, the pupils huge. 'I can't.'

'It's OK.'

'No.' She shook her head from side to side vehemently, her hair swinging over her face.

'It's all right. You don't need to say anything.'

Hannah wrapped her arms around her battered body. 'Please,' she said.

Frieda touched the wrist of her right hand, where the simple tattoo of a red flower spread up towards the palm. 'This is new, isn't it? But I remember this one, the snake.'

Hannah sat up slightly and unwrapped her arms so that they hung loosely by her sides. Her expression was blank.

'And these.' Frieda touched the three crosses on the side

of her elbow, with the circles drawn unevenly at their tops. 'I remember these.'

Hannah lifted her hand and touched the larger cross with her index finger. 'Me,' she said.

'They're people,' said Frieda. 'Of course, I see now.' Crude stick figures, three of them, side by side. 'Then who's this?' She touched the middle one.

Hannah put her finger there. 'Him,' she said. A strange noise came from her and then a single tear ran down her broad cheek.

'Oh.' Frieda nodded. 'That's Rory, isn't it? Your brother.'

'Rory,' said Hannah. 'Rory.'

'But then who's this?' Frieda touched the third stick figure, so little it looked like a plus sign with a dot on top.

'No one. Never. All gone.'

She wrapped her arms back around her bulky body and began to rock, backwards and forwards, backwards and forwards, a faint keening sound coming from her and her eyes fixed on nothing.

On her way out, Frieda stopped in Christian Mendoza's office.

'You should have made an appointment,' he said.

'I don't need an appointment to say this. Hannah is a patient under your protection. She is being repeatedly beaten. Each time I have seen her, her condition is worse. I don't know who is doing it, the staff or other patients.' She put a hand up and spoke over his protests. 'But at the very least there is a wanton disregard for her safety and her well-being. It must stop. Keep Hannah from harm, Dr Mendoza.'

Josef was waiting outside in his van, and Frieda could see as she approached that he was singing along to something on the radio, tapping out the time on the steering-wheel.

'Home?' he asked, as she climbed in beside him.

'No. Can you drive me to Walthamstow, please? I told Jack I'd drop in on the way back. I'll give you directions.'

Her mobile vibrated in her pocket. 'Hello?'

'It's Tom Morell. I missed your call.' Frieda had tried him twice and only got through to voicemail.

'Yes. Is this a good time to talk?'

'Maybe we could meet.'

'OK.'

They made an arrangement to meet in two days' time at Number Nine. As soon as she finished the call, another came through.

'Yvette?'

'I got hold of the medical records.'

'And?'

'I think I can tell you why Aidan Locke no longer gave blood.' She paused.

'Yes?'

'In 1999, he had a course of chemotherapy.'

'That makes sense. If you've had chemo, you can't be a blood donor. So he'd had cancer.'

'Testicular cancer. It was quite advanced. He had his testes removed.'

'Poor man. Was he in remission?'

'As far as I could make out.'

'I see.'

'I looked at her medical records as well.'

'Deborah's?'

'Yes. There was nothing significant there.'

'Thanks, Yvette.'

'I don't see what this has to do with him being killed.'

'Maybe it doesn't. I don't know.'

Frieda ended the call. Something was bothering her, a faint tingle in her brain, like an itch she couldn't scratch.

Josef dropped her off outside Chloë's workshop and she made her way to the shed. Jack looked round from a battered leather armchair as she entered. He had a Thermos beside him and a mug in his hand; there was a storage heater in the corner that had made the air warm and dry. Near to him was a small fold-out table with a deck of cards on it and a paper opened at the crossword.

'Don't get up.'

'Coffee? And there are some biscuits as well.'

'I'm fine.'

'Or there's wine in the cooler.' He gestured towards the square bag at his side.

'Not right now. I'm glad you're making yourself comfortable.'

'Chloë gave me one of their chairs.'

'Good. How's it going?'

'I can't say I've unearthed anything very interesting. Rory was dyslexic. I've just read through a very long report by an educational psychologist. Hannah used to be very good at tennis and cross-country running. Deborah was on their school's PTA. Aidan was fined for speeding. They went skiing as a family a few times. They had a pest-control person out to their house a month before they died because they had a problem with mice. They had several quotations for a new boiler. Rory was going to go to a paintballing party the day after he was killed. You?'

'Aidan Locke had testicular cancer two years before his death.'

'That doesn't sound good. But does that get us anywhere?'

'I don't know. There's something . . .'

'What?'

318

'I'm not sure.'

Jack tipped the last of his coffee into his mouth, shook the drips from the mug, then reached into the cooler and pulled out the bottle of wine, pouring a small amount into the mug. 'Cheers.'

'Have you seen much of Chloë?'

'Chloë? Oh. You know.'

'I don't.'

'Some.' He fidgeted uncomfortably in his chair.

'How is your thinking about your future going?'

'I thought about taking a year out and seeing what it felt like. I might do a boat-building course.'

'Really?'

'Something with my hands. Chloë says it's therapeutic.'

'Do you like boats?'

'I went on a ferry to France.'

'Last time we talked about this, you said you might want to be a gardener.'

'They're both outside.'

'Do you like being outside?'

'When it's nice weather. That's not the point, Frieda. I need to step out of my own life for a while. I feel I've been suffocating in myself, if that makes sense.'

'It makes sense.'

'Good.'

Frieda looked at the open door. Outside it was getting dark and the wind gusted in the yard, rattling at the bins and scraping pieces of wood and litter over the paving-stones. 'I've got to go,' she said.

'Where are you going?'

'There's someone I need to see, though I don't think he'll be very pleased to see me.'

*

Brenda Docherty opened the door. She was wearing a soft grey cardigan and a pair of comfortably baggy trousers; her greying hair was rumpled. 'He's not here,' she said.

'I saw him through the window.'

'Then you'll know that, when I say he's not here, I mean go away.'

'There's one question I want to ask him, and then I will.'

Brenda Docherty folded her arms. 'What is it you don't understand about the words, *go away*?'

'Why is Seamus so unwilling to see me? His son and his ex-wife were murdered, his daughter's in a hospital for the criminally insane. What could be worse than that?'

'I'll tell you what could be worse: someone like you coming and opening up old wounds, making him remember it all over again.'

'I don't think Hannah killed them. Isn't that worth opening old wounds for?'

'That's ridiculous.'

'Why? Why are you so sure that she did?'

'I'm a social worker. I meet lots of people like you.'

'What kind of person is that?'

'You have a mad theory and then you make things fit into it, and of course, you can always make things fit if you're ingenious enough. You're like those people who believe Shakespeare isn't Shakespeare or that the Twin Towers weren't really demolished by a plane.'

Frieda nodded. She thought of Erin Brack and her ragbag of conspiracies. Then she looked into Brenda Docherty's face; she seemed frightened as well as hostile. 'I won't come back after this,' she said.

'There is no "this". I don't want you to come in.'

'Let her in.'

Seamus Docherty stood in the hall in the shadows, his

320

thin shape wrapped in a bathrobe. Brenda shrugged and stepped back and Frieda entered the house.

'Thank you.'

'Come through. Give us a few minutes, Brenda.'

'You don't want me to sit in on this?'

'No.'

Frieda followed him into the living room and he gestured to a chair, then sat opposite her.

'My wife is protective.'

'I can understand that.'

'She thinks I've been hurt enough. Why have you come back again? Have you discovered anything?'

'I want to ask you something. About Deborah.'

'Go on.'

'Do you know if she had a third child?'

A faint wince tightened his expression. 'A third child? No, she didn't.'

'Or Hannah? Was Hannah ever pregnant?'

'Not as far as I know. Or as far as Debs knew. I think she would have told me.'

'Did Deborah have an abortion?'

'I'd like to know why that is any of your business. She's dead. Murdered. Haven't we all suffered enough?'

'So she did.'

Seamus sighed. He rubbed his bony hands on his bony knees. 'It was distressing for her. She thought she was too old to get pregnant. It was quite late on.'

'When was this?'

'Shortly before she was killed.'

'It wasn't in her medical records.'

'She had it done privately.'

'Because it wasn't Aidan's.'

'What?'

'Aidan was infertile. He'd had chemotherapy, and also an operation.'

'I knew he'd had an operation but it didn't occur to me he was infertile. But that makes sense. There you are, then.'

They sat for a moment in silence. Frieda could hear Brenda clattering pans in the kitchen, making sure she was heard.

'Who was the father, Seamus?'

'I don't know.'

'She told you things. You'd remained close in some ways. You knew about the abortion.'

'I don't know,' he repeated.

'You can't give me any idea?'

'No.'

'Was it you?'

'No.' He stared at her, then repeated the word more insistently, 'No.'

'All right.' Frieda stood and he did too. She saw how exhausted he looked, his eyes deep in their sockets. 'Last time we met, you said you'd nothing else to tell me. Now this. Is there anything more?'

'No.'

'Truly?'

'I wanted to protect her.'

'Who from?'

'I don't know. Stupid, really.'

'Does Brenda know about all of this?'

'No.'

'You're sure?'

'I never told anyone.'

'OK.'

'Goodbye,' he said.

'It wasn't Hannah.'

An expression passed over his face, like a shadow falling. Frieda couldn't make it out – grief, fear, resistance?

'You don't understand,' he said. 'You don't know what it's like to lose your children.'

'You lost Rory. Hannah is still alive and still your daughter.'

'She died thirteen years ago. Let it all go. Leave us in peace.'

On her way out she met Brenda in the hall. The woman stared at her. 'Leave us alone,' she said. 'We're happy. After everything, we're happy.'

Frieda thought of Hannah with her bruised mouth. 'Sometimes that's not what matters,' she said.

'Leave us alone.'

Karlsson swung his way into her house on his crutches and settled in front of the fire. His leg in its cast stretched out in front of him. It had been newly decorated with stars and hearts, a rudimentary rainbow; his children, Bella and Mikey, had signed their names underneath.

'You're getting quite agile.' Frieda passed him a tumbler of whisky.

Karlsson rapped on the cast as if it were a door. 'It feels like an alien object, something that doesn't belong to me but that I'm dragging around with me. It's hard to imagine I used to run several times a week.'

'When does it come off?'

'Weeks yet. My leg will be a shrivelled white thing.'

'You'll have to do lots of physio.'

'I know. At least it's raining outside. And this is nice.' He nodded towards the fire. 'Just what I need.' He lifted his tumbler. 'Here's to spring.'

'To spring.'

'You've bought yourself new clothes.'

'Bit by bit I'm restocking.'

'You look nice.' He said it awkwardly, glancing away from her as he spoke.

'Thank you.'

'What's happening with the Docherty case?'

'Deborah Docherty was having an affair – or had had a sexual encounter at the very least. We know that Aidan was infertile after his testicular cancer, yet she had a late abortion shortly before she was killed.'

'But you don't know who the man is?'

'No.'

'Perhaps it isn't connected to the murders.'

'That's possible.'

'Perhaps it was Hannah after all.' His tone was gentle.

'Someone killed Erin Brack. That wasn't Hannah. Meanwhile, she's shut away, and every time I see her she looks worse. Time isn't on her side. I need to find out who did it.'

'What about Dean?'

'Keegan's put a friend of his onto it. He's going round upsetting people.'

'And you just have to wait?'

'Yes. You know how much I love waiting.' She looked at Karlsson's attentive face and then into the flames. 'Everything feels so dark and still. Like an ambush is coming.'

Hannah Docherty goes to a group-therapy session twice a week where she never speaks. In the afternoon she works in the garden, digging, pulling up weeds. She eats in the dining hall. She sleeps in a secure dormitory. She's under special measures, always accompanied, always watched.

'We can't get at her.'

'Just wait,' says Aggie.

THIRTY-FOUR

Jack was late to the shed. He'd been out the night before and had difficulty in getting out of bed. It was so warm in the cocoon of his duvet, and outside it was gloomy; he could hear rain still falling. His eyes felt glued together and his head throbbed slightly. But it didn't matter: he'd been through everything already and there wasn't really anything left to do. He was unwilling to give up yet, though. Frieda seemed so sure there was something there. He pushed away the thought of Chloë, who came by several times a day, nonchalantly cheerful, squatting beside him as he leafed through papers.

It was mid-afternoon and nearly dark again by the time he unlocked the shed door, then fumbled for the lights, which flickered on. He stared, blinked a few times, took a step into the shed. There was a coiling in his stomach. He sat down heavily in the chair.

'What the fuck?' he said. He sprang up again and ran towards the workshop, shouting for Chloë.

'Was this you?'

Frieda looked at her phone to check it wasn't a wrong number. It really was Jack talking.

'Was what me?'

'Clearing everything out? You and Josef?'

'I don't know what you're talking about.'

There was a silence, except that Frieda could hear Jack's deep breathing. He sounded tired or stressed.

'Where are you?' he asked.

'At home.'

'Stay there.'

'What's this about?'

But the line had gone dead. She rang him back. There was no reply. She knew it was pointless but she rang him again and left a message. Was he coming straight over? It seemed certain. She had been seated by the fire with a piece of paper and a pencil, concentrating, writing down names connected with arrows. But she couldn't think now. She couldn't even sit down. Instead she walked around the house. She would have tidied, but she had already tidied so much that there was nothing to do, except to rearrange objects. She fed the fire, and kept looking at her watch. How long could the journey be? It shouldn't have taken more than half an hour but after forty-five minutes he still hadn't arrived. Had she misunderstood him? The conversation had been so brief.

An hour passed. He still hadn't arrived. Frieda looked at her watch again: it was nearly six. Should she do something? Finally, there was knock at the door. Frieda opened it and Jack pushed past her without a word, without even looking at her. He was carrying a leather shoulder bag that brushed against her.

'What took you so long?'

Jack was walking up and down Frieda's living room. He looked like a wild cat in a cage. When he spoke it was in a highly caffeinated stream of words.

'What took me so long? Is that what you want to know? All right. I didn't come the short way. I changed trains twice and then I got out at Euston so I could mix with the crowd. So that's why it took me a long time. Is that clear enough?'

'Jack, stop with this. What's wrong?'

'It's gone. All of it.'

'What's gone?'

'The Docherty stuff. I arrived to do some more work on it at about half past four. The door was locked. I opened it, went in. Nothing. I assumed you had done it. I thought, It's the kind of thing Frieda would do, and if she did it, she wouldn't tell me in advance. So when I rang you and found out it wasn't you, I was out of there.' He paused. 'It wasn't you, was it?'

'It's gone?' said Frieda, slowly, trying to make some kind of sense of it.

'It's not some kind of joke? Or did you suddenly get worried and not want to tell anyone? If there's something you need to tell me, then tell me, because it's doing my head in.'

'Of course it wasn't me.'

'Then someone broke in and took it. So they know about it and they know about you. And me. And all of us.'

'Was there any sign of forced entry?' asked Frieda.

'Nothing that I could see. But I didn't spend time checking. There's only one way in. Whoever did it knew what they were doing.'

'And nothing was left behind.'

'Nothing that I could see. It's a bloody disaster.'

'There's one thing,' said Frieda.

'What's that?'

'There was something important in there.'

'You say it like it's a good thing,' said Jack, in an agitated tone. 'What if Chloë had been there when they broke in? According to you, they've already killed one person.'

'I didn't say it was a good thing. I said that's what we've learned. Clearly we've got to be more careful.'

'More careful than what? What else could we have done? Who knew about this?'

'I don't know. Did you talk about it to anyone?'

'Of course I didn't. Who would I tell?' Jack continued to pace around the room. 'I thought this was just like sorting out an archive. I didn't know something like this would happen.'

'I didn't either.'

'We need to call the police.'

'Sit down,' said Frieda. 'And calm down. You'll drive yourself mad, walking around like that. Or you'll drive me mad. Or you'll bump into something.'

'Fine. I'll sit down.' Jack took off his jacket and sat in an armchair with his shoulder bag on his knees. He started to tap it until Frieda gave him a look and he stopped. 'So. The police.'

'I don't think we can call the police. What would we say?'

'We'd say there's been a burglary and that it was probably done by whoever killed Erin Brack.'

Frieda thought for a moment. 'I'm imagining trying to explain this to the police. Erin stole family papers that didn't belong to her, or she helped herself to rubbish that didn't belong to her. It relates to an inquiry that has just been closed for the second time. We had the material but we don't own it. If there even was a break-in . . .'

'Of course there was a bloody break-in. I've just come from there. Everything's gone.'

'Was there any damage?'

'I told you.' Jack was sounding sulky now. 'They must have undone the lock, then locked it again. This wasn't just kids messing around.'

'I'm not doubting you. I'm just saying what the police will say. I've been here before. There's nothing to report. So what good would it do?'

'Well, wouldn't it be good if the police caught the burglar, who is probably the person you're after? Or persons.'

'That's all I want. I've been trying to get the police to do this so that we don't have to and I've failed. But now the collection that might have provided a clue has gone.'

Jack mumbled something in response but Frieda couldn't make it out. 'What's that?'

'I said, I might be able to help you with that.'

'What do you mean?'

As he spoke, Jack took his laptop out of his bag, opened it up and switched it on. 'All that stuff, the bits of paper, the receipts, was unmanageable. You could only arrange it in one way at a time. So while I was sorting it out, I put the details on here in a series of spreadsheets.'

Frieda sat next to him as he walked her through the various files and how they could be arranged by person or by time or by category. There were pie-charts showing how time in individual days might have been spent, there were Venn diagrams demonstrating where friendships overlapped, there were dizzying graphs with four differently coloured lines representing each member of the family's movements, zigzagging through each other. Graphs of financial expenditure, outgoing and incoming, even a pictogram to represent a typical day in each of the family's lives.

'This is fantastic, Jack. How long did it take?'

'I don't really know. It was boring at first, but after a while it became a bit hypnotic, just looking at these people's lives and re-ordering them in different ways, turning them into different stories.'

Frieda watched Jack as he clicked from window to window. 'When you were looking at those different stories, did anything stick out? Anything odd? Anything that shouldn't have been there?'

Jack shook his head. 'What I mainly felt is that it was just the stuff that an ordinary family had.'

'That's not the way to look at it.'

'Oh, I'm sorry about that.'

'No, I didn't mean you. I meant me. The solution isn't going to leap out. We need to ask the right question.'

Frieda stood up and walked to the kitchen. She came back with a bottle of wine, cold from the fridge, and two glasses. She unscrewed the top and poured wine into the glasses. She handed one to Jack. 'I'm probably not very good at saying thank you. Or well done.'

Jack responded by murmuring something and looking embarrassed.

'Have you seen any mention of Justine Walsh?'

'No,' said Jack. 'But if you're having an affair with someone, you're probably going to keep quiet about it.'

'I'm not convinced about this affair. Her daughter, Shelley, is adamant her mother was in no sort of state to have an affair. And if you're having an adulterous liaison with someone, do you conduct it in the person's house while one of the person's children is in the next room?'

'God knows. Going by what I've heard from patients in the last few years, I wouldn't rule out any weird behaviour at all. And have you got any better explanation for being found in a bed, in a nightie?'

'I find that even stranger. If you did actually have this assignation for adulterous sex, would you wear a nightie? And why would Justine Walsh wear Deborah Docherty's nightie?'

'Maybe Aidan Locke got turned on by it.'

'Oh, please. What's puzzling is that there's no evidence Locke had an affair . . .'

'Having a woman in your bedroom is some kind of evidence.'

'But he was the one who'd had testicular cancer and

Deborah Docherty was the one who got pregnant. It all seems the wrong way round.' Frieda's phone rang and she looked at the screen. It was a withheld number. It was probably someone trying to sell her double-glazing but she answered anyway.

'He's clever, your Dean.'

'Who is this?'

'Stringer.'

'That's how he's managed to stay out of sight for all these years.'

'It's harder than you think.'

'It's not harder than I think. As you know, I was forced into trying it myself. I had friends to help me and even so it was impossible. So are you saying that you won't be able to find him?'

'No, I'm not saying that. But he knows how to cover his tracks. Really cover them, I mean. Sometimes covering your tracks is just another way of leaving tracks. He's different. But I've talked to someone at that building firm.'

'You mean Josef?'

'No. I talked to him but he didn't have anything. But there was an electrician there, Micky. He spent some time with him and he had another name. However sly you are, there's always something. I thought I'd let you know how things are going. The next time we talk, I may have some good news.'

'The question is, what we do with that good news?'

'That's not my problem. I'll be in touch.'

Frieda put her phone back in her pocket.

'Is everything all right?'

She looked round at Jack. For a moment she had forgotten he was there. 'All right? Not really. You just stay there and I'll find us something to eat. Unless you've got somewhere to go.'

'No, no, that's great, I'd love it.'

There wasn't much in the fridge, but Frieda assembled a salad and found some cheeses and a packet of water biscuits that didn't seem too stale. Suddenly she heard Jack calling from the other room. She walked through.

'I want you to look at something,' he said. She sat down beside him. 'I was flicking through my file of their credit-card receipts. It's the normal sort of thing, supermarkets, some holiday flights, but I saw the name of a restaurant called La Strada. Sounds Italian. It rang a bell, so I did a search. She went there at least thirteen times in the fourteen months before she died.' He paused.

'I don't know what I'm supposed to think,' said Frieda. 'Don't lots of people have their favourite restaurants?'

'I cross-checked it with the timeline I made for Aidan. On the fourteenth of October Deborah spent sixty-two pounds eighty-five at La Strada. Aidan was at a conference in New-castle. On the tenth of February Deborah spent seventy-eight pounds at La Strada. Maybe she bought an extra bottle of wine. Meanwhile Aidan had a petrol receipt placing him in Manchester just after six on that evening.'

'I suppose he could just about have driven back in time.'

'I checked on Google Maps. No, he couldn't. I haven't had time to check all the others but there are at least three when Aidan definitely wasn't in London.'

'I'm going to play the role of the boring, awkward person,' said Frieda. 'There could be a family tradition. Aidan goes away, Deborah takes the children – or child – out to the local Italian.'

'I checked. La Strada is up in Bermondsey, near the river. It's five miles away. It's not exactly her local Italian. Is that where you're going to take a child on a school night, rather than somewhere nearby?'

Frieda sat back in her chair and thought for a moment. 'That's great, Jack,' she said. 'You should be doing this for a living.'

'Who does this for a living?'

'So we know that Aidan was infertile and Deborah got pregnant and had an abortion. And it looks like she was having an affair, rather than just a fling.'

'It may or may not have been an affair. She went to an Italian restaurant occasionally without her husband.'

'But accepting it as a hypothesis: who does that make angry?'

'Hannah Docherty.'

Frieda frowned at Jack. 'That wasn't what I wanted you to say.'

'I know. I'm being your devil's advocate.'

'Thank you, but I don't need any more of those.'

There was a sudden hammering at the front door. Jack started as though he'd been bitten. 'Who's that?'

'I don't know yet,' said Frieda.

'It might be him.'

'Who?'

'Whoever took everything.'

'I don't think so,' said Frieda. 'Wait here.'

She opened the door and Reuben stood there, with an exaggerated smile on his face, a bottle of wine in one hand and whisky in the other, which he held out to her.

'Come in,' she said, taking both bottles from him.

He stepped over the threshold and took off his damp overcoat. She saw that he was wearing his favourite jacket and, under it, the embroidered waistcoat he put on for special occasions. He did not remove the patterned scarf that was wrapped around his neck.

'Come and sit by the fire. Jack's here.'

'Have you come from some grand occasion?' asked Jack, eyeing the baroque waistcoat, the jacket.

Reuben was still smiling. It was starting to look like a silent, frozen shout.

'Here.' Frieda held up both bottles. 'What do you want to drink?'

Reuben pointed at the whisky. She poured him a slug and handed it across. He tipped it into his smiling mouth. His eyes watered.

'Tell me,' said Frieda.

'You know anyway.'

'Yes.' She glanced at Jack, who was staring at Reuben and pushing his hands through his disordered hair. 'You've had bad news.'

'Shall I go?' asked Jack.

'It doesn't matter.' Reuben poured himself some more whisky. 'I have cancer.'

'Oh, God, Reuben. I'm sorry.'

'Cancer,' repeated Reuben. 'Me. *Me*!'

'Do you want to tell us what the doctor said?'

'Not really. I'd prefer just to drink whisky.'

'OK.'

So that was what they did, sitting by the fire as the night darkened, not speaking, watching the flames.

THIRTY-FIVE

'Is this a good time to talk?' said Yvette.

'We seem to be talking anyway.'

'I was worried you might be busy with something. Or asleep.'

'It's ten o'clock.'

'It is Sunday.'

'Yvette, what is it you want to say?'

'I've got someone who wants to see you.'

'Who?'

'Detective Chief Inspector Ben Sedge.'

'Why has he gone through you?'

'Why shouldn't he? Don't you want me involved?'

'I don't mean that. Just tell him that if he wants to see me, he can see me. There's no trick to it.'

'I'll tell him. Is it all right if he comes straight over?'

'Of course it's all right.'

'He won't be long.'

Frieda barely had time to gather her thoughts when there was a ring at the door and Sedge was there, alone. He looked different, wearing trainers, jeans and a tracksuit top.

'I know it's Sunday. You probably have things to do.'

She gestured him inside. 'What I don't understand is why you have to approach me through Yvette. You've got my number. You only need to call me.'

'Do you want to go out for a coffee?'

'I can make coffee.'

As Frieda filled the kettle and ground the coffee beans, she was conscious of Sedge walking around, looking at pictures on the wall, picking up objects. She felt she was being scrutinized and she didn't much like it.

'Nice place,' said Sedge. 'It's good to live centrally. Do you have trouble parking?'

'I don't have a car.'

'Sensible.'

Frieda poured them both mugs of coffee and they went out and sat in the little yard behind the house. It had been raining during the night but now the sun was out.

'Lovely spot.'

Frieda sipped her coffee. 'So why didn't you just call me direct?'

'Do you want the short answer or the long answer?'

'I don't particularly want any answer,' said Frieda. 'I want to find out the truth about Hannah Docherty. That's all I really care about.'

'I'm back at work but I'm still being investigated,' said Sedge, as if he hadn't heard what Frieda had said. 'You probably already know that.' He waited, but Frieda didn't reply. 'I'm not going to make excuses. When I joined the force, everything was different. The police used to mix with the people they investigated. Sometimes it was difficult even to tell them apart. They went to the same pubs, the same clubs. My first boss used to say that if anyone stepped out of line, he'd be dealt with. Sometimes it worked, but you ended up with some coppers crossing a boundary. You probably don't understand that.'

'I think I do,' said Frieda. 'I'm a psychotherapist. We have the same problem.'

Sedge laughed. 'I doubt that very much.'

'It's true. Therapists start to identify with their patients — they want to be liked by them, they almost want to become their friends. They can delude themselves that getting emotionally close to their patients is a way of helping them.'

'That's exactly what I'm talking about,' said Sedge. 'But part of our job involves grey areas. You talk to criminals. Money changes hands. You let someone get away with small crimes as a way of sorting out bigger crimes. You make trade-offs and sometimes they're hard to justify.' He laughed again. 'It looks like I'm giving you the long version. I don't mean to sound like I'm justifying myself to you.'

'You don't need to. That's not what I'm here for.'

Sedge narrowed his eyes and looked at Frieda more closely. 'You're good at this.'

'Good at what?'

'Getting people to talk,' he said. 'I suppose that's your job. You sit there silently and you don't seem to be doing much and people just talk to you about themselves. I've done that myself sometimes in interview rooms. You go in there, you sit down opposite them and you don't speak and you wait. People don't like silence. It makes them uncomfortable, so they start to speak to fill the silence and they give themselves away.'

'There hasn't been much of a silence here,' said Frieda. 'But you still haven't told me why you've come.'

'I contacted you through DC Long because I wanted this to be on the record. There's been enough meetings off the record and unofficial investigations.'

'I don't really mind whether it's on the record or off the record.'

'I do, though. As I've tried to tell you, there are things I've done that can be made to look bad. I think I can defend them but you never know how it'll turn out. Senior people have given me a wink and a nod and said that, if I choose to take early retirement, I can get my pension and no questions will be asked. I'm not going that easily. But I've been thinking about my past, about the Docherty case. I followed the law, I built the case, I got a conviction. It's easy to hide behind that and I've spent a lot of my career doing that. I've still got some of my old sources, some contacts. All I'm saying is, if there's anything I can do . . .'

'Why?'

'You mean, why do I want to help you when you've wrecked everything in my life?'

'Yes.'

'I don't know. To feel a bit less shitty about myself. To be able to look at myself in the mirror.'

'I went to see one of your officers,' said Frieda.

'Which one?'

'Jane Farthing.'

Sedge frowned with concentration. 'She left the force, didn't she?'

'As a result of what she saw in the Docherty house.'

'They're not just numbers,' said Sedge. 'You never get used to it. People see murder scenes on TV, but they don't know what it's like, the smell of it, bodies that are still warm.'

'Jane Farthing said that.'

'I understand why she left. A lot of people do. Maybe the sane ones.' There was a pause. 'So. If you need anything, ask.'

Frieda thought for a moment. 'Did you interview the neighbours?'

'Which neighbours?'

'Sebastian Tait and Flora Goffin, at number fifty-six.'

'As far as I remember, we talked to them to find out if they had heard or seen anything.'

'And had they?'

'All I can say is that if they had it would have been a significant part of the investigation. Why? Is there something I should know?'

'They were an interesting family, the Dochertys. They got involved with people in complicated ways . . . they affected them. They left a trail.'

'Of destruction?'

'You could see where they'd been.'

'But the crime itself,' said Sedge. 'Where are you with that?'

'How do you mean?'

'I mean that it doesn't seem to make sense. Or, at least, the only thing that makes sense is that it would be done by someone insane.'

'You mean like Hannah?'

'That's a possibility. You must see that.'

Frieda shook her head. 'Whoever did the murders – she or he or they – wasn't insane. But, then, I don't think Hannah was insane.'

'But none of it makes sense now,' said Sedge.

'Yes, it does. It just depends how you tell it.'

'Like how?'

'I'm going to tell you the most plausible story I have come up with so far. It might not be entirely accurate, but as far as I can tell, it works. So, somebody wanted to kill the Docherty family, including, strangely enough, their child. I imagined doing it myself, simply as a practical problem. It's difficult to kill a whole family except with a gun, and guns are hard to get, difficult to get rid of and they make a lot of noise. So I kill Aidan somewhere else and bring him back in the boot of my car. I go to the Docherty house, but there's a problem. Deborah Docherty isn't there but Justine Walsh is, presumably to talk about their problem daughters. What can I do? I can't postpone the killing. Aidan is already dead. I have to kill Justine Walsh. And Rory Docherty. But what do I do with Justine Walsh's body? Do I take it away and dispose of it somewhere? Then I have an idea. I drag Justine's body upstairs, dress her in Deborah Docherty's nightie.'

'Bloody hell,' said Sedge. 'Is that even possible?'

'There are still a couple of challenges. I have to damage Justine Walsh's face so badly that it isn't recognizable.'

'Jesus,' said Sedge, almost in a whisper

'And I have to find Deborah Docherty, kill her and hide her body. She really mustn't be found. That would ruin everything.'

'This makes a sort of horrible sense.'

'It does.'

'But the whole plan depends on Justine Walsh being identified as Deborah Docherty. By her daughter.'

'That's right.'

'I don't want to be the guy who's still trying to defend his fuck-up – pardon the language – but if Hannah did actually do it then all she needs to do is to make the identification herself and she's home free.'

'Hannah couldn't drive. How would she bring her stepfather's body back? How would she dispose of her mother's body?'

Sedge thought for a moment. 'That crowd she ran around with. Did one of them have a car? They'd already stolen from the house. They could have had a plan to get everything.'

'And kill Rory as well?'

'A hundred per cent is a lot better than fifty per cent.'

'You see, this story explains things that have bothered me.'

'Such as?'

'Why there was a difference between the time Aidan Locke was murdered, and the murders of Rory and

Deborah, or the woman we thought was Deborah but, in fact, was Justine. It explains why Justine Walsh was killed when she seemed to have no connection with the family, except that Shelley and Hannah were both living in the squat. It explains Hannah's blood-covered clothes.'

'Come again?'

'The clothes that were found in a bin-bag five doors down from the Docherty house were Hannah's all right, but they weren't the kind of clothes she had taken to wearing.'

'Oh,' said Ben Sedge. His face wore a bemused expression.

'It explains Hannah's bizarre alibi, which has always puzzled me. She said she was supposed to meet her stepfather but she met her mother instead. Didn't that seem odd to you at the time?'

'It did – except that we thought she was mad.'

'Yes. So I'm assuming that whoever killed Aidan got him to call Hannah and arrange to meet her. That way she only had an alibi that didn't hold up and she could be framed.'

'But what about her mother?'

'I don't know.'

'Maybe her mother went to see her after she'd talked to this Justine Walsh,' suggested Sedge.

'You mean, because she was worried?'

'It's a thought. She might have known where Aidan and Hannah were meeting and gone to find them.' He gave a sudden smile. 'This is all make-believe, though. It's just one story. There must be dozens of others we can come up with.'

'I can't,' said Frieda.

Sedge leaned forward, frowning. His blue eyes were intent. 'OK. How about this? Have you turned it the other way round and wondered if Deborah Docherty might have killed them all because she was depressed or something, or because she'd discovered Aidan was having an affair and was maddened by fury? And then when she realized what she'd done she killed herself?'

'And someone else buried her?'

'There is that.'

Frieda was starting to reply when her phone rang. She answered it with a wave of apology at Sedge. It was Stringer. As she talked, they both stood up and walked inside.

'I've got some news.'

'Good news?'

'Interesting news. I'll be at the King's Arms on Camden Road at two o'clock.'

'Can't you just tell me?'

'I'll see you at two.'

And the line went dead. Sedge looked at her curiously. 'Has something happened?'

'It's about something else.'

Sedge took a card from his pocket and wrote on the back of it. 'This is my private mobile,' he said. 'You can call me any time.' He placed it on the table in the living room.

'I'll be in touch,' said Frieda. 'I want to know more about what you know. But I need to think about the right questions to ask.'

'I'll be waiting,' said Sedge.

'I'm glad you're doing this. I just wish it had been a few years ago.'

Sedge shook his head. 'It may not be much use to Hannah. God help me if I've been wrong.'

An hour or so later, Frieda left her house and headed north through Regent's Park, crowded on that sunny, blustery Sunday. She crossed the bridge over the canal and walked down to the towpath. As she approached Camden Lock, the crowd got denser and denser, tourists and students. Frieda liked markets but not this one. A few years ago, it had burned down and Frieda had rather hoped they wouldn't rebuild it, but they had, the same as before. She pushed her way through the punks and the Goths on Camden High Street and in a few minutes had arrived at the King's Arms. She looked at her watch. She was five minutes late. The pub was crowded, with people spilling out onto the pavement in spite of the chill and the sky that promised rain. It took her ten minutes to walk through both bars, past the tables, out into the little garden at the back, then out onto the pavement to see that Stringer wasn't there. It felt wrong just to stand there, so she went to the bar and bought a glass of sparkling water for two pounds. She sipped at the water, then walked slowly through the pub again, checking all the places she had already checked.

She went into the garden at the back again. A man approached her and asked her if she was there alone but Frieda gave him a look and he backed away. She glanced at her watch. Half past. Very carefully she made her way back through the pub, making sure that she checked every single person. Then she stood outside on the pavement and peered in both directions. There was no sign of Stringer but, then, the road was so crowded that it was difficult to see more than a few yards. She looked up at the sign. He had said the King's Arms, hadn't he? Not the King's Head or the Queen's Arms? And it was definitely the King's Arms in Camden? There were King's Arms pubs all over London. But this was all ridiculous. She was sure. And she didn't have a number for him: he'd been careful not to give her one.

She counted off the minutes, and at three o'clock, she decided there was no point in waiting any longer. She couldn't bear to go back through the market. Instead she walked south and cut across until she reached the Outer Circle and made her way home.

As soon as she let herself in, she stopped. She didn't know what it was. She just felt something was different. It was like a change in the weather, the feeling that a storm may be coming or that the storm has gone and everything looks a little sharper or a little blurrier. There was a smell, a sawdusty sort of smell she couldn't identify, something that was either very faint or very distant. She looked at the little card on her table that Sedge had left for her. It was facing away from her, so that the numbers were upside down. She thought that maybe she remembered the card being the other way round when she had left, but she wasn't sure. She wasn't sure at all. The locks had all been changed but the locksmith had said that no lock, however strong or complicated, could ever be totally secure. And why would someone pick those locks, come into her house and turn that card around?

There had been a few moments in Frieda's life when she had glimpsed what it would be like to lose her mind. This was one of them.

The full moon shines through the bars of Mary Hoyle's cell so brightly that it feels almost like day. She is often awake at this time of the night. Chelsworth is quiet. The screams have subsided. There is the hooting of an owl, or is it the hooting of two owls, searching out one another? There in the dark she lives in her memories, children's faces, children's voices. Each one has its own soft charge, like when she was herself a child, touching the terminal of a battery with her tongue. She thinks of the future and freedom and what she can do with that freedom. And she thinks of the present. She thinks of Hannah Docherty and what is going to be done to her. She doesn't need to see it. She doesn't need to do it herself. It is enough to anticipate it and to know it is being done and then, once it has been done, to imagine it, over and over and over.

Freedom would be good: there would be so much she could do with it. But the real freedom is in Mary Hoyle's head.

THIRTY-SIX

Walter Levin wasn't at the house but Keegan was.

'What's up?' he asked.

'It's Stringer.'

'What about him?'

'He's disappeared on me.'

Keegan smiled. 'That's what he does.'

'He arranged to meet me yesterday at a pub and he never turned up.'

'That's not like him.' But Keegan didn't sound unduly worried. 'He probably had a lead.'

'He said he had something to tell me, and that's the last I heard from him. Can you contact him for me?'

Keegan looked at her. 'You're worried about him?'

'Concerned.'

'He's never the one you need to worry about. I told you, he's good at what he does. The best.' He rose from the desk. 'Wait here,' he said, and left the room.

Jude popped her head round the door. 'Long time no see. Coffee?'

'No, thank you.'

The head disappeared. Frieda waited. She heard doors upstairs opening and closing. After about ten minutes Keegan came back.

'No luck,' he said. 'I'll keep on trying. I'll let you know when I find him.'

'Is it odd?'

'He doesn't follow normal rules.' His expression was

neutral, but then he said, 'You got all those locks changed, didn't you?'

'Of course.'

'Good, good.'

It was always easier to talk while walking. Frieda and Karlsson made their way round Highbury Fields in the blustery wind, Karlsson swinging along rapidly on his crutches, his face creased in thought.

'You're saying that you and Jack have found nothing,' he said.

'Not nothing. We know that Aidan had an affair with his neighbour. That shortly after this ended, he had an operation and chemo for testicular cancer and was therefore bound to be infertile. We know that Deborah got briefly entangled with her first husband after their divorce – he says it was brief, anyway. And that she had an abortion shortly before she was killed. He says he wasn't the father. We infer that this was an affair, rather than a simple sexual encounter. But we haven't found anything that would remotely explain why Erin Brack's house was burned down with her inside. There was nothing we found in the collection of stuff that incriminates anyone. Maybe all we've found is evidence of a marriage going wrong. Or maybe it wasn't even going wrong, just had its own rules.' Frieda paused. 'And yet someone killed Erin Brack to stop me seeing the stuff she'd collected.'

'Not necessarily.'

'What do you mean?'

'The fact that someone was willing to kill the poor woman to stop you looking through what she'd collected doesn't have to mean there was anything there.'

'What does it mean?'

348

'That they thought there was something. That would be enough. I've looked at her blogs. They're full of grandiose statements about her own importance, hints about things she might know.'

'But only in the most general terms. Is that enough to kill someone? It's quite a risk.'

'It's a thought. It's possible you and Jack have been searching for something that simply isn't there, and what's important is that the very act of searching confirms its significance. That's why it was taken.'

'Yes,' said Frieda. The wind was carrying rain. Old sodden leaves swirled at her feet. 'You're right.'

Jack called her. He said he'd been trawling online and found that Erin Brack had done an interview with her local paper shortly before she died.

'It's sort of both short and rambling at the same time.'

'Send it to me.'

'There doesn't seem to be much in it.'

'Thanks, Jack,' said Frieda. 'But now I think you should return to your real life. You've done more than enough for me.'

'What's my real life?' asked Jack, but didn't wait for her answer.

She looked at the interview. It was written by a journalist called Derek Blythe and accompanied by a small photograph in which Erin Brack appeared to have her eyes half shut. She was described as a 'colourful local character' and a 'collector', her house as 'cluttered'. There was almost no mention of the Docherty case: Blythe had focused more on the things she had found on the riverbed when the tide was low.

Frieda rang Blythe at the paper and he agreed to see her

the following morning. Then she put on her coat and walked to Number Nine.

Tom Morell was already there, sitting at a table for two in the corner in his slightly shabby tweed jacket and his double-knotted, stout brown shoes. She ordered coffee for them both and sat down. 'I'm probably wasting your time. I didn't really want to talk about it over the phone.'

'That's OK. I might be wasting yours. You said Hannah told you something.'

'Not told me exactly. Said something. When she was crying after, you know . . . It was the most intimate bit of the night, not the sex but when she cried in the dark and I tried to comfort her.'

'So what did she say?'

'She was sobbing and saying something about everything falling apart.'

'In her life?'

'I thought so. I mean it was, after all. But now I think she may have meant back at home. Her old home, I mean. She might have run away but she was still so tangled up with her family.'

'So she said things had fallen apart there?'

'Yes. I don't know in what way. Maybe with her brother, or her mother.'

Frieda thought about Deborah's late abortion. She thought about Guy Fiske. When she had met him in prison, he had talked about 'little Rory'. She looked at Tom Morell's round, sombre face and tried to imagine Hannah lying in the darkness next to him, sobbing her heart out.

'Have you heard from Stringer?' said Keegan on the phone.

'No. I'd have told you.'

'You say he told you that he'd found something.'

'He said he'd found something interesting. And then you told me not to worry.'

'Did he say what?'

'No.'

'It's a pity you didn't ask.'

'It's a pity he didn't tell me he was going to disappear.'

'I'm sorry,' said Keegan. 'We're on the same side here. Do you know who he had seen?'

'I know the names I gave him. I don't know if he followed them all up. But he talked to my friend, Josef, and my sister-in-law, Olivia Klein. And he said he'd talked to a builder called Micky, who'd worked with Dean Reeve. I directed him towards Joanna Vine, the woman Reeve had kidnapped as a little girl and later married. And also Caroline Dekker, the wife of his twin brother, Alan, whom he killed and then impersonated. Should I contact them and see if he was in touch?'

'All right. Let me know if you hear anything.'

'Of course. Are you going to tell me not to worry?'

'No.'

Joanna Vine was rather drunk and was not happy to see Frieda. She said that every time Frieda turned up in her life, she did damage. She blamed Frieda for ruining her life because it was Frieda who had understood that Dean had not only abducted a little boy, he had abducted Joanna so many years earlier. Joanna hadn't wanted to be rescued, and neither had she thanked Frieda for insisting that she was Dean's victim rather than his collaborator, although that had meant she hadn't been charged with a crime. Now she gestured wildly at Frieda, ash dropping from her cigarette onto the carpet. Her make-up was smeared and she'd put on weight. Frieda thought she seemed wretched and chaotic, and for a moment she imagined she could glimpse the terrified child this woman had once been, who had been snatched out of her ordinary life and plunged into another world. In a way she still hadn't escaped it.

'Have you been visited by a man called Bruce Stringer?' she asked Joanna Vine.

'That was your doing, was it?'

'When was he here?'

'I don't know.' She stubbed out her cigarette and immediately lit another. Her eyes looked slightly yellow and her face swollen beneath the make-up. 'I told him to get lost.'

'Is that all you told him?'

'I should be the one who can't get Dean out of my system, but it's you. I know you're meant to help mad people, but you're the one who's touched in the head.'

'Did you give him any names or places where Dean used to go?'

'Nope. I told him where *he* could go, and then I shut the door in his face.'

The next visit was less quarrelsome and more distressing. Frieda hadn't seen Carrie Dekker for more than three years and she hadn't heard anything about her since Jack had stopped being her therapist. It was she who had recommended Jack, after Carrie had discovered that her beloved and helpless husband had been killed by Dean, and that she had let Alan's murderer into her bed. Carrie had liked Jack and they had done well together, but a year ago she had said it was time to move on.

She knocked on the door. It was early evening, and dark. Rain came in gusts; the branches of the tall plane trees writhed in the street and every so often a half-moon sped out from behind the heavy clouds, then disappeared once more.

A dog was yapping, and when Carrie opened the door, she had a small, shaggy mongrel at her feet.

'You,' she said, not hostile – although once she had been very hostile towards Frieda, blaming her for the death of Alan.

'I hope it's all right just to turn up like this.'

Carrie stepped back and Frieda went inside.

Frieda saw at once that everything had been decorated. The room that used to be divided by large doors had been opened out; all the shelves that had been full of Alan's clutter were gone.

'I thought I should stop living in a museum.'

'Good.'

'Jack was very helpful.'

'I'll tell him you said so. When did you get your dog?'

'Just a few weeks ago. He's a rescue dog. When we were trying for a baby, Alan used to say we should get a dog. He's a bit like a child, a child who'll never grow up and leave me.'

Frieda gave the dog a tentative pat and he immediately rolled over on his back and stuck his legs into the air, his tail banging gently on the floor. 'I'm here for a reason.'

'Yes.'

'Did you meet a man called Bruce Stringer?'

'A few days ago. He was rather mysterious about what he was doing.'

'He's looking for Dean,' said Frieda.

Carrie bent down and stroked the dog's stomach. 'Any luck?' she said at last.

'Stringer's disappeared.'

Carrie met Frieda's gaze, and for a moment she didn't say anything. 'Do you think something's happened?'

'I don't know. Did you give him any information?'

'I just told him what had happened. He was easy to talk to.

He wasn't shocked. He wasn't pretending to care. It was just a clue, nothing else.'

Frieda nodded.

'I gave him a few photos of Alan, because that seemed as good as giving him photos of Dean. And I told him things that Alan liked doing, though I don't think he was interested in that. But I didn't give him any actual names because I didn't have any.'

'Thank you,' said Frieda.

'When I imagine him still out there,' said Carrie, 'I think I'll go mad.'

Frieda's last stop was at Reuben's house. He and Josef were both there. Josef was cooking some rich, meaty casserole and Reuben was smoking a cigarette and drinking red wine out of a vast goblet.

'I can smoke without guilt now,' he said. 'It's already done the damage. And don't lecture me.'

'I wasn't going to.'

'I'm not going to be a brave patient, you know. Don't expect me to be because you'll be disappointed.'

'That's all right.'

'You'd be irritatingly stoical, not me. No one's going to say, "He lost his brave fight against cancer."'

'You haven't lost it yet, anyway.'

'They're not going to say that because I'm not in a fucking battle. I'm the battleground. That's what. You remember that. Dying isn't a moral failure. It's not a sign of weakness.'

'I agree.'

'Good. Wine?'

'Please.'

Josef brought over the bottle and a glass. As he put them down, his phone rang on the table. She saw his eyes glance at the caller ID; then he reached down and turned the phone over so the screen was hidden.

'You should tell her,' said Frieda.

'What?' He spread his palms out; his face wore a look of bemused innocence. 'Tell who?'

'You should tell Emma Travis that you cannot see her any more.'

'I don't want to make big upset.'

'It's much kinder than not answering her calls.' She poured herself some wine, then said, 'There was something I wanted to ask you. The man who came to talk to you about Dean.'

'We drink vodka together.'

'What did you tell him?'

'I tell him names of other people at house,' said Josef. 'Builders and painters and electricians.'

'That's all?'

'All. Why?'

But Frieda didn't want to tell Josef that Stringer had disappeared. He felt bad enough already about Dean. She clinked her glass against his tumbler of vodka and took a sip. 'To spring coming,' she said.

'I rather like these storms and floods,' said Reuben. 'It feels Biblical.'

'You like them because you're safely inside.'

Derek Blythe was stick-thin with jug ears and looked like an ageing schoolboy. His suit was too big for him. He sat behind his desk in a small office that was empty, apart from a large man in a glass cubicle at the far end.

'What a thing,' he said. 'Who'd have thought when I met her that she was about to die?'

'You met her at her house, is that right?'

355

'What a tip. It sounds bad to say, after everything, but she was a bit of a nutter.'

'Did you spend a long time with her?'

'Ages. It was just for one of our little items on local characters, so I didn't need much, but she wouldn't let me go. I suppose she was lonely.'

'I think so.'

'I know why you're interested in her.'

'She probably talked about it.'

'Course she did. She was excited about you.'

'There's not much about it in the piece you published.'

'Like I said, it was just a small item and we were looking at a local angle.'

'Did she say anything about the case that wasn't in the piece?'

'She said she was in possession of important evidence but she didn't say what it was. But you must know that.'

'Do you have any idea of what she meant by "important evidence"?' Frieda stopped abruptly. She frowned across at Blythe. 'What do you mean, I must know that?'

'From your colleague.'

'I don't understand. Which colleague?'

Blythe looked at her in puzzlement. 'One of your lot came before.'

'My lot?'

'Someone came in. I wasn't here. He spoke to one of my colleagues and looked through my notes. I could have saved him the trouble: there wasn't anything, just ramblings and insinuations. He said he was looking into the case.'

'What do you mean "looking into"? Was he a policeman, a journalist, a lawyer?'

'I don't know. I didn't meet him. I was out of the office.'

'Who did he speak to?'

'I think he talked to Sally or Dawn.'

'Can you put me in touch with them?'

He looked amused. 'I think I can manage that. Follow me.'

Blythe led her along a corridor into an office where two young women, who were about Chloë's age, were drinking coffee. One was dressed in jeans and a black sweater, the other in a onesie, elaborately patterned with a design that looked like wallpaper. Blythe introduced them and explained who Frieda was. The first was Dawn, the second Sally.

'Derek said a man came in to ask about the Erin Brack interview.'

There was a silence.

'Erin Brack?' said Dawn.

'The fire,' said Blythe.

'I vaguely remember,' said Sally. 'I think.'

'The man?'

'The fire. Was that the tyre dump?'

'No, the house in Thamesmead,' said Blythe.

'It doesn't matter,' said Frieda. 'A man came in to see Derek about the interview. He says he talked to one of you.'

The two women looked at each other.

'Was it that man with curly red hair?' said Dawn.

'That was about cycle paths,' said Sally.

'Did he have a shaved head?' said Dawn, looking at Frieda.

'I don't know anything. That's why I'm asking you. Do many people come in?'

'Loads,' said Sally. 'They're always bloody complaining.'

'Or doing some campaign,' said Dawn.

'Or trying to get us to cover some stupid thing,' said Sally.

'This is really, really important,' said Frieda. 'It's about a murder. Anything you can remember would be crucial.'

'Are you sure it's a man?' said Dawn.

'Derek said it was,' said Frieda.

'No, I didn't,' said Derek. 'Or, at least, I didn't mean it. I thought Sally had said it was a man.'

'No, I didn't,' said Sally.

'I've got an idea,' said Dawn.

'What?' said Frieda.

'You're a psychiatrist. You could hypnotize us into remembering.'

Frieda gave up. She took their numbers and left.

There was a fire in the tiny grate, giving out no heat. Outside the rain dripped from gutters, and the sky was low and dark. Walter Levin sat at his desk, his shirtsleeves rolled up. He had a cafetière of coffee in front of him and a slice of cake, which looked homemade, on a plate. It was all very cosy, thought Frieda, as she closed the door behind her.

He looked up at her. 'What a pleasant surprise.'

Frieda sat down opposite him, told him what she knew and outlined her scenario: that Aidan had been killed earlier in the evening and brought to the house; that Deborah had not been there, but Justine Walsh had, presumably because of her worries about Shelley, so they'd had to kill her as well; that Deborah was killed later; that Rory was just collateral damage. He listened, his chin propped on his steepled fingers. 'That sounds possible,' he said.

'There's one other thing.'

Frieda told him about her visit to Derek Blythe. When she had finished, Levin simply looked puzzled. 'And?' he said.

'It wasn't you, was it?'

'I don't understand. How could it be me? I haven't even heard of this man. And if I had heard about him, what possible interest would I have in talking to him?'

'I don't know.'

'I mean rationally.'

'Yes.'

'You have to think rationally.'

'So people tell me.'

'You sound a bit frustrated.'

'I am, a bit.'

'The question remains simple: who would kill an entire family?'

'A member of that family,' said Frieda, reluctantly. 'But it wasn't Hannah.'

'So who else?'

'There's the father, Seamus Docherty. I don't know what I think about him. And then there is Deborah's lover, the father of the child she aborted.'

'Whose identity you do not know.'

'That's right.'

'And you can't discover who that is.'

'I don't think I can. I've reached a dead end.'

'So perhaps you're looking at it in the wrong way.'

'Can you suggest the right way?'

'Not immediately.'

'Then I'm done.' She rose to her feet.

'Am I no longer under suspicion?'

'I wouldn't go that far.'

'I'm going away,' said Maria Dreyfus.

'Are you? How long for?'

'I don't know. I'm going to Spain to stay with a friend I used to be very close to but then lost touch with. She had her busy life and I had mine. And then I thought I'd visit places I've always meant to see but never got round to, like the Alhambra, and Córdoba. Just me, on my own. It's been decades since I travelled alone.'

'Sounds good.'

'I'm a bit scared. But in a good way. I've put myself on hold for too long and I don't even know if it's still there.'

Frieda looked at her intently. 'But you're coming back?'

'I'm going away, not running away.'

'I hope it goes well for you.'

'Thank you. Is it still all right if I come to see you when I return?'

'Of course.'

'In here, I can talk about things and think about things and feel things that are impossible to talk about or think about or feel anywhere else. It's my safe and secret place.'

*After group therapy, Dr Styles approaches Hannah. 'How are you?'
she asks. 'Is there anything you want to talk to me about?'*

Hannah doesn't reply.

*'Hannah. I wonder if we couldn't give you a bit more freedom. You
could mix more. See people.'*

*Dr Styles doesn't notice a shape behind her, in the doorway. By the
time she turns around, it has gone.*

*Aggie finds them in a group, smoking, out under a tree in the garden,
unsupervised.*

'Tonight,' she says.

THIRTY-SEVEN

Frieda was told that Hannah wasn't available for a routine visit and was sent away. She called Levin on her mobile, told him, and he said he would look into it. Five minutes later he rang back and said he couldn't help.

'You can help when you want to help,' said Frieda.

'I've tried the official channels.'

'What about the unofficial channels?'

'I think that's more your department.'

Frieda rang Professor Andrew Berryman.

'So, what do you want from me?' he said.

'Why should I want something?'

'Nice as it would be if you were ringing up to chat and get together, I think you're after something.'

'Chelsworth isn't a prison. It's an NHS hospital.'

'That's right. The clue is in the name. Chelsworth Hospital.'

'We're doctors. We should be able to visit a patient, even if they're in solitary confinement.'

There was a pause on the line.

'I suppose that's technically true, except Hannah isn't your patient. But you're telling me this why?'

'I was thinking about who might know someone at Chelsworth. Or know someone who knows someone. And you're a neurological researcher.'

'All right, I get it. I'm not very flattered but I get it. The short answer is that I don't know anyone at Chelsworth.'

'Oh, I'm sorry.'

'Wait, though. Let me think for a second.' Frieda counted slowly in her head. She got to eight. 'I'll see,' said Berryman. 'There's a couple of people who might have contacts. I can't promise anything but I'll try.'

'It's also very urgent.'

'Did you hear the bit about not promising anything?'

The following day, Frieda and Berryman were sitting at Reception when a man emerged from behind a swing door. He had a shaved head and an artfully shaped reddish-brown beard. He wore blue linen trousers and a white shirt with the sleeves rolled up to the elbow. He walked forward. 'Dr Berryman?'

Berryman stood up, shook his hand and introduced Frieda.

'I'm Dr Charles Stamoran. I gather you worked with Onslow.' He spoke eagerly to Berryman as if Frieda wasn't present.

'A couple of years ago.'

'Maybe you saw my paper on minimally conscious states.'

'I heard about it,' Berryman said cautiously.

'It's a promising field.'

'Very much so.'

'So you want to visit Hannah Docherty?'

'We'd be grateful. We've seen her before.'

'Yes, I know. She's been put in a different part of the hospital. Have you signed in?'

Frieda and Berryman held up their plastic-covered passes. Stamoran led them back through the swing door into what might have been a corridor in any hospital, pictures of the Alps on the wall and posters for quiz nights and film shows. But they turned a couple of corners and then it stopped feeling like a hospital and started feeling like a prison. Stamoran knocked on a heavy door of metal bars. A security guard came forward, inspected their passes and opened the door, with the scraping and banging that, to Frieda, always sounded like a caricature of a prison door. They followed Stamoran down a set of stairs. They were in a corridor with a row of doors. Another guard was sitting at the far end.

'They're here for Docherty,' said Stamoran.

The guard was tall, pale, with greying red hair and a strange grin of welcome. 'Something up?' he said.

'Why is she here?' asked Frieda.

'Don't ask me,' said the guard. 'Why are *you* here?' He had a rural accent that took her back to where she'd grown up, and he addressed Berryman, as if he were the one in charge.

Berryman looked at Frieda. 'Good question,' he said.

'If you could just let us in,' said Frieda.

'I'm the one with the keys.' The guard bared his teeth in a smile once more. He slid back the metal plate over the grille in the door and peered through. 'Away from the door,' he said sharply. 'There's a good girl.'

It took two keys to open the door, which swung inwards. Hannah was backed into one of the corners. The room was white, brightly painted. There was a bed, a lavatory, a wash-bowl and nothing else. She was dressed in grey tracksuit trousers, a maroon sweatshirt and white trainers. Berryman and Frieda stepped into the cell. When Stamoran made as if to follow them, Frieda stopped him with a look. 'If you could just give us a moment,' she said.

He shrugged and stepped back outside. The door was pushed shut but there was no sound of a key turning in the lock. Frieda looked at Hannah. Her eyes seemed red and inflamed but that might just have been the brightness of the light in the cell. Around one of them was a circular purple and yellow bruise. She had a large plaster on one cheekbone.

Her lip was split and swollen. There were dried bloodstains round one nostril. There were bruises on the backs of both hands and on the knuckles, red and purple, and mottled marks around her neck as though someone had squeezed it. When she opened her mouth, Frieda could see two teeth were newly missing.

'Back in solitary,' said Berryman, almost to himself. 'And look at the state of her.'

'What's been happening, Hannah?' asked Frieda.

She just shook her head. It was more like a twitch, as if she was trying to dislodge something. Frieda stepped closer but Hannah tried, impossibly, to squeeze herself further into the corner, so she stopped.

'I hoped we could talk.' Frieda spoke softly. 'I hoped we could help each other.'

Hannah gave no sign of having heard. She continued moving her head from side to side. Now Frieda moved slowly closer, as if she were approaching a terrified wild animal. When she was just inches away she put up her hands and held Hannah's head with them. 'It's all right. You're safe with us.'

'It's no good,' said Berryman. 'She's entirely non-responsive. You can see it in the eyes.'

'She can respond in different ways.' Frieda took her hands from Hannah's head and stepped back. 'Hannah, can you show us your tattoos? All of them.'

Now Hannah raised her head and looked at Berryman, then back at Frieda.

'Go on,' said Frieda. 'It'll be all right.'

Hannah took a few shuffling steps forward until she was in the middle of the room. She reached down, took hold of the edge of her sweatshirt and, wincing from the pain in her ribs, pulled it over her head. Underneath, she had a floppy blue T-shirt. She took that off in the same way. She wasn't wearing a bra.

'I'm not sure I'm comfortable with this,' said Berryman. He turned so that he was looking into an opposite corner.

'We're both doctors,' said Frieda.

'We're not doing this as doctors.'

'Yes, we are.'

Hannah kicked off her trainers, pulled down her trousers and stepped out of them. She was wearing only grey socks and faded white knickers. She reached for the waistband of the knickers.

'That's all right,' said Berryman, who had turned his head. Hannah stopped. 'Unless you think we're likely to miss a crucial tattoo.'

Hannah stood in the centre of the room. The harsh light illuminated her from above, emphasizing her extreme pallor, her injuries, and the blue and black, red and green garishness of the tattoos. They were everywhere, even on her bruised ribs, her breasts: her pale brown nipples were the centres of intricate lines. Frieda walked round her, observing her from every angle. She saw that there were cigarette burns on Hannah's shoulders and thighs.

'I don't like this,' said Berryman. 'It feels like the Victorian age where doctors displayed patients like freaks.'

'You're talking about Hannah as if she wasn't here.' She looked at Hannah, who met her gaze properly for the first time. 'Thank you for showing us these. They're beautiful.' She looked round at Berryman. 'Tell me what you see.'

Berryman walked closer to Hannah and faced her directly. 'We're looking at you because we want to help you. Do you understand?'

Hannah looked away but it didn't seem like a refusal, so Berryman shifted his attention from her face to her body.

'There's a dragon, surrounded by flames. I guess that figure there' – he pointed at her upper back – 'is the devil or some sort of demon. Complemented by a skull on the other side. And a butterfly and some Chinese lettering. I'd always worry about having one of those. You have to take it on trust and hope it isn't something crazy.'

'Those are your family,' said Frieda, pointing to the three wonky crosses. 'You and Rory and the foetus who was never born. Around that shape are teardrops or almonds or I thought they may represent the pomegranate seeds that condemned Persephone to the underworld. And on your stomach, you've got a coiled snake. And on your breasts an abstract pattern, like a spider's web or a dreamcatcher. What were they for, Hannah? What do they mean to you?'

Berryman picked up Hannah's clothes and handed them to her. 'Thank you for that,' he said.

She pulled them on.

'I'll be back,' Frieda said to her. 'Soon.'

As they stepped out of the cell, and the door was shut and locked, Frieda and Berryman looked at each other.

'She didn't do those tattoos herself,' Frieda said.

'I don't understand you.'

'What do you mean?'

'You're a psychotherapist. You're a doctor. You've just seen that damaged girl, locked in solitary confinement, away from people, away from the outside world. And you're thinking of, what? Evidence? Clues? Doesn't Hannah Docherty just need help?'

'Showing that she didn't kill her family looks like the best we can do for her.'

'I think it may be a bit late.'

'But it might help her to get somewhere safer, more comforting.'

Berryman paused. His expression was bleak. 'All right,' he said finally. 'Clearly she couldn't tattoo a dragon on her own back. So what?'

Frieda turned to the warder. 'Hannah's tattoos look professional. Someone in here must have done them.'

The warder looked wary. 'Tattooing's against the rules. They do it anyway. No stopping them.'

'I don't care about the rules. The woman who did it. Is she still here?'

'Why would you want to know that?'

'We need to see her. And, by the way, when is Hannah getting out of solitary?'

'She should be out already. The paperwork got lost.'

'Please find it,' said Frieda.

'It's for her own good.'

'Does it look like that?'

Kaz Hoolihan was seventy but she looked much older. She was gaunt, and half her teeth were gone, so that she whistled and wheezed while she talked. Her hair was so thin that the scalp was plainly visible. When the warder led them to her, she was sitting on a bench outside, smoking a roll-up.

'It's good she's allowed out alone,' said Frieda.

'She's all right, Kaz is,' said the warder. 'They've kept her here for her own good, really. It's like her home.'

The warder left them and Frieda and Berryman approached her. They introduced themselves and sat on either side of her. Small and wizened, she was almost lost between them.

'We've just seen Hannah Docherty,' said Frieda. 'We saw your work on her. Your tattoos.'

Kaz had finished her cigarette. She took a cigarette paper from her pocket and a pack of tobacco, then assembled a new one. Her hands were trembling and there was the occasional breath of wind so the process was halting and spasmodic. Frieda and Berryman watched her in silence until the new cigarette had been lit.

'How does it work?' Frieda continued. 'Do people design their own tattoos?'

'Depends.'

'What about Hannah's?'

'Long time ago mostly.'

'I wanted to know why she chose those tattoos.'

'Ask her.'

'You know we can't ask her.'

'You can *ask* her,' said Kaz. 'Won't say nothing.'

There was a strange wheezing, coughing sound, which Frieda realized was a laugh.

'She has a dragon on her back.'

'I do lots of dragons.'

'Why do people want them?'

Kaz looked up at Frieda in disbelief. 'Fucking locked up, aren't we? Dragons are freedom.'

'Then there was a devil. What was that about?'

'It's your demon.'

'You mean, like your personal demon?'

'No. Like you deal with your own demons, right?'

'Is that something Hannah particularly wanted?'

Kaz shook her head. 'They've all got their demons. There's lots of demons here.'

'Then there was the skull, which I suppose is death.'

'Maybe. But they all like skulls. I do good skulls.'

'And the butterfly.'

'The butterfly's girls. You know, and . . .' she moved her hands around '. . . like life. Like going from one thing to another, like a butterfly. Things change.'

'We're not getting anywhere,' said Frieda. 'Wasn't there

369

anything Hannah specially wanted? Something that was personal to her?'

'That was years ago. Don't see her much. She's funny.'

Frieda closed her eyes and tried to remember all the marks on Hannah's pale skin. There was so much clutter, so much noise. What was left? What hadn't she thought of?

'There was a little one,' she said. 'Not much more than a line. And a little scrawl at the front. A pattern.'

'A locket,' said Kaz.

'What?'

'I just remembered when you said. A locket. That's what she asked for.'

'What for?'

'It was her ma.'

'You mean it reminded her of her mother?'

'It was her ma's. She found her dead. All she knew her by was her locket. She wanted it on her neck. Couldn't have the real one.'

'But . . .' Frieda began, and then she stopped. Suddenly she stood up. 'We've got to go.' She looked at Kaz. 'Thank you for your help. But we have to go. I've got something to do.'

Kaz muttered something that Frieda couldn't properly make out.

'What was that?'

She muttered again.

'Trouble?' said Frieda. 'Did you say that Hannah is trouble?'

Kaz shook her head. 'She's *in* trouble.'

'You look well,' says Hal Bradshaw.

'I feel well,' says Mary Hoyle. 'I feel very well.'

THIRTY-EIGHT

When Levin saw her he said simply, 'Well?'

'I've got it.'

He nodded at her. 'Good.'

And then Frieda understood – like a light going on in a room that had been wrapped in shadows, and she could see clearly at last.

'You always knew,' she said.

'I'm sorry.' He took off his glasses and polished them. 'I don't know what you're talking about.'

'That's what I was brought in for. Nothing to do with ticking boxes. You knew all along. I'm right, aren't I?'

He beamed at her.

'You knew I wouldn't stop.'

'And you didn't.' His tone was still genial.

'You used me.'

'If you've found the answer, isn't it worth it?'

'That's not the point.'

'It's always the point.'

Without saying another word, Frieda took the file he was holding and walked briskly back to her house. She needed the walk to calm herself down, to settle herself down, to prepare herself.

She arrived at home, threw off her jacket, then opened the file and spread the contents – the photographs of the Docherty crime scene – on her table. She started to arrange them. What was it that Jane Farthing had said? The photographer had been working in the area, so he had arrived very quickly. One by one she put the photographs of Rory Docherty and Aidan Locke back in the file until she was left with those of Deborah Docherty. That was the name written on the back of the prints but, of course, they were really of Justine Walsh.

She leaned down and looked closely. It was growing dark and she couldn't see clearly enough. She went upstairs, fetched her desk light, plugged it in, placed it on the table and switched it on. There. There were three photographs showing the battered head. Then, slowly and deliberately, she moved the photograph on the right to the left. And then she knew. She picked up her phone and dialled Ben Sedge.

'Can you do me a favour?' she asked.

Frieda, Ben Sedge and Yvette Long were shown into a conference room. It had a long, laminated table, ten leatherette chairs and a view over West Norwood on a rainy Tuesday morning: car showrooms, superstores and the steel framework of a tall building flanked by giant cranes. The three sat down at the table.

'Thanks for sorting this out,' said Frieda.

Sedge gave a nod of acknowledgement.

'What's this about, Frieda?' asked Yvette.

'I already told DCI Sedge. I'm done with this. I just wanted to pass on a couple of things and move on.'

'Move on?' said Yvette. 'Since when do you move on?'

The door opened and two men in suits came in. They looked impatient, as if the meeting had already gone on too long. One of them was DCI Waite. The other was heavily built, with dark hair, parted on one side. His face was jowly, with pockmarked skin. 'I'm DCI Lumsden,' he said. 'DCI Vic Lumsden. And I'm in a hurry.' He nodded across the table. 'Good to see you, Ben.'

'Likewise. Thanks for seeing us.'

'No problem. But we'll have to be brief. I've got a meeting.'

Lumsden and Waite sat opposite them. Frieda felt as if she was trying to sell them something they didn't want to buy. She looked at Waite. 'I'm glad you could come too.'

'I didn't think I'd be seeing you again,' he said.

'How's the Erin Brack investigation going?' she asked.

'Don't push it.'

'I'm just asking as a citizen.'

'I said don't push it.'

'Hang on,' said Lumsden. 'I think you'd better tell us what this is about.'

'I've been wanting to meet you,' said Frieda. 'You're the officer who didn't reopen the Hannah Docherty case.'

'That's right. I know about you too. I don't really understand why you're involved in this case but you'd better say your piece and we can get on with our work.'

With exaggerated care, Lumsden removed his wristwatch and laid it on the table in front of him. The clock was running.

'I went to see Hannah Docherty yesterday. She wasn't very communicative. She's not in a good way.'

'I've heard that,' said Lumsden.

'But I looked at her tattoos.'

There was a pause. Lumsden looked at Waite, then back at Frieda. He seemed to be barely suppressing a smile. 'Her tattoos? Anything to report?'

'One of them is around her neck. I talked to the inmate who drew it. She told me it represents the locket that was on the body when Hannah saw it. It was what she used to identify her mother.'

'And this is interesting?'

'When I heard this I remembered the inventory of what

was found on the bodies in the Docherty house. There was indeed a locket.'

'All right.'

'Here's a photograph of the body at the crime scene.' Frieda took a photograph from the file she had brought with her and slid it across the table. Lumsden looked at the picture and flinched slightly. 'I know,' said Frieda. 'It's horrible. But I meant you to look at the locket round her neck.'

Lumsden pushed the picture back to Frieda. 'All right. Hannah has a tattoo of the locket. The locket is mentioned in the inventory. The locket duly appears in the crime-scene photo. What is the problem?'

'What I expected you to say was something like, "Hang on, the body isn't Deborah Docherty, it's Justine Walsh. Why is the locket on her neck?"'

'Because the murder was staged,' said Lumsden.

'So what you're saying,' said Frieda, 'is that whoever killed Deborah Docherty, removed the locket from her neck and placed it on the neck of the dead Justine Walsh in order to aid the false identification. Is that what you're saying?'

Lumsden thought for a moment. 'Yes, that's what I'm saying.'

'Good. I agree.'

'Well, I'm glad you agree, Doctor. But we already knew that the murder was staged. We already knew that whoever killed Justine Walsh also killed Deborah Docherty. You're telling us nothing new.'

Frieda pushed the photograph back across the table. 'The photograph is time-coded. What time does it say?'

Lumsden took a pair of glasses from his pocket and put them on. 'Two thirty-eight,' he said.

Frieda took another photograph from her file. 'Look at the time on this one.'

He leaned down. 'It's earlier. Two eleven.'

'Look more closely.'

'At what?'

'At her neck. At the locket.'

Lumsden looked up. 'What the fuck?'

'It's not there.'

Lumsden passed the photograph to Waite. 'What's that mean?' he said.

'Think about it,' said Frieda.

'I am thinking about it and it makes no sense.'

Slowly Frieda turned her gaze to Ben Sedge. 'Mostly, when people commit murder, they go blank. Sometimes they don't even remember doing it. They go haywire. But you didn't.'

Everything was happening in slow motion. The faces of Lumsden and Waite clicked through expressions: incomprehension, incredulity, and then a strange dawning. Sedge stared at her. He opened his mouth and from his chest came a booming sound. He was laughing, but it didn't sound like laughter. 'You are certifiably insane,' he said.

Frieda gazed at him, into his blue eyes. 'It wasn't an impetuous crime, and even when things went a bit wrong, you kept thinking clearly all the way through. When you arrived at the Docherty household with the dead body of Aidan Locke, you found Justine Walsh there instead of Deborah.'

'You are insane,' repeated Sedge. 'This is ridiculous. Vic, tell her to shut up.'

Lumsden didn't move. His jaw hung loose. She could see sweat on his forehead.

'Justine Walsh was looking for her daughter and you killed her. You then dressed her in Deborah Docherty's nightie and arranged her as if she were Deborah Docherty, in the bed beside her dead husband.'

Sedge rose. 'I'm not staying to listen to this crap.'

But Yvette had now stationed herself by the door and the big man stood in the centre of the room, his arms hanging by his sides. He looked like a bull trapped in a bull-ring.

'Stay where you are,' said Frieda. 'We talked about different stories last time we met. This is the true story. You killed Justine Walsh. You killed Rory Docherty. I think that might have been hard. You put him face down: probably you couldn't bear to look at his face. After all, what had that little boy done to you?'

'Vic,' said Sedge. 'Vic, you don't believe this, do you? This is *me* she's talking about.'

Lumsden stared at him, his face wiped clean of any expression. The silence in the room was absolute. 'Go on,' he said to Frieda.

She nodded and looked back at Sedge. 'You smeared Rory's blood downstairs, just to confuse things. Which it did. Then you had to find Deborah Docherty, kill her and bury her. Her locket. That was another inspiration. You make an anonymous call to the police and make sure you're first on the scene and put the locket on Justine Walsh. All you need is to get poor, troubled, traumatized Hannah to make the identification and you're free. There was a bit of a problem, though. A junior officer, Jane Farthing, went straight up to the room and called in reinforcements. The photographer was in the area and arrived too early. But you made a fuss about him contaminating the scene, got him out and put the locket on. But you didn't realize he'd already taken a photograph.'

'It could have been anyone,' said Sedge. 'Anyone.' His voice cracked. 'It could have been anyone,' he repeated.

'Jane Farthing?' said Frieda. 'The photographer? I'm sure DCI Lumsden will check. And DCI Waite could check with the staff at the *Thamesmead Gazette*: someone came asking about Erin Brack and what she knew. Because, of course, there was a fifth murder, thirteen years later.'

'Vic?' repeated Sedge. 'Vic?'

'Yes,' said Lumsden, slowly. 'I will check.' He gazed at Sedge with an expression of puzzlement.

Frieda had seen dynamite demolish buildings from her consulting-room window. After the explosion they would stand for a few moments, holding their shape, then their edges would lose solidity and all of a sudden the edifices would waver, then dissolve into a shower of bricks and mortar. Now Sedge's face lost its fixed expression of outrage; his body seemed to fold in on itself. He no longer looked tall, bulky and strong, but diminished. For a moment he staggered backwards. Yvette stepped forward, pulled his chair out for him and he sank on to it. He lowered his head into his hands. No one said anything. There was no sound in the room, except for the hum of the heating and the drip of rain outside.

When he looked up at last, he spoke to Frieda. 'My wife said I was a good man,' he said. 'And I am. I am. I joined the force because I wanted to make the country a better place. I'm a good man who's done bad things.'

Frieda stared at him. She was thinking of all the people she had known who somehow managed to separate what they did from who they were – as if there was a single, irreducible self that was untouched by experience. Sedge had killed five people and wrecked the life of a sixth, yet he still believed that his true self, the self he felt to be fundamentally good, was intact.

'I loved her,' said Sedge.

'Deborah.'

'And she loved me. We met because of Hannah. She came to the station once when Hannah had got into trouble again and we talked.'

'That wasn't in the records.'

'It was. It isn't now.'

'You are entitled to a lawyer,' said Lumsden, suddenly, his voice gravelly. 'If you're going to make a statement, you can call someone.'

'I'm not making a fucking statement, Vic. I'm making a confession.' He nodded at Frieda. 'I'm making a confession to you.'

'What for?' Frieda felt almost dulled by the misery of it. 'Who is there left to forgive you?'

'We were in love. She was like no one I'd ever met. She made me alive. I was going to leave Laurie and she was going to leave Aidan. If she'd kept to her promise, this would never have happened. But then she changed her mind.'

'Because of Rory?'

'There was that business with his bastard of a teacher. He was in a bad way.'

'And she also had a late abortion. I assume you were the father.'

'I'd always wanted a child. Laurie couldn't –' He broke off. 'Deborah thought she was too old to get pregnant, but it happened. It was meant to be. Then, without even talking to me about it, she murdered our child. She did that and then she left me.'

'So you killed her.'

'I needed to show her what it's like to lose everything.'

'And Rory? What had he done?'

Sedge looked entirely impassive. 'She killed *my* child.'

'And Hannah? Was she just collateral damage?'

'There had to be someone to blame. She was on the way down anyway.'

'So she basically deserved what she got?' said Frieda.

'Deborah told me that Aidan was going to see Hannah to

sort things. Playing happy families. That was my chance to really show them.'

'But you didn't know Deborah would go to see her as well, when he didn't come back.'

'It worked out all right.'

'And then poor deluded Erin Brack.'

'You know how it is. You plug one leak and it just starts somewhere else.'

Mary Hoyle lies awake, happy in the knowledge of what is happening elsewhere. It's like she's doing it with her own hands, as if she's wielding the blades herself.

And then she's asleep and then, for a moment, she doesn't know if she's awake or asleep. She can feel a pressure on her chest and on her neck. A face is looking down at her, eyes looking into hers, as if in curiosity.

'Look,' says Hannah Docherty.

Look at what?

'The children,' says Hannah Docherty. 'Think of children.'

Mary Hoyle could say to Hannah Docherty: I think of the children every night. I think of them and I don't care. But she can't say it and she can't call out or scream because there is something around her neck, a cord or a wire. Her arms are flapping helplessly, uselessly. It's all too late.

She wonders how Hannah Docherty can be here and she sees a glimmer of keys, a rattle.

She sees a flash of something else. She sees that it is metal and that it is a blade and then she has time to wonder if it is one of those blades, the Stanley knife, the scalpel . . . What were the others? Hannah Docherty leans in close. Sweet breath. A flash of the blade.

'Your blood,' says Hannah. 'You're tasting.'

Yes. It is wet and warm and tastes of iron.

'Think of the children,' says Hannah. 'You're first I've killed. First.'

First. That sounds strange to Mary Doyle. And it's the last word she hears and Hannah Docherty's face, blurry in the darkness, is the last face she sees.

THIRTY-NINE

As soon as she arrived at Chelsworth Hospital, Frieda knew something was wrong. Everyone seemed to be expecting her, yet how could that be? She'd called Josef from the police station and he'd driven her straight there and for once she hadn't objected when he broke the speed limit. It had felt, after Hannah's thirteen years of incarceration, as if every minute counted. At Reception, the man behind the desk just nodded when he heard her name and lifted the phone. He said that Christian Mendoza and Charles Stamoran would see her immediately. He gave her the pass and she was led through the security barriers, down corridors, up the winding staircase, and into Mendoza's large and light-filled office.

'How did you know?' asked Mendoza. He was thin-lipped and sombre; he wasn't wearing his round spectacles and his eyes looked small and defenceless. She saw he still had on his bow-tie.

'I don't understand,' said Frieda. It felt like the wrong question.

'How did you know about Hannah?'

'I always felt there had been a miscarriage of justice, but I've only just found out exactly what happened. How did *you* know?'

Mendoza peered at her as though he were having trouble making her out clearly. 'What are you talking about?'

'I'm just puzzled how you already knew I had discovered the real murderer. I've told no one, so who told you?'

'I think you should sit down,' said Stamoran, uneasily.

'I'd like to see Hannah at once.'

'You don't know about her?' Mendoza frowned.

'I know that the officer in charge of the inquiry thirteen years ago killed the Docherty family and framed Hannah. I know that Hannah has been held here for thirteen years for a crime she didn't commit.'

'You're too late,' said Stamoran, in a soft voice.

'What do you mean?'

'We thought you were here because you'd heard.'

'Heard what?' Neither of the men answered. 'Heard *what*?'

Mendoza looked down at some papers on his desk, then back up at Frieda before speaking.

'Last night, Hannah Docherty injured two other patients.'

'Severely,' said Stamoran.

'Yes, very severely,' said Mendoza. 'She then gained entrance to the secure room where a woman called Mary Hoyle was being kept. She stabbed her with a Stanley knife.'

'Is she badly hurt?' asked Frieda.

'Oh, she's dead,' said Stamoran.

'So,' said Mendoza, 'your news makes no difference.'

'Last night,' said Frieda. She looked out of the large window, onto the lawns and beyond them the woodland. She had imagined walking out of here one day with Hannah by her side, taking her back into the world. She could feel the blood beating in her temples.

'The hospital's in lockdown,' said Mendoza.

'You knew she was being bullied and abused,' said Frieda to him. 'You saw her covered in bruises, with a broken rib. You let it continue.'

'That's not true.'

'This isn't the end. Hannah was pushed beyond what any human could endure: beaten up, drugged, placed for weeks on end in solitary confinement. Whatever terrible things she did last night, she cannot be held responsible for them.'

'It's not about fault,' said Stamoran. 'It's about capacity.'

'What do you mean?'

'Do you think any doctor, legal body or politician in the country would find her fit to be released?'

'Listen.' Frieda put both hands on the wooden surface and leaned towards the two men. 'Thirteen years ago, when she was barely an adult, Hannah's entire family were savagely murdered. Imagine how she would have felt. And then she was charged with the crimes and found guilty. Imagine that. She was sent here, to be kept safe from herself and from others, to be cured, and has been repeatedly assaulted and tortured. Do you think I'm going to walk away from this?'

'I've no idea what you'll do,' said Mendoza.

'I want to see Hannah.'

'I'm not sure that's a good idea.'

'I don't care what you think. I want to see her. I'm not leaving until I do.'

'Why not?' said Mendoza, suddenly. 'What harm can it do now?'

Hannah was in the same little room as she had been the last time Frieda and Andrew Berryman had seen her, and was sitting hunched up in the far corner, her knees under her chin, her arms around them, her hands pushed into the opposite sleeves of her oversized top, her matted tangle of dark hair hanging over her face, like a curtain.

'You can go,' said Frieda to the male nurse.

'It's not safe.'

'Ask Dr Mendoza if you need his permission. Or watch us through the grille if it makes you happier.'

Frieda stepped into the room and the door shut with a small clang. Hannah didn't move. There was a heavy, rancid smell in the room: blood, sweat, shit, fear.

Frieda sat on the floor beside Hannah. 'I know what happened last night.'

From behind the greasy fall of hair she heard a muttering sound, but could make out no words.

'Can you hear what I'm saying, Hannah?'

Hannah lifted her head. Her face was mashed almost beyond recognition, her nose swollen, one ear bandaged, a stitched gash running like a terrible smile from her mouth. There was blood even on her teeth. Her dark eyes glittered.

'I know about it,' said Frieda. 'I know why you did what you did.'

Hannah took her hands from her sleeves and held them out. At first Frieda thought they were still red with the blood of her victims, but then she saw that they were lacerated and bruised, with a torn nail.

'I showed them,' she said, in her low voice, gravelly from disuse.

Frieda tried to keep her face clear of expression. 'I want you to listen,' she said, slowly and clearly. 'I came this morning about something else. I know who killed your family, Hannah. I know it wasn't you and so do other people now.'

She looked across. Hannah was staring straight ahead. Frieda took Hannah's face in her hands. 'Just once, I want you to look at me. Look me in the eyes as I say what I'm going to say.' And the two women looked at each other as

Frieda told her what she'd discovered, and Frieda felt she was speaking to herself as well as to Hannah.

When she had finished, Hannah made no response. Frieda put out a hand to touch her arm. 'Your mother loved you, in spite of everything that had happened between you. She was worried and that's why, that evening, after she'd talked to Justine Walsh, she went to find you.' She had started the story hesitantly, but now she felt on sure ground. She knew how it had all unfolded, could almost see it. 'The alibi you gave was true, though of course no one believed it, because no one knew she wasn't the woman lying in bed beside your stepfather. She loved you, and you loved her. You didn't kill her.'

Hannah made a small noise, like the beginning of a word, then stopped. Her eyes shone in her ruined face, her ripped mouth worked.

'And you didn't kill Aidan. However complicated your feelings were towards your stepfather, you didn't harm him.'

She stopped. Silence filled the little room. Frieda could feel the tick of her heart.

'You didn't kill Rory,' she said softly.

'No,' said Hannah – or Frieda thought that was the word she had spoken.

'You always looked after Rory. You protected him. You fought for him. You didn't kill him.'

'Not me,' said Hannah. Perhaps it was a question.

'Nothing can bring him back, or your mother. Nothing can bring back your lost years. But I want you to know that, although last night you killed a woman, I will do everything in my power to help you leave this place.'

It was very still in the room, and the floor was cold. The lights above them flickered briefly.

'Hannah, do you understand?'

'Doesn't matter.'

'What do you mean?'

'Doesn't matter.'

'It does.'

'No.' As if she was the one who was the comforter, Hannah took Frieda's smooth hand in her cut and swollen one. 'All done.'

FORTY

Frieda asked Josef to drop her at St Pancras station and from there she walked towards the little church. It was drizzling, but that didn't matter. In the twilight, the world around was grey, with a low, dull sky and the outlines of buildings blurred. Frieda walked into the churchyard, under the great plane trees, past the monuments and graves, and was at last in front of the Hardy Tree. One hundred and fifty years ago, graves had been moved to make room for the railway line, and now stood in an overcrowded circle around an ash tree, whose roots dug down into the bodies beneath. It was like a small city of the dead. She didn't think, but thoughts drifted through her; she didn't feel, but emotions shifted in her blood.

Frieda stood for a long time, staring at the tree, until the light faded. The wind blew in squalls across the grass, and clouds billowed in the dark sky. She turned, and as she did so, she saw them through the dusk. Five figures walking towards her – no, seven. Behind Reuben, Josef, Sasha, Chloë and Jack came Karlsson on his crutches and Yvette walking beside him. Josef must have gathered them all.

She waited as they made their way through the grave-stones towards her. No one said anything, for what was there to say? Karlsson took off his coat and draped it round her shoulders. Sasha took her arm. Chloë gave one loud sob, then stopped herself. Frieda looked from face to face.

'You're done,' said Reuben.

*

The fire was lit. She had a glass of whisky beside her and now she sat at her little chess table. She would play through an old game, clear her mind of everything except the felted click of the pieces, the mathematical reconfigurations, advances and retreats. But she couldn't quite settle. There was a faint odour in the air, a sweet stench. She moved through the rooms, trying to work out where it was coming from, and at last rang Josef.

'Sorry, I know it's late.'

'I help?' Always so eager.

'I think there might be something up with my pipes. Or maybe I've got mice or something. Can you help?'

'I come now.'

'Tomorrow's fine.'

'Now,' Josef said, and the phone went dead.

'Is not pipes,' he said, sniffing the air suspiciously. 'Is here.'

They were standing in the living room.

'Could a rat have got under the floorboards? And died?'

'Is possible.'

Josef knelt down on the floor and looked where it touched the wall. He licked his finger and dabbed at a joint between the floorboards. He lifted and showed it to Frieda.

'What's that?'

'Sawdust.'

'It must be left over from the work you did.'

'Not me,' said Josef. 'Is fresh.' He opened one of the large tool cases he had brought. He took out a crowbar and a heavy screwdriver, then everything became grainy and slow, happening far off and happening close up, in her home, under her feet. He levered up a board. Frieda could hear him saying something, in a hoarse whisper, which she couldn't make out, and then her senses were overwhelmed by the foul smell,

389

spilling upwards. There was a white tennis shoe. A grey-yellow ankle. A heaving billow of maggots. A hand holding a shrivelled daffodil. A face of puddled flesh, whose mouth slipped and whose open eyes stared in dead surprise. Bruce Stringer looking up at her with yellowy dead eyes.

'Dean,' said Frieda.

'No, Frieda,' said Josef, still whispering. 'Is that man. Stringer.'

'Dean Reeve did this to him. To me. For me.'

Frieda heard Josef's voice on the phone calling the police. She knelt beside the hole and closed her eyes and then she opened her eyes and made herself look at the mouth pulled open into a rotting smile. She stood up and stepped back until she felt the wall against her, holding her up. She was aware of Josef saying things to her, but she couldn't respond, couldn't make out what he was saying. And then there was a scrape of tyres outside, flashing lights outside her front window, heavy footsteps. The world outside was coming for her.

THE FIFTH THRILLER IN THE FRIEDA KLEIN SERIES

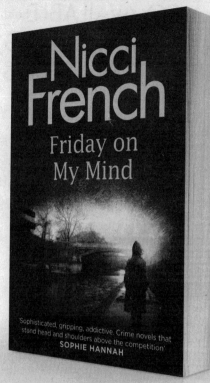

When a bloated corpse is found floating in the River Thames the police can at least be sure that identifying the victim will be straightforward. Around the dead man's wrist is a hospital band. On it are the words Dr F. Klein . . .

But psychotherapist Frieda Klein is very much alive. And, after evidence linking her to the murder is discovered, she becomes the prime suspect.

Unable to convince the police of her innocence, Frieda is forced to make a bold decision in order to piece together the terrible truth before it's too late either for her or for those she loves.

Rich in intrigue, intensity and atmosphere, *Friday on My Mind* is classic Nicci French – a dark, gripping and sophisticated masterclass in psychological suspense in which nothing is quite what it seems . . .

Out Now

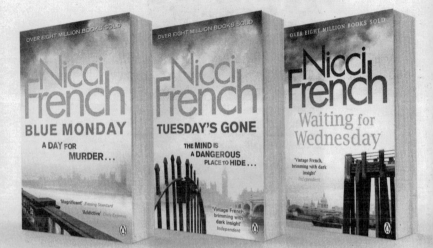